STONEKING

BOOK THREE OF THE GEMETA STONE

STONEKING

BOOK THREE OF THE GEMETA STONE

DONNA MIGLIACCIO

StoneKing: Book Three of The Gemeta Stone
SECOND EDITION

Copyright 2018 by Donna Migliaccio

ISBN: 978-1-7338389-4-8

Cover design by Melissa Williams Design

Interior formatting by Melissa Williams Design

Edited by Vicki McGough

Published by Donna Migliaccio

donnamigliaccio.com

For Joan, Phil and Rikki

ACKNOWLEDGEMENTS

To my literary agent, Cynthia King, and to Roger Yoerges and J. Fred Shiffman at Capital Talent Agency, thank you for your ongoing support, particularly during the lunacy that was 2017.

To my editor Vicki McGough, a thousand thanks for your persistent attention to detail. To Catherine Lenderi, thank you for your sharp eye and assistance with the Kentávron language. To Michelle Argyle of Melissa Williams Design, thank you for another wonderful cover.

To Rikki Boyce, Philip L. Harris and Joan C. Lillard, my trusty beta readers – thank you for continuing to say "yes please!" when I sidle up to you with another manuscript.

Thanks to Macallister Stone and the community at AbsoluteWrite.com for providing a great atmosphere to learn, be inspired or just procrastinate when I should be writing.

To the readers of Kinglet and Fiskur: you're the reason I write. I'll try not to let you down. Thank you and bless you for your support and enthusiasm.

And to my husband John, with all the love there is: thank you for being there, through the lows as well as the high. I could not do this without you.

CHAPTER ONE

The Reaving stretched toward the horizon, splintering the frozen earth, pointing at the sunrise like an accusing finger. Kristan Gemeta stood over it, sick with the desire to stamp on it, shriek at it, piss on it, claw his fingers into it, find its heart and tear it out.

He did none of those things.

Instead, he stared into the distance, one gloved hand on Malvo's bridle and the other beneath his fur-lined cloak, clutching the Gemeta Stone at his chest. *Control, control, control,* he told himself, as he had a thousand times before, for a thousand different reasons. *Breathe. Count your breaths.*

The churning nausea receded, leaving him light-headed. Malvo let out a rumbling sigh, but Kristan only shut his eyes against the bitter wind and waited for the strength to face another day.

He did not know how long he had been standing in numb silence when a sense of being watched crept over him. He opened his eyes. A dozen paces away stood an old woman, heavy and stolid, swaddled in a blanket and wincing in the frosty air. Beside her was a tabby cat.

Kristan blinked and looked again. A wavering, transparent haze surrounded the cat, as if the little creature was somehow radiating intense heat. *Wiche,* he thought, and tensed. *By the Stone, what sort of trickery is this?*

"A cold morning for standing afield," the old woman said.

Kristan nodded. The cat took a few steps toward him, angling to his left. Now that the morning sun was no longer behind it, the flickering blur had a distinctly human shape; small, slight and somehow feminine.

"Pay her no mind," the old woman said. "Curious creature, but she means no harm."

A blast of wind made them all flinch. Malvo shuddered and stamped. Cat and shape skittered backward in perfect unison.

"Are you of the castle?" the old woman asked.

Are you of the castle?

Bright fragments jangled in the ruins of Kristan's memory: a spring morning, the smell of fields freshly green, the ring of tack and the thunder of Malvo's hooves. Beneath those shining shards other, more ominous memories shifted, and Kristan twitched his attention back to the pair before him.

"Can you not speak, sir?" the old woman asked.

"I can speak." Kristan jerked his chin at the cat-thing. "Is she yours?"

The old woman chuckled. "As much as such creatures can be."

The cat moved toward him again, with more confidence. It lifted a paw, as if to pat at his leg, just as the shape spouted a foggy protrusion that reached toward his cloak. He recoiled and bumped against Malvo.

"Never fear," the old woman said. "Such a little cat can do you no harm."

Kristan snorted. "Does she speak?"

Both the cat and the woman froze, but then the old one chuckled again, although this time the laugh sounded forced. "Speak? That would be strange indeed."

"Why? Is she a simpleton?"

With a loud hiss, the cat disappeared, snuffed like a candle's flame. In the same breath, the shape solidified into an adolescent girl. She stumbled backward and fell, and the old woman leaped in front of her, arms outflung as if to ward off a blow.

When Kristan did not move, the woman slowly relaxed. "You saw her?" she asked, her voice scarcely above a whisper.

"I saw her. Who is she, your granddaughter?"

"My great-niece. Daughter of my sister's daughter." The old woman brought one hand from beneath her blanket and rubbed her face, as if dazed. On her wrist was a bead-studded bracelet of braided leather thongs, and on the back of her hand were strange tattoos. From the rubble of Kristan's mind's eye more fragments rose: the smoky smell of a little campfire, feet squelching in wet boots, a bent and wrinkled woman offering him a tattered blanket to dry himself. In an instant they were gone, obliterated by more powerful memories: shadowy, gore-splattered, horrifying. Panic and rage twisted Kristan's guts. *Control, control, control*, he told himself. He took a deep breath and brought all his senses to bear on the woman before him. "We've met before."

"No," said the old woman.

"You were here with your sister on this very field, nearly three years ago. You frightened my horse. I fell in the lake." He pointed to the ground. "You showed me this Reaving. You told me it was an omen. And now you come back and try to dupe me with your Wiche tricks."

The woman's mouth dropped open. She stepped toward him. The girl stood up and peered at him over the old woman's shoulder. She was no more than thirteen, with straggly brown hair and amber eyes.

"You're much changed," the old woman said. She studied the welts striping Malvo's shining black hide, then shifted her gaze to the scar that disfigured Kristan's face. "You and horse both. You wear Reavings of your own now."

"I don't like to be stared at," he answered gruffly. She raised one hand, as if to stroke his mutilated cheek, and he flinched away.

"Nor to be touched, either," she said. "You was a pretty boy then. Mannerly to a pair of old women trespassing in the royal fields. Willing to listen to their Wiche stories."

"I was green as grass."

"We warned you of the Great Amiss. Told you to pass on the warning."

"And I did. I told my father. It earned me only anger and disgrace, and in the end, changed nothing."

The woman raised her eyebrows. "It changed you. The innocent boy has become the Gemeta, the StoneKing, lord of four countries and conqueror of the Wichelord." The girl let out a little peep of surprise, and the old woman laughed. "Yes, that's why you couldn't fool him, kitten. Beneath that fine fur cloak, he wears his family's Stone. It protects him from all things Wiche, even baby tricks like yours. Bow to the StoneKing, child."

They bent into clumsy curtsies, but the homage only made him uncomfortable. "Get up. Have you eaten?"

"Not for days," the girl said.

Her voice was high-pitched with want, and at last Kristan noticed the starveling hollows in both faces. Another cold gust slammed into them, and as they huddled deeper in their blankets, a grudging pity cut through Kristan's own misery.

"Come with me, then." He turned to the old woman. "I can put you on my horse, if you like."

She shook her head. "I'll walk alongside of you."

The four of them—man, girl, old woman and horse—turned southwest, leaning into the wind. Kristan led Malvo, the old woman walked beside him and the girl trailed behind. Standing in the cold had stiffened Kristan's bad leg, making his limp even more pronounced. The wind tugged his hood askew and blew his hair back from his forehead. From the corner of his eye, he saw the old woman scrutinizing the marks that still ringed his hairline. "You've been used hard, StoneKing," she said.

He pulled his hood forward again. "I told you, I don't like to be stared at. Where's your sister?"

The old woman's chin trembled. "Dead. During the last full moon."

"Was she ill?"

The old woman shook her head. "She was trying to protect the child."

"From what?"

"A mob."

"Explain yourself."

"The girl shifts. You saw it. She takes cat form, mostly. When she was small, she'd do it by chance—if she was scolded, mayhap, or frightened. Chance or no, her parents punished her for it." The old woman sighed. "Coming of a Wiche family, you'd think her mother would have been kinder, but she herself was born without the gifts. And it was a time when all Wiche was scorned and its believers mocked—as you know your own self," she added, looking at Kristan slantwise. "So my sister taught the child how to control the shifting; no more. But after the Wichelord took power, those of us with the gifts were respected; feared even. And suddenly poor Nolle here, who'd had the shifting nearly slapped out of her, was kissed and cossetted and urged to shift all the time.

"My sister taught the girl what she could. Nolle can do more than cats, now. If she thinks hard and says the words just so, she can even shift others. Make a boy look like a dog, or a dog like a boy. It don't last, though, and it's only the look of the creature that changes, not its nature." The old woman chuckled. "A sow may look like a lady, but it gives the game away when it roots in the mud with its nose, eh, Nolle?"

"It wasn't my fault the man was fooled," Nolle said, looking sullen.

"Was that the reason for the mob?" Kristan asked.

"No, the mob was for different." The old woman lowered her voice. "Everything changed after the Wichelord fell. Nolle's parents turned her out, along with her grandmother. The three of us wandered, through village and countryside alike, and everywhere we were turned away, refused a place to sleep or food to eat. We would have starved, but for Nolle's other gift. In addition to the shifting, she has light fingers, Gemeta. She stole only what we needed—a coin or two, a bite of bread, a blanket—but one day she was distracted, and let the shift slip. They chased her, and would have caught her, but my sister stood in their path. Nolle got away, but the mob beat my sister so badly that she died of it." The old woman sighed again. "So now it's just the two of us, wandering. For me it's nothing new; I've been on the outside all my life, but for Nolle it's hard. She's young and needs a place to call home."

They were on the outskirts of Kingsmere now. Inhabitants of the castle town were already about their business, bundled from head to foot against the sharp wind. They bowed to Kristan and called out morning greetings, but studied his two companions with unabashed curiosity. Kristan glanced over his shoulder at Nolle. The girl's lips were moving, her amber eyes had grown strangely fixed and her gait was shifting from a heavy-footed trudge to a supple glide. "Stop it," he said, and she stiffened. "No Wiche foolishness. No gulling my people."

"Come up here and behave, kitten," the old woman said. Nolle hurried to join her, shooting a glare at Kristan.

"Good morning, my lord!"

Even though the greeting came from a man muffled up to the eyes, Kristan recognized Lyko Yeomans, master mason of Kingsmere. "I saw you at dawn, riding out to the east," Lyko continued, as he fell into step with them. "It's a cold morning to be afield."

"So I'm told," Kristan said.

"Not too early to be thinking about spring planting, though."

"Not in that field."

Lyko winced. "Of course not. Not there. Never there."

"Why not?" Nolle asked. "Reaved fields can be harvested."

"It's not because of the Reaving, child," Lyko said in a low voice.

"Then why?"

Lyko only pulled his head deeper into his woolens, like a

turtle pulling into its shell. "What's wrong with the field?" the girl insisted.

"You brought the subject up, Lyko; now finish it," Kristan said.

His voice was harsh, and Lyko flinched. "I'm so sorry, my lord—"

"Tell her why."

Lyko sighed and turned to Nolle. "It's one big grave, child. The Daaznans buried all the dead of the castle and town there, after Fandrall fell. To plow it would disturb their bones." He looked at Kristan, his face wrung with misery. "I'm sorry, my lord."

Kristan jerked his chin toward the castle. "Your workmen will be waiting for you, Lyko. Good morning."

Lyko hurried ahead of them up the castle road. Kristan sensed the girl and the old woman sneaking glances at him, but he kept his gaze fixed forward. The castle's drawbridge was just ahead, and waiting near the gatehouse were half of the knights of Kristan's personal retinue: gruff, dependable Geoffrey, grave, dutiful Kennet, and Walter, wearing his usual irrepressible grin. They greeted Lyko as he approached, and the master mason paused long enough to exchange a few words. *No doubt warning them that the StoneKing is in a foul mood*, Kristan thought. *Again.*

The three knights met them on the drawbridge. "Good morning, my lord," Sir Walter said. "I was just about to ride out to see if you wanted company, but I see you've already found some. Good morning," he added to the women.

The guards came to attention as Kristan passed through the gatehouse. The keep towered ahead, and Kristan's spirits drooped further at the sight of it. Repairs to the outside had been completed in late autumn, but the delineation between the bright new stonework and the soot-stained lower walls was a constant reminder of the destruction that had greeted him on his return.

His mood soured still more at the sight of Quinn Logan waiting on the keep steps. The councilor's face was carefully expressionless, but his lean figure tilted forward, as if already poised with the first questions of the day. With him were two more knights: golden-haired Matthew and Mitchell, the youngest of Kristan's retinue.

"Shall I stable Malvo for you, my lord?" Sir Kennet asked. Kristan nodded and handed off Malvo's reins, and Kennet led the great black horse away.

As Kristan mounted the steps, Mitchell and Matthew gripped the handles of the great keep doors and opened them. Quinn Logan's lips pursed. Kristan knew his councilor was irked at the sight of knights doing the work of page boys, but Quinn merely bowed as Kristan passed into the keep, with the women and knights behind.

The air in the entryway was already thick with grit and sawdust, and the great hall beyond rang with the banging of masons' hammers and the screech of carpenters' saws. Scaffoldings crawled with workers, hard at work pulling out the charred remains of the upper floor. As Kristan watched, one man swung himself down and hurried to Sir Randolf, eldest of Kristan's knights and overseer of the restoration work.

"I'm having your breakfast laid in the northwest anteroom, my lord," Sir Geoffrey said, as he took Kristan's cloak and gloves. "It's less noisy there this morning."

Kristan did not answer. The workman was handing something to Randolf, but through the dust and distance Kristan could not make out what it was. The old knight cocked his head at the object in his hands, then asked the workman something Kristan could not hear. In response, the man pointed toward the northern wall.

At that moment Randolf caught sight of Kristan. He dismissed the workman with a nod and hurried over. "Good morning, my lord. One of the workmen just found this, up in the floorboards of what used to be your bedchamber. Perhaps you know what it is."

Randolf held out the object. It was a large, deep box, coated with dust and soot. Its lid was hinged on one side and fastened on the opposite with a rusted hasp.

"There's something on the lid," Sir Mitchell said. The five knights, Quinn Logan and the two women all craned their necks to look. Kristan rubbed one hand across the lid. Beneath the grime, two uneven letters were carved into the wood: *KG.*

"Well, look at that," Randolf said.

"Is it yours, my lord?" Mitchell asked.

Kristan knew the box was his, and that he had hidden it away, long ago, but his memory was so crippled that he could not remember why, nor what was inside. Worse, he was afraid to open it; afraid that whatever he found inside would stir up fresh horrors to torture his brain and twist his guts and rob him of what little sleep was still left to him.

"Well, what's in it?" the girl Nolle demanded.

"Hush, you," the old woman said, but she was looking at Kristan. All of them were looking at him. Many of the workers had stopped what they were doing to watch. He felt pinned by all the eyes. *Stop looking at me,* he wanted to shout, but instead he bit down on his tongue and fumbled the hasp open.

The hinges creaked as he lifted the lid. Everyone leaned forward to look inside.

The box was full of a child's treasures: a little wooden top, a horse carved of stone, a few coins, three buttons made of horn, a pair of small brass rings that might have come from a pony's bridle, a lopsided leather ball streaked with mold.

And there were two more items, each wrapped in soft cloth: one large and round, one long and flat. Kristan lifted out the flat one and turned back the cloth.

Randolf caught his breath.

Within the cloth was a lock of hair. It was black and curly and so long that it had been looped upon itself several times and tied in the middle with a bit of silky ribbon.

. . . waxy white face drowning in a sea of dark curls; his father's eyes red and swollen with weeping; flash of a knife and his father's hand thrusting the single long lock at him, crying 'take it then boy, take it to remember her by . . .'

"Is that your own hair?" Nolle asked.

"No, child," Randolf said quietly. "It's his mother's."

. . . controlcontrolcontrol . . .

Kristan shrouded the hair in its cloth and laid it back in the box. He picked up the round item. It was surprisingly heavy for its size and so smooth and slippery within its wrapping that he nearly dropped it. The cloth fell away and he found himself holding a ball of shining blue glass. This time it was the old woman who gasped.

"A scrying ball," she whispered.

. . . the smooth and shining ball held close in Simeon's heavy-knuckled hand; his gray eyes suddenly steely and frightening; hissing 'take it Avama, look at it again, what do you see, what do you see . . .'

The room seemed to shift beneath Kristan's feet. His vision blurred. Nolle pushed closer, her pinched little face suddenly bright with avarice. "Ooo, pretty," she whispered, fingers twitching toward the ball. The old woman caught her wrist and pulled her back.

"I remember that," Randolf was saying. "That's the ball Simeon gave you. The one Daazna stole . . ." His voice trailed off.

Kristan fumbled the cloth around the ball, put it in the box and closed the lid. As he took the box from Randolf, the pity in the old knight's face galled him. "Enough idling," he snapped. "Get these men back to work."

Randolf ducked his head. "Yes, my lord. Sorry, my lord." He hurried back into the great hall, bawling orders, and the sudden burst of hammering and sawing made Kristan's ears ring.

He tucked the box under his arm. "Sir Walter, please see that these two are given breakfast and someplace warm to rest," he said, nodding at the two women. Walter's eyes brightened with curiosity, but he only murmured his assent and hastened the two away. Exchanging a glance, Matthew and Mitchell followed in their wake.

Geoffrey cleared his throat. "Shall I have your breakfast served now, my lord?"

"I'm not hungry," Kristan said.

Geoffrey bowed, but not before Kristan saw the despairing look he shot at Quinn Logan. "Shall I send your scribe to you, my lord?"

Kristan nodded. With Quinn at his heels, he crossed the great hall. The room that served as his work chamber was tucked well back in the northern portion of the keep. It was a humble, drafty space that had once served as a sewing chamber, but Kristan had chosen it because of its good light and distance from the racket of rebuilding. He knew Quinn Logan hated it, and all the paucities of Fandrall's court, and he also knew that a lecture on the subject was in the offing.

"You must hire more staff, my lord," Quinn said. "It isn't right to ask your knights to do servants' work."

With an effort, Kristan kept his voice level. "I haven't asked them to."

"What are they to do? Stand by and watch as their lord opens his own doors and stables his own horse and fetches his own meals? It isn't right."

"You said that."

"And they should have their own squires."

"Then they should hire them. I pay them enough."

"Money isn't the issue. If the king of the realm doesn't have a squire, then it would be presumptuous for his knights to have them." Quinn hurried ahead, opened the door to the council chamber and scowled. "It's freezing in here. There's no fire."

Kristan brushed past him. His scribe Bastian had tidied the room at the end of the previous day, but the work table was still piled high with ledgers, scrolls and loose parchment. Kristan found a place for the box on a side table, and then crouched before the hearth, grimacing at the pain from his knee.

"Let me do that, my lord."

"You couldn't light a decent fire if your life depended on it." Kristan dug in the tinderbox for kindling and Quinn threw his hands up in frustration.

"That's what I'm trying to say, my lord! You don't pay me to light fires. You pay me to be your councilor—right now your only councilor. You should have more. You should have more of everything. You're the lord of four countries, and yet you live like a pauper here in Fandrall while in Hogia, Dyer and Norwinn your Reaches have every comfort. Why?"

Kristan finished laying the logs and lit the kindling with a firesteel. "Are appearances so important to you, Quinn?"

"With respect, my lord, they are, and they should be to you as well."

"Then think on this." As the kindling began to crackle and snap, Kristan dusted off his hands and with difficulty, pushed himself to his feet. "Two years of Daaznan occupation destroyed my kingdom and impoverished my people. You know how poor their harvests were this autumn. Should I surround myself with pomp and splendor while they struggle through the winter to put bread in their mouths?"

"You've bolstered Fandrall's economy out of your own pocket." There was an unusually dogged glint in Quinn's eye. "You bought seed for winter crops and gave it to farmers without charge. You replenished their herds and flocks, again without charge."

"They'll repay me from the spring births and summer harvests. That was our agreement."

"Of course. But after you showed them such generosity, would they begrudge you a proper household?"

More eyes watching me, Kristan thought; *more mouths yammering at me.* He sat down at the table and pulled the treasury reports from the nearest stack of paper.

"We can't keep limping along this way," Quinn went on. "Everyone is so preoccupied with menial tasks that they can't focus on their real work. My lord, experienced servants are available in Norwinn and Dyer. Instruct your Reaches to send the best of them here. And recruiting in Hogia has gone so well; why not ask Lady Heather to send you some likely candidates for squire?"

Kristan's heart gave a sudden heave and just as abruptly, sank. *Heather,* he thought. *It only needed the mention of her name to make this miserable morning complete.*

With all the discipline he could muster, he put the papers down and fixed Quinn with a cold stare. From the corner of his eye he saw old Bastian hesitating in the doorway. "I've told you no," he said.

"My lord, see reason—"

Kristan slammed his hand on the table, and both men jumped. "By the Stone, will you leave off?" Bastian started to sidle away, but Kristan stabbed a forefinger at him. "Come back here. Quinn and I are finished with this discussion."

"With respect, my lord, we are not," Quinn said. His high forehead was flushed and his chin jutted at a defiant angle. He snatched up a scroll and shook it. "Look at this. This is the third message from King Lockward of Malchea in as many months. He's eager to establish relations with you—"

Through his rising anger, Kristan sneered. "He's eager to foist his daughter off on me."

A muscle jumped in Quinn's jaw. "He wants to send a special envoy, my lord, but your court cannot receive official visitors in its present condition. It would be an insult."

Eyes wide with dismay, Bastian shook his head at Quinn.

"An insult?" *Controlcontrolcontrol* resounded through Kristan's brain, but the warning was drowned by the roaring in his ears.

"Yes, my lord, and a humiliation for you. Your empathy with the poor of your kingdom is laudable, but you are not one of them. You are the StoneKing, the lord of an enormous realm. You must show the appropriate display of might and majesty, and conduct yourself in a manner befitting your position."

Kristan got slowly to his feet. Acid rose in his mouth; his insides writhed like a sack full of snakes. "Get out," he said. His throat was thick with rage; he could barely push the words out. "Get out now."

"My lord—"

"GET OUT!" Kristan grabbed one of the heavy ledgers and threw it; it crashed against the door, just missing Bastian. The scribe fled. As he strode around the table, Kristan caught up a heavy iron candlestick; Quinn's eyes went wide, and he bolted from the room. Kristan slammed the door shut, hurled the candlestick against the far wall, and then flung himself at the table. He shoved a mound of papers one way, a stack of ledgers the other, and then the first spasm seized him like a giant hand. It shook him so hard his feet went out from under him. As he fell, he hit his chin on the edge of the table and saw stars. He tried to get to his feet, tried to get his hands on the Stone, but the nausea overwhelmed him. On hands and knees, he gagged and retched, his whole body jerking with the effort, but he could not vomit. One last paroxysm convulsed him: his tortured muscles locked, his eyes rolled up into his skull, and everything went black.

CHAPTER TWO

Ravelin Seachlan, Reach of Hogia, crossed his arms over his bare chest and leaned against the window frame. In the bed behind him, Isobel heaved a breathy, affected yawn he knew was for his benefit, but the fact that she was awake and receptive did not entice him. Instead, he studied the troops marching toward the castle from the north. A cluster of mounted knights led them, with a slim figure on a white filly front and center. An animated conversation was going on between the horsemen, with much pointing, arm waving and martial gesturing, and even at a distance Ravelin could make out their broad grins.

"Good morning, my lord," Isobel said. She was the only one who still called him that, but only when they were alone. Some days the title excited him and some days it only made him sullen. Today was a sullen day, and he did not answer. A moment later Isobel was snuggling against him, her naked body wrapped in a fur-lined blanket, her narrow face set in a coquettish simper. "Ooo, you're cold, my lord. Let me warm you up."

She tried to envelop him, but he shrugged free. "Leave off. What's our heroic Lady of the Sword up to this morning?"

Isobel's lips pushed out into a pout. "Oh, her." She leaned against the opposite side of the window frame, holding the blanket to her chest with one arm. The pose squeezed her breasts upward, making them look larger and plumper, and accentuating her pale pink nipples peeping through the fur. The pose was deliberately seductive, but the effect was ruined by the morning sun, harsh on the fine lines ringing her lips and eyes and the goose pimples the cold air raised on her skin. "The knights were going to show her some of the battle maneuvers from the Stratheden war."

Ravelin snorted. "As if they'd know anything about that."

"Indeed, my lord." Isobel dropped her voice to a confidential purr. "You'd think the stupid girl would ask the one person in this castle with firsthand knowledge of the campaign—but then, you'd never tell her, would you?"

The little army was passing just beneath Ravelin's window and he could see their commander more clearly. Heather Demitt rode astride, easy in the white filly's saddle. In her thick leggings, quilted tunic, boots and heavy cloak, it was easy to mistake her for a young man. Her hair was hidden beneath her hood, but for the bright fringe across her forehead. "Look at her," Isobel sniffed. "A common merchant's daughter, at the head of Hogia's army. It's an outrage, the way the Demitt family wormed its way into the Gemeta's good graces."

Lady Heather gestured as she posed a question to Sir Jerrold, her eyes a bright, inquisitive blue in her cold-reddened face. Ravelin preferred his women shapely, comely and compliant, but there was a certain appeal in Heather's youth and wiry energy. Her men clearly adored her; every eye was fixed on her, every mouth ready to smile. *She controls the military,* Ravelin thought, *and whoever controls the military controls the kingdom.*

"Has she taken any lovers yet?" he asked. "Any of her knights, perhaps?"

Isobel rolled her eyes. "Not her. Dallying with someone under her command would be bad for discipline. Anyway, her heart is already lost."

"Really? To whom?"

"The Gemeta, of course. Rumor has it they were lovers."

"Does he return her feelings?"

"He left her behind when he went to Fandrall, so there's your answer. I'll tell you this, though." Isobel's mouth twisted into an unpleasant smirk. "When he gave her a title and appointed her commander, he elevated her out of the reach of most men. He might not want her for himself anymore, but he made certain no one else can have her."

Ravelin grunted. Below, Lady Heather was giving orders, her clear voice ringing through the mullioned glass of the window. The little army separated into three smaller units, each headed by a single knight. As the troops hurried off on their missions, their young commander lingered, watching them go. As she took up her filly's reins, she raised her eyes toward the castle battlements. Ravelin had just enough time to grab Isobel's blanket, shove her out of view and cover himself before Heather's gaze fell on him.

"My lord!" Isobel whined.

"Shut up," Ravelin said out of the corner of his mouth.

At the sight of him, Heather's pensive expression turned frosty. In the months since the Gemeta had taken control of Hogia, Ravelin had hidden his bitterness beneath a smiling face and false cordiality, but to no avail. The Lady of the Sword did not trust him, although she was too polite to display the outright contempt of her father Colin, Hogia's steward, or the cool disdain of her cousin Alister, the castle's head scribe. *These damned Demitts*, Ravelin thought, not for the first time. *All three stand between me and my throne.*

Before his usual unctuous smile could take form, he was struck by a new idea. *She's a fierce little warrior. Perhaps playing the toadying courtier is the wrong choice. Perhaps a change in tactics is in order.* He raised one hand quickly to his forehead, covering his eyes. He could still see Heather through his fingers; her stern expression was softening. *Enough*, he told himself; *don't overdo it.* With shoulders slumped, he half turned from the window.

"What's the matter?" Isobel hissed.

"Shut up," he said again. "Peep out and tell me what she's doing, but keep out of sight."

Isobel crouched down and peered from the lower corner of the window. "She's watching you," she reported.

"How does she look?"

"Puzzled. A little uneasy."

Ravelin grinned behind his hand.

"She's turning her horse. Now she's riding off, but she keeps looking back this way. There, she's gone." Isobel squawked as Ravelin grabbed her by the hips and crowded her face-first against the window. "Wait, my lord, wait—"

"Shut up," Ravelin said through his teeth. He pressed up behind her, kneading her breasts with both hands, pinching and tweaking the nipples.

"Ooo, not so hard, my lord!" Isobel's flirtatious giggle turned into a yip of dismay as Ravelin shifted his grip to her buttocks. "Wait, no; not here, my lord; let's go back to the bed where it's comfortable—ow!" Her voice spiraled into a yowl as he crammed himself into her, thrusting so hard that her feet left the floor and her forehead banged against the glass. "Ow, ow, ow! My lord, we're going to break the window!"

He let out a guttural laugh. "We don't want that, do we?" He reached over her shoulder, unlatched the window and pushed it open. A blast of frigid wind seared his face.

"Don't, don't! Someone will see!" Isobel cried.

"Hold your tongue and no one will notice." Ravelin's next thrust shoved her halfway out the window. Isobel let out a single strangled yelp and began to struggle, pleading with him in a screaming whisper. He grabbed the back of her neck and pinned her against the broad window ledge. With eyes shut, he savored Isobel's whimpers, imagining that it was the Lady of the Sword he held there instead. He drew back until he was nearly out of her, and then slammed into her again and again, his hot breath hanging in a fog around his smiling mouth.

* * *

"Good morning, daughter," Colin Demitt said through a mouthful of food.

Heather breathed a little sigh. Her father was surrounded by papers and the remains of an enormous breakfast; beside him, her cousin Alister nibbled a crust of bread as he took notes. The stress of the Demitt family's new responsibilities had manifested in different ways: her father, formerly moderate in all things but temper, had become a voracious eater, while Alister, plump during his days as an apprentice, had lost so much weight that he was almost slender. The old Wichearte Phelan sat at the table with them, a cup of some herbal brew cooling before him as he stared absently at the ceiling.

"Good morning," she answered. As she took her seat, a servant hurried to fill her tankard with ale and her bowl with the hot porridge she favored after a cold morning ride. She murmured her thanks, drained half the tankard in a single swallow and applied herself to the porridge with gusto. It was rare that she was this hungry, but exercise had whetted her appetite.

"So, do you want to raise the taxes or not?" Alister asked Colin.

"I do, but now isn't the time, in spite of what Reach Seachlan says," Colin said, with a disdainful snort. "Most folk in this country are barely scraping by. We'll raise them in the spring, after the early harvests. Maybe by then some of the livestock will start to bear as well, and trade will pick up."

"In the spring, then," Alister said, making a note.

"Spring," Phelan repeated under his breath. He raised one hand and traced a graceful shape in the air. "*Vere, varen, chuntian.*"

A single blossom, pink and white, materialized, dropped to the table and was just as quickly gone, leaving only a damp spot on the wood and a lingering fragrance. "As fleeting as that," Phelan said, and went back to smiling at the ceiling.

"As fleeting as your wits," Colin muttered, and focused his attention on his papers.

Alister turned to Heather. "How was your drill this morning?"

"Interesting, but not entirely successful," Heather said. "My knights have studied the battles of the Stratheden war, but they were all too young to have taken part." She shook her head as she scraped up the last of the porridge. "Everything felt stiff and formal, as if we were doing some sort of court dance. I've got a lot to learn before I can call myself a strategist."

"You spend too much time in the saddle," Colin said. "You're going to end up bowlegged."

"And you spend too much time at the table," Heather shot back. "Your little friend Annys is going to have to make you a new tunic soon—you're about to burst the seams of that one."

"You're not too old to get the back of my hand, my girl," Colin answered, but his gruffness lacked any real anger. Heather and her father still squabbled on occasion, but without the fury and bitterness of years past. "You're getting as cheeky as that horse of yours—Scrappy or Stroppy or whatever you call her."

"Her name is Skapi and you know it."

"Skapi. What kind of name is that?"

"Olaf called her *skapstór*—it means temperamental," Alister said. "But the stablehands can't pronounce it and call her 'Skapi' instead."

"I like it," Heather said.

"You would." Colin applied himself to the rest of his meal, and Heather finished her porridge and signaled to the servant for more. The mention of Olaf Sigurdson had made her smile, but already the smile was fading. *I wonder where he is*, she thought. *I wonder how he does. I miss him. I miss Torrin. And Nigel and Melissa.*

And Kristan . . .

Overwhelmed with sudden melancholy, she pushed her bowl aside and stood up. "Eyes bigger than your stomach?"

Alister said, without looking up from his notes.

Phelan's eyes flicked toward her. The sudden bright clarity in his gaze made her feel as if the old Wichearte could see straight into her heart. "I've had enough," she said. She hurried out of the small anteroom the Demitt family used for private meals and headed through the great hall with her head down, winking back tears. *You great fool,* she scolded herself. *There's no use crying about it; what's done is done.*

She could not avoid hearing Kristan's name; it came up constantly in documents, messages and meetings. She had trained herself to bear that pain, but casual conversations were different. A passing comment could awaken memories that were like stabs to the heart, and it took every ounce of her self-control to hide her feelings.

She was halfway up the stairs before she was able to raise her eyes, and then it was only to catch sight of Ravelin, on his way down. She braced herself for his usual ingratiating smile and greeting, and was surprised when he hesitated, swallowed hard, and then hurried past with scarcely a nod. She suddenly remembered seeing him in his window, looking oddly forlorn.

"Good morning, Reach Seachlan," she said to his retreating back.

For a moment she thought he would continue down the stairs without responding, but then he stopped. "Good morning," he said, without looking at her.

"Are you quite well?" she asked.

He turned to her then, his mouth pinched tight and his eyes bright with hurt. "Well?" he repeated in a choking whisper. "How could I possibly be well, knowing the contempt you have for me?"

Speechless, Heather gaped at him.

"You dislike and distrust me," he went on. "I don't blame you for that. But this morning you and your knights drilled the army in maneuvers from the Stratheden campaign. None of you know anything about those maneuvers beyond what you've read, but I do—I carried them out on the battlefield." He took a deep, shuddering breath. "I could have helped you, but clearly my help wasn't wanted. You didn't even show me the courtesy of pretending to want it. If ever I was uncertain just how low I've fallen, I'm certain now." He started down the stairs again.

"Ravelin." His first name felt strange on Heather's tongue. Again, he paused, looking at her over his shoulder. "The exercise went poorly," she said. "We didn't know what we were doing. You're right—I should have asked for your help. I'm sorry."

He held her gaze for a long moment, then jerked his chin in a curt nod.

"We were going to try the drill again in a few days, weather permitting," Heather said. "If you'd come along to advise me, I'd be grateful."

He studied her, his sharp features softening. "You and I got off on the wrong foot, months ago. I've regretted it ever since. I would be happy to lend my assistance, if it's genuinely wanted."

"It's genuinely needed," Heather said, with a wry smile.

"Very well, then. At your service . . . my lady." To Heather's surprise, he bowed deeply before continuing on his way. She stood looking after him, her head on one side.

CHAPTER THREE

Nigel Demitt paced back and forth before the door of the bedchamber. Within, Steffen was speaking in a low, soothing voice, but Melissa had not made a single sound. She had not made a sound since early morning, when she had rolled over in the bed, stiffened and cried out for him to fetch the healer. Steffen had come at the run, trailing several of his assistants and a pair of female servants; they had shut the door, leaving Nigel frantic on the opposite side.

It was now well past noon. A procession of courtiers had kept watch with Nigel, bringing him water, wine and ale which he did not drink; toasted bread, porridge and sausages which he did not eat; words of comfort and advice which he did not hear. The kingdom's chief councilor, Vadden Yale, had been sitting in the little antechamber with him for some time now. Vadden's good-humored face was creased in dutiful commiseration, but he held a small stack of papers in his lap, and occasionally Nigel caught him riffling mournfully through them.

"You look as if Moordock is sinking into the Mor," he finally snapped. "Say what's on your mind."

Vadden shrugged in apology and waved the papers. "I know you're worried about your wife, First Advisor, but there have been more of these raids on our coastal villages. These reports arrived this morning. Judging by the locations of the raids and the nights they occurred, it looks as if the two ships are moving west now."

Nigel dug the heels of his hands into his eyes. "Maybe there's been a mistake. Maybe the descriptions of the ships are wrong."

"Every report describes them the same way, Sir Nigel. I realize it's a delicate situation; I know the princess is reluctant to tell her brother what's happening, but as Reach she must think of the people of Norwinn first."

"All right, all right," Nigel said. "I'll talk to her as soon as . . . as soon as I can."

Vadden sighed and stood up. "Sir Nigel, I'm not heartless. I'm concerned for the princess, too. Is it . . . do you think it's another—"

Before Nigel could answer, the door to the bedchamber opened and Steffen's assistants hurried out, carrying stained linens and a covered basin. None spoke. Steffen followed more slowly, his arms folded into his sleeves, his expression pensive. "A word with you, First Advisor," he murmured, and Vadden bowed and left them alone. Nigel followed the healer into the far corner of the anteroom.

"It's as I feared," Steffen said, keeping his voice low. "Another miscarriage."

Nigel groaned. "How is she?"

"It's hard to tell. She scarcely whimpered through it all— barely spoke after I told her what had happened. It seems to be a Gemeta trait to suffer in silence."

"Is there nothing to be done?"

Steffen raised his eyebrows. "The child is lost, Sir Nigel."

"No, no, not that. For her. For Melissa."

"The worst of the cramping has subsided, but the flow of blood may continue for a few days. She should be kept quiet and warm and as comfortable as we can make her. The women with her are experienced in these things. They'll look after her." Steffen cleared his throat. "Sir Nigel, it would be best if you didn't attempt relations with her for a while—at least until after her next menses. She'll need time to heal . . . and to grieve."

Nigel nodded, his throat too constricted to speak. Steffen

patted him on the arm and left.

Within the bedchamber, one of the women crouched before the hearth, stoking the fire, while the other held a cup at the bedside. "Drink the milk, Princess, while it's nice and warm," she said, but the little figure burrowed beneath the covers did not answer. The woman at the fire straightened up and saw Nigel as he entered.

"Ah, here's your husband," she said. "Come along, Tilda. Put the cup back on the hearth to stay warm."

As the two left the room and closed the door, Nigel came to the bed. Melissa lay on her side, facing the fire. She seemed as small as a child, and her heart-shaped face was pale to the lips. Nigel crouched beside her and stroked her tangled dark hair from her brow. "I'm so sorry, Missy," he whispered. "So terribly sorry."

She did not look at him. "I was careful this time," she said in a toneless voice. "I didn't ride or dance or even walk fast. I drank milk and ate bland, boring food. I did everything Steffen told me to do, but it happened again. Why?"

"I don't know, my love. You're very young. Perhaps too young."

She looked at him then. Her brown-eyed gaze, usually merry or tender, was cold. "What does that mean?"

"It's just that, perhaps in a few years' time—"

"I'll be mature enough to bear a child, is that it?"

"Missy, you're only—"

"Any kitchen slattern of fourteen seems to be able to bear a brat without even missing a day's work. Am I so fragile a flower?"

"Be patient, darling—"

"Why does it have to be my fault? It couldn't possibly be because of you, could it?"

"Me?" Nigel almost laughed. "Don't be silly. I got you with child twice, didn't I?"

He instantly wished the thoughtless words unsaid. Melissa's

mouth twisted into a bitter smile. "Yes, you're quite the stallion. But you're also a Hogian. Maybe you carry the Hogian curse."

"What?"

"The Hogians are cursed with barrenness. That's what everyone says. Ravelin couldn't sire an heir. There are hardly any children in the whole countryside; you saw it for yourself last summer. They say it's because of the Reavings. The whole kingdom is barren, right down to the cattle in the fields and the sows in the mud and the chickens on their empty nests."

Nigel sat back on his heels. "Do you really believe that?"

"I don't know. I don't care." Melissa shut her eyes. "I don't want to talk about it anymore."

Nigel got to his feet and went to the window. The sky above was the same leaden color as the River Mor below. The room was silent but for the crackle of the fire.

"What did Vadden want?" Melissa asked at last.

"Nothing of importance."

"I heard him whining. What did he want?"

"It can wait."

She let out a weak laugh. "On what? Until I'm better? I've nothing to do but lie here with a headache and a wad of linen stuffed between my legs. Give me something else to think about."

He winced at the bitterness of her tone. "You sound like Kristan."

"Leave my brother out of it."

"I'm afraid we can't. There have been more coastal raids." Nigel turned his gaze to the town of Moordock, huddled at the foot of the cliffs on which the castle stood. "Vadden says you need to take action. He wants you to inform Kristan."

Melissa shifted in the bed, and he turned to look at her. She had rolled onto her back and was staring at the ceiling. "No," she said. "Not until I'm absolutely sure."

"Vadden says the descriptions of the ships are the same. It's got to be Olaf and his brother."

"The news will break Kristan's heart. I have to be sure."

"Then perhaps you should send someone to make sure."

"Perhaps I should." She glanced at him, and then looked at the ceiling again. "I want you to go."

"Don't you want me to stay with you? Until you're better?"

"No."

In three quick strides, Nigel crossed the room and knelt at her side. "Missy, I know how sad and disappointed you are. I am, too. But once you're better, we'll try again, and we'll keep on trying—"

"No. I'm sick of trying. I'm sick of feeling life stirring, and then having it torn from me. I can't do this anymore."

Nigel reached for her but Melissa slapped his hand away. The blow was like a stab to the heart. "Missy!"

"Don't touch me." Melissa's breath hitched on a sob. "Go away, Nigel. Go look for Olaf. Find out what's going on. Just go—go away."

Her words seemed to hang in the silence like a thick fog. "As you say," Nigel choked out. He spun on his heel and strode from the room. With every step he expected her to call his name, to fling out a plea for forgiveness, like a lifeline that would draw him back to her side. But she was silent, and he kept on walking.

* * *

Raul Ferrador waited in the council chamber, drumming his fingers. The tabletop beneath his hand was highly polished and inlaid with a huge mosaic portraying the busy harbor of Seagirt, but Raul had stopped seeing the riot of color and detail long ago. He regarded his fidgeting fingers with irritation. The hard, knotted callouses and burn scars were still visible, but the ground-in dirt under the nails, put there by years of blacksmithing, was gone. *I've washed more in the past few months than I have in my entire life*, Raul thought, and found the idea vaguely unsettling.

His fingers paused in mid-drum at the approach of soft, rather aimless footfalls. A few moments later Dell Curry ambled into the room, arms crossed over his chest, head bowed in thought. His sleeves and the front of his fine tunic were wet.

"Where have you been?" Raul asked. "You missed the meeting!"

Dell looked up with an expression of distant surprise. "I did? I thought it was at noon."

"It's long past noon, you nitwit. Marcus never showed up, either. What kept you away this time?"

"I was with Captain Ommald. He was out in the harbor trying some new waterborne catapults, and I suppose I lost track of time."

"Since when have you been interested in war machines?"

"I'm not." Dell drifted to a chair at the opposite end of the table and sat down. "But every time a shot landed in the water, it stunned the sea-creatures below, and when they floated to the surface, I scooped them out to have a look at them." He regarded his own hands, spangled with fish scales.

"You look a mess. Weren't you cold, out there in the wet?"

Dell shrugged. "A little, but Dyer's winters aren't like Hogia's. Ommald and his men were stripped to the waist, and I just had a light cloak on. Everyone else in Seagirt is bundled to the eyes."

"Thin-blooded," Raul grunted.

"Just different. Everything here is different." Other footsteps sounded in the hall, and Dell cocked his head. "There's Marcus."

"How can you tell?"

The footsteps faltered. A crash followed, then a good-natured guffaw. Dell looked at Raul and raised his eyebrows. A moment later, Marcus Tasgall stumbled into the chamber, hair uncombed, clothing askew, reeking of wine. His eyes were bloodshot, but he was grinning. "What ho, fellow Reaches!" he cried, and then looked around the room with an expression of mock surprise. "Oh, dear. Either I'm very, very early or very,

very late."

"Late, and you know it," Raul said. "So was Dell. Piri Neff and I had to meet with Mali Uzuri and Fedro Vincenze and the rest of them by ourselves. It looked bad."

"I'm sure you conducted business in your usual efficient fashion." Marcus threw himself into a chair, tipped it back and propped both long legs on the table. "Did I miss anything important?"

"It's all important," Raul said. "You and Dell and I are supposed to be partner Reaches. That means we share the work."

"You don't need us," Dell said, without rancor.

"Of course I do."

"What utter shit," Marcus said. He was still grinning, but his lips curled with sarcasm. "Neff rolls his eyes and sighs every time Dell or I try to speak, but he defers to you. So do most of the guild masters."

"If you want to be treated equally, put in equal effort instead of spending so much time with that little Seagirt slut."

Marcus' grin widened—more a baring of teeth than a smile. "Watch yourself, my friend."

"It's the truth." Raul thumped the table with his fists and stood up. "You spend your time carousing through the city with her while Dell wanders around staring at fish and rocks and the sky. Neither of you takes your duties seriously, and I'm left to handle it all."

"And that's how you like it," Marcus said.

"Marcus and I only get in the way," Dell added. "We tried at first, Raul; you know we did. But anything I proposed got brushed aside, and Marcus—"

"These thin-skinned Dyerians don't care for my jokes," Marcus said. "They prefer Reach Ferrador's honeyed tongue."

"You're shirking your duties because your feelings are hurt?" Raul demanded. "If you want to be taken seriously, then be serious. Don't insult the guild heads, and don't waste their time with nonsense."

"I didn't think my proposals were nonsense," Dell said quietly.

"Suggesting they remove the harbor's breakwaters wasn't nonsense? Man, they're the very lifeblood of this place!"

"They've been causing the harbor to silt up for years, and the newest jetties are adding to the problem. Ask any of the fishermen. Don't they deserve some consideration as well?" Raul opened his mouth to answer, but Dell went on: "And what about the fish themselves?"

Marcus hooted, and Dell shot him a cold look. "Yes, I know you think I'm foolish. But my concern for the harbor's condition is no more foolish than your concern for the taxes levied on the taverns and doxy-houses."

"The taverns and doxy-houses pay more taxes than any other Seagirt business. Is that fair?"

"They require more regulation—healers to keep the passage of disease at bay; soldiers to break up fights. You seem to have a vested interest in—"

"Stop it, both of you," Raul said. "As Reaches we have to concern ourselves with the whole of Dyer—not just our pet issues. And that means all of us have to be present at council. Piri Neff is so vexed with the situation that he wants me to write Kristan about it."

"Are you going to tattle on us, Raul?" The mockery in Marcus' voice was unmistakable.

"I'll do what I have to."

"Then by all means, do it." Marcus kicked back from the table and stood up. "I'm off."

"We're supposed to go over the harbormaster's report with Piri this afternoon."

"I have another engagement."

"That woman is going to be the ruin of you," Dell said.

"Oh, I most fervently hope so." Marcus started from the room, but at the door he turned back. "The two of you need to loosen up—get a bit of enjoyment out of life. Perhaps you should visit her house." He winked at Dell. "There's plenty to choose from—male as well as female. They'll get your mind off your fish."

"Marcus—" Raul started to say, but Marcus was gone. Dell ducked his head and hurried out by a different door, fists clenched white, cheeks flaming. Alone once more, Raul sank back into his chair, propped his elbows on the table and buried his face in his hands.

CHAPTER FOUR

The cook thumped a loaf of bread and a large covered pot onto the middle of the table. The men leaned forward as he lifted the lid, revealing a steaming brown sludge.

Sir Mitchell groaned and slumped back in his chair. "Stew again, Dru?"

"But I put kidneys in this time," Dru said. "They give it a nice tang." His gaze fell on the single empty chair, and his hurt expression deepened. "He's not eating? I did the kidneys special for him."

No one answered, although a few sidelong glances were directed at Bastian and Quinn Logan.

"Well, I'll dish up, then," Dru said.

"Leave it," Sir Geoffrey said. "We'll serve ourselves."

Grumbling under his breath, Dru left the room. In silence, the scribe, the councilor and the six knights of Fandrall addressed themselves to their humble meal. After only a few bites, Quinn Logan pushed his plate aside. "How did he look, Geoff?" he asked in a low voice.

"Didn't see him," Sir Geoffrey said. "He answered me through the door. He sounded more like himself, though; that's something."

Sir Walter grunted and tore a hunk from the loaf of bread. "He didn't eat breakfast. Nothing at noon. And now no dinner. The boy is wasting away."

"Don't call him boy," Sir Kennet said. "It's disrespectful."

"No disrespect intended. I only mean that he's young—and this everlasting work is killing him. I woke in the middle of the night and heard him pacing the floor again, like a horse that's been left alone in its stable too long."

"He's pulled tight as a bowstring," Sir Matthew muttered. "If only he'd hunt, or game, or even get drunk and go whoring . . ." His voice trailed off, and in the ensuing silence every eye went to the empty seat at the end of the table.

"I've never seen him like that," Bastian said in a near whisper. "He's lost his temper before, but never like that. He was like a wild animal."

Quinn sighed. "It was my fault. I pushed him too far this morning. I saw the warning signs, but I just kept pushing." He rubbed his brow wearily. "He'll probably send me back to Norwinn."

"You only said what we were all thinking," Kennet said. "He's king of the realm. He needs a household in keeping with his position. It's not right."

"More people around is probably the last thing he wants," Geoffrey said. "You know how he hates it when someone comes up on him suddenly; never mind touching him. I swear, sometimes I'm afraid to speak to him for fear of getting my head snapped off." He shrugged. "But he's always been a hard fellow, distant and cold."

"You didn't know him when he was young," Sir Randolf said, so sharply that they all turned to him. He was staring into the depths of his tankard. "He was the kindest, sweetest-tempered boy before . . . before the Wichelord came. Soft-spoken, gentle manners, nimble as a bird and as beautiful as a young man could be. The women were mad for him. Ask Lyko Yeomans; his daughter Tansy and Kristan were sweethearts, until my son Owen came between them. But now Owen is dead, and Tansy is gone, and so is the Kristan Gemeta I knew." The corners of the old knight's mouth crimped downward. "What Daazna did to him . . . what he suffered . . . it was beyond any cruelty you could imagine."

"We heard he was beaten—" Matthew started to say.

"It was worse than that. So much worse."

"Well, what happened, then?" Mitchell asked. "No one has ever said."

Randolf would not meet their eyes. "And that's as it should be. But I'll tell you this much: if the StoneKing is ill-tempered, or jumps at shadows, or flinches if he's touched, he has every right, and you can thank Daazna for it."

Geoffrey drained his tankard and put it down with a bang. "Well, I never thought I'd say it, but I wish Lady Heather was here. She's a brash creature, but she could always bring him out of his black moods."

"She still writes him," Bastian said. "Beyond her usual reports, I mean. He used to answer her letters, if only in the most cursory way, but now he doesn't even do that."

They all took care not to look at Kennet. Although the topic was never discussed, it was common knowledge that the knight had proposed marriage to the Lady of the Sword and been refused. Kennet's habitually grave expression grew even more somber.

"Odd, him bringing that pair of women to the castle this morning," Matthew said. "What did you do with them, Walter?"

"Turned them over to Dru. Told him to feed them and give them hot water for a wash and a place by the fire. He wasn't any too pleased about it."

Geoffrey snorted. "He wouldn't be. He's an army cook and runs his kitchen by the book."

"I wish his book had a few more recipes in it," Quinn muttered.

"Do you think they're Wiche?" Mitchell asked. "The old one is all over tattoos, and the child has a spooky look."

"I can't imagine the StoneKing wanting Wiche around him."

"He treated that old Wiche Phelan very well."

"But he left him behind in Hogia, didn't he?"

Kennet rose from his seat, a finger to his lips. A soft, uneven tread was approaching, and the group abruptly quieted. A moment later, the StoneKing limped into the room, his old wooden box tucked under his arm.

"Good evening, my lord," Kennet said. The rest of the men stood. Mitchell hurried to pull out the StoneKing's chair. Putting his box to one side, the StoneKing sat down. With a weary flick of his hand, he gestured everyone back to their chairs.

"May I serve you, my lord?" Sir Matthew asked.

"A little, please." He looked at the pot in the middle of the table. "What is that?"

"Stew, my lord. With kidneys."

The StoneKing's pale face went a shade paler. "A very little, then."

"I can send to the kitchen for something else."

"No, it's fine. Thank you." He gazed without enthusiasm at the plate Matthew placed before him. Sir Walter poured him a tankard of ale, and he accepted it with a nod. Dark circles ringed his eyes and there was a bruise on the point of his chin that had not been there that morning. They watched as he drank from the tankard, then put it down and stared at it as if he had never seen it before.

"My lord, I—" Quinn Logan started to say.

The StoneKing lifted one hand, as if in warning. Quinn sagged back, the muscles in his jaw twitching. No one spoke. No one moved.

"Bastian," the StoneKing said at last, "tomorrow morning post notices in Kingsmere and nearby villages that the castle is hiring. Randolf and Geoffrey, you'll be in charge of filling vacancies for house servants and kitchen staff. Kennet and Walter, you have responsibility for the squires and pages. Matthew and Mitchell, find stablehands and groundskeepers."

The knights murmured their assent, darting pleased looks at each other.

"If you don't find what you need in Fandrall, then have

Bastian write to Norwinn, Hogia and Dyer to ask for suitable candidates. Quinn, you'll be responsible for determining rates of pay. Allot the funds as you see fit."

"Yes, my lord." Quinn cleared his throat. "My lord . . . may we . . . do you want us to hire your personal attendants as well?"

The StoneKing rubbed his forehead. "Do what you want, only don't trouble me about it."

There was an uncomfortable silence, broken at last by Randolf. "Don't you worry, my lord. Geoffrey and I will find you a dependable, trustworthy fellow like William." The StoneKing gave him a blank look, and Randolf's reassuring air faltered. "You remember William? Your father's manservant?"

"William." The StoneKing's hand rose toward his chest. His fingers knotted tight around the Gemeta Stone. "Yes. Someone like William. That would be good. Thank you, gentlemen." It sounded like a dismissal, but as they began to rise, the StoneKing took a deep breath. "One more thing. My behavior this morning was inexcusable. Please forgive me."

Quinn let out a broken sound, halfway between a sob and a laugh. "No, my lord, it was my fault—"

"I lost control," the StoneKing said, as if he hadn't heard. He looked at each of them in turn, with an expression of terrible weariness. "I can't lose control. Not again."

"Once we get a proper staff in place, all this fiddly, everyday rubbish will be off your shoulders," Geoffrey said. "Then you can concentrate on what's important."

"What's important . . ." the StoneKing murmured. He stared at the wooden box for a long moment, then gave himself a shake. "Well. Good night, gentlemen."

At the far end of the great hall, well out of earshot, the men grouped together in an anxious cluster.

"Do you think he's all right?" Mitchell whispered.

Bastian shook his head. "I don't like the look of him."

"Nor I," Kennet said. "I'm going to wait out here until he goes up to bed. I'll find some excuse to be afoot until then."

"I'll wait with you," Walter said. "The rest of you, go along. We've got a busy day tomorrow."

* * *

Kristan put the scrying ball on the table. He folded his arms before it and rested his head on them, careful of his bruised chin. He had not experienced a seizure in many months, and he had forgotten how the weak, shivery feeling lingered afterward.

The light from the dying fire and guttering candles danced across the ball's smooth blue surface. Kristan touched it with one forefinger; rolled it a little to the left, a little to the right. He concentrated on the smooth feel of it. *How different my life would be, little ball, if you'd never come into it. Why did Simeon give you to me?* He closed his hand around the ball and shut his eyes.

He did not realize he had fallen asleep until some small sound woke him. The room was nearly dark, the fire almost out, and his fingers around the scrying ball were stiff with cold.

"You should be in bed, StoneKing."

He jerked upright. Sitting across the table was the old Wiche woman, wrapped in her blankets and smiling. "All the castle slumbers but you and me," she went on. "Even your two faithful knights on watch outside this room are sleeping . . . now."

"Did you spell them?"

"They were nodding off anyway. I just gave them a little nudge so I could slip past."

"You take great liberties in my house, madam."

She grinned at his curt tone. "If you're going to be all lordly, boy, that puts an end to any comfortable chat. And you're longing for a comfortable chat, aren't you?"

He opened his mouth to retort, then shut it. She was right. He could not remember the last time he had spoken to anyone except as lord and ruler.

She nodded at the ball. "Do you See?"

"See?" It took a moment before Kristan realized what she meant. "Oh. No. I never could. Can you?"

He rolled the ball across the table. She caught it in her tattooed old hand, lifted it to the light and turned it this way and that. "It's a pretty thing, but the Sight has never been one of my skills. How did you come to have a scrying ball, Gemeta?"

"It was given to me when I was a child. I never understood what it really was. Never knew its true purpose until someone told me last summer. I don't know why it was given to me. I have no Wiche skills—no magic."

She chuckled. "Every child has a little magic, if only because it doesn't know any better. Every child is full of *yes*, until elders and experience fill it with *no*. Whoever gave you this ball must have seen a great deal of *yes* in you." She rolled the ball back, squinting at him. "Now, of course, you're full of *no*. All grown people are, but you—you're brimful, poor boy. No wonder you spent half the morning all aswoon on the floor."

Kristan's skin prickled. "How do you know that?"

She ran her tongue out and in, so suddenly that he jumped. "Tasted it," she said. "Tasted what led up to it, too. So bitter it almost choked me. Does it happen often?"

"No," Kristan said. "Usually I can feel it coming on and control it."

She grunted. "Control it? I can taste what it is. *Tabi'a*. True magic. You can't control that."

"And yet I do," he said, and knew he sounded arrogant.

She only smiled at him kindly. "I think you know better."

He looked down at the scrying ball, unable to bear her gaze. "Can you . . . do you . . ."

"Know how to fix it? No, boy; I don't have that learning. But I can taste the state you're in." She closed her eyes and put her tongue out again. "I taste the Stone's power. I taste the *Tabi'a* it keeps imprisoned. And I taste the hands that made those marks on your head, too. A terrible spell, that. What did he take from you?"

He could not keep his voice from trembling. "My past. He took every happy memory and left me only pain and sorrow."

"Poor boy." She tasted the air again and winced, as if it burned her. "But that terrible hurt wasn't enough, was it? He stalks you yet."

Kristan's breath caught in his throat. "Daazna is dead," he whispered.

She opened her eyes. "Everyone else believes that, but you don't. In your dreams you see his face, his eyes; feel the grip of his fingers on your brow. Even when you're awake you can still hear his laughter."

"How . . . how do you know?"

"Much as you do, I suppose. My very bones tell me, even though reason and everyone around me says different. It's your burden, boy, and your choice to make, and naught you can do about it until the moment is ripe."

"What choice is that?"

"You'll know when the time comes."

"But when will that be?"

"I expect you'll know that, too."

"And then what must I do?"

"Make your choice."

Kristan scowled. "Why can't you Wiche say anything without making a riddle of it?"

The old woman only smiled and flicked the air with her tongue once more. "I taste your names," she said. "I taste Kinglet and the flutter of little wings, insignificant in a great forest teeming with life, but still, that fluttering may cause a leaf to shiver and drop. I taste Fiskur, all shining slippery scales, bigger than Kinglet but still only one shimmering form in a wide ocean of fish, and yet the flick of a tail makes a ripple that can grow ever wider until it laps against the shore. And I taste StoneKing, a name so ponderous that it cracks the spine of its bearer. I taste these names and others, too: loving names like Princeling, mocking names like Wet Nurse, harsh names like

Fool and Coward and . . ." The old woman's voice trailed off. "And *Avama*," she said at last. "I taste *Avama*."

Kristan shuddered. He saw the old woman mark it, and sneered to show he did not care. "And which of these names is the right one?"

"All, and some, and none," the old woman said. She heaved herself out of her chair and picked up the pack at her feet. "I'm glad we got the chance to talk, Gemeta. Goodbye."

"You're leaving? Now? It's the middle of the night."

"The night and I are old friends."

"What about Nolle?"

"She might cry a bit, when she finds I'm gone."

"You can't leave her. There's no place for her here."

"You're hiring, aren't you? Give her a little job, a warm place to sleep, her meals and a coin or two on occasion, and she'll earn her keep." The old woman shouldered her pack. "I warned her about her light fingers. She'll behave herself. Maybe. She might bring you luck. You look as if you could use some luck. Goodbye, StoneKing."

"Wait." Kristan stood up, unwilling to let the old woman and her air of comforting familiarity go. "Wait until morning."

She only smiled. "Look after my girl. And look after yourself, Gemeta."

In the morning, on discovering her abandonment, Nolle did not cry. She did, however, startle everyone by turning immediately into a cat and fleeing high into the scaffolding in the great hall, where she stayed until Kristan coaxed her down with the promise of kind treatment and work that would not be too hard. Randolf put her under Dru's watchful eye, and the old army cook taught her to chop vegetables and pluck chickens and turn meat on the spit in front of the big kitchen hearth. Although Dru was strict with her, he was also protective, and fended off the curious and the unkind. Nolle gave no more trouble, and as the castle began to fill with new faces, Kristan forgot about her.

CHAPTER FIVE

Ravelin traced his forefinger along the map. "The Stratheden forces were lined all along the ridge here, so they had the high ground, you see? And here's the valley below."

The Lady of the Sword studied the map, arms crossed and lower lip caught between her teeth. He was pleased that she was finally standing beside him as he explained the strategy of this particular battle; in the past, she had been careful to keep the table between them.

"Why didn't you use catapults against the Stratheden forces? Here and here," she said, thrusting a forefinger at the map. "They would have given you an advantage."

Some cream may coax this cat closer. "Clever of you to see that. How do you know about catapults?"

"Kristan used them in our first battle with the Daaznans," she said, and with the mention of the Gemeta's name her face grew wistful.

Isobel was right, Ravelin thought; *the girl does pine for the StoneKing.*

"That battle was on the Plain," he said. "It's the perfect terrain for catapults. But for this battle, getting the equipment up the high mountain passes would have taken all our strength and resources, and we had little enough to spare."

"What made you think of an assault over the mountains?"

He couldn't help grinning. "I knew Aldo wouldn't think of it. We were outnumbered, and with the mountains at his back, he felt protected."

"Wasn't it risky, to divide your limited forces that way?"

"It was a risk I was willing to take."

"But the men you sent into the valley to lure the Stratheden forces down—what about them?"

He shrugged. "We had to bring the enemy into position for the rear assault to succeed."

"You knew you were sending them to their deaths. They must have known it, too."

He regarded her with a raised eyebrow. "You are so young."

"What's that supposed to mean?"

"The Hogian army of my youth was different from the one you command now. The men were career soldiers. Fearless. Ruthless. They took commands without question and went into battle with terrible joy." A knot of sudden anger rose in Ravelin's throat, and he had to turn away to collect himself. *All that has been stolen from me*, he thought; *stolen by a boy king and the children he commands.*

He felt Heather's hand on his arm. When he turned back, he was startled by the compassion in her bright eyes. "It must have broken your heart to lose them."

He realized she had mistaken his anger for grief over the lives he had sacrificed. *Oh, you little fool*, he thought, and had to fight back a grin. "It was a great loss, but it gave us the advantage at last. Aldo's casualties were enormous. Once we gained the ridge, he knew it was only a matter of time before we'd be hammering on his very gates. He was quick to negotiate a truce."

She turned to look at the map, gnawing on her lower lip again. "I'm not sure I could have done it."

He had done it without a second thought, but he shook his head in sham regret. "Great victories come at great price. I came back to Hogia a hero, but it was a hollow triumph."

Heather flicked a glance at him. "I heard."

He had been referring to the lost soldiers, but it was clear that her cautious sympathy was meant for some other hurt. All at once he grasped what she meant, and an acid bile rose in his mouth. "Who told you?" he almost snarled.

"Phelan," Heather replied.

The flesh of his face and neck felt as if it was burning. A red haze fogged his vision and through it Heather's blue eyes took on a violet cast. He wanted to grab her by the throat and squeeze until those pitying violet eyes bulged. Instead, he clutched the edge of the table and held onto it with all his strength.

"What was her name?" Heather asked.

"Liana." A bitter laugh burst from his lips. "Look what you've made me do. I swore I'd never speak her name again."

"Why?"

"You have to ask? She slept with my father."

"Did she have a choice?"

"And then she let that Wiche fool put his hands on her."

"Your father used her and you rejected her. She was desperate and in mortal pain. She went to Phelan for help."

He knew he was in danger of losing what little ground he had gained with her. He tried to meet her gaze, but was overwhelmed by memories of his father's triumphant smirk, of Liana's pleas for forgiveness, of his cold, proud anger as he turned his back on her, and his grief and guilt on learning of her death. "My pain is my own," he spat. "Would you like it if I prodded and quizzed you about the Gemeta?"

She gasped. The sound freed him, and the anguish in her face supplanted his pain with cruel satisfaction. "Your pardon, my lady, but I was raised a warrior. When I'm pushed, I push back."

"So you do," she said through tight lips.

The little victory turned his own mouth wet with desire. He wanted to grab her, rip away her ridiculous mannish clothing, throw her screaming and struggling to the table and take her. Instead, he leaned over the map, concealing his rising hardness beneath the table's edge. "It would be easier to explain the intricacies of this battle if I could show you the actual terrain. I built a fine hunting lodge nearby after the war was over—the one where my courtiers lived after they fled from Daazna." He pointed to the map. "It would be about two days' march. We could take your troops there and carry out some war games— weather and the StoneKing permitting, of course," he added, with a meek inclination of his head. "The lodge belongs to him now."

"I can write him and ask," Heather answered. Her face was carefully expressionless.

"The exercise would benefit your troops. And I could use a change of scenery myself. Long winters on this Plain can be tedious."

"I'm used to them."

Her tone was brusque, but Ravelin only smiled. "Of course you are. You're a Hogian, born and bred. But large as this castle is, there are times when the walls seem to draw in very close, don't they?"

She swallowed hard before answering. "They do indeed."

As he rolled up the map, he studied her. He could tell the attention made her uncomfortable; she shifted from foot to foot and finally lifted her chin with an air of defiance. "Well, what?"

He shook himself, as if waking from a reverie. "I beg your pardon. I was only thinking . . . I used to find your choice of clothing peculiar, but I see the sense of it now. You've succeeded brilliantly at making your men see you as their commander. It would be a mistake to remind them that you're still a woman, and a young one at that."

"Nonsense." There was a growing fire in her eye. "My men are disciplined. I can wear whatever I want."

"To be sure," he answered, letting the merest hint of doubt color his tone. He handed her the map and gave her his court- liest bow. "I hope the Gemeta will send his permission quickly so we can make plans."

Someone knocked at the door, and they both turned. Sir Bran was standing in the doorway. "Your pardon, my lady," he said, shooting a cold look at Ravelin, "but can you come? There's been a fight amongst the cesspit workers. Uklet is dead."

Heather blew out a sigh. "I can guess what happened. Where is Staub now?"

"Sir Jerrold is taking him back to his cell."

"I'll deal with him later, then. Show me the body."

The knight hurried out, and the Lady of the Sword followed, rapping the rolled map irritably against her leg. Ravelin caught up with her, fixing his features into an expression of concern. "Uklet and Staub? Who are they?"

"You should know," she said gruffly. "They were your soldiers, once."

The urge to strike her was strong, but he made himself sigh instead. "I'm sure I should. But after Iele . . . I don't always remember what I should."

It was an untruth; when he had been king, he had rarely bothered to learn the names of either soldiers or servants. All the same, Heather's face softened. *Little fool*, he thought.

"They're two of the Wichelord's One-Eyed Men—the soldiers he spelled for the attack on Fandrall's castle," she said. "One in their unit resisted the spell, and the rest were somehow damaged when Daazna punished the offender."

Ravelin pursed his lips. "I remember now. I saw it happen. It turned my stomach sick."

"None of them were right in the head afterward. When the Wichelord was killed, the few who still lived were too violent and untrustworthy to be restored to ranks like the other Daaznans, so they've been imprisoned below stairs ever since. They were never fit for anything but cesspit duty, and that under guard. There were five of them, originally, but one hung himself, another was trampled by the cess-wagon's horses, and the third was killed when he tried to attack one of the guards. Staub and Uklet were the last of them. Now there's only Staub."

They were passing out of the keep now, wincing at the slap of icy air. A small crowd clustered near the southwest corner of the courtyard, by the cesspit opening in the keep wall. "Make way," Sir Bran told them. They stepped aside, revealing a dead man lying on his back. His throat had been cut from one ear to the other, and the blood pooling beneath his head and shoulders steamed faintly. Another knight, Sir Eaden, stood nearby with the cesspit overseer. "I'm sorry, my lady," he said, as Heather joined the crowd. "Uklet and Staub were muttering at each other all morning, and finally Uklet tried to hit Staub. It was over before we realized what was happening."

Heather crouched by the body and Ravelin peered over her shoulder. The dead man's lips were curled back from his teeth in a snarl and his single eye stared sightlessly at the snow-heavy sky. "Was anyone else hurt?" Heather asked.

"No, my lady. The regular workers got clear, and the guards were able to subdue Staub before he could do any more harm." Sir Eaden produced a long sliver of metal and handed it to her. "Who knows where he got this, or how long he'd been honing it in secret."

"Did Uklet have any family?"

"None, my lady. At least, none that would own him."

"Arrange for him to be buried in the common graveyard, then. And get all these gawkers back to work."

The overseer hustled his wide-eyed workers away as Sir Eaden called for assistance with the body. Heather turned and strode back toward the keep, so quickly that Ravelin had to hustle to stay with her. "May I see that makeshift knife?" he asked, and Heather passed it to him without comment. He ran his thumb along its edge. "He must have worked on this blade for a long time. It's as sharp as a razor. What are you going to do with this Staub now?"

"I don't know. Clearly, he can't be trusted any longer." She fell silent, and Ravelin slipped the crude knife into his belt. They reentered the keep, crossed the great hall and headed downstairs toward the soldiers' hall. The door was closed, and Heather rapped a distinctive rat-a-tat on it, hesitated for a few moments, then threw it open. As she descended into the hall, the men were already at attention, although some were surreptitiously twitching leggings straight or fastening tunics. Only the men of rank were housed here; the common soldiers occupied barracks in the courtyard. "As you were," Heather said absently, but they remained at attention as she crossed to the door at the far end of the room.

"You didn't give them much notice," Ravelin said, as they went down the final flight of stairs. "What if you caught them undressed?"

She shrugged. "I've seen naked men before."

What had been the interrogation room of the castle's lowest level was largely empty. The tall scaffolds that had occupied it for years had been disassembled and stacked along one wall. Beyond lay the corridor of little prison cells. The first cell had no door on its battered hinges and stood open and empty, but the next cell was shut, and a terrible wailing echoed from within. Sir Jerrold, Lady Heather's second in command, waited with two guards in the corridor. "We locked him in, my lady," he said, "but he's been shrieking and acting the fool as usual."

"Unlock the door, please," Heather said. "Guards, have your pikes at the ready." With an officious rattle of the keys, Jerrold unlocked the door and threw it open, and with the guards behind her, Heather stepped into the cell. Ravelin crowded into the doorway, ignoring the disdainful look Sir Jerrold gave him.

The man Staub was squeezed into the far corner, his one eye rolling, his face and filthy tunic smeared with Uklet's blood. He was thumping his head repeatedly against the wall.

"Stop it," Heather said. "What do you have to say for yourself, Staub?"

To Ravelin's surprise, Staub obeyed. He even tried to draw himself to attention. "Lady," he whispered. "Lady of the Sword. Good morning, Lady."

"It's not a good morning, Staub. You killed a man. You'll have to be punished."

Staub wailed again and fell to his knees. "I had to! I had to! He kept coming into my cell at night!"

"Nonsense. He was locked in his own cell, the same as you."

"He came at night! He muttered things when I wanted to sleep. Lady, I couldn't sleep. He kept me from sleeping!" Staub crawled toward her, as if to grasp her feet, but one of the guards brandished his pike in the man's face. Staub cringed back, his hands over his face. "Don't hit me, don't hit me again."

"No one's hit you, fool, but someone will if you don't control yourself," Sir Jerrold said.

"Quiet," Heather said. She stooped so she could look Staub in the eye. "Staub, no doubt others will say you should pay for the life you took with your own. I don't see the point in that. But you're going to have to stay in your cell until I sort out what to do with you."

Staub groaned. He thrust his hands between his thighs, as if to warm them, and began to rock back and forth. "Lady, please let me out. Let me out to work. I don't mind the cesspit; truly I don't, but don't keep me here in this cell in the dark. Not with the whispering."

"You'll be alone now. No one will whisper."

"Lady, let me out. Let me out and I'll be good. I'll be your dog, your good dog. I'll fetch your things and lie by your bed at night and lick your hands . . ." Staub began to massage his crotch, and his grimace twisted into a wild-eyed grin. "I'll lick your feet, and your ass, and between your legs where the saddle chafes you—"

Heather straightened up, mouth tight with disgust. Ravelin grabbed one of the guard's pikes and struck Staub across the back with the butt of it. Staub cried out and began to blubber. "Shut your mouth," Ravelin barked, and with a show of outrage, turned on Sir Jerrold. "Shame on you, to stand here and let this scum talk such filth to your lady commander."

Sir Jerrold flushed bright red and started to stammer out an apology, but Heather silenced him with an upraised hand. "Everyone out of this cell," she said. "There's no reasoning with Staub when he's like this."

They filed into the corridor, and Staub shrieked as the key rattled in the lock again. "Get back to your posts," Heather said to the guards, then turned to the crestfallen knight. "Sir Jerrold, I'm sure you have other duties to attend."

"But Staub—"

"I'll deal with him later, when he's had time to settle down." She waited until guards and knight had gone, then turned to Ravelin. "I'm sure you meant well, Reach Seachlan, but I don't need your protection."

Such a fierce little warrior, Ravelin thought, fighting back a smirk. "My apologies," he said, "but I couldn't let him speak to you that way."

Heather's brows knotted. "I've heard worse. I'd appreciate it if you wouldn't interfere in future."

Ravelin bowed. "As you wish, my lady."

He watched her go, amused by her stiff spine, her squared shoulders, her long stride. *You may be a warrior, but you're still a woman, and every woman has her weakness. Now that I know yours, I'll find a way to use it.*

"My lord," a voice whispered. Ravelin turned toward the cell door. Two grimy fists gripped the bars of the little window, and Staub's single eye peered at him from the darkness within. "I know you, my lord. I was your man, once; your loyal man. I did your bidding, and was proud to do it. I let the Wichelord spell me, and see where I am now. Let me out, my lord. I can't bear the whispering anymore. Help me."

Ravelin smiled. "Perhaps we can help each other, Staub." He drew the crude knife from his belt, stood on tiptoe and placed it on the lintel above the cell door. Staub peered toward it longingly, but it was out of both sight and reach. "I'll leave your knife up there while I think things over," Ravelin told him. "It'll remind you to behave yourself and wait patiently, like the good soldier you are."

"All right," Staub said in a choking voice. "All right, my lord, I'll wait. I'm your loyal man, my lord. But don't keep me waiting. The whispering . . . it gets louder all the time. I can't bear it much longer."

"Be patient," Ravelin said. "Think about the knife, and keep silent, and I'll be calling on you sometime soon."

He turned away, and as he left the dark corridor and ascended to the soldiers' hall, he heard Staub weeping.

* * *

Alister was perched at his tall writing desk, scribbling furiously, but when Heather strode into his work chamber, he looked up. "You look like a woman with a mission. To what do I owe this visit?"

Heather handed him the rolled-up map. "This can go back into your library. Do we have any messengers headed to Fandrall?"

"Their runner just arrived. I was going to give you this at dinner." He handed her a letter sealed with plain wax, and she blew out an irritable sigh at the sight of Sir Kennet's handwriting.

Alister wagged his quill at her. "For shame. He's a faithful correspondent, whatever else you may think of him."

"Nothing else for me?"

"Sorry, no." Alister's tone was brisk, but his gaze was sympathetic. "The runner won't start back for another day, at least, so you've plenty of time to answer Kennet's note."

"I need to send a message to Kristan."

"He hasn't answered your last few letters, cousin."

The words stung, but she let them pass. "This isn't a letter; it's an official request. In fact, you can write it for me." She waited until Alister had a fresh piece of parchment in front of him.

"Tell him I'd like permission to use his northeastern hunting lodge—the one in the mountains near the Stratheden border."

"Since when have you been interested in hunting?" Alister asked, as he bent over the parchment. His writing was elegant, much finer than her own hurried scrawl.

"It's not for hunting. I want to take some troops up there for a training exercise."

"Are you sure that's wise? Winter isn't over yet."

"Barring a blizzard on the way there or back, we should be fine." Alister completed the message and handed her the quill; she signed her name at the bottom. "Besides, my men need some fresh challenges and I'm sick to death of this place."

"Coward. Running off to leave Uncle Colin and me to deal with Ravelin alone."

"I'm taking Ravelin with me." She raised her hand as Alister began to protest. "You should be thanking me."

"Heather, you know how Kristan feels about him. You know he's not to be trusted."

"I don't trust him. But I need to keep picking his brain about the Stratheden campaign. There's nothing else I can glean from maps and old reports."

"Uncle Colin won't like it—you and all those men."

"I'll take Bayla."

"One maidservant isn't much of a retinue for a Lady. Why not take Annys or Lily? Or Isobel?" He grinned at Heather's glare. "If you managed to lose her along the way, you'd have the thanks of the entire castle."

"This isn't a pleasure trip."

"It wouldn't be, with her along."

Exasperated, Heather threw up her hands. "Just send the message, would you?"

"As you command, Lady of the Sword." He folded the parchment, dripped red wax onto the opening and pressed Hogia's official seal into the warm blob. "Done. I'm sure he'll answer this one, cousin." He picked up his quill and turned to his work, then hesitated. "If it's any solace to you, no one gets personal correspondence from the StoneKing. Uncle Colin and I sometimes put the odd little note to him into official packets—nothing of importance, just enquiring after his health or passing on a greeting—but he never responds."

You didn't have what we had, Heather thought, but she only nodded. "Thanks, cousin."

Upstairs in her bedchamber, she found her maidservant Bayla sitting before the fire. One of Heather's gauntlets was in her lap, and a curved needle was sunk into the leather, as if ready to take the next stitch, but Bayla's attention was fixed on the letter in her hand. She jumped a bit as Heather stepped into the room. "There you are, my lady. You missed lunch. If you're hungry, I can fetch you something."

"I had a big breakfast. Go on with your letter, Bayla." Heather sat at the other end of the bench and began to work her boots off. Bayla put the letter aside and knelt to assist her. "Is that from Sir Walter?"

Bayla nodded, a slight flush coloring her cheeks, and Heather was both amused and touched. Her maidservant's tall figure had gained much-needed flesh over the past six months, and her haunted expression had softened. *She's grown quite lovely,* Heather thought; *all the men look at her when she passes now, but Walter saw her beauty first.*

"What's the news from Fandrall?"

"The reconstruction of the castle is going well," Bayla said, grunting a bit as she yanked at Heather's boot. "Sir Walter says the floor above the great hall is laid at last and the framing of the interior walls has begun. Once the upstairs is finished, the StoneKing and his retinue will finally have better quarters. They've been living in the eastern wing of the castle, sharing what used to be the bachelor knights' chambers—not at all appropriate for men of their rank." The boot came off and Bayla turned to its mate. "And he says the StoneKing has finally begun hiring in earnest. Walter says the castle is so full of servants that you can't turn without stumbling over someone new. There's a Wiche girl among them that can change into a cat."

"A Wiche girl?"

"The StoneKing returned from a ride one morning with two of them in tow: the girl and an old woman. Walter says the old woman moved on, who knows where, and left the girl behind."

"How old is she?"

Bayla pulled off the second boot, picked up her letter and perused its pages. "He doesn't say."

Heather felt a pang of jealousy and was instantly ashamed of herself. "Any other news?"

"Candidates for squires and pages are being sought." Bayla nodded at Kennet's letter, still unopened, which Heather had set aside. "Walter says Kennet wrote to you about it."

"Oh, good heavens," Heather said, and quickly broke the seal. "I thought this would be one of his usual letters. I haven't even looked at it."

She extended her stockinged feet to the fire and warmed her toes as she read. Kennet was prone to long passages about lonely nights, flowery descriptions of Heather's hair and eyes and the occasional attempt at poetry, but this letter was much more businesslike. "He and Walter are conducting the interviews. He's putting me on notice that if they don't find what they need in Fandrall, they've been instructed to bring in candidates from the Reach countries." She blew out a sigh. "We're short of decent squires and pages ourselves. There just aren't enough boys in Hogia to fill the need. This country has been barren for so long; I hate to think what we're going to do for fresh recruits in a few years."

"Strange," Bayla said. "I thought, with the Wichelord dead, everything would come right again."

Heather put the letter aside. "Maybe we just need to have patience—and hope." *Hope holds the key*, she thought, suddenly remembering the battered old book of verses that had been the start of last summer's journey. *I wonder where that book is. Burned up with the rest of Daazna's things, no doubt. Maybe it was for the best.*

She stared at her toes, lost in thought. At last Bayla's voice broke through her reverie. "Would you like to change for dinner, my lady?"

She was about to say no, but remembered telling Ravelin that she could wear whatever she wanted. Her response had been bold, but after the incident with Staub she wondered if he was right. "I think I will," she said. "It's been ages since I've worn a dress."

Bayla's mouth dropped open, but she quickly recovered her composure. "Any particular gown, my lady?"

"Oh, it doesn't matter. You pick one."

As Bayla rummaged through the big storage chest, Heather stood before the fire and pulled off her padded tunic and bulky leggings. She had designed the clothing herself, for warmth and ease of movement, but now she wondered if she had made herself look freakish. "But you are a freak, lady commander," she muttered to herself.

"Let's try this one," Bayla said, pulling out a russet gown. "It was big on you last summer, but maybe it'll fit now."

"Have I gotten fat?"

Bayla grinned at her consternation. "Far from it, my lady. Your waist and hips are as slender as a boy's. But your shoulders have gotten broader."

She helped Heather into the dress, and then stepped behind to lace it up. Heather stood as still as she could against Bayla's yanking, but after spending so much time in her work garments, the dress felt odd—constricting through the chest and disconcertingly airy around the legs.

"How do I look?" she asked, as Bayla came back into view.

Her maidservant surveyed her with a critical eye. "Well . . . perhaps you should see for yourself."

Heather turned to the mirror on the far wall. She rarely looked at herself and was startled by what she saw: a dress that sagged at the waist and hips but was so tight through the bodice that it mashed Heather's modest breasts flat. The muscled expanse of her shoulders and neck were exposed, along with the thick scars left by Iele's teeth.

"The dress barely meets across the back," Bayla said. "It was all I could do to fasten it. I'm afraid your other dresses will be worse. You were so thin last summer."

Heather raised her hand to the scars, grateful that the marks from Iele's knife were low on her back. "I look like a grizzled old warrior."

"Not at all. Look here." Bayla worked Heather's hair loose from its coronet of braids and shook it out across her shoulders and breasts, veiling the scars and ill-fitting bodice. "No man has hair like yours, my lady. Such a beautiful color, and so thick."

Heather flicked at the fringe across her forehead. "And so unbecomingly cut."

"There are women in Needwood who've cut their hair the same way, in your honor."

"And were no doubt sorry for it afterward. I know I was."

"You should wear your looks with pride. You earned them with courage in the StoneKing's service. I wish I'd done as you did. I wish I'd taken up arms instead of—"

Bayla's voice broke. She started to turn away, but Heather caught her arm.

"You earned your scars, too," she said quietly, "but you wear them on your heart." A faint smile crossed Bayla's face, and Heather went on: "As for taking up arms, any fool can do that. At least I was stubborn enough to demand that someone teach me, and fortunate to find a good teacher." She smiled through a stab of sorrow at the memory of her lessons with Kristan in O Tópos. "If you want to learn to use a sword, I can pass on what I learned."

"I'd like that," Bayla said. "For now, though, I'd better see if I can make this dress presentable."

"Let it go. It's clear I'll need some new ones, and until we can make them, my work clothes will have to do."

She reached for her discarded clothing, but Bayla was faster. "No, you don't," she said. "These need a good sponging and brushing before they're fit to wear. Put on your dressing gown until I come back. I don't care what kind of clothes you wear, my lady, but if I have anything to say about it, they'll be clean."

CHAPTER SIX

"Have mercy," Kristan said under his breath.

"My lord?"

Sir Kennet stood at Kristan's left, watching him closely. All the knights were watching him, as well as Bastian and Quinn Logan. Lyko and his band of masons were taking their noon meal perched on the rough-finished steps of the new staircase; Kristan felt their eyes on him, too. Worst of all were the combined gazes of the candidates for squire, a round dozen of them: tall, muscular boys in their mid-teens, brought from their plows and anvils and millwheels for a chance to be the StoneKing's squire. *Big strong boys, the pride of their villages and the cream of Fandrall's youth*, Kristan thought, but in every towering form he saw Owen's cocksure posture and in every face, Owen's cruel eyes. With an effort, he pulled himself back to the present. "Nothing," he said to Kennet. "Carry on."

Kennet nodded to Sir Walter. Starting at the head of the line, Walter introduced each boy with his name, place of birth, training and skills. Each boy stepped forward and greeted Kristan with the proper obeisance before returning to his place in the line. The similarity in their deportment and words made it clear they had been carefully drilled. It was only after Walter moved on that the boys' true natures showed; they glanced slantwise at each other, smirking in triumph or scowling in challenge. The sight made Kristan feel old and weary.

In the anteroom beyond the great hall, the keep's main

doors slammed open, admitting a blast of cold air and the roar of the storm outside. Kristan winced, and Walter broke off in mid-introduction to glare toward the disturbance. Bastian hurried out, hissing a reprimand. Walter cleared his throat pointedly, bringing Kristan's attention back to the squires, but before the knight could continue, Bastian returned, clutching an open scroll. Behind him strode a tall, handsome man, snug in a thick-furred cloak and hood. A gawky, shivering, ill-clad boy followed in his wake, gaping as he looked around the hall. Bastian hastened to Quinn's side and the two of them held a whispered conversation over the opened scroll. The tall man caught sight of Kristan and pulled up short. He bowed low, and the boy ran straight into his backside. With an oath the man turned, lips drawn back from his teeth, one hand raised to strike.

Startled, Quinn and Bastian looked up. "Sir, do not discipline your servant in the StoneKing's presence," Quinn snapped.

"He's not my servant," the man protested. "He must have slipped in behind me. Go on, boy, get out of here."

The boy did not even look at the knight. He stared at Kristan, snow melting in his mousy hair. His small eyes shone in his homely, freckled face. "Are you the StoneKing?" he asked. His voice snagged somewhere between the flute of the child he had been and the deeper tones of the man he would become. Bemused, Kristan nodded, and the boy beamed. "Hello, sir. I want to be your squire."

One of the older boys guffawed, but stifled it at Walter's glower. The whole room burst into motion. Fire in his eye, Sir Randolf stamped toward the main entrance, where the newly-hired doorward and his two pages stood heavy-footed with guilt. Sir Geoffrey hurried to speak to the tall man, who was studying the rough staircase and the raw wood of the ceiling above with dismay. The boy took a few steps toward Kristan only to be intercepted by Sir Mitchell and Sir Matthew. Suddenly, Quinn and Bastian were at Kristan's right elbow. "My lord," the councilor hissed. "My lord, I must speak to you immediately."

"My lord, the candidates—" Kennet said.

"My lord, this gentleman—" Geoffrey interrupted.

"My lord, I bring—" said the tall man.

"My lord, the boy—" Sir Matthew said.

"My lord, the message—" Quinn insisted.

Kristan resisted the urge to clap his hands over his ears. Instead, he raised a finger, and everyone quieted. "Kennet," he said, "have the candidates wait. Matthew, let the boy wait as well. Geoff, see to our visitor's cloak. Quinn, Bastian—come with me." He limped to the far side of the room, flicking a warning glance at Lyko on the staircase. The master mason hustled his workmen up to the landing, out of sight and earshot beyond the new walls.

Kristan turned to Quinn and Bastian. "Well, what's so important?" he said, keeping his voice low. "It had better be news of a plague or a declaration of war."

"It's worse than that, my lord," Quinn said. "It's a special envoy from Malchea—from King Lockward."

"Who, the tall fellow?"

"No, my lord," Bastian said. "He's Sir Velios, sent in advance of the envoy. Their wagons are mired in the mud some miles away. The envoy decided to leave them behind and come ahead on horseback."

"That's it? That's the reason for all this uproar?"

"The envoy, my lord," Quinn said. "It's . . . it's Lockward's daughter."

"She's coming here?"

"Yes, my lord. Sir Velios says she should arrive before dark. My lord, where are we going to put her? The upstairs rooms aren't finished yet, and there's nothing else suitable—"

"What was Lockward thinking, sending his daughter on such a journey in the dead of winter? Never mind," Kristan went on, as both Bastian and Quinn opened their mouths to respond. "Bring that Velios fellow here. And fetch Sir Randolf and Sir Geoffrey."

The three knights came hurrying. "Sir Velios, welcome," Kristan said, but he could not keep the edge out of his voice. "I understand the princess is on her way."

"Yes, my lord."

"I thought I made it clear that my castle was badly damaged during last summer's siege and won't be fit to receive visitors until the spring. Why did King Lockward ignore my message?"

"My lord, it was Princess Jelena's idea." Sir Velios shifted from foot to foot. "The princess is . . . is . . . well, she's a very determined young woman, my lord."

"We'll see how determined she is once she sees the state of this castle. I assume she travels with a retinue?"

"Yes, my lord."

"How large?"

"Oh, it's small, my lord, quite small—"

"How large, Sir Velios?" The knight hesitated, and Kristan stamped his foot. "Answer my question, or by the Stone I'll have her and you and the rest of your party housed in the stables."

"Three dozen, my lord," Sir Velios blurted.

"Three dozen?" Geoffrey repeated. He knotted his hands in his bristly hair as if he wanted to yank it out. "We can't accommodate three, my lord."

"Most of her company will come later, once the wagons are freed," Sir Velios said. "For now, it's just the princess, her elderly aunt, two female attendants and an escort of five knights. And me."

Kristan brushed past him and strode to the foot of the staircase. "Lyko!" he shouted, and the master mason appeared on the landing. "Lyko, can those upstairs rooms be occupied?"

Lyko gaped at him. "My lord, the first coat of plaster on the walls isn't dry. And the floors are just raw wood."

"Are the windows sound? Are the doors hung? Do the flues work?"

"Yes, my lord, but it's still terribly cold and drafty."

"Never mind. Get all your workmen and their equipment out of there." Kristan turned to Randolf. "As soon as the rooms are clear, get them swept and have fires laid in the hearths."

"My lord, you can't put the princess in an unfinished room," Quinn protested, and Sir Velios nodded vigorously.

"I'm not. The princess will have my chamber in the eastern wing, and her retinue the rooms below. They're not elegant chambers, Sir Velios, but at least they're warm."

"But where will you sleep?"

Kristan jerked his head toward the unfinished rooms overhead.

"Upstairs?" Randolf squawked. "My lord, you might as well sleep out in the open. It's that cold up there."

"I'm no stranger to sleeping in the open." He waved the other knights over. "Gentlemen, we're about to be invaded by the princess of Malchea. She'll be arriving with part of her retinue before nightfall. We'll house them in the eastern wing, so all of us—including Bastian and Quinn—must clear out of those rooms. I'm moving upstairs. You can do the same, or bunk in the barracks with the soldiers where it's warmer; it's all one to me. Walter, put all those young squire brutes to work fetching bedframes, mattresses and bedding. Randolf knows where to find such things. Matthew, have my belongings carried upstairs and see that all the vacated chambers are presentable: fires laid, new candles, fresh linens on the beds. Geoffrey, tell the kitchen staff to prepare for additional mouths to feed. Check our stores and arrange for the necessary provisions. Mitchell, find room in the stables for our guests' mounts. Kennet, assemble men for whatever sort of official greeting is appropriate. I'm sure Sir Velios can advise you."

Walter hesitated as the knights hurried off. "My lord, what about that boy? Shall I throw him out?"

"No. Put him to work with the others. There's plenty to do." Walter grinned and was gone, and Kristan pinched the bridge of his nose as he tried to think what to do next.

Quinn cleared his throat. "My lord, perhaps a bath and more suitable clothes would be in order. And a shave. I can send to Kingsmere for the barber."

Kristan's skin crawled at the idea of someone's hands on his head. "I can shave myself."

"Your hair has grown quite long, my lord. Perhaps the barber—"

Quinn's voice died as Kristan turned a cold stare on him. "I've told you before; I have no interest in Lockward's daughter. Don't try to groom me like a prize ram."

Quinn twisted his long fingers together. "My lord, I . . . all of us . . . we take pride in our service to you. It would give us such pleasure to see you receive Malchea's envoy looking your best."

"Oh, very well," Kristan said crossly. "Arrange for the bath and fresh clothing in my work chamber, out of the way of all this fuss. I'll be there shortly."

He limped up the stairs, watching his footing on the uneven patches. The workmen, carrying down armfuls of tools and supplies, stood clear as he ascended. Lyko waited on the landing, his brow knitted. "My lord, I have an idea. May I show you?"

"Please do." It was so cold he could see his breath.

Lyko led the way down the hall. The doors to every room stood open; scaffolding had been raised here and there and the air was thick with the smell of damp plaster. Outside, a blast of wind rattled all the windows, and Kristan's mouth tightened at the thought of anyone being fool enough to travel through such weather.

The largest chamber was at the end of the hall, and Lyko stepped aside to let Kristan enter first. With his hands tucked into his armpits for warmth, Kristan scrutinized the room. The generous space, with its many windows, double hearth and lofty ceiling, was a reconstruction of his father's bedchamber. He closed his mind against remembering more and concentrated on the master mason, who was gesturing at the walls.

"You'll need fires in the hearths up here, my lord, but there's a good chance the heat might cause the plaster to dry too fast and crack. If we use scaffolds to enclose the area around the hearth and hung covers on them—canvas, old hangings and blankets, whatever's available—that would shield the walls from the heat and make a snug space for sleeping. It'll look a mess, my lord, and you won't have much room, but—"

"That doesn't matter," Kristan said. "Good thinking, Lyko. I'll have coverings sent up and you and your workmen can arrange things as you see fit."

As they returned to the landing, they met a bevy of servants ascending with brooms and firewood. Lyko squeezed past them, calling for his workmen. Kristan stepped aside to let them go by. Below, the squire candidates were carrying bed frames and mattresses across the great hall. "I left home to get away from this kind of work," one of them was complaining.

"Then why not leave?" another candidate said. "The Gemeta won't be picking you, clod hopper."

"Nor you, cobbler boy."

"What a wreck this place is," someone else said.

The small, freckled newcomer poked his head from behind a teetering pile of bedding. "Oh, no, it's beautiful," he said. "It's the most beautiful place I've ever seen."

The first boy smirked and stuck his foot in the other's path. Boy and bedding went flying, to a chorus of guffaws. At that moment one of the candidates caught sight of Kristan on the staircase and hissed a warning. As Kristan descended, they attempted to bow in spite of their burdens.

"Get on with your work," Kristan said, without a glance.

The would-be squires continued up the stairs, leaving the freckled boy on his knees, clumsily trying to fold the linens. "Four hands make the job easier," Kristan said, picking up one of the sheets. "Stand up and take the other end."

The boy's eyes went wide in his tear-streaked face, but then his smile burst out again. "Oh, yes, sir! Thank you, sir."

"What's your name, boy?"

"Serle Cordell. I'm from eastern Fandrall, sir, from a village near the Mor. I'm twelve, sir; I know that's too old for a page and too young for a squire but I'll work hard, sir; I swear I will. I'll be a good squire, sir, and then you'll make me a knight and I'll ride across your lands and do your will. I remember when you came back last summer, sir; I wanted to be on the shore when you landed but I couldn't leave my sheep; we don't have so many sheep but what we have are wily, sir; wily and fast, and no one around to help since they'd all gone chasing the Daaznans—"

Serle kept up a steady stream of chatter, barely pausing for breath, and Kristan let him ramble, amused by his enthusiasm. As Kristan heaped the boy's arms with the refolded linens, Sir Matthew hurried into the great hall, carrying Kristan's wooden box and followed by a procession of servants bearing the rest of Kristan's belongings.

"How goes it?" Kristan asked.

Matthew's mouth was solemn, but his eyes twinkled. "Organized madness, my lord."

"Well, when you're through with this task, I've another one for you. Find out where all the old tapestries and wall coverings were stored and have them brought to the upstairs rooms. Lyko will know what to do with them." Kristan turned and nearly collided with the boy, still waiting with his armload of bedding. "Serle, get back to work."

"Yes, sir," the boy said.

"You call the StoneKing 'my lord,'" Matthew told him, not unkindly, and gave him a little push toward the stairs.

Another group of servants hustled through the great hall, with Quinn barking orders behind them. They headed toward Kristan's work chamber, bearing pails of hot water and a bathing tub. The girl Nolle was with them, carrying a basket of linens and soaps, but her amber eyes were on Sir Matthew as he mounted the stairs two at a time. *And why not?* Kristan thought;

he's a good-looking fellow. He had no more time to think about Nolle; Geoffrey and Dru arrived with a list of potential dinner courses, and on their heels were Kennet and Sir Velios, to have the greeting ceremonies approved. Kristan had no sooner sorted through those problems when Quinn appeared at his elbow. "Your bath is ready, my lord. Shall I assist you?"

"Great heavens, no. See to your own preparations."

It was with a certain relief that Kristan closed the door on the chaos. Everything in his work chamber had been pushed aside to make room for the tub, which steamed before the hearth. Linens, soap, a razor and a small mirror lay on a table within arm's reach. Fresh clothing was folded neatly on a nearby bench.

Kristan stripped, shivering. A new fire crackled merrily in the hearth, but it had not yet warmed the room, and the hot water felt good as he stepped into the bath.

He washed quickly, as he usually did, trying not to see or feel the scars crisscrossing his body, the hard knots beneath his flesh where broken bones had knitted, the indentation where Daazna's knife had pierced his side. Afterward, he soaped and rinsed his hair. Six months had done nothing to lessen the tenderness of the bruises at his hairline, and even the touch of his own fingers made Kristan feel a little sick. Outside the room the racket continued, and he decided to allow himself a quiet soak before the bathwater cooled.

He slid down until he was chin-deep, shut his eyes and delved warily into his memory, trying to recall what he could of the princess Jelena. His cautious probing turned up nothing, and he was about to open his eyes when a sudden memory materialized.

. . . halfway up the stairs to the council chamber; hesitating as a voice echoed from above . . .

"She's a beauty indeed, but older by several years and already headstrong. She'd lead him a dog's life, I fear. Too much woman for our gentle little Princeling."

Laughter then; mocking laughter, with Robert Gemeta's voice ringing clearly over them all . . .

Kristan stood up abruptly, sloshing water onto the floor. He stepped out of the tub and dried himself with such force that his skin stung. He propped the mirror on the mantelpiece and shaved quickly, nicking himself in his haste. With a whispered oath, he pressed one end of his towel to the nick. With the other end he dried his hair.

Finally, he put on the clothing Quinn had chosen for him: dark leggings, fine black boots and a high-necked, plum-colored tunic of rich padded velvet, trimmed with fur and embroidered with neat whorls of gilt thread. He did not remember purchasing any cold-weather clothing of this splendor, and it was not until he was fastening the tunic that he realized the clothing was part of King Landon's wardrobe, sent from Norwinn with the rest of the old king's possessions. He settled the Stone in its customary place over his heart and took a quick look at the mirror. His haggard, fierce-eyed face glared back at him. "Good enough," he muttered, and opened the door into the great hall.

CHAPTER SEVEN

The figure stood in silence as the women peeled away layer after layer of fur-lined garments. It extended first one foot, then the other, so that the thick boots could be slipped off, providing a glimpse of finely turned ankles and delicate slippers. It held its arms out while the mitts were removed, exposing gloves of soft red leather beneath. These, too, were taken off, revealing pale, shapely hands with slender, beringed fingers. A rich, flowery perfume filled the air. The old aunt, stooped as an ancient stork, turned back the heavy hood, slid off the cloak and drew away the white veil shielding the face.

Someone caught their breath.

"Lord Gemeta," said Sir Velios, unmistakable pride in his tone, "may I present the princess Jelena."

The princess dipped into a deep curtsey, but her head remained erect and her hazel eyes locked on Kristan with the unwavering stare of an archer aiming at a target. Her full lips curved into a perfectly shaped smile. "Greetings, Lord Gemeta."

Kristan bowed. "Welcome to Fandrall."

She put out her hand, and Kristan had no choice but to take it. "My father sends his best wishes." Her voice was light and melodic. "He apologizes for his presumption in sending me without notice."

As well he might, Kristan thought, but he had resolved to keep his temper in check. "I'm honored that he trusts me with his daughter's safety and well-being. I hope your journey wasn't too difficult."

Jelena laughed, showing fine white teeth. "Fandrall's mud took us by surprise. My wagons are mired to the axles."

Her fingers were still in his, making his flesh creep. "I can send men to help dig them out."

"No need; I have plenty of men. Sir Velios will return in the morning to supervise them." She flicked a look at the knight, and Velios blushed to the ears.

Jelena released Kristan's hand at last and began to introduce her retinue. Aunt, ladies and knights alike were bedraggled and clearly exhausted from their journey, in sharp contrast to Jelena's vitality and immaculate appearance.

Kristan studied her with an impartial eye. She was a head taller than he, with a proud bearing that made her even more imposing. Her face was a perfect oval, the skin without blemish, the features even and pleasing. Her dress was the color of fresh cream, carefully fitted to emphasize her full breasts and hips. Around her narrow waist she wore a honey-gold sash embroidered with pearls. Her rich brown hair was arranged high on her head in an intricate pattern of loops and coils, crowned with a circlet of gold etched with vines and embellished with more shining pearls.

She's beautiful, Kristan thought, *but it's a studied beauty, as if she's practiced every smile before a mirror.* Heather's unaffected grin rose in his memory, but he forced the vision aside and busied himself introducing his men. The princess acknowledged their beaming faces and deep bows with a polite nod, but her gaze kept returning to Kristan, roaming over his face, his hair, his clothing. Her scrutiny made him want to squirm.

"You must be tired after your journey," he said. "Your company's chambers are ready, if you'd like to rest and refresh yourselves. You've plenty of time before dinner."

"Oh, thank you—" the aunt started to say.

"I'm not tired," Jelena said.

Her aunt cast a woeful look at the female attendants.

"And I'm terribly hungry," Jelena went on. "It's difficult to enjoy even a morsel when traveling through a storm. If it's not inconvenient, dinner would be most welcome now."

It's exceedingly inconvenient, and she knows it, Kristan thought. "As you wish," he said aloud.

"I'll inform the kitchen." Geoffrey's voice was calm, but there was a wild light in his eye, and as the knight hurried off Kristan wondered wryly what kind of mad scramble was in store for the kitchen staff. Quinn busied himself helping the old aunt out of her cloak; Walter and Matthew did the same for the two ladies, while Mitchell, Bastian, Randolf and Kennet assisted the gentlemen. Without invitation, Jelena tucked her fingers into the crook of Kristan's arm, and it took all his self-control not to jump like a frightened rabbit. Teeth clenched, he led the party into the great hall.

Three long tables had been set up in the shape of a horseshoe. At the head table was a single high-backed chair, flanked by two less imposing seats. Eight more chairs ranged along each of the side tables. Servants hurried in carrying long tapers. As the lamps and candles blazed to life, their warm yellow light flickered across the immaculate table linens and the plates and goblets of silver washed with gold. The old aunt murmured appreciatively. "Tribute from the merchants of Dyer," Quinn told her. "In gratitude for their freedom from Daaznan occupation."

"How lovely," Jelena said, but a faint crease rose between her silky brows as she looked around the room. "But I thought your reconstruction would be further along, Lord Gemeta. Where is your throne?"

"Fandrall's throne was destroyed during last summer's fire." He spoke evenly in spite of the sudden heartache. "The great hall's central beam fell in and crushed it."

The old aunt clucked in sympathy.

"What a shame," Jelena said. "But it was for the best, don't you think?"

"I beg your pardon?"

"My father told me your family's throne was carved from a block of plain stone. A green-blue granite quarried from the mountains near my own country. With respect, Lord Gemeta, a man of your power should have a grand throne—and a fine crown." Jelena flicked a teasing look at Kristan's head. "Why don't you wear one?"

Kristan's stomach twisted at the thought of a crown pressing against his bruised head. The squire candidates were hurrying forward to assist the guests into their seats, and he used the disturbance as an excuse not to answer. Once they were seated, with the princess on his right and the old aunt on his left, Jelena persisted. "Surely Fandrall has a crown, Lord Gemeta."

"My father's crown is battered beyond wearing."

"But the crowns of your other kingdoms—"

"Are in the treasury." Kristan's hand sought the comforting shape of the Gemeta Stone. "I wear this."

"Oh, is that the Stone?" Jelena asked. "It's far plainer than I expected. And with the Wichelord dead, you don't really need it anymore, do you?"

The echo of a chuckle hissed through Kristan's brain. He repressed a shudder. *Breathe*, he told himself. *Count your breaths.*

Jelena was still smiling, but there was a hint of mockery in the curl of her lips. "I suppose, with so many crowns and thrones, you place little value on them. But a man of your power should, at least, outfit yourself more suitably." She caught up the fabric of his tunic sleeve and rubbed it between thumb and forefinger.

Breathe. Count. "Is something wrong with my clothing?"

"Oh, the fabric is lovely, and no doubt costly, in its day. But the cut and embellishments are sadly out of fashion, and far too conservative for a young man like you."

"It was my cousin Landon's."

"An old man's cast-offs? Well, no wonder! You should

indulge yourself in a new wardrobe, Lord Gemeta. I doubt you have smart tailors here in Kingsmere, but you should be able to bring in someone from Dyer who can advise you. And a proper barber." She reached toward the nick on his face. "Look here. Whoever shaved you did a terrible job."

His hand rose of its own volition, to push hers away, but suddenly a bowl of warm, herb-scented water was between them, and Jelena began to dabble her fingers delicately, still talking of hair and clothes. Kristan breathed a silent sigh and concentrated on the hands holding the bowl. They were some-how familiar. A white towel hung from each wrist, and his gaze wandered past them up the bony arms to the thin shoulders and finally into the face of the Wiche girl Nolle. She was staring at the princess' pearl circlet, her lips slightly parted, the picture of avarice. Kristan cleared his throat softly, and Nolle's strange amber eyes flicked to him. He gave his head a slight shake.

"Give me the towel, girl," Jelena said. The sudden sharpness of her tone startled both of them. Muttering an apology, Nolle fumbled a towel into Jelena's hands. The princess patted her fin-gers dry and eyed Nolle with a coolness that was at odds with her enchanting smile. "Offer the bowl to your lord now, little fool."

Nolle scowled and turned to Kristan so abruptly that the water nearly slopped from the bowl. He bathed his hands, dried them and returned the towel with a nod. Nolle tossed her head and stalked off. The old aunt, her hands lifted for washing, blinked in confusion. Red-faced, Randolf excused himself and hurried after Nolle.

Jelena rolled her eyes. "Servants. Useless and stupid, and that one is surly into the bargain. I'm surprised you keep her."

"She's quite new," Kristan said.

"And that one?" Jelena tilted her head toward the foot of the table, where the boy Serle was clumsily pouring wine for one of the Malchean knights.

"Also new."

Jelena laughed. "Oh, you dear man. You mustn't hire locally."

Kristan's insides began to curdle. "Why?"

She laughed again. The sound jangled in his ears. "You may be the StoneKing, Lord Gemeta, fierce in battle and ruthless in negotiation, but you know nothing about hiring servants."

"I don't?"

"Your people are farm folk. I'm sure they're fine in the kitchen, or the gardens or stables, but they can't do the delicate work of waiting on a royal table. It's like expecting an ox to run like a deer." She turned in her chair to face him and tapped his thigh with flirtatious fingers. "I'm up to my eyes in well-trained staff. I could easily spare you fifty of them, and you could let these people go back to their plows."

Controlcontrolcontrol.

"Fandrallians learn quickly."

"Well, for your sake I hope so." With another lilting laugh, she waved toward Serle, who had overfilled the goblet and was trying to mop up the resulting mess with his sleeve.

I'd like to slap this foolish bitch out of her chair, Kristan thought. His hand rose again, as if eager to carry out the wish, but instead he made himself take hold of the Stone. It was cold beneath his fingers. *Breathe,* he thought. *Breathe and control it.*

At the far end of the room, a manservant swooped in with a towel, elbowing Serle out of the way with a hissed reprimand. Jelena watched with interest. "He's made a terrible mess. Are you going to punish him?"

He deserves punishment, stupid boy.

Jelena touched his leg again, more lingeringly. "I can do it if you'd rather not trouble yourself with such petty matters."

He bit down on his tongue. *Control it. Control it. Use it.*

He crooked his finger at Serle. The boy was gazing sorrowfully at the mess he had made, but the manservant saw Kristan's gesture and shoved Serle toward the head table. Bearing the pitcher and an anxious, apologetic smile, Serle came to Kristan's side. Jelena cocked her head and smirked, as if ready to be entertained.

"What happened, Serle?" Kristan asked.

"The pitcher was too full, sir—my lord."

"Is it too full now?"

Serle hefted it experimentally. "No, sir—my lord."

Kristan picked up Jelena's goblet. "Then fill this for the princess, if you please," he said, and held it deliberately over Jelena's lap.

Quinn let out a faint gasp. The old aunt leaned close to watch; Kristan felt her breath on his neck. Jelena sat upright, her perfect smile gone, her jaw slack with consternation. Serle raised the pitcher again. Its lip rattled against the brim of Jelena's goblet.

"Take your time," Kristan said. Serle tilted the pitcher a bit more, and a feeble rivulet of deep red wine trickled into the goblet. "Well done. Now fill it up."

Jelena glared at the stream of wine, as if willing Serle's hand to be steady. When the cup was brimful, Kristan put his head on one side and studied it. "Perhaps a little over-full, Serle," he said, and with one smooth, sure movement, placed the goblet on the table. Jelena's tense posture relaxed, but only for a breath as Kristan held his own goblet over her cream-colored lap. "This time pour less."

Serle plied the pitcher again, this time stopping with a fingertip's worth of room to spare. "Thank you, Serle," Kristan said, and raised the goblet to Jelena. "We may be farm folk, but we learn quickly. Your health, Princess."

He waited, his goblet suspended, and at last she reached for her brimming cup. Despite her care in lifting it, some of the wine spilled over and ran down her hand. She ignored it and raised her cup in a gesture that mirrored Kristan's. "And yours, Lord Gemeta."

A few drops of wine pattered onto her lap, staining the pretty dress. As they drank, they locked gazes over the rims of their goblets. Bewilderment and anger mingled in Jelena's eyes.

Dinner was served soon after, a dizzying array of dishes,

some successful, some not: soft cheese baked in a delicate crust, overcooked and oversalted fish, boar roasted to perfection and garnished with chestnuts, root vegetables so heavily sauced that they had turned to mush. Kristan ate and drank sparingly, as he always did; Jelena said little and picked at her food, but often gestured for more wine. The old aunt applied herself to her meal with such vigor that she had no breath for small talk, so the head table was nearly silent. The courtiers, however, kept up a steady hum of polite conversation. Red-faced and sweating, Dru had accompanied the roast from the kitchen, trailing a sulky Nolle in his wake. He carved the boar himself, with an evil-looking knife, and kept Nolle hustling to refill plates even when the company was sated.

The final dish was a towering and wildly decorated confection; impressive, but so sweet that it made Kristan's teeth ache. Most of the company took a polite taste and pushed their plates aside, but Jelena ate her share and then gestured to Nolle for more. After a few bites, she suddenly stood up, her face an alarming yellowy-green. "Excuse me," she said, took two steps away from the table and vomited all over the floor.

"Ew," Nolle said.

The room erupted. The old aunt, Sir Velios and the female companions yelped and rushed to Jelena's side. Quinn called for servants, Dru bellowed for a mop, several of the squire candidates began to giggle, Serle added to the commotion by dropping his pitcher, and Nolle backed all the way to the staircase, her nose wrinkled with disgust.

Kristan waved Randolf and Geoffrey over. "Please show our guests to their rooms, and make certain the princess is shown every kindness."

"I hope she isn't going to need a healer," Randolf said under his breath. "All we have is the army's man."

"She's just worse for drink," Geoffrey muttered. "I've never seen a girl her age pack it away like that."

"Do as I ask, Geoff, preferably without commentary,"

Kristan said. His triumph over the princess suddenly seemed hollow and stupid, and his shame made him cross. Jelena's retinue escorted the staggering, white-faced princess from the room, with Geoffrey leading the way and Randolf bringing up the rear. At a barked order from Dru, the servants and squire candidates began to clear away the remains of the meal.

"My lord, I'm terribly sorry." Dru was at his elbow, breathing equal parts wine and regret. "I could have done better if I hadn't been rushed, I swear I could—"

"My lord, I know she was rude, but—" Quinn was saying.

Sir Walter was laughing helplessly, his eyes crinkled above his curly beard. Sir Kennet looked stunned, Sir Matthew amused.

"She was a right bitch," Sir Mitchell observed solemnly, which made Walter laugh even harder.

A slow pounding rose behind Kristan's eyebrows. "Quinn, what have I done?"

Quinn's expression was prim. "Nothing that can't be undone, my lord, with the proper apology."

"Apologize?" Bastian blurted. "She insulted his people!"

"She didn't mean to," piped a young voice.

They all turned. Serle was on his hands and knees, mopping up vomit and wine. "She didn't know," he went on, in a reasonable tone that contrasted sharply with his revolting task. "She's from outside, sir—my lord. She doesn't know about Fandrall. So, she was in the wrong, judging. And you were in the wrong, making her pay for the slight. Sorry to say it, my lord, but there it is."

He went on wiping up the mess, oblivious to the horrified stares of the court. At last Kristan turned to Kennet. "This one," he said, and pointed at Serle. "I want this one for my squire."

"My lord, we know nothing about this boy," Kennet protested. "I doubt he's trained. I doubt he has any skills at all."

"Oh, we can all help train him," Walter said.

"But the other lads—"

"You knights can share out the rest," Kristan said. "I want this one."

Sir Velios hurried into the room, followed by Geoffrey and Randolf. "My lord," he said, bowing before Kristan, "the princess sends her regrets for ending a lovely dinner on such an unpleasant note."

"Does she need a healer?" Kristan asked.

"No, my lord. Her aunt has put her to bed. I think a night's rest will put her right." Velios heaved a little sigh. "A night's rest will benefit all of us."

"I hope your rooms are acceptable."

"They're warm and comfortable, my lord, and you've no idea how we appreciate that. The rest of our company won't be so fortunate tonight."

"My offer of assistance still stands."

"Thank you. I'd be grateful for some shovels and a few additional men tomorrow."

"I'll see to it, my lord," Geoffrey said.

"Thank you. I have an early start, so I'll say goodnight." Velios bowed again, then hesitated. "My lord, I hope you won't think ill of Princess Jelena. She's willful, and can be tactless at times, but she meant no disrespect."

Kristan snorted. "My own behavior was less than exemplary. Good night." As the knight departed, Kristan turned to his own men. "Well, gentlemen, as Sir Velios said, a night's rest will benefit all of us. I hope our makeshift lodgings won't be too much of a trial."

Sir Geoffrey took Serle by the shoulder. "Come along, lad. You can start your squiring work by helping me get our rooms ready upstairs. You know how to make a fire, don't you?"

"Oh, yes, sir. I make fires all the time out in the pastures; to keep warm and scare wild animals away—"

Serle's prattle faded as he and Geoffrey disappeared up the stairs. "Where would you like the boy to sleep, my lord?" Kennet asked.

"Isn't there room with the servants?"

With an expression of great patience, Kennet clasped his hands behind his back. "If he's to be your squire, my lord, his place is with you."

"Couldn't he sleep in the barracks instead?"

"My lord, a squire should be ready to wait on his master at all times. Common practice is to have him sleep at his master's bedside—"

Kristan shook his head. *Too close. I couldn't bear having him so close.*

Kennet's eyebrows bobbed up. "Well, sleeping in the hall across your doorway is also acceptable."

"Upstairs?" Mitchell protested. "The hallway will be freezing."

"Enduring privation is part of a squire's training."

Walter snorted. "A frozen squire is no use to anyone."

"I was often cold when I was a squire."

"Ah, but you had some harsh masters," Matthew said. "Even if I'd been consigned to the doorway, once my knight was asleep I could usually slip away to a warm bed."

"With a nice warm companion in it," Walter said.

Chuckling, the knights began exchanging stories about their squiring days, but Kristan was too troubled to be amused. He was not surprised when Randolf, always better at reading his mood, sidled up to him. "My lord, we can arrange the scaffolding in your chamber to make a little nook for the boy. With a mattress and some warm covers, he'll sleep snug enough. You'll have privacy, but he'll still be close enough to attend on you when needed."

Kristan was about to say no when he realized everyone else had stopped talking to listen. His irritation rose afresh. "Oh, very well. Put him in my room, Randolf. The rest of you, go get settled. Quinn, a moment, please."

As the servants gathered up the last of the dinner detritus and the knights and Bastian went upstairs, Kristan retreated to the far side of the room with Quinn on his heels. "All right, how bad is the situation?" he asked.

With his arms crossed and his weight on one hip, Quinn stood considering. "Bad, but not irredeemable. I believe she was flirting with you."

"Flirting? Challenging and insulting me was flirting?"

"In some courts such behavior is considered charming, although by Fandrall's standards it was excessive," Quinn said. "While it's clear Jelena has been indulged, she's not a fool. Tread carefully, my lord. I wouldn't want to lose Malchea's goodwill."

"As you say. We'll see what tomorrow brings."

"First, we have to deal with tonight," Quinn said, as they climbed the stairs. "I know you're accustomed to the cold, but I confess I'm dreading it."

"Do what you must to be comfortable," Kristan said.

"That would mean suffocating Bastian. We're sharing a room and he snores. Good night, my lord."

I believe he just made a joke, Kristan thought.

At the door of his own chamber he met Randolf coming out. "All set, my lord," the old knight said. "The boy couldn't be happier. He says he's never had a room and a bed to himself. If we were all so easily satisfied, this world would be a simpler place."

"Indeed. Good night, Randolf."

Kristan closed the door and leaned against it, suddenly bone-tired. The chamber still smelled strongly of damp plaster. The unfinished walls and the greater part of the room had been blocked off with the draped scaffolding, creating a smaller space dominated by a bed on a simple frame. Kristan pressed his hand into the mattress and heard the crinkle of straw. *I hope the princess enjoys my feather bed*, he thought sourly. Near the eastern wall, a jog of scaffolding formed a little niche, like a kennel. When Kristan peered into it, he found Serle sitting cross-legged on a woven straw pallet. The boy had draped his blanket around his shoulders as if it were a fine cloak, and he looked up at Kristan with a wide-eyed smile. "I've had plenty of woolen covers, but never one with fur lining," he said. "It's lovely and soft, my lord."

As Kristan inspected the rest of the chamber, Serle followed him, chattering like a squirrel. "I've turned down your bed. It's right by the hearth, so you'll be nice and warm. A good fire, too; I made it myself. Candle on the table at your bedside, my lord, for light, and your little wooden box next to it. Chest with your clothes in it at the foot of the bed, sir—my lord. Sir Geoffrey told me I should help you out of your clothes and put them away."

In his eagerness he took hold of Kristan's sleeve. Before he knew what he was doing, Kristan jerked free and turned on the boy, hand raised to strike. Serle recoiled, flinging his arms over his face. "Sorry, sir, sorry!"

For a long moment, Kristan could neither move nor breathe. His pulse hammered in his ears and the floor beneath his feet seemed to throb. At last he dropped his hand. "Don't do that," he said, his voice little more than a hoarse snarl. "Don't ever touch me."

"Sorry, sir." Serle still cowered, his face averted.

Kristan sat down on his bed. He put both hands to the Gemeta Stone and pressed it against his heart. It was unpleasantly cold. *Control,* he told himself. *Controlcontrolcontrol.*

The floorboards creaked; when he looked up, Serle was creeping into his kennel. "Come back here," he said. When the boy was before him again, cringing like a beaten puppy, Kristan took a deep breath. "Serle, you seem like a good-hearted boy, so I'll be honest with you. I don't want a squire. I especially didn't want one of those big, swaggering fellows, but I had to choose someone, or my men wouldn't give me a moment's peace."

Serle's lower lip trembled. "But I want to be a good squire, my lord. I want to serve you and learn everything so I can be a knight."

"And I'll make certain you're taught all a knight should

know. But in return, I want two things from you. One is discretion. Do you know what that means?"

"No, sir."

"It means that whatever I say or do, here in my own room, is my own business. I have very little privacy, Serle, and what I have I hold dear. You're not to gossip with the servants or the knights or anyone about what I say or do. The first time that happens will be the last time. Understood?"

"Yes, sir."

"The second thing I want is distance. I don't want you touching me or watching me or dogging me with questions. In here, you can keep things tidy and tend the fire, but otherwise stay out of my way." Serle's shoulders sagged, and Kristan made an effort to soften his tone. "Outside this room, I welcome your assistance. You can bring me my cloak and gloves when I go out. You can fill my goblet at the table. You can look after my horse, Malvo. Do you know anything about horses?"

"No, sir." The boy's mouth trembled. "Only sheep."

"You'll have to be taught, then. If you want to be a knight, you'll have to know about horses: how to ride them, groom them, saddle them and care for their tack. You'll have plenty to keep you busy, never fear. Now, warm yourself up at the fire, and then get in your bed and go to sleep."

"Yes, my lord." Serle hesitated. "Could I . . . could I at least look after your cat, sir?"

"My cat?"

"The pretty tabby, sir. It's such a nice cat, sir; it let me stroke its ears a bit. It was up in the scaffolding earlier, but it went under the bed just before you—"

Kristan crouched to look beneath the bed just as something scrabbled out the other side. When he straightened up, the tabby cat was flinging itself at the chamber door, the girl-shaped haze flickering around it.

"Stop that," Kristan snapped.

The cat froze facing the door, and Serle laughed. "Look at

that! A cat that obeys!"

"She's not a cat, and she certainly doesn't obey. Nolle, take your true form."

The cat did not move, although the haze around it shivered and pulsed.

"Take your true form this instant, or I'll make you do it." Kristan took a step forward. The cat spun, reared onto its hind legs and with a hiss, disappeared as Nolle's form solidified. At the same moment, something round and wrapped in cloth fell from beneath her skirts. As it rolled toward Kristan, the cloth slipped away, revealing the blue glass of the scrying ball.

Kristan picked it up, never taking his eyes off Nolle.

"She's . . . she's . . ." Serle stammered.

"A girl, yes; and Wiche, and a thief into the bargain. Come here, Nolle." Nolle came slowly to stand before him, flinching as if expecting to be struck. "Give me one good reason why I shouldn't have you punished."

"I only wanted to see it close up," Nolle whispered.

"Well, was it worth the risk? Worth punishment? Worth losing an easy job and plenty to eat and a warm bed?"

Nolle's lower lip trembled. "I thought maybe I could See with it."

It took Kristan a moment to understand what she meant. "And did you?"

She shook her head. Her cheeks had gone crimson.

Kristan looked at the scrying ball, overwhelmed with sudden anger. *This is all I have of Simeon,* he thought. *All he left me. And this girl was going to steal it. I should punish her. She deserves to be punished. I should have her beaten—*

His stomach heaved, and he knotted his hands around the ball. *Stop. Controlcontrolcontrol.* "Get out," he said, his voice little more than a growl.

She stood unmoving, as if unable to believe her ears.

"Go on," he said. "Go back to the kitchen. Get out of my sight before—"

She darted from the room before he could finish. "Close the door, Serle," he said, and wrapped the ball in its cloth again. He put it in the box, closed the lid, then sat on the bed and buried his face in his hands. In the long silence that followed, he could sense Serle's eyes on him. "What?" he said gruffly. "What is it?"

"My lord, how did she—"

"She shifts, Serle. All Wiche have a particular skill, and that's hers. No more questions, now. Get in your bed and go to sleep."

"Yes, my lord." A series of bumps and grunts followed as Serle crawled into his little alcove and made himself comfortable. When everything was quiet, Kristan got up, stripped off his clothes (*old man's cast-offs*) and climbed into bed. He moistened finger and thumb and pinched out the candle at his bedside.

"Good night, my lord," Serle whispered.

For some time Kristan lay staring at the ceiling, his fingers laced across his chest. The smell of damp plaster was overlaid with the scent of wood smoke, and beneath that, the faint pong of unwashed boy. Kristan reminded himself to have Randolf arrange a bath and some clean clothes for Serle. In the far corner of the room the boy's breathing deepened to a gentle snore. Kristan closed his eyes and tried to slow his own breathing, but it was no good. No matter what some freckle-faced shepherd boy might think, he could not sleep in such an exposed position.

With a silent sigh, he burrowed beneath the covers and arranged himself in the only position he found comfortable: huddled on his right side, with his left hand clutching the Stone at his chest and his right arm curled protectively around his head. Beneath the blankets an array of fresh smells filled his nostrils: the crisp grassy scent of the straw mattress, the soapiness of clean linens, a faint whiff of herbs from the chest where they had been stored. A trace of Jelena's perfume rose from his fingers, and to his surprise he was suddenly aroused. He rarely had the energy or even the inclination to indulge himself in thoughts of the flesh, but now the curves of Jelena's body rose in the darkness behind his closed eyes. He imagined running his hand along those curves, cupping and squeezing the supple flesh beneath the cream-colored gown. *Stop it,* he scolded himself. *Everything she wore, everything she said and did was devised to seduce you.* He focused his mind's eye on Jelena's too-perfect smile, her calculating eyes. He listened to the dull thud of his own heartbeat. Eventually, his weariness overtook him, and he dozed off.

* * *

He followed the cream-colored gown up a steep, narrow staircase. The figure wearing it was only a step or two ahead of him, filling his view with the pleasing sight of shapely thighs and buttocks moving beneath the fabric. He was so close that he could smell the perfume rising from the flesh beneath. Rigid with desire, he reached for the figure before him, but it eluded his hands. Jelena's mocking laugh echoed as the figure ascended into the darkness. He followed, and suddenly found himself in a small room. The figure in the cream-colored dress stood with its back to him, silhouetted in the feeble light of a banked fire. Somehow Jelena had grown smaller, slimmer, and her hair, tumbling loose down her back, glowed red in the firelight.

His tongue felt too big for his mouth and his groin was so heavy with lust that he could barely walk. "Turn around, you provoking slut," he muttered.

The figure turned. It was Heather.

Her expression was so grave that he was ashamed of his crudeness, his craving, the ponderous weight of his privates. He fumbled for an explanation but found none. He tried to step forward but could not move. As he struggled, a hand moved from the darkness behind Heather. Long fingers slithered across her belly and thighs, stroking the fabric taut, revealing the outline of her navel and the cleft between her legs. A second hand crept, spiderlike, across her right breast. At that moment, Daazna's face loomed over her shoulder. His mouth opened and his tongue rolled out of his mouth like an eel sliding from its hole. He ran it up the side of her neck, leaving a slimy trail. Heather shuddered but could not seem to flee. Daazna's hand roamed up from her breast, caught her chin and twisted her face toward his. His thumb pressed into her lower lip, forcing her teeth apart, and then his long tongue plunged into her mouth. He sucked and mumbled at her, grunting like a calf at its mother's teat. His fingers knotted in the creamy bodice of her dress and with a long, slow pull, ripped it from neckline to hem. Heather's flesh broke out in goosebumps as Daazna's hands explored her nakedness. With a wet, sucking pop, he released her mouth and grinned at Kristan. "You can watch," he whispered. "Would you like that?"

And he let out a low, throaty chuckle.

With a screaming gasp, Kristan jerked awake. He was sitting bolt upright in bed, the Stone clasped in both hands. He stared from corner to dark corner of the room, the echo of Daazna's laughter still pulsing through his brain. With an effort he controlled his panicky breathing. *Only a dream*, he tried to tell himself, but while his lips moved, he made no sound.

At that instant, he realized Serle had stopped snoring. *Stay where you are, boy, and don't speak*, he thought, but at the same time ached for the comfort of a human voice.

"My lord?" Serle whispered. "Are you all right?"

Sleep was impossible now; he knew that. With the boy listening, pacing the floor was impossible as well. Without answering, Kristan lay back on the crinkling straw mattress, still clutching the Stone with both hands. He counted his breaths. He counted each pop and snap of the dying fire. When Serle began to snore again, he counted the snores. All through the long night he lay with his eyes open, counting and waiting for daylight.

CHAPTER EIGHT

"We still have to go over the latest trade reports from Dyer," Quinn said. "And there are your own finances to review; you keep putting that off."

"The courier arrived with Hogia's packet yesterday afternoon, but in all the tumult I was only able to glance through it," Bastian said.

"Anything urgent?" Kristan asked, with a briskness he did not feel. He was exhausted, but had thrown himself into the morning's work to distance his thoughts from his nightmare.

"Just the usual reports, I think."

"Let it wait, then. Is the Malchean party stirring yet?"

"Sir Velios was on his way at first light. Since the weather's improved, they should able to dig out and be here by midafternoon. Matthew and Randolf are in the barracks trying to make room for the newcomers. The old aunt and some of the Malchean knights were having breakfast a little while ago; I think the rest are still in bed."

"With luck they'll stay out from underfoot long enough for us to get some work done," Quinn muttered.

The councilor's usual cool efficiency was absent, and the dark rings beneath his eyes spoke eloquently of a poor night's sleep. *That makes two of us*, Kristan thought, as he turned to the next document. *Bastian must be a champion snorer indeed.*

"Where's your new squire, my lord?" the scribe asked.

"With Walter and Kennet in the stables, learning how to

care for Malvo. He told me this morning that he doesn't know how to read or write, so I'd like you to teach him."

"Can't read or write, knows nothing about horses, hasn't a clue how to wait at table and can't even remember how to address you properly," Quinn said. "My lord, what kind of squire will he make?"

"With luck, a quiet, obedient one."

Before Quinn could respond, Sir Mitchell appeared in the doorway. "I'm sorry to disturb you, my lord, but the princess has requested a private audience with you."

"That sounds rather significant," Quinn said. "Would you like us to stay, my lord?"

Kristan shook his head and turned to Mitchell. "Tell the princess I'm happy to meet with her now."

Mitchell left, with Bastian and Quinn on his heels. Kristan continued to read and sign papers, meanly glad that he had rebelled against his dated finery and was clad instead in an old, ink-stained tunic. Light, unfamiliar footsteps approached, and he deliberately dipped his quill afresh and bent his head over the document before him.

"Good morning, Lord Gemeta." The princess sounded subdued, and the smell of her expensive perfume was far less evident.

"Good morning," Kristan responded, without looking up. "Won't you sit down while I finish this? I won't be a moment." A faint creak told him she had taken the chair across from him. He read through the document, scratched his name at the bottom, set it aside, put the quill in its holder, and only then, raised his head to look at her.

His fear of being aroused by her presence was immediately allayed. In place of the luxuriant cream-colored gown, Jelena wore a more severe dress of soft gray-green. Her flawless complexion had an unhealthy yellow cast. Her eyes were bloodshot, her full mouth pinched, and her expression, so self-assured the night before, was wary.

"I hope you're well," he said.

"I've felt better," Jelena said, with a dry smile.

His own lips quirked. "It's a new day, Princess. I think we should put last night behind us and start afresh."

Jelena nodded. "Agreed. I know now you have no patience with games of flirtation, and I also see you're busy, so I'll speak frankly. My father grows concerned about the giant on his doorstep."

"I beg your pardon?"

"You, Lord Gemeta. He worries about you, and your armies, and your reputation."

Kristan sat back in his chair. "What reputation is that?"

"Don't be coy. You're the master of four countries. Fandrall was your birthright, of course, and perhaps Norwinn was, too, but you were quick to snatch up Hogia and Dyer when the opportunity presented itself."

"Hogia was spoils of war."

"And Dyer?"

"Dyer was . . . agreeable. And necessary."

One shapely eyebrow rose, but Jelena merely laced her fingers together and studied him. "My father desires a stronger bond between our countries."

"Is that why he sent you, instead of a traditional envoy?"

A slight flush crept up her cheeks. "There was a time when our fathers talked of a match between us. My father favored it because he'd heard you were a meek boy and might be easily managed."

"Time and circumstances have changed many things."

"They have indeed. Now, Father wants the match to ensure Malchea's safety."

Kristan propped one elbow on the arm of his chair and leaned his cheek on his fist. "Princess, Fandrall's border skirmishes with Malchea are well in the past. As far as I'm concerned, the treaty our fathers made long ago still holds. Tell King Lockward my plate is full. I have no designs on Malchea."

"What if Malchea was . . . agreeable?"

Kristan stared at her. "Are you proposing marriage to me, Princess?"

"Don't you find me desirable, Lord Gemeta? Most men do."

"You're quite beautiful."

She laughed at his flat tone. "I'm more than a pretty face, sir. I'm heir to my father's throne. I've sat in council with him for years. The match would benefit both of us. It would mean a fifth kingdom for you and for Malchea, a highly advantageous alliance with an extraordinarily powerful man." She heaved a little sigh. "Besides, there are few marriageable men of appropriate status available to me."

"Is status so important to you?"

Jelena lifted her chin. "I won't marry some piddling prince, nor one of my father's underlings."

Kristan's head was beginning to ache again. "Why not marry for love?"

A bitter laugh burst from her. "Don't tell me the ruthless StoneKing believes in marrying for love?" He said nothing, and her laughter faded. She put her head on one side. "Perhaps your tastes lie in other directions. Some men prefer the charms of other men."

"I'm not one of them."

"Or perhaps you have a penchant for young flesh, like that little serving wench last night."

Kristan grimaced. "Madam, please."

"Or perhaps what I heard is true."

"What did you hear?"

"That the StoneKing had an affair with a commoner who fought at his side. That in return, he elevated her to Lady and gave her the command of his army in Hogia."

Kristan did not trust himself to speak, and she shrugged at his silence. "I would never expect one woman to satisfy a man of your reputation, Lord Gemeta. If you want to keep a mistress after we're married, I don't mind."

"You and I have very different ideas of what marriage entails," Kristan said, very quietly.

For a long moment neither spoke. "You're an odd fellow, StoneKing," Jelena said at last.

"So I'm told."

"You have no interest in the match at all?"

"Princess, you've great beauty, and intelligence to equal it. I value King Lockward's regard and my alliance with Malchea. But as I've said, my plate is full."

A tight little smile curled her mouth. "Then why do you look so discontented?"

Before he could answer, voices echoed in the great hall and Jelena cocked her head toward the sound. "It sounds as if Velios is back with the rest of my escort. My father sent you a fine gift, Lord Gemeta; it's been stuck in the mud with everything else, but with luck it won't be any the worse for wear. May I give it to you now?" She rose and held out her hand. He stepped from behind the table and offered her his arm instead. With a gracious nod, she slid her fingers into the crook of his elbow. Her touch reminded him uncomfortably of his dream, but he settled his face into what he hoped was a pleasant expression. Just outside the door they passed Quinn and Bastian. *Eavesdropping,* he thought. *I expect Quinn's nails are bitten down to the quick.*

Sir Velios met them by the keep's main doors. He was breathless and mud-splattered but a jubilant smile warmed his face. "We got back as quickly as we could, Princess."

Jelena barely looked at him. "I hope Lord Gemeta's gift made the trip without incident."

The knight's expression faded to utter dejection. *He loves her,* Kristan thought. *How sad.*

The pages swung open the keep doors and Kristan winced at the slap of cold air. In the courtyard, the Malcheans were unloading wagons and hurrying parcels through a side door under Randolf and Geoffrey's supervision. As Jelena stepped outside, she drew herself even more upright and raked her people with an imperious gaze. They halted in their work to bow deeply, but she only sniffed and flicked a pale hand at them. "Disgraceful. There's mud on everyone and everything. Captain, show the StoneKing my father's gift."

One of the soldiers waved a tall wagon forward. It was completely covered by heavy canvas tied down tightly at each corner. As the Malchean men began working the knots loose, Sir Velios hurried out with Jelena's cloak, but the princess waved him away. With a loud rattle, the canvas cover was pulled off, revealing a barred cage with a large form huddled in the far corner. Kristan caught his breath. It was a female centaur.

She darted a single look at him from haggard dark eyes, then averted her face. She clutched a ragged blanket about her shoulders and breasts. Her matted hair and tail were black, her shaggy hide a silvery dapple.

"How did you . . . where did she come from?" Kristan said, his voice little more than a croak.

"A sea trader arrived in our port with a dozen of the creatures, just as I was making ready to journey here," Jelena said. "He said he stopped for water on an island well west of Malchea, discovered the creatures there and captured them. We'd heard you already had a male. I hope you still have it; Father picked out the strongest female so you'd have a breeding pair."

"By the Stone . . ." Kristan breathed.

Jelena smirked. "Then my gift is a success?"

"Where are the rest?"

"So greedy! Aren't you going to thank me for this one?"

He yanked his arm from her grasp. "Stop acting the fool! Where are the rest?"

Her eyes narrowed to resentful slits. "I don't know. The trader said he was headed south to Dyer. I wish him luck selling them; he was asking a ridiculous price."

Kristan hurried down the steps to the cage. "Be careful, Lord Gemeta," the captain said. "She's very wild."

As Kristan came close, the centaur shot him a savage glare

and staggered to her feet. Standing, she was too tall for the cage, and it turned Kristan's heart sick to see her hunched shoulders and bowed head. Her hocks were covered in sores from the cage's rough floor and her legs trembled as she moved to the opposite corner.

Kristan clenched his fists around the cage bars. "I'm so sorry," he whispered. The female only huddled deeper into her blanket. Kristan tried to recall any words of the centaur language, but the ashes of his memory produced nothing. He angled around the cage toward the female, but she turned her back on him. "I won't hurt you," he said. "I swear I won't hurt you."

Jelena snorted. "Surely, you don't expect an answer. The thing only speaks gibberish."

Kristan turned to the captain. "Let her out."

"She'll run for it, Lord Gemeta. Every chance she gets, she tries to run—"

"I said let her out!"

"Do as he says," Jelena said.

The captain fumbled a key from beneath his cloak and fitted it into the lock of the cage door. The centaur tensed. There was a metallic ring of tumblers turning, then the creak of metal on metal as the captain opened the door.

The centaur charged toward it with such force that the entire wagon rocked, nearly knocking Kristan off his feet. The captain ducked and the rest of the Malcheans scattered as the centaur leaped from the cage and landed in the courtyard, no longer a pitiful trapped creature but a huge, menacing beast. Her hair whirled about her shoulders as she wheeled, looking for escape. Her large slanted eyes fixed on the castle's gatehouse and she lunged toward it. The guards, already on alert, brought their pikes to bear. A single word burst from Kristan's shattered memory and was on his lips before he knew it.

"*Chaírete!*"

She skidded to a halt and stared at him over one shoulder.

Kristan struggled to remember more words but the only thing that came to mind was an expression Torrin sometimes used. "*Astéria mou*," he said, stepping forward with what he hoped was a reassuring smile.

Her face twisted into a snarl. He had only enough time to throw his hands over his face before she was on him, pounding him with knotted fists. "*Pós xérete to ónomá mou?*" she shouted. "*Pós to xérete?*"

He slipped on the icy flagstones and fell heavily on his back. The centaur woman reared. "Stop her!" Geoffrey shouted, as her hooves slammed down a hand's breadth from Kristan's face. Bowstrings hummed overhead as the guards on the parapets took aim.

"Don't shoot!" Kristan cried. "Don't hurt her!"

The centaur was rising onto her hind legs again. At that instant, Serle thrust himself in her way, his scrawny arms raised. "Bad! Bad horse lady!" His reedy voice echoed around the courtyard. "Bad, bad, BAD!"

As Serle advanced, shaking his finger at her, the centaur woman backed away. "*To paidí eínai treló*," she muttered. Pikemen, knights and Malcheans were advancing on her from all sides with weapons at the ready. Kristan rolled to his feet, gestured them away with one hand and grasped Serle's thin shoulder with the other. "Enough, Serle," he said, and turned to the centaur woman. "*Chaírete.* We mean you no harm. Please don't be frightened."

"*Pós xérete to ónomá mou?*" the woman said again, but this time her voice trembled.

Kristan turned his hands up. "I'm sorry, I don't understand." Sir Mitchell stood gape-mouthed among the onlookers, and Kristan beckoned to him. "Mitchell, do you remember any *Kentávron?*"

"*Kentávron?*" the centaur woman repeated, her eyes wide.

"Almost none, my lord," Mitchell said. "My visits with them were so short."

The centaur woman stamped one hoof. "*Pos xérete ti glóssa mou?*"

Kristan patted his mouth with his fingertips. "*Kentávron,*" he said, and then extended forefinger and thumb held close together. "Only a little. I'm sorry." He pointed toward the keep doors. "Please—come inside and get warm. Come inside."

"Come inside," Serle said, mirroring Kristan's gesture. The centaur narrowed her eyes at them. Finally, she nodded.

With Kristan, Mitchell and Serle backing up before her, she crossed the courtyard, mounted the steps and passed into the keep. Her hooves slipped a little on the stone floor, but when Kristan put out a hand to steady her, she flinched back. "It's all right," Serle said, extending his own hand. "We're not going to hurt you. I'm sorry I said you were bad. You're not bad at all. You're just scared, aren't you? Come on, then." He twitched his fingers, and the centaur woman slowly put her hand into his. She towered over Serle, but he kept up his cheerful, soothing prattle as they backed across the great hall. "That's the way. Just one step at a time and we'll get there soon enough. It's a big room, isn't it? That's why they call it a great hall. I'd never seen a room so big before. I like the way it echoes, don't you?"

The centaur woman glanced at Kristan. "*To paidí eínai treló,*" she said again, but this time a dry smile curved her lips.

"Randolf, where are you?" Kristan asked in a low voice.

"Right here, my lord," the old knight said from somewhere behind him.

"Stoke the fire in my work chamber and make room for her in front of it," Kristan said, without taking his eyes off the centaur. "Find some cushions for her to rest on. Mitchell, help him. Geoffrey?"

"On your left, my lord."

"Send to the kitchen for something to eat and drink. I don't know what she'll want; bring whatever's hot and fresh. Matthew?"

"Here, my lord."

"Get bandages and salves from the healer. Walter and Kennet, keep everyone else away."

"Yes, my lord," they chorused, from somewhere out of his line of vision.

"Serle?"

"Yes, my lord?"

"Stay with her. Keep talking to her."

They made their slow, halting way across the great hall, leaving behind the staring eyes and suppressed murmurs of courtiers, servants and Malcheans alike. At each strange sound or sudden movement, the centaur woman froze, but Serle's bright chatter seemed to reassure her, and at last they were in the hall leading to the work chamber. Out of the corner of his eye Kristan could see figures darting in and out, but by the time they reached the door, only Randolf was there, puffing slightly. "All ready, my lord," he murmured.

Kristan nodded his thanks and backed into the room. The chairs and his work table had been shoved aside and all his carefully-arranged documents were jumbled into tilting, disorderly stacks, but the room was warm and everything he had asked for was in place. "Come in," he said, gesturing to the cushions heaped before the fire. "Come in and rest." Serle led the centaur woman to the fire, and Kristan stepped to the door. "Keep everyone away," he said to Randolf. "Make certain news of our visitor doesn't travel any further. I don't care if you have to gag everyone in the castle—this is not to be gossiped about beyond our walls."

He closed the door, and the centaur let out an anxious grunt. "It's not locked," Kristan said. He opened and closed the door several times to demonstrate. "You can leave whenever you like, see? But you'll be safe in here for now."

Serle knelt and patted the cushions. "See how soft they are? And the fire is nice and warm." He pointed to the crackling flames. "Fire. We call this fire. Fire."

"Fi-yer," the centaur woman repeated.

"Yes, fire!" Serle nodded and clapped his hands with delight. "Fire. What do the Kenta . . . Kentra . . ."

"*Kentávron*," the centaur woman said, but she was watching Kristan as he lifted a pitcher of wine from a tray on the table.

"Yes, *Kentávron*," Serle said. He pointed at the fire again. "*Kentávron* . . . fire?"

"*Fotiá.*"

"*Fotiá*," Serle repeated, and then pointed as Kristan poured wine into a goblet. "That's wine. Wine."

"Wy-yen."

"Yes! Wine! *Kentávron* . . . wine?"

"*Krasí.*" She accepted the cup from Kristan and sniffed at its contents.

"*Krasí.*" Serle held up one of the cushions. "What do you call—"

"Serle," Kristan said, "too many questions."

"Sorry, my lord."

With the goblet at her lips, the centaur paused. "Milor?" she said. "*Eínai Milor to ónomá sas?*"

Kristan shook his head. "I don't understand."

"*Eínai Milor to ónomá sas?*" she repeated, with a touch of impatience. With her free hand, she pointed at Serle. "Serle, *naí?*" She tapped the goblet. "Wine, *naí?*" She indicated the fire. "Fire, *naí?*"

Kristan nodded. "Yes, that's right."

She pointed at him again. "Milor, *naí?*"

"Oh! No, no." Kristan put his hand to his chest. "Kristan."

The centaur woman nodded solemnly. "Kreestan. Yes."

He pointed to her. "What is your name?"

"*Nómiza óti to xérate*," she said in a low voice. She pursed her lips thoughtfully, but at last she patted her own chest. "*Astéria.*"

"Astéria!" Serle crowed. "You called her that before! How did you know her name?"

"I didn't," Kristan said. "It's something a friend of mine likes to say. I don't even know what it means. No wonder she was

startled." Astéria cocked her head as if expecting enlighten-
ment, but he could only shrug helplessly. "Perhaps later I'll be
able to explain. Right now, there are more important things to
discuss. Serle, see if she'll sit down and eat something. I need a
few moments."

He rummaged among his papers while Serle settled Astéria
before the fire and offered her the tray, explaining the various
dishes and giving his considered opinion of each. Astéria ate
a few distracted bites, but her attention was on Kristan as he
knelt before her and spread a large map on the floor. It was a
beautiful thing, extravagantly illustrated and tinted, and both
the centaur woman and Serle peered at it with interest.

Kristan put his finger on the drawing of a little castle centered in a wash of green. "Fandrall," he said, then patted the
floor beside him. "Fandrall."

She nodded. "Fandrall, *naí*."

He put his finger on the drawing of Malchea's castle in the
northwest. "Malchea."

"Malchea. *Naí*."

There was a small bowl of honeyed walnuts on the tray;
Kristan placed it on the map off Malchea's western shore.
"Ship," he said, and then pushed it across the blue-tinted parchment until it reached Malchea's castle. Astéria's brows knotted.
Kristan pursed his lips in a faint whistle and repeated the gesture. "Ship," he said again, then plucked a single walnut from
the bowl and held it up. "Astéria," he said. He placed the nut
on Malchea's castle and with one finger, pushed it east until it
reached Fandrall's castle. "Astéria in Fandrall, *naí*?"

She nodded. Kristan glanced at Serle, who was concentrat-
ing so hard that a faint sweat had broken out on his forehead.
"Serle, I have to speak privately with Astéria. Please leave the
room."

Serle's face fell. "Yes, my lord."

He started to rise, but Astéria grabbed his hand. "*Óchi*," she
said, shaking her head. "*Afíste ton na meínei, Kreestan*."

Kristan shook his head. "Serle must go, Astéria."

"*Afíste ton na meínei*," she repeated. She pulled Serle down beside her and patted his knee. "*Ton sympathó.*"

Serle beamed. "She likes me!"

"She certainly seems more at ease with you in the room." Kristan blew out a sigh. "Very well. Serle, what you're about to hear can never be shared with anyone, understand?"

"I promised I wouldn't gossip, my lord."

"This isn't gossip. What I'm about to tell Astéria is a secret, so important that I made everyone who knew it sign a paper swearing they'd never tell. The secret is of such magnitude that even I swore not to talk about it, but I have to tell her."

"I'll never tell, my lord," Serle almost whispered. "I swear it. I swear it on my sheep."

Kristan put his finger on the map again, this time on the gray, featureless expanse of the Exilwald. "Astéria, look here. *Kentávron.* Many *Kentávron* here, in a place called *O Tópos.*"

Her mouth dropped open. "*Apokleíete*," she said in a low voice, her disbelief almost palpable. "*Eímaste oi mónoi pou éxoume apomeínei.*"

"Many, many *Kentávron.*" Kristan poured the rest of the walnuts onto the gray part of the map. He patted his chest, pointed to her, and then to the pile of walnuts. "I'll take you there. Take you to the *Kentávron.* Do you understand?"

"*Óchi*," Astéria whispered, eyes wide. She shook her head, slowly at first, and then with more vehemence.

"Look." He picked up the lone walnut and started to place it with the others. "I'll take you there—"

"*Óchi!*" Astéria shouted. "*Prépei na vro tous sympatriótes mou! Tin oikogéneiá mou!*" She grabbed a handful of the nuts, counted eleven into the bowl, pushed it out onto the painted sea and jabbed her finger at it. "*Eínai kratoúmenoi! Prépei na tous vreíte, prépei na tous apeleftherósete!*" She slapped her chest several times and pointed at the bowl again, tears welling in her deep brown eyes. "*Voithisé me na vro tous sympatriótes mou!*"

"Hush now, hush," Serle said. He offered her the goblet, but she ignored it and extended one pleading hand to Kristan.

"*Voithíste me*," she whispered. "*Voithíste me*."

Serle looked from Astéria to the bowl and back again. "I think those are supposed to be her people, in the boat on the sea. She doesn't want to go to that gray place. She wants to find her people. She's asking you to help her."

Kristan sat back on his heels, thinking hard. At last, he picked up the bowl and rose, dragging the map with him. Nuts scattered across the floor. "Serle, encourage her to eat something and tend those sores on her legs if she'll let you. I'll be back in a while."

Kristan struggled to roll up the map one-handed as he hurried across the great hall. Servants were rushing in and out of the keep, their cheeks reddened with cold, their eyes bright with curiosity. Quinn, Randolf and Bastian stood just within the great hall doors, shoulders hunched against the cold drafts that blasted through the keep every time someone opened a door. Quinn turned to say something to the scribe and caught sight of Kristan. "There you are, my lord. The princess—"

"I need you both," Kristan said. "Right now."

"My lord, Princess Jelena—"

"Randolf, gather the rest of the knights and meet me in our dining chamber."

"But the princess—"

"What?" Kristan demanded. "What about the princess?"

"The princess is leaving," said a cool voice behind him.

He turned. Jelena was pulling on her red leather gloves, while her aunt and ladies hovered nearby, holding the rest of her extravagant traveling attire. "Leaving?" Kristan echoed. "But your people just arrived."

Jelena waved her attendants off. Exchanging anxious looks, Quinn, Bastian and Randolf retreated with them.

"This visit has gone awry in every possible way," Jelena said, adjusting her gloves with elaborate care. "Rather than linger and wear out my welcome further, I'm going home. I believe you're sincere when you say you have no designs on Malchea. I'll tell my father so. I expect he'll be relieved. I am as well. Although a political match between us would have been ideal in theory, the reality is that marriage to such an ugly, ill-mannered little man would have been unpleasant indeed. Goodbye, StoneKing." With her perfect smile fixed on her lips, Jelena swept from the great hall. Her retinue scurried after her.

For some moments, Kristan stood with the unfurled map slack in one hand and the bowl of walnuts tilting in the other. At last Quinn, Bastian and Randolf edged up to him. "What did she say to you, my lord?" Quinn asked.

With an effort, Kristan collected himself. "Nothing of importance. Come on." He led the way to the small dining room, where the other knights had already assembled. "Close the door," he said, and as Randolf obeyed, he flung the map on the table. "Here's the situation. Astéria—that's the centaur woman's name—has refused my offer to take her to O Tópos. Instead, she wants me to find the rest of her people." He placed the bowl on the blue-tinted sea again. "This is the sea trader who captured the centaurs. The princess said he was headed south to Dyer." He pushed the bowl south along Malchea's coast, and then southeast toward the great city of Seagirt in Dyer, marked with a drawing of a large, elaborately-towered castle. "The princess also said the sea trader was asking an outrageous sum for the other centaurs, so my guess is that he'll sail past all these little ports and make straight for Seagirt, where he stands the best chance of finding someone with both the money and the appetite for such an exotic purchase. I've no idea when the trader left Malchea, what kind of ship he sails, or the weather he's been sailing through. All I know is that if I'm going to outrun him to Seagirt, I have to leave right away."

"Leave?" Quinn repeated. "You mean you're going to travel to Dyer?"

"Yes. It's a straight route south from here. With luck and

decent weather, I might be able to make the trip in four days. Don't argue with me, Quinn; I'm going."

To his surprise, Quinn shrugged. "I'm not going to argue; it's well past time you visited that part of your realm, although traveling in winter is scarcely ideal. You'll have to have an escort, though; you simply cannot travel alone."

"Fewer people will mean less notice and fewer questions," Kristan said.

Quinn fixed him with a fierce stare. "You must have the protection of an escort. What if something happened?"

"Very well. I'll take Mitchell; he has experience with the *Kentávron*."

"Let me come, my lord," Sir Walter blurted. Kristan glared at him, and he shrugged apologetically. "My lord, you may need some muscle on the way."

The other knights began to claim places with him as well, but Quinn's testy voice cut through the noise. "Take all of them. It's time these big oafs had a mission instead of hanging around the castle. Bastian and I can take care of things here. Just leave me Randolf; between the three of us we can get this place running smoothly by the time you return."

"Are you going to take the centaur woman?" Bastian asked.

"She knows what the trader's ship looks like," Kristan said, "and she's the only one who can communicate with her people. Once we have them all, I'll take them straight to *O Tópos*."

"If you think an escort will draw attention, imagine what traveling with a centaur will be like," Quinn said.

"If we took a unit of horsemen, we could hide her among them, the way we hid Prince Torrin last summer," Matthew suggested.

Walter shook his head. "That unit traveled within an army and was easy to overlook."

"The Malcheans left her cage behind," Kennet said. "She could travel in that and be hidden."

"A covered cage would draw attention, and it's a heavy, awkward thing," Geoffrey said. "It would slow us down."

"If I were her, I wouldn't want to be stuck in there again," Mitchell said. "And how could we make her understand she wasn't still a captive?"

"How else can we disguise her, my lord?" Randolf asked. "She's every bit as big as Prince Torrin."

"She is, isn't she?" Kristan stood with his hand to his chin, musing. He looked down at the map, at its wash of blue ink symbolizing the western sea. *So much blue. I hope that sea trader is having a slow voyage.* A sudden image of the blue scrying ball popped into his head, along with an idea. "Ha," he said aloud.

"Did you think of something, my lord?" Matthew asked.

"I did. Bring Astéria here, please. And Randolf, fetch that little Wiche girl."

CHAPTER NINE

Nolle gaped at Astéria. The centaur stared back, eyes narrowed. "Can you do it?" Kristan asked.

Everyone seemed to be holding their breath. Even though she still clung to Serle's hand, Astéria's size and sheer presence were daunting.

"I . . . I think I can," Nolle said. "But I'm not sure how long it'll hold. I can stay a cat for a long time, but I can't always hold the shift for others."

"Well, give it a try, girl," Sir Randolf said. "You won't know until you try."

Nolle swallowed and lifted her hands. Astéria scowled at her. "Wait," Kristan said. "We can't spell her without explanation. She'll be terrified."

For what seemed like the hundredth time, he raised the upturned goblet and exposed the single honeyed walnut beneath. Astéria blew out a frustrated sigh. He felt like sighing himself. His head ached, and his fingers and the map were sticky from his attempts at explaining the route south to Seagirt, and how Astéria would be hidden during the journey.

"Do it to me first," Serle blurted.

"What?" Nolle said.

"Change me into something—a frog or a mouse or something. And then change me back so she can see that it doesn't hurt and isn't forever."

Nolle looked at Kristan. He nodded. Serle patted Astéria's

hand reassuringly and released it. "All right," Nolle said. She raised her hands again, locked her gaze on Serle and began to mutter under her breath. A damp, green smell filled the air. Nolle thrust her hands at Serle, as if to push him away. "*Marra, marra, marrapatta*," she whispered.

Serle shuddered and his scrawny figure began to waver. As he faded to transparency, a small greenish form materialized where his feet had been. Astéria cried out and the others gasped. "My mother's little mustache," Walter muttered.

"I take it the spell is a success," Kristan said drily.

"You can't see?" Walter looked puzzled, then suddenly grinned. "Oh, of course—the Stone. Yes, my lord, young Serle makes a handsome little frog."

Astéria was pointing at the frog and making incoherent sounds of dismay. "Nolle, change him back before Astéria goes mad," Kristan said.

Nolle made a subtle twirling gesture with her forefinger. Accompanied by the familiar hissing sound, the frog disappeared and Serle's shape solidified once more. He turned to Astéria with a smile, although his face was so pale that the freckles stood out more than ever. "See, Astéria? No harm done."

"Are you all right, boy?" Geoffrey asked in a low voice.

"I feel a little sick," Serle said through his grin. "See, it's just a game, Astéria. Like hide and seek."

Astéria shot a glance at Kristan. "*To agóri eínai treló.*"

"She keeps saying that," Serle said. "I wonder what it means."

"We'll find out another day," Kristan said. "Nolle, are you ready to try?"

Biting her lip, Nolle nodded.

"Your turn now," Serle told Astéria, and stepped away.

The centaur cringed against the wall as Nolle raised her hands again. "*Marra, marra, marrapatta*," she said again. Astéria's eyes went wide as her lower half began to flicker and fade. Within the vague outline of her centaur form, a human figure was shaping: pale, female, and stark naked.

"Oh my," Kennet murmured, averting his eyes.

Astéria looked down at herself in horror. "*Óchi!*" she cried. She leaped forward, as if to escape, but her legs buckled and she fell with a crash.

"You have to put clothes on her, stupid!" Serle shouted at Nolle.

Nolle did not answer him. Sweat beading her upper lip, she concentrated on Astéria, who was kicking and struggling to regain her feet. "She's fighting me. I can't hold her."

"Then let go," Kristan said. Astéria's helpless writhing, coupled with the wavering blur of her centaur form, made him feel a bit sick himself.

Nolle twirled her finger, the familiar hiss rustled in the air, and the transformation was over. Astéria sprawled on her side, panting. Serle crouched beside her, patting her shoulder and making comforting noises.

"What happened?" Matthew asked. "Why did she fall?"

Astéria rolled upright and slapped one foreleg. "*Pódia. Den ypárchoun arketá.*" As Serle helped her stand, she held up two fingers. "*Dyo*," she said, shook her head emphatically and held up four fingers. "*Téssera.*"

Geoffrey grunted. "She's used to four legs. She can't walk on two."

"Imagine trying to teach her how to ride," Walter said. "It'll have to be the cage, then."

"Nolle, what if you did just the opposite?" Kristan asked. "What if you changed her into a horse?"

Nolle twisted her fingers together. "I could try. She might hate that, too. She wouldn't have hands and she wouldn't be able to talk."

"I'll try to make her understand. Astéria, look. Horse." He extended his first fingers and placed them at the sides of his head. She only stared at him blankly. "Horse," he said again. Feeling foolish, he scuffed the floor with one foot and blew through his lips. "Horse? Yes?"

"*Ena álogo?*" she said. Her chin trembled for a moment and tears shimmered in her eyes, but then she seemed to steel herself. "Horse. Yes."

"Go ahead, Nolle," Kristan said.

For the third time, Nolle lifted her hands and muttered the spell. The room filled with the scent of grass and fresh-cut hay. Astéria's arms squeezed tight to her sides and her upper half faded to a blur as a horse's head and black-maned neck took its place. The hide was the same silvery gray as Astéria's lower half, but for a bright white blaze that ran down the horse's nose.

Walter let out an admiring whistle. "What a beautiful animal."

The horse form shuddered and let out a high, weak whinny. Kristan blinked. Deep within the quivering haze around the horse's head, Astéria's eyes were wide with fear. Nolle breathed a little sigh. "She's scared, but at least she's not fighting. I can hold the spell, at least for a while."

"All right, Astéria?" Kristan asked. He backed up a few steps and gestured for her to follow, and after a moment's hesitation, the horse clopped toward him, her head held stiffly erect. The others stood back as he walked her around the table, but as she passed the third time, Walter reached out to stroke the horse-form's neck. "Don't—" Kristan said, but Walter's caressing hand had already landed. The horse whipped its head around, ears laid back, and buried its teeth in Walter's arm. Walter cried out and pulled free as Astéria recoiled and collided with Kristan. With a hiss, the spell collapsed.

Astéria held out both hands to Walter, her face wrung with remorse. "*Lypámai, lypámai.*"

"No, it was my fault," Walter said, trying to smile. "You made such a pretty horse, I couldn't help myself."

"The spell is only a mask," Kristan said. "Beneath it she's still Astéria. Nolle, how was it that time?"

The Wiche girl was scowling. "Not so hard, but the further

away she gets, the harder it is to hold the shift. And you can't touch her or you'll ruin everything."

"You address the StoneKing as 'my lord,'" Quinn snapped.

"That's settled, then," Kristan said. "Nolle will have to come with us."

"What'll you give me if I do?" Nolle said.

Randolf snorted. "I'll give you a boot up the rear if you don't. How d'you like that?"

"You'll do as the StoneKing says, girl," Kennet said.

"What'll you give me?" Nolle insisted. Kristan said nothing, and she rolled her eyes. "Oh, all right. *My lord.* It's going to be a lot of work. I should get something for my trouble. That's only right."

"Fair enough," Kristan said. "If you come with us, and if you give no trouble, and if we're successful—then I'll reward you."

"With what?"

Walter laughed. "She's a persistent little brat, isn't she?"

Nolle ignored him. Her amber eyes bore into Kristan, and he suddenly realized what she was after.

"Very well," he said. "I'll give you the scrying ball."

Just saying the words made his heart ache, but Nolle smirked. "That'll do," she said.

"Go gather what you'll need for the journey and tell Dru he'll have to do without you for a while." Serle let out an involuntary whimper, and Kristan blew out a sigh. "Yes, Serle, you're coming, too. You can look after Astéria. Keep her calm and help her any way you can." With an effort, he put the loss of the scrying ball from his thoughts. "Quinn, Bastian, Randolf: we'll need to go over what happens here while I'm gone. Serle, we'll be using my work chamber, so take Astéria upstairs to my room to rest. Nolle, once you've made your preparations, please join them and practice shifting with Astéria. The rest of you knights, make the arrangements for our journey. I want to leave at first light and move fast, so don't encumber us with a lot of gear. Nolle and Serle are novice riders; make sure the stable master chooses suitable horses for them and that they have proper clothing for the journey. Everyone meet me back here for dinner and we'll finalize our plans then."

* * *

"And there's a request from Lady Heather asking permission to use your northeastern hunting lodge as a base for some training exercises." Bastian was still fumbling through papers as he, Randolf and Quinn trailed Kristan across the great hall.

"I didn't know I had a northeastern hunting lodge," Kristan said. The doorward hurried up with Kristan's furred cloak and gloves.

"One of Ravelin Seachlan's former holdings," Quinn said, and frowned as Kristan heaved the cloak around his shoulders. "My lord, your squire should be helping you with that."

"Serle is outside attending to Astéria."

"You'll never make a proper squire out of him if he's always looking after someone else."

Kristan looked at him slantwise. "By the Stone, you're petulant when you haven't had any sleep. Once I'm gone, you should go back to bed."

"I have to make my notes on Princess Jelena's visit while it's still fresh in my mind. Are you sure you don't have anything else to tell me? Your final conversation with her seemed rather . . . strained."

Kristan snorted. "She was blunt, which was refreshing."

"Are you sure you want those extra troops on the Malchean border, my lord?" Randolf asked, as Kristan worked his fingers into his fur-lined gauntlets.

"Yes. Use whatever pretext you wish. I doubt we have anything to fear from King Lockward, but I want him to remember that he has a great deal to fear from me." Kristan nodded to the doorward, who nodded in turn to the sleepy-eyed pages, who opened the keep doors onto the cold murk of early dawn.

"Lady Heather's request, my lord?" Bastian said, wincing in the sudden bitter draft.

The nightmare vision of Heather in Daazna's arms swelled in Kristan's memory. "Approved," he said, more sharply than he intended. "You can approve whatever requests she makes."

"Yes, my lord."

They followed him out onto the keep steps. In the courtyard, the little company bound for Dyer was already assembled. Serle and Nolle were mounted on ponies and looking dubious about the experience. Astéria stood close beside them in horse form, the outline of her head and shoulders shimmering in the thin light. "Good morning, my lord," Sir Kennet called. "Everything is ready, and the weather looks to be cold but fair."

"My lord, please send word when you reach Dyer," Quinn said.

"I wish old Phelan was here, with some of his magical messenger crows," Randolf said. "It would make things so much easier."

"Perhaps not," Bastian said. "Alister wrote that the old man is more addled than ever. He's so preoccupied with his papers and books that he sometimes forgets to eat."

"He's not the only one," Quinn muttered, with a pointed look at Kristan.

"With luck we'll be able to find this sea trader, recover Astéria's people and get them all to O Tópos quickly and without incident," Kristan said, ignoring the look. "In the meantime, gentlemen, I'm entrusting the day-to-day affairs of the realm to you, along with the castle's reconstruction."

"Never you fear, my lord," Randolf said. "When you get back, you'll have a proper bedchamber, a trained staff and everything in order."

"Safe journey, my lord," Bastian said.

"Don't take any foolish risks," Quinn added.

Mitchell held out Malvo's reins as Kristan descended the stairs. "He's keen to go this morning, my lord. The other horses have been skittish around Astéria, but old Malvo never paid her any mind. He's had his eye on the gate."

Kristan mounted up and took a quick look at the rest of his little cavalcade. In accordance with his instructions, there were only two pack ponies moderately loaded, and the eight mounts carried just a bedroll and a pair of saddlebags each. "Ten horses altogether," Mitchell said, following his gaze. "Eleven, if you count Astéria. No tack or saddlebags for her, of course. We'll just have to tell folks she's a pet or something."

The guards saluted as the company passed through the gatehouse and across the drawbridge. Kingsmere was stirring to life, and the early risers watched curiously as Kristan and his escort made their way through the town. Lyko Yeomans with his wife Feva smiled and murmured greetings from the doorstep of their modest home as he passed, but Kristan only nodded, his focus on Astéria.

As they headed south, the outlying farms of Kingsmere gave way to fields and valleys. The road ahead grew more and more deserted. At first, Astéria stayed close to Serle and Nolle, but as the sun rose, she began to move ahead, first at a cautious trot, and then into a canter and finally into a full gallop, stretching her legs and tossing her head. Serle tried to keep up with her, but he tended to panic and grab at his horse's mane whenever the pace quickened. "The more you do it, the easier it is," Walter told him. "Look, I'll show you. Sit square in the saddle, tighten your knees and find your mount's rhythm." He nudged his horse into an easy canter, caught up to Astéria, circled around her teasingly, and then trotted back. Astéria followed him, but rather than go back to Serle, she came alongside Malvo. The great black horse snorted a cloud of steam from his nostrils, but paid her no real attention. As Astéria matched Malvo's gait, she looked at Kristan sidelong. The wavering outline of her human head nodded and her horse's head bobbed in tandem.

Kristan glanced over his shoulder at Nolle, awkward in her pony's saddle, her gaze locked on Astéria. "How goes it with you?"

"Not too bad. She's accepted the shift; as long as she doesn't stray too far, I can hold it. I'm getting tired, though."

With her ears upright and tilted forward, Astéria watched Serle receiving instructions from Walter, Matthew and Geoffrey all at once. The flickering haze surrounding her made Kristan's head ache, and he turned his attention to the road ahead. He was tired himself, but any hope of a light doze in the saddle was dashed when Sir Kennet drew up on his right.

"What are we going to do with her once we reach Seagirt, my lord?" Sir Kennet asked.

"What do you mean?"

"Well, if she's in horse form, my lord, they'll want to stable her with the rest of our mounts, won't they?"

"And there's Nolle to think of, my lord," Mitchell said, reining up on Astéria's far side. "If she needs to be near Astéria to hold the spell, she'd have to sleep in the stables with her."

"I'm not sleeping in any stable," Nolle muttered behind them.

Kristan repressed a sigh. "I hadn't considered that. Thank you, gentlemen; I'll give it some thought. Kennet, would you ride ahead with Mitchell? If you spot anyone on the road, or see dwellings ahead, send word back. Tell Serle to stay with Astéria. Ask Geoffrey to take up the rear position; Walter and Matthew to the right and left with the pack ponies. I'd like to give Nolle and Astéria some relief from the spell, but only if there's no one around to see." When everyone was in place, he turned in the saddle and crooked his finger at Nolle. She nudged her horse up to join Serle and Astéria. "As soon as we get word that it's safe, you can release Astéria," Kristan said. "While she's in her true form, you and Serle talk to her. Teach her more of our words; learn what you can of hers. Be ready to shift her the moment other people approach, understand?"

Kennet and Mitchell had already disappeared over a rise in the road, but a moment later the younger knight returned.

Grinning, he held out one fist, thumb pointed up, then turned his horse and headed back the way he had come. Kristan nodded to Nolle, and as the Wiche girl made the now-familiar twirling motion with her forefinger, he nudged Malvo forward so he could be alone. He let his head sink into the depths of his furred hood and closed his eyes. The voices of Astéria and the children faded to a soft drone as he drowsed in the saddle.

"Head!"

"*Kefáli.*"

"Hand!"

"*Chéri.*"

"Hair!"

"*Malliá.*"

Only a few miles down the road, Sir Mitchell woke him with news of a village ahead. With Astéria in horse form and the knights gathered close, the group moved past the little houses and shops without stopping, receiving only curious looks and the occasional polite nod from villagers going about their business. Once it was safe, Nolle changed Astéria back again and the lessons went on.

"'My name is Astéria.' Say it. My . . . name . . .'"

"Moi nem—"

"'My name is Astéria.'"

"My name ees Astéria."

"Good!"

With the sun at its zenith, they stopped to eat and rest the horses. Geoffrey tapped a little keg of ale from their stores and served out savory meat pies, so carefully packed that they were still warm. Everyone made appreciative noises as they bit into the sturdy crusts. "Dru may not be much for dainties," Geoffrey said, "but at this kind of soldiers' fare no one can match him. Enjoy it while you can. There's enough for dinner tonight, but after that we'll be eating porridge and what we can hunt or snare."

"Why?" Nolle asked. "Didn't we bring food?"

"A little, but mostly we're carrying grain for the horses. We can hunt for our meals, but there's not much browse for horses in the wintertime."

Serle pointed to Astéria's cup. "Ale," he told her.

She took a sip and nodded in satisfaction. "*Zýthos*."

"Ale," Serle said again. He smacked his lips and rubbed his belly. "The ale is good."

"D'ale is *goooood*," Astéria said, mocking his enthusiastic inflection.

"I am eating," Nolle said through a mouthful.

"I yam ating."

"No, eating. 'I am eating.'"

"I am eating."

Nolle pointed to Serle. "He is eating."

"He ees eating."

Nolle pointed at the horses munching the sparse grass. "They are eating."

"Dey are eating."

Nolle waved her arms at the group. "We are eating."

"We are eating."

"We are happy to be eating," Walter said. Astéria looked at him curiously. "Happy," the knight said again, and turned up his mouth in an exaggerated grin.

"Ah, *eftychisménos*," Astéria said, and smiled.

"That's a mouthful," Walter said. "Eff-tee-keesh-men-osh."

"Goooood," Astéria said, and they all laughed, except for Kennet, somber as always, and Kristan, who sat a little apart from the others, too weary even to smile.

Mitchell pulled his face into an extravagant scowl. "Angry!" he said.

"Angry," Astéria answered, mimicking both word and expression. "*Thymoménos*."

"The-mo-me . . ." Mitchell shook his head. "I've never had a head for languages. I'm sorry."

"Aym sorree?" Astéria repeated, with a look of confusion.

"*Ti simaínei aftó?*"

"It's an apology," Matthew said. "Look here." He jabbed Walter in the ribs with his elbow, and then drew back in comic dismay. "Oh, I'm sorry!"

Walter cuffed the side of Matthew's head, and then clasped his hands in mock contrition. "I'm sorry!"

The two knights snickered as they poked and swatted each other, apologizing profusely after each blow. Geoffrey grunted and jerked his thumb at the pair. "Stupid," he said to Astéria. "They are stupid."

"Dey are stooped," Astéria repeated.

Walter had his arm locked around Matthew's neck and was knuckling the blond knight's scalp fiercely, but he left off long enough to point at Geoffrey. "He is grouchy," he said, drawing down his brows and sticking out his lower lip.

"Heeyis growchy," Astéria said. She pointed at Kennet's grave face. "Heeyis growchy, yes?"

"Oh, no, no," Walter said. "Kennet is stern." He released Matthew, drew himself upright and composed his features into solemnity. "Stern."

"Kennet ees stern." She pointed at Mitchell, who blushed. "Meetchell ees . . . ?"

"Mitchell is shy," Matthew said. He covered his own face with both hands, and then peeped through his fingers. "Shy."

"Meetchell ees shy." Astéria turned to Nolle. "Nolle ees . . . ?"

"Nolle is crafty," Geoffrey said, and tapped his forehead with a knowing look.

"Nolle ees craftee." Astéria swung her hand to point at Kristan. "Kreestan ees . . . ?"

The knights' playfulness faded. Kristan knew that if he would only smile, their lighthearted mood would return, but he could not. An uncomfortable silence fell and Astéria looked from face to face, clearly puzzled.

At last, Kennet cleared his throat. "King," he said, and bowed deeply to Kristan. "He is king."

"He is king," Walter repeated. He and the others bowed as well.

"Kreestan ees king," Astéria echoed, sudden comprehension brightening her eyes. She put a hand to her chest, extended a graceful foreleg and inclined her head. "*Den íxera*. I yam sorry, *Vasiliá* Kreestan."

"It's time we were on our way," Kristan said.

The journey resumed, more quietly. The knights positioned themselves as before, while Serle, Astéria and Nolle continued their lessons. As the afternoon wore on, a raw wind blew out of the northwest and the clouds clumped and mounded, blocking out the wan winter sun. Gradually, an enormous darkness spread across the southeastern horizon. "Is that a storm ahead?" Matthew called to Walter.

Walter rose in his stirrups to look. "I don't think so, but it certainly looks forbidding."

"It's the Exilwald," Kristan said, and even speaking the word was difficult.

"It's huge," Matthew said. "I had no idea."

Painful memories were crowding into Kristan's brain, and he was grateful for the distraction of Kennet and Mitchell, approaching at a gallop. "Village ahead, my lord," Sir Kennet said, as they drew up.

Kristan turned to Nolle, but she had already cast the shifting spell and Astéria's glum face was fading behind the horseform's bright white blaze. "I'm getting better at it," Nolle said.

"I'm afraid you've more work ahead. I've been thinking it over, and I don't see any way we can do what's necessary in Seagirt unless Astéria can pass as a human woman."

"She's not going to like it," Nolle said. Astéria was tossing her head irritably, and in spite of the cold, a fine sweat broke out on Nolle's brow.

"It can't be helped. When we stop for the night, I want you to try that shift again. Serle, I'll depend on you to help Astéria when she needs it."

Serle nodded importantly and turned to Nolle. "You'd better remember to put clothes on her this time."

"Don't tell me what to do," Nolle snapped.

"Well, you scared her."

"She scared herself."

"Quiet, you two," Matthew said. Both children fell silent, but they still glowered at each other over Astéria's back as the company passed the village. With outlying farms still on either side, the two began a muttered bickering, and Kristan felt the familiar sick swirl of anger in his gut. "Kennet," he said, "Serle has yanked at his horse's bit all day. You and Mitchell take him ahead with you and teach him how to use the reins properly."

Kennet smiled in grim satisfaction. "With pleasure, my lord."

Mitchell crooked his finger at Serle and the three trotted ahead. Astéria started after them, but Kristan stopped her with a raised hand. "Stay here," he said.

The horse's head turned, and for one startling moment Astéria's glaring eyes seemed to leap at him from the haze. Nolle let out a grunt and screwed up her face, and just as abruptly, the eyes faded back. "Phew," Nolle said. "She tried to break out, just then."

"I saw."

Nolle cocked her head. "What did you see?" He shot her an exasperated look, and she rolled her eyes. "My lord. What do you see when you look at her?"

"I see a blur around the shift-shape, and on occasion, her true form within."

"And that's because of the Stone?"

"Yes."

"If I tried to shift you, would it work?"

"No."

Nolle's eyes glittered, and she raised her hands.

"Don't you dare," Walter said, pushing his horse and his own imposing bulk between them.

"I wasn't going to—"

"Don't you even think about it."

"But he said it wouldn't—"

"I don't care what he said; you're not casting any spells on him."

A rebuke was on Kristan's lips, but then he saw how pale and grim Walter was.

Nolle's chin jutted at a truculent angle. "Fine," she muttered. She put heels to her horse and trotted ahead, jouncing in the saddle. Walter glared after her.

"Easy, my friend," Matthew said gently.

Walter gave himself a shake and tried to smile. "Sorry. Sorry, my lord. But the look on her face . . . well, it made my skin crawl." He shuddered again and added in an undertone: "She reminded me of Daazna."

Beneath his good humor he's as damaged as I am, Kristan thought, *and yet he came between Nolle and me.* The realization sapped him of any lingering anger. "I don't think she meant any harm, but thank you all the same."

"Doesn't it bother you, my lord?" Matthew asked. "After what you've been through, I'm surprised you can tolerate having Wichie folk around you."

"Wiche," Kristan corrected absently. "And no. I had a Wiche teacher when I was a child."

He said no more, and the knights let him be. Even though the Exilwald was far away, its forbidding mass kept reminding him of Gabriel and Martin, of how they had died; how he had let them die. *Their blood is on your hands,* Colin Demitt had once told him, and the words kept hissing through Kristan's head, like a snake threatening to strike. To distract himself, he began to count again. First, he counted Malvo's hoof beats, but they were too steady to provide a real diversion. He counted the few sheep in the meadows they passed, using his right hand to track them, and on his left hand he counted the number of times Walter laughed. It was still not enough. At last, he set himself the mental task of listing all the courtiers, commanders and captains in his realm, filling his brain with names to crowd out any other thoughts.

As the road angled southwest, the Exilwald finally receded from sight, but Kristan's relief from that misery was short-lived. The sky grew leaden and a sharp-edged wind began to buffet them. "It's coming on for dusk," Sir Matthew said. "Shall we look for a tavern, or some sort of house where we can spend the night?"

"I think either would be risky," Kristan said. He nodded toward a sizeable stand of trees well off the western side of the road. "We'll make camp there. There are plenty of evergreens to provide shelter from the wind."

"It's going to be a miserable night, my lord."

"I know, but camping will be easier than trying to sort out arrangements for Astéria. Ride ahead and let Kennet and Mitchell know we're stopping. Walter, wait here with the pack ponies for Geoffrey to catch up, then follow us. Nolle, come with me." He quirked his finger at Astéria. "Astéria, you come, too."

"Shall I release her from the spell?" Nolle asked.

"Not until we're certain we'll be alone in these woods."

He dismounted with difficulty. His whole body ached from the long, cold day in the saddle, and his bad knee throbbed as soon as he put weight on it. Nolle alighted, almost as stiffly, and the two of them stumbled toward the trees, leading their horses. Astéria came behind, tossing her head and leaping over hummocks as if untroubled by the cold and happy to be finished with their first day's journey.

They made camp in a clearing ringed with study fir trees, which provided some respite from the rising wind and blowing snow. Kristan set to work building a fire as Kennet and Matthew went off to scout. Geoffrey tended the horses, with Serle providing more hindrance than help. Mitchell gathered long branches to provide the framework for a lean-to, while

Walter produced a hatchet and cut down fresh limbs of evergreen to make a roof for the shelter. Nolle spread the softest, springiest branches under the roof to make a foundation for their bedrolls. "That'll make for pleasant sleeping in spite of the cold," Mitchell said, as he helped her lay the last branches. "Nothing like a sweet-smelling mattress of fir boughs on a cold night."

"I've slept outdoors enough to last me a lifetime," Nolle said crossly. "I'd rather sleep in a real bed."

"Gotten used to the soft life of the castle, have you?"

"I like sleeping outdoors," Serle said. "Unless it rains."

"Snow isn't any better," Nolle sniffed.

Astéria snorted and stamped one hoof, as if calling attention to her shifted state. "I know," Nolle told her. "I'm tired of it, too. But we have to wait until Kennet and Matthew tell us it's safe."

"And it is," Matthew said, as he and Kennet pushed through the trees to join them. "There's no one in these woods but us."

Kristan nodded to Nolle. As soon as the spell was lifted, both she and Astéria heaved a sigh of relief, and Nolle sagged into a crouch. "Glad that's over," she muttered.

"*Ki egó*," Astéria said. She stretched out both arms and wiggled her fingers, then smoothed her hair over her shoulders.

"Later on, after we've eaten and rested, I want you to try shifting Astéria into a human," Kristan said.

Nolle groaned and flopped onto her back.

"*Ti symvaínei?*" Astéria asked, narrowing her eyes.

Nolle held up two fingers. "*Dyo podia*," she said, and Astéria let out a groan of her own.

"Don't forget to put clothes on her this time," Serle said, and received a glare in reply.

"There's a stream at the far edge of the woods, my lord," Kennet said. "It hasn't iced up completely; we can still get water."

"Plenty of rabbit droppings nearby," Matthew added. "I'll set some snares when we water the horses. If we're lucky, we'll have fresh meat for breakfast."

With the horses watered, fed and blanketed for the night, the company dined on the rest of Dru's meat pies, now cold and slightly mashed but still tasty. The wind whistled in the treetops above, and snow still filtered through the branches, but in the lee of their shelter it was not unpleasant. After they were finished eating, they all sat staring at the fire, too tired for conversation. At last, Kristan roused himself from his stupor. "Don't fall asleep yet, Nolle. We still have to practice the spell."

"What do you mean, *we*?" Nolle said under her breath.

"Mind your tongue," Kennet snapped.

Nolle sighed and poked Astéria, who had stretched out on her side with all four legs tucked up against her body. "Wake up. Time for *dyo podia*."

Astéria rose, head drooping and shoulders slumped. Nolle got to her own feet, yawned hugely, and then raised her hands.

"Don't forget the clothes," Serle said, then yelped as Geoffrey swatted him across the top of his head.

"Quiet," Kristan said. "Go ahead, Nolle."

Nolle licked her lips and fixed Astéria with a steady gaze. "*Marra, marra, marrapatta*," she said. Astéria's body began to glow and pulse. Her hindquarters faded to transparency while her forequarters, torso, shoulders and arms were slowly masked by a soft, pale light that finally solidified into a cream-colored gown with a sash of gold at the waist.

"Ha!" Serle cried. "That's the dress the princess wore!"

"Shut up," Walter said through his teeth.

Nolle's arms trembled as she perfected the shift; Astéria's long black hair coiled and looped upward, forming itself into the same intricate hairstyle Jelena had worn, crowned with a duplicate of the princess' gold and pearl circlet. With a shuddering gasp, Nolle lowered her arms and stepped back.

"Now that's a beautiful woman," Matthew said softly.

"A hundred times better than that princess," Mitchell said.

Astéria looked down at herself, and with a tremulous smile, raised her hands to stroke the soft fabric smoothly over her breasts and hips. "*Ómorfo*," she said.

She was very tall for a human female, and Kristan could still see the wavering outline of her true form, but judging by the looks on the faces of his men, the transformation was a success. "Is it all right?" Nolle asked, her voice tremulous. "I'm sorry about the dress, but it was all I could think of."

"It's fine," Kristan said. "Well done."

Astéria pinched her skirt between thumbs and forefingers and raised it, enough to expose graceful feet in elegant slippers. She peered down at them, then raised one foot as if to examine it more closely. Even that slight movement threw her off balance; she teetered and began to wave her arms wildly. Everyone leaped to their feet, but Matthew reached her first, catching her about the waist as her legs buckled.

"*Adýnaton*," Astéria cried, struggling and shaking her head. "*Den boró na to káno.*"

Kristan shot a glance at Nolle. The Wiche girl was pale to the lips and shuddering from head to foot as she fought to keep the shift in place. *She's going to faint*, Kristan thought. "*Óchi!*" he shouted. "Astéria, stop it!"

Astéria froze in Matthew's arms. Kristan pointed at Nolle. "Look. You're hurting her. You're hurting Nolle."

"*Lypámai*," Astéria whispered, her eyes wide. "*Lypámai,* Nolle.*"

"I know you're frightened, but you've got to try," Kristan said. "Serle, get on her other side. Help her stand upright. That's the way. Now, Astéria, just slide your feet like this." He demonstrated, shuffling his feet across the loamy forest floor. "Just a little bit at a time."

Astéria nodded and took a deep breath. Leaning heavily on Serle's shoulder, and with Matthew's arm firmly about her waist, she made her way around the fire; once, twice, three times before her wobbling knees gave out. Matthew and Serle lowered her to the ground and she sat there like a dropped doll, legs extended awkwardly before her.

Nolle was swaying a bit, and Geoffrey helped her sit down next to Astéria. "Well done," he said, and gave her a clumsy pat on the head.

Panting, Nolle and Astéria looked at each other, and burst into weak giggles. "*Poly kalá,*" Astéria said. "Well done, Nolle."

Even Kennet laughed then, but Kristan had to look away. The wavering of Astéria's true form, combined with the shift form clad in Jelena's clothing, made his head spin. "That's enough for one night. Release her, Nolle. We should all get some sleep."

"I'll take the first watch," Walter said. "My lord, why don't you sleep in the center of the shelter? It'll be coziest."

The idea of being squeezed in the middle of the company, all huddling together for warmth, made Kristan feel even sicker. "No, thank you," he said. "Let Astéria and the children take the middle. I'll sleep at the far end."

CHAPTER TEN

"What's she up to now?" Ravelin muttered.

Isobel said nothing. She sat before the fire in a loose robe, her arms folded and her back to him. Ravelin shrugged and peered out the window again. Isobel's small bedchamber overlooked the kitchen courtyard, where Heather stood side by side with her maidservant Bayla. Both were bundled against the cold and carried a sword—Heather the beautiful weapon that had been presented to her by the StoneKing, Bayla a battered practice sword. Heather was gesturing toward her boots as she demonstrated what Ravelin quickly recognized as basic footwork for a beginning swordsman. After a moment, Bayla nodded, and the pair began to pace through the moves together.

"I'll be damned," Ravelin muttered. "She's teaching her servant to fight."

Isobel sniffed and tossed her head. Ravelin barely noticed. Fascinated, he folded his arms and leaned against the window frame. Bayla seemed to be catching on fairly quickly, but sometimes she tripped on the hem of her gown, throwing off her timing. Finally, she put her sword under one arm and tucked up her skirts, providing Ravelin with a fine view of trim ankles and shapely calves, albeit clad in thick woolen stockings. "Nice legs on that maidservant," he said.

"Half the Wichelord's army was between them," Isobel snapped.

"Don't be spiteful, my dear; it's not becoming. Perhaps, if you made an effort to be pleasant to the maidservant, her mistress would be open to a friendship with you."

"Why should I be friends with her?"

"Because it would be helpful if Lady Heather saw you as a confidante."

"A confidante? Ha!"

"Doesn't she ever talk to you or Annys or Lily? Chat about clothes or jewelry or men or whatever it is you women like to talk about?"

"Her? You can see how much she cares about clothes and jewelry. She's nothing in common with the ladies of the court. She says good morning or sometimes remarks about the weather, but that's all."

"Then perhaps you should take an interest in what she does. Ask her to teach you swordplay, too."

Isobel gaped at him. "Are you joking?"

"Not a bit. A little exercise wouldn't hurt, my dear; you're getting a bit pudgy."

"Perhaps you're starting to prefer your women shaped like boys."

"I've told you before: I find her repulsive."

"Then why do you spend all your time watching her?"

He shrugged. "She's a challenge. And until she trusts me, I can't make any progress. Now do as I say. Put on your clothes, run downstairs and present yourself as a willing pupil."

"I will not."

He crossed the room in three long strides and yanked her to her feet. "Do as I say," he snarled into her face. "Get Lily and Annys to join you. Do it now."

He pushed Isobel from him and went back to the window. The two women below were still pacing through their footwork, and once again Ravelin absorbed himself in the scene, ignoring Isobel's sniffles as she dressed.

Even with her skirts rucked up, Bayla was still clumsy, and

soon, red-faced and panting, she stopped and shook her head. Heather put an encouraging hand on her maidservant's shoulder and spoke to her. Bayla nodded and squared her shoulders, and the women began to move through the exercise once more. Heather was light on her feet, which was not unexpected given her slight build, but Ravelin was surprised by the aggression of her advances and lunges. *Someone taught her well,* he thought, *but beyond that, she takes pleasure in the drill. A warrior's pleasure.*

The chamber door opened and slammed shut, signaling Isobel's exit from the room. Ravelin smiled and turned from the window. He washed his face in the basin by the fire, and then put on his clothes, taking his time. When he was dressed, he cracked open Isobel's door and looked carefully up and down the hall, making sure no one was about before he slipped from the room. He went downstairs to the kitchen, where he helped himself to a bowl of porridge and stood in front of the fire to eat it, paying no heed to the cook's glare. He left the empty bowl on the mantel and made his way to the kitchen's rear door. It was slightly ajar and a few scullery maids were peering through the crack. "Look at them stumbling around," one of the girls said. "I could do better."

"Yes, I'd like to see you plodding through those moves in your clogs," an older woman answered. She caught sight of Ravelin and hissed a warning to her fellows. They bobbed into offhand curtsies, but Ravelin was too curious about what was going on outside to care. He brushed past and stepped out into the raw morning.

"That's it," Heather was saying. "That's it. Advance with your right foot, close with the left."

Lily, Annys and Isobel had joined Bayla in the exercise, and Heather stood facing them as they drilled. Bayla was moving with greater confidence and Lily and Annys were working hard to master the moves, but Isobel was barely trying. Within her fur hood, her eyes and mouth were pinched tight. "Keep your weight centered," Heather went on. "Isobel, if you really throw yourself into the exercise, you'll warm up quickly."

Isobel's surly expression deepened. She opened her mouth as if to retort, but Ravelin cleared his throat pointedly, and she jumped. All the women hesitated. Heather recovered first. "Concentrate," she called. "Don't let the Reach distract you. Advance, advance, advance . . . and *thrust*." She lunged forward, demonstrating, and Ravelin admired the clean, sure lines of her body, taut from toes to sword point. He ambled around the little courtyard, taking full advantage of the opportunity to observe the women: Lily graceful, slender and faintly blue about the lips with cold; Annys wide-hipped and bosomy, with a red spot rising on either cheek as she huffed and puffed through the drill; Isobel sluggish; Bayla scowling with concentration but with every move growing less awkward. Up on the battlements the guards paused to watch, leaning on their pikes. Heather looked up and arched an eyebrow, and the men hastily resumed their posts. "That's it," she said, turning her attention back to the women. "Bayla, give your sword to Annys. Lily, take mine. Try the drill again and see how different it feels with a weapon in your hand." From the bin next to the kitchen door, she caught up two long, thin sticks of firewood and handed them to Bayla and Isobel. "Use these for now. Next time I'll bring enough swords for everyone."

"When is next time?" Annys panted, struggling to keep her sword point up as she paced through the exercise.

"First thing tomorrow, before breakfast. I always have a greater appreciation for my meal if I have to work for it. Face me, ladies, and let's try the drill again."

She worked the women briskly, but with a genial enthusiasm that had all but Isobel smiling even as they gasped for air. Ravelin's muscles twitched in response to each drill, and finally he could not resist snatching up a stick for himself and joining the line. Heather said nothing, and he threw himself into the exercise with a will, stretching muscles grown stiff and unresponsive from lack of use. By the time the sun crept over the curtain wall, a small crowd of servants, knights and off-duty soldiers had gathered to watch. Most surprising, Heather's father and cousin were among them. Colin Demitt looked vaguely displeased, but Alister was grinning.

"That's enough for one day, ladies," Heather finally announced. "Any more and you'll be too sore for a decent practice tomorrow. Slow and steady, that's the way. Go enjoy your breakfasts. I expect you'll have a good appetite for them."

There was a pattering of applause from the onlookers. Lily returned Heather's sword with a little curtsey and Annys handed the practice sword to Bayla. Isobel cocked her arm as if to hurl her stick into the woodpile, but at a sharp look from Ravelin, she dropped it instead and curtsied to Heather, murmuring a few words of thanks.

As students and observers dispersed, Heather sheathed her sword and went to the well. "Thank you for allowing me to take part in your exercise," Ravelin said, as he joined her there. "I hope I wasn't intruding."

Heather took a long drink from the dipper and wiped her mouth with her sleeve. "You made the women uncomfortable."

"I'm sorry. I felt the need to join in. I'm out of practice."

"Yes, you are."

Her brusqueness made him bristle, but he forced a laugh instead. "Was it so obvious?'

"You're heavy-footed and slow to recover from your lunges."

She started across the courtyard, as if finished with the conversation, but in a few quick strides Ravelin caught up to her. "I'd welcome the chance to drill with you."

"My knights and I sometimes practice in the afternoons. It might be better if you joined us, rather than drill with the women."

"I doubt Sir Jerrold and the others who were Lost with me would welcome my participation."

"Perhaps not at first." Heather stopped and faced him. "But

if you make the same effort with them that you make with me, they might be friendlier."

Toady to them as I do to you, Ravelin thought, but made himself nod and smile. "You may be right. Perhaps I'll join you this afternoon, then."

"As you like," Heather responded, but she was looking past him. Ravelin glanced over his shoulder. One of the scullery maids was at the kitchen well. She had drawn up the bucket and filled her ewers, but instead of carrying them back to the kitchen, she was clumping through one of Heather's exercises, a stick of firewood in one hand.

Ravelin smirked. "Ah, the plodding plow horse yearns to run."

Heather did not smile. As she studied the girl, she munched on her lower lip, a habit Ravelin found repellent. Just then, a servant stuck his head out the kitchen door and bawled at the girl to hurry up. Tossing aside her stick, she grabbed the ewers and hustled inside.

A strange light brightened Heather's eyes. She nodded to herself and struck off toward the stables.

"Going for a ride?" Ravelin asked, as he hurried after her. "Shall I come with you?"

"Thank you, no. I doubt you'd be interested."

"Perhaps I would. Where are you going?"

"Into Needwood."

"What for?"

"To look at plow horses. Good day, Reach Seachlan."

* * *

Skapi was a white horse, but it was a white that seemed to alter according to her mood. Some days her hide was pearly, with an iridescent sheen that made Heather catch her breath. On pearly days Skapi was as mannerly as an elderly noblewoman. Other days it looked more like milk, with a creamy richness that invited touch, and on those days Skapi was affectionate and playful.

And some days Skapi's hide seemed murky, like a lead-tinged winter sky, and on those days Skapi's peculiar blue eyes and her disposition were shifting and untrustworthy. *Today is a murky day*, Heather thought; *I'll have to keep her under control.*

She heaved a little sigh. It was an inconvenient time for Skapi to be temperamental; Heather's errand in town required delicate handling. She had been born and raised in Needwood, but during the rebellion against Daazna, her family and friends were often at odds with others in the town. She sometimes wondered which of her Needwood neighbors had whispered accusations against the Demitts into Daaznan ears. She couldn't blame them; it had been an unsettled, fearful time, with fingers pointed simply to deflect attention elsewhere. Now that she was Lady Heather and commander of Hogia's troops, she was even further removed from life in Needwood. Truth be told, she did not miss it, but today she needed to seem part of that community again.

At this time of day many of the town's women would be gathered around the well that was Needwood's physical and social center. It was a large, fine well. A waist-high stone wall ringed it, a tiled roof overhung it and a carved stone trough was hard by it, so thirsty livestock could drink at the same time as their owners. As Heather and Skapi approached, a dozen women were already clustered beside it, noses and cheeks red with cold. They jigged up and down and breathed into their work-chapped hands while their buckets and pitchers and jugs stood idle. One of the women leaned on a herding staff as her flock of goats drank at the trough. Another switched absently at the geese milling around her legs. But every woman's attention was on a thickset girl with arms crossed defiantly at her waist. "You have to tell him," an older woman in a stained apron was saying.

The young woman shook her head. "I don't want to burden him."

"He's your husband," said the goatherd. "He should know."

"I don't want him getting his hopes up again," the young woman said. "The last time grieved him so."

"What about your grief, child?" the woman in the apron demanded. "Do you have to suffer it alone?"

Skapi snorted, causing the geese to gabble and honk. Startled, the women looked up. "Good morning," Heather said, smiling.

As she dismounted, the women backed away, bowing. Some looked friendly enough, but others wore disapproving frowns. Heather realized how outlandish she must look to them, in her tall boots and baggy leggings and thick, padded tunic. Too late, she wished she had left her sword behind.

"Some water for your horse, Lady?" asked the woman in the apron.

She bore a strong resemblance to the young woman. *Mother and daughter*, Heather thought. "If you please," she said aloud.

The goat's owner used her staff to push her charges aside as the aproned woman filled the trough. While Skapi drank, eyeing the goats and geese with a disdainful air, Heather examined the faces around her. Since Daazna's death and Kristan's appropriation of Hogia's throne, newcomers had inundated Needwood, looking for work, a new home, a fresh start. Most of these women were strangers to Heather, but one face was familiar. "Good morning, Mistress Duncan."

"Good morning, Lady Heather." The wife of Needwood's goldsmith gave her an obsequious smile and curtsey. "What brings you into town today? My husband is in his workshop if you have need of him."

"Not today," Heather said. "I wanted to speak with some of Needwood's women. I need some opinions."

The women drew closer, murmuring.

"You all know how scarce soldiers are in Hogia these days," Heather said. "Many of the men who served the Wichelord were killed or deserted. Of those that remained, most were absorbed into the StoneKing's service and scattered throughout his realm. Our army here is adequate, but just barely. If something were to happen—if I had to station more troops on the Stratheden border, for example—I'd barely have enough soldiers left to man the castle, and I'd be hard-pressed to protect Needwood."

"Do you think Stratheden will attack us?" the goose woman asked.

"I think it's unlikely, but there's always a chance."

"The StoneKing should hire mercenaries to protect us, then," Mistress Duncan said.

"Mercenaries are in short supply, as are the funds to pay them," Heather said. "It would be better if we could protect ourselves. I was thinking that the women of Needwood could learn to fight."

The women stared at her.

"What do you mean?" asked Mistress Duncan. "Use a sword like you?"

"Perhaps. In time."

"Do you think any of us have swords?" the goatherd demanded.

"I'm thinking more about training with what you have on hand. Your herding staff, for example."

"What, fend off a Stratheden soldier with this?"

"Why not? It's got twice the reach of my sword."

The aproned woman snorted. "And none of its edge."

"She could stand well out of harm's way and still fetch me quite a wallop," Heather said.

The goatherd weighed her staff thoughtfully. "That's true."

"If you all had some instruction—"

"It's not natural," Mistress Duncan burst out. "I don't mean any offense, my lady, but it isn't right for women to take up arms, nor go into battle, nor lead men." She eyed Skapi. "Nor to ride unnatural animals."

"It isn't natural for so many of us to be alone, either," the goose woman said. "It's not just the army that lacks for men."

"And most who have men are still barren," the aproned woman said. "Why doesn't the StoneKing do something about that?"

"What would you have him do?" Heather asked. The woman scowled, and she added quickly, "I'm not mocking you. I really want to know. What do you think he should do?"

The woman shot a glance at the thickset girl. "I wish I knew, Lady. With the Wichelord gone and with the Gemeta and his Wiche Stone on Hogia's throne, we thought things would change. We thought the Cracks would close and the kingdom would be fruitful again. But the barrenness continues." She looked Heather up and down pointedly. "Maybe for some that's no great loss. For those who'd rather ride and fight and act like a man."

"There's no call to be rude, now," the goatherd said.

Heather blew out a sigh, and Skapi tossed her head as if she shared Heather's frustration. "Ladies, I learned how to ride and fight because I had to. Not only to protect myself, but to help the StoneKing defeat Daazna. In return, the StoneKing entrusted me with command of his army in Hogia and the protection of his people. If I'm to do that job and command men, then yes, I have to ride and fight and sometimes even act like a man. But that doesn't mean I'm not a woman underneath, and well aware of a woman's troubles." Even as she said the words, she wondered when she had last had her menses. *Months*, she realized. *It's been months.*

The realization was troubling, but she made herself go on: "Daazna's presence was like a poison to this land, and we're not going to be cured of that poison overnight. Until nature rights itself, there's little the StoneKing or anyone else can do about it. I'm sorry for that. In the meantime, I'd hoped you'd be open to learning something new and doing things a little differently. But if you won't, you won't."

She swung herself into the saddle and turned Skapi back

toward the castle. "Wait, Lady," the goatherd called. "Would we have to march? Drill with the other soldiers?"

Skapi skipped with impatience as Heather reined her in. "No. What I'm proposing is a home guard. I'm not asking you to enlist; I'm asking that you learn to defend yourselves, your families and your homes." The women muttered among themselves, and she pressed on: "Some of the ladies of the castle are already learning. You could join them."

"Well . . ." said the goose woman. "It's not like I have little ones at home to mind. But there's my geese—"

"If you come up to the castle to train, I'll make sure your geese are looked after." The goatherd harrumphed. "The goats, too," Heather added rashly. "I won't keep you long, I swear it. What do you say?"

Mistress Duncan averted her eyes, and several women shook their heads, but the goose woman nodded, and the goatherd smiled grimly and thumped her staff on the ground. "I'm game. I'd do it just for the chance to watch some of those castle ladies break a sweat."

Heather grinned. "Very well. Any of the rest of you?"

A few of the other women raised their hands. Heather looked at the thickset young woman. "What about you?" she asked.

The woman shook her head and clutched her arms around her waist, as if suddenly chilled. "I'd . . . I'd better not. I'm sorry." She hurried away, with the woman in the apron in her wake.

Heather shrugged and turned back to the other women. "Weather permitting, we'll practice in the castle courtyard tomorrow at noon. I'll let the gatehouse guards know to expect you. And I'll have some food and drink ready when we finish, as payment for your time." The women looked pleasantly surprised. Some murmured excitedly, and for the first time Heather noticed that more than a few looked as if they could use a good meal. "Tomorrow at noon, then. Let your friends know. Good day to you."

That's a job well done, she thought, as she nudged Skapi back to the castle, leaving the women chattering around the well. *Many will only come out of curiosity, and may never come again, but if at least a few stick with it, I may be able to make this peculiar idea work.* A wry smile twisted her mouth. *Can't wait to hear what Father has to say about it.*

As it turned out, she had to listen to what her senior knights had to say about it first. All three were idling in the courtyard when she returned. "There you are, my lady," Sir Jerrold said, hustling to her side as she dismounted. "I thought you'd want to know that the runner from Fandrall just arrived."

"Maybe there's an answer to your request to use Ravelin's—I mean the StoneKing's—mountain lodge," Sir Bran said. "For our war games."

Heather's heart began to pound, as it always did whenever there was a chance of communication from Kristan. *You simpleton,* she told herself, doing her best to keep her composure. *When will you stop hoping?* "I wanted to talk to the three of you first," she said aloud. "I've invited some of the Needwood women to the castle tomorrow at noon, to teach them some basic defensive drills."

Sir Jerrold pursed his lips. "I heard you were giving instruction to some females this morning, my lady."

"Do you disapprove of women using weapons, Jerrie?"

Jerrold's eyebrows bobbed up. "And me with a lady commander? No, ma'am, it's just that if we have permission to use the lodge, we'll all be off to the war games."

"Not all," Heather said. "Someone will have to be in command here at the castle."

All three knights straightened up as she eyed them. Eaden and Bran's faces were suddenly bright and eager, but Jerrold looked merely dutiful. *Well, now I know who'd rather go on maneuvers.* "Whoever stays behind in command will be expected to continue with the women's instruction," she went on, and Eaden nodded, while Bran's enthusiasm seemed to wane. *And now I know who to leave in command*, Heather thought, controlling the urge to smile. "But that's getting the cart well before the horse. I'd better find out if we've got the lodge first."

The exchange with her knights had calmed the fluttering of her heart, and when Alister met her in the great hall and handed her a packet with Kristan's seal on it, she was able to take it with a steady hand. She waited until she was in the anteroom she used as a work chamber before she opened it.

To her surprise, it was the same request for the lodge Alister had written for her five days past. At the bottom, in Bastian's elegant handwriting, was a single word.

Approved.

There was nothing else: no instructions, no stipulations, no commentary, no questions. Nothing to show that anyone had given her request more than a moment's thought. Nothing to show that Kristan had even seen it.

Approved.

Heather laid the parchment on her worktable, on top of a map of the Stratheden-Hogia border she had been studying the previous day. She bowed her head and gripped the edges of the table for support. A single tear rolled down her face and landed on the parchment, wetting and blurring the writing.

"So, do we have a response?"

Heather quickly wiped her face with one hand; with the other, she held out the parchment to Ravelin, keeping her head bent over the map. He took it from her, and was silent for some moments. She swallowed. The sound seemed loud and ugly in the quiet room.

"He's sparing of paper," Ravelin said.

Heather did not trust herself to speak. Ravelin put his hand on her shoulder. It was warm and surprisingly gentle. "Strange, how a single word can make you feel so unimportant."

She shrugged off his hand and stood up straight. "It's my own fault for expecting more. Anyway, we have our permission now, and the weather has been cold but fair. I'll give the order to start preparations for the journey."

She turned to go, but Ravelin caught her by the elbow. "I'm sorry, Heather. Truly, I am."

"You needn't worry about it."

"I can't help but worry. You're a strong woman, but you're also very young. I hate to see you wounded like this."

"It doesn't help to talk about it."

"Perhaps it would. You could talk to me. You and I work well together. A month ago, I wouldn't have thought that was possible."

He was standing a little too close to her. Her impulse was to step away, but she stood her ground.

"You're such an unusual woman," he said. "So different from other women I've known."

"Perhaps you never took the time to really know them," Heather said, a little too sharply.

"Before I bedded them, you mean? I suppose you're right. But I was angry then; I'm less angry now. I enjoy your company, Heather. You and I, we see things the same. We're pragmatic." He turned from her a little. "I was thinking—perhaps you and I should marry."

Her mouth went dry; her tongue was like a block of wood in her mouth.

"I know you don't love me," he went on. "It's clear where your heart lies. And you know I lost mine, long ago. But I'm lonely, and I think you are, too. I like you. We could be good companions, good for each other and good for the kingdom. If your father didn't dislike and distrust me so much, I could be more useful. Useful is all I want to be right now. Useful . . . and perhaps not quite so alone."

"But why must we marry at all?" Heather said, finding her voice at last.

"Don't you know what they say about us, now?"

She shook her head.

"The same thing they used to say about you and the Gemeta." Ravelin smiled a bit thinly. "I'll try not to interpret your look of dismay as a personal insult. You're strong, Heather, independent and hardheaded, but you're unworldly, too. There will always be talk, when a woman and a man spend time together—particularly time alone."

"I don't care what people think."

"Admirable, but that sort of carelessness can damage one's reputation. If it wasn't me, then people would talk about you and someone else—one of your knights, perhaps, and that would be bad for discipline. You're in a unique and difficult position, and you must protect yourself. Think of me as a buffer between you and your detractors."

"I don't love you."

"Nor I you."

"It would be wrong to marry without love."

"And yet people do it all the time. They marry for money, or security, or position. Even the Gemeta has to think about position. That's no doubt why he entertained the princess of Malchea. Ah, you didn't know," he added, as she stood bolt upright, feeling as if all the blood was draining from her face. "There was a line or two from Quinn Logan about it in the message from Fandrall. Princess Jelena isn't far from his age and it would be an advantageous match."

She clenched her jaw and turned away. Ravelin put his hand on her arm. "I don't say these things to hurt you, Heather. But life is what it is, the Gemeta is who he is, and we all have to carry on." His fingers closed about her wrist. "Tell me you'll think about it, at least."

She felt as if a wall was closing all around her, a wall of loneliness and despair, too high to climb and too thick to break, and Ravelin the only door in that wall. She felt her girlhood dwindling away, and she hardened her heart against that girl's anguished wail. "Very well," she said. "I'll think about it."

If he had smiled, if he had uttered a single tender word, she would have hardened her heart against him. He did not. He raised her hand to his lips and kissed it solemnly, with lips that were cool, dry and passionless. Then, he released her and left the room without another look.

For a long time, she stood stroking the spot he had kissed. She remembered how Kristan had kissed her hand, back in the long-ago summer; how soft and warm his lips had been. She let the tears flow down her face and did not try to hide them. She wept soundlessly, and when she had no more tears left, she wiped her face carefully and thoroughly on her sleeve. She found a quill and some ink. With a single diagonal line, she struck through the writing on the parchment, and then turned the paper over. On its blank side she wrote:

My lord Gemeta,
Ravelin Seachlan has proposed marriage to me.
Unless you have some objection, I will accept his offer.

Heather Demitt
Lady Commander of Hogia

She folded the parchment, with the new message turned inside, and carried it to her cousin Alister in his workroom. "A request for the StoneKing," she said, handing it to him. "Would you seal it and send it out with the next messenger for Fandrall?"

Alister raised his eyebrows. "I could have given you a fresh sheet of parchment, Heather."

"It's only a small thing."

He shrugged and carefully sealed the message with a blob of red wax. "There. It'll go out tomorrow." Alister peered into her face. "Is everything all right, Heather? You're very pale."

"I'm fine. I've been given permission to use the StoneKing's hunting lodge for our war games, so I have a lot on my mind."

"When do you plan to set out?"

"Weather and preparations permitting, I'd like to leave

within the next seven days. Do you think I'll have a response before then?"

"Oh, the StoneKing generally answers very quickly. He keeps the messengers flying between Kingsmere and Needwood, I can tell you. If the weather stays fair, you should hear back well before you leave."

"Very good," Heather said, smiling although her heart was as heavy as a lump of iron. "Thank you, Alister. Now let me leave you to your work. I have to go tell my knights to make ready."

CHAPTER ELEVEN

*A*nother miserable sleepless night, Kristan thought, *another cold morning, another endless day on the road.* He eased out of his bedroll, wincing at the ache of his chilled muscles. The upright bulk of Geoffrey, on watch near the fire and bundled to the eyes, turned toward him. The knight grunted a good morning, jerked his chin first toward Nolle's tumbled and vacant blankets, and then to the west. Kristan nodded in response, pulled on his boots and cloak, and took the opposite tack into the trees, to relieve himself in privacy.

It had been three nights since they had last slept amongst trees, and he knew he should be grateful for a more comfortable camp. Two nights had been spent in open fields; the first in the lee of a hill and the second behind a thicket, neither of which had provided much shelter from the winter wind. The third evening they had camped near the outskirts of a village, hoping to avoid notice. Even though their travel clothing was simple and unremarkable, Kristan had not thought to order their horses into plainer tack, and in consequence the fine leather saddles and brass and silver-trimmed bridles had piqued the villagers' interest. So many came to spy on their camp that Nolle had been forced to maintain Astéria's shift well past dark, taxing her strength and Astéria's patience to the breaking point. As a precaution, Kristan ordered a double guard, taxing the weary company still further and making the most recent leg of their trip a hard slog. After dinner, they'd fallen asleep quickly—all but Kristan, who had spent an uncomfortable, dream-troubled night on the very edge of their communal bed.

He was so exhausted that even the rattle of his piss against the dead leaves of the forest floor set his teeth on edge. He quickly diverted the flow against the nearest tree. Finished, he adjusted his clothing and started back to camp, but a sudden clatter of wings made him jump. A small bird, surrounded by a blur of wavering light, darted clumsily past him and plunged into a nearby thicket of brambles. Hard on the bird's tail was an owl, yellow eyes intent on its prey, but at the last moment it spotted Kristan, veered sharply away and disappeared through the trees. Kristan was still staring after it when a giggle burst from the brambles, followed by the rustle of branches and a muttered curse.

"That was foolish," Kristan said.

Nolle winced as she tried to disentangle herself from the thicket. "If I'd known it was going to be all over prickles, I wouldn't have flown in here."

"That's not what I meant, and you know it." He pulled some of the branches aside, and Nolle wiggled free. "That owl nearly had you. Why didn't you just shift back?"

"I was scared," Nolle said, picking twigs out of her hair. "The shift locked."

"What do you mean, locked?"

"You remember that time I was up in the scaffolding, the morning after my aunt left?"

"You turned into a cat and wouldn't come down."

"It was because I was scared. When I'm really scared, I can't think. I can't remember how to undo the spell, and I get locked in the shift form. Everyone was chasing me and yelling, but you climbed up and spoke to me quietly and that calmed me down enough to remember." She put her hand to her face and flinched. "Ouch."

"You've got a thorn in your cheek." With one finger, Kristan turned her chin to one side and looked closer. "It's just a little one. Hold still." Using his thumbnail, he began to scrape the thorn from beneath her skin.

"You're touching me," Nolle said.

"What of it?"

"Everyone says you don't like to be touched."

"Everyone is correct. There, it's gone."

"Why don't you like to be touched?"

"Why did you think it was a good idea to shift into a bird?"

Nolle's lower lip went out. "You never answer my questions."

"I don't have to answer your questions. You, however, have to answer mine. Why did you shift into a bird, here in the forest? Surely, you knew it was dangerous."

"I wanted to try flying. I've tried before and couldn't go more than a little ways, but this time I went further and higher, but then the owl came after me, and I locked. I saw you and I flew toward you." She examined a tear in her sleeve, then shrugged and grinned. "It was worth being scared. I flew. I really flew."

"Congratulations," Kristan said, but he was already several steps ahead of her.

Nolle hurried after him. "And yesterday I held Astéria's shift for a long time, longer than I've ever held a spell before. I'm getting stronger. Next, I want to try holding two shifts at once, hers and mine."

"Wait until we've stopped for the day."

"Why?"

"Because maintaining multiple spells is tiring."

"How would you know?"

Her disdainful tone irked him. "I've had more than a little experience of Wiche ways."

"I know, I know," Nolle said, rolling her eyes. "You had a Wiche teacher."

"I also have a good friend in Hogia who's a Wichearte." *Why in the world are you arguing with this child?* he scolded himself. The camp was in sight; Kennet was feeding the horses and everyone else was gathered around the fire. The air was redolent with hot porridge.

"We should go to Hogia," Nolle said, skipping a bit. "Maybe your friend could show me some new spells. Aunt and Grandmother didn't have many to teach."

"I don't have time to go to Hogia. We've got to find Astéria's people and take them all to . . . to another place. After that we go back to Fandrall."

"But first you'll keep your promise and give me the scrying ball," Nolle announced. She pushed past him to the campfire, where Geoffrey was dishing up the morning's meal.

"She shouldn't talk to you that way, my lord," Kennet said in a low voice.

"I know," Kristan said. "But I'm willing to put up with a little impudence if it keeps Astéria safe."

"Were you cold last night, my lord? When I took over the watch, you had your blanket pulled tight over your head. Did you sleep well?"

As well as any child terrified of the dark, Kristan thought. Malvo rumbled and thrust out his long black nose, eager for a caress, but Kristan evaded him and went to the fire, filled with sudden self-loathing. *Can't even stand to be touched by your own horse, you little coward.*

"Good morning, my lord," Geoffrey said, proffering a bowl and spoon. "Some porridge?"

"It's good and hot," Walter said. "Just the thing, on a cold morning like this."

"Goooood," Astéria said, cocking an impish eye at Serle. The squire was scooping porridge into his mouth as if starving, but he looked up and smiled.

"My beard, boy, slow down," Geoffrey said. "You're getting food all over your face."

"No, not that side, the left," Matthew said, as Serle wiped his cheek on one sleeve. "How do you manage to get food on just the left side?"

"Because he's left-handed," Kristan said absently.

They all turned toward him. "How's that, my lord?" Mitchell asked.

The weight of their combined gazes was almost more than he could stand, but he forced himself to answer as pleasantly as he could. "He grips the spoon overhand and dips deep," he said, demonstrating with his own spoon. "Then, he lifts it square to his mouth, with his elbow pointed out. Food on the handle smears onto his left cheek."

Sir Walter mimed the motion and grunted in surprise. "Well, I'll be skewered. I'd never have noticed such a thing, myself."

"Time for some lessons in table manners for you," Sir Matthew said to Serle.

"You have a sharp eye, my lord," Sir Kennet said.

It was plain to see, if you'd bothered to look. The spiteful words rose in Kristan's mouth, but he swallowed them with a spoonful of his breakfast. Geoffrey had chopped some dried sausage into the porridge, but while the others seemed to appreciate the addition, the salty chunks mixed into the thick gruel turned Kristan's stomach. *And of course, Geoff has given me the lion's share.* He forced down a few more bites, all too aware that the knights were darting furtive glances at him. *By the Stone, can I not even eat without being scrutinized?*

Serle's spoon clattered as the boy scraped up the last bits of porridge from his bowl. He darted a hopeful look toward the cook pot on the fire, but it was empty. "If you didn't gobble it down, it would last longer," Nolle said. She raised her spoon and licked it as daintily as a cat.

"Serle *eínai laímargos*," Astéria said, shaking her head at the squire. "Greedy boy."

"Here," Kristan said, holding out his bowl. "Take mine."

Serle started to reach for the bowl, but every knight turned toward him, glowering. "You've had more than enough, boy," Geoffrey said.

Serle blushed bright red and drew back. "No, thank you, sir," he said to Kristan.

"You call him 'my lord,'" Sir Kennet said through his teeth.

Serle ducked his head. "No, thank you, my lord. I'm full, my lord."

"Take it," Kristan said. "I've had all I want."

"But you barely touched it, my lord," Mitchell said.

"You don't eat enough to keep a bird alive," Matthew said.

"Eat up, my lord," Walter said, grinning. "When we get to Seagirt today, you'll need your strength to deal with all those slippery Dyerians."

The knights chuckled, but Kristan was suddenly furious. "By the Stone, are the five of you knights or nursemaids?"

Serle's head snapped up. Astéria's eyes widened. The knights went quiet.

"Uh oh," Nolle muttered.

Kristan shook his bowl. "Do you want it or not, Serle?"

"No, my lord," Serle whispered.

"Fine." Kristan slung the porridge into the fire and thrust the empty bowl at Geoffrey. "If the rest of you are finished with your breakfasts—and your commentary—let's get moving."

For a long, uncomfortable moment, they stood staring at him. "Yes, my lord," Geoffrey said at last. "Sorry, my lord."

He took Kristan's bowl. In near silence, the company began to break camp. Geoffrey poured water over the campfire, and Kristan's stomach heaved as the sickening smell of burnt porridge steamed up from the hissing embers. Walter, Kennet and Mitchell began saddling the horses. Matthew and Astéria shook out the company's blankets and rolled them neatly. Nolle and Serle took the empty water skins and headed toward the stream. The knights followed with the horses, leaving Astéria and Kristan alone in the clearing.

Feeling the centaur's worried gaze on him, Kristan bent to his pack. The Stone swung into his line of vision, its chain dragging heavily at his neck. He caught it in one hand. The cold, disapproving weight of it made his flesh creep.

And now you judge me as well? His voice, at its most sarcastic, rang through his head. *Should I be ashamed of myself for asserting my authority? For being a king?* He tucked the Stone inside his tunic, and the chill of it against his bare skin set him shivering.

"Kreestan?" Astéria's voice was timid and oddly far away. "You are sick?"

"I'm fine," Kristan said.

He busied himself breaking up the last glowing embers of the fire. When the others returned from the stream, they were still subdued, although the knights occasionally murmured among themselves while darting cautious glances his way, as if trying to gauge his mood. As they loaded the horses, Kennet sidled up to him.

"Your pardon, my lord," he said, "but what form should Astéria take this morning?"

"Form?"

"Yes, my lord. Horse or woman?"

Horse, you idiot, Kristan was about to retort, but Kennet hurried on: "I'm sure you know that even some miles out from Seagirt, the land is thickly settled. We'll be passing through a number of villages, with little privacy. Perhaps we should arrive at Seagirt with Astéria already in . . . in whatever form you think best."

Idiot, Kristan thought again, but this time he was addressing himself. *Didn't think about the horses' tack; didn't think about how to bring Astéria into Seagirt.* He considered the problem for a few moments, acutely aware that everyone was waiting for his response even though they kept their eyes averted.

"It'll have to be the woman's form," he said at last. "And she should take it now."

"*Dyo,*" Serle said to Astéria, holding up two fingers. The centaur nodded, and Nolle raised both hands.

"Wait, wait," Kristan said. "We haven't addressed how she's to travel."

"My lord?" Kennet said.

"We've spent all our time teaching her how to walk. But she can't walk all the way to Seagirt, can she?" *Should have thought ahead; should have had her try riding before this. Idiot!*

Walter let out a low whistle. "You're right, my lord. We could unload one of the pack ponies and put her on that, I suppose."

"She makes too tall and elegant a lady, to ride a pony," Matthew said.

"Astéria could ride Nolle's horse, and Nolle the pony," Kennet suggested.

Nolle scowled. "Why do I have to ride the pony? Why not Serle?"

"Quiet," Geoffrey snapped.

Matthew patted Nolle's shoulder. "You can pretend you're Astéria's maid."

"I'm no one's maid," Nolle said under her breath.

Geoffrey glared at her. "I seem to recall you peeling turnips in Dru's kitchen."

"Geoff, please," Kristan said, before Nolle could answer.

"*Ti symvaínei?*" Astéria asked, gripping Serle's arm anxiously.

Serle patted her hand. "It's all right. You'll be riding today. Riding." He mimed holding reins and rocked his body slightly, as if in the saddle. Astéria's eyes went wide.

"Very well," Kristan said. "Nolle, which pony do you prefer?"

Nolle kicked at the loamy forest floor. "The one with the white forefeet, I guess."

"Mitchell and Matthew, distribute that pony's load amongst the other horses and prepare it for riding. Walter, bring Nolle's horse here. Astéria, are you ready?"

"*Naí,*" Astéria whispered. "Yes."

Kristan nodded to Nolle. The Wiche girl raised her hands, and as she muttered the spell, Astéria's figure began to waver. Kristan's mouth filled with the salty saliva of nausea, and he averted his gaze as the blended Astéria-Jelena shift formed.

"Well done," he managed to say. "Walter and Matthew, help her mount and give her some basic instruction. The rest of you, finish loading the other horses."

Everyone fell to work, much more cheerfully than before. Kristan checked Malvo's tack, hindered more than helped by Serle, who came to assist after a hard glare and a push from Geoffrey. The squire was so excited that he was chattering. "Astéria makes such a pretty lady, doesn't she, my lord? She's very graceful in the saddle."

Kristan snuck a sidelong look at Astéria as she rode past. Walter led her horse by the bridle, and Matthew walked alongside to assist, but Astéria was sitting upright and smiling. "Kreestan, look!" she called. "I am riding!"

She was sidesaddle, and seemed secure enough. The blur of her horse-half spread over her mount's loins, and the animal kept rolling its eyes and twitching its head, as if trying to see its rider for itself. *The horse knows something is amiss,* Kristan thought.

Walter eyed the animal with some trepidation. "My lord, perhaps I should lead the horse for her, in case . . . well, just in case."

"Please do," Kristan said. "Since we'll be entering more populated areas, let's keep close today, rather than spread out along the road. Nolle, can you maintain the shift through the day?"

Nolle smirked. "Of course."

"Very well. Let's get going."

They set out in improved spirits. Astéria chattered happily with the knights and Serle, in an amusing commingling of *Kentávron* and the common tongue, and nearly unseated herself a time or two, trying to see her human feet in their dainty slippers. For appearance's sake, Matthew had provided her with a cloak, but she wore it slung carelessly from her shoulders with the hood back. Kristan envied her imperviousness to the cold.

As was his custom, he rode a little apart from the others, deep in thought. *What if the merchant ship has already come and gone? We'd have to take a ship and go after them. Worse yet, what if it was never bound for Seagirt at all? We'll never be able to find them, and all this effort will be for nothing.*

His worries circled through his brain like a pack of hounds pursuing the elusive scent of some half-familiar prey, only to lose it amongst brambles and thickets. It was not until early afternoon that he was brought out of his anxious ruminations, and then only by a sudden damp touch on his cheek and the faint tang of salt in the breeze. He looked up and found that everyone else in his company had thrown back their hoods to breathe in the soft air. "We're close," Sir Geoffrey said. "You can smell the sea."

"It's a lot warmer here," Serle said.

"There's Seagirt, on the horizon," Sir Kennet said. "You can see the palace towers from here."

Kristan pushed his hood back. In spite of a light fall of large, wet snowflakes, he was able to make out the slender columns in the distance, more like spires than battlements. Beyond, the waters of the harbor reflected the blustery gray sky.

All around them were shops and houses, their occupants moving sedately about their business. Astéria leaned forward, one hand pressed to her breast, a sudden blaze of hope in her eyes. "We are there?"

"Very nearly," Sir Geoffrey said.

The other knights kept a wary watch on the people they passed. For their part, the Dyerians gazed back with condescending, yet calculating eyes. "High and mighty," Nolle said under her breath.

Kristan had to agree. He was accustomed to the simple attire of Fandrall's farm people, but while the Dyerians they passed were clearly common folk, every one of them wore colorful clothing embellished with embroidery, frills, fur, fringe and shiny bits of cheap metal. A goatherd shooing his flock out of their way paused at the roadside to study them, and Serle gaped at the boy in astonishment. "He's got gilt tassels on his shoes," he whispered. "He must be rich."

"Look again," Sir Matthew said, keeping his voice low. "Those shoes are worn right down at the heel, and his elbows are nearly coming through his coat. Tassels may be pretty, but they don't keep out the cold, do they?"

"Dyerians like to make a show of themselves," Sir Walter said. "And this is just the backside of Seagirt. Wait until you see its face."

Astéria shrugged off her cloak and handed it to Serle. "No more. Ees not cold."

"No indeed," Walter said, unfastening his own cloak. "It's almost balmy here."

Geoffrey let out a derisive snort. "This whole place is soft as butter. Not even a good honest winter."

Kristan alone did not take off his cloak; in fact, he pulled his hood forward to hide his face. *With luck this will all go smoothly,* he thought. *With good luck I'll be home again within a few days, away from all these staring eyes. With the best of luck, the merchant ship will already be in the harbor with its cargo intact, and I can turn right around, take them to O Tópos and avoid Seagirt altogether, although Quinn Logan will be annoyed.* He tried to think of every possible outcome of the problem looming ahead, listening with only half an ear to the murmured conversations of his party. The clamor of his thoughts soon drowned out even that.

When Kennet touched his arm, it startled him so that he jumped, and then flinched again at the commotion surrounding him. "Sorry, my lord," Kennet said, raising his voice over the din, "but I didn't think you'd heard me."

Kristan pushed his hood back. They were on a cobbled street, lined with tall whitewashed buildings topped by sloping roofs of warm reddish tile. Many of their windows were framed by shutters painted in bright colors; others were bedecked with striped awnings. Shop doors were hung with bells that jangled each time someone exited or entered. Litters, borne by pairs of burly servants and curtained with elaborate hangings to hide the passenger within, jockeyed for position with horse-drawn carts strung with still more bells, while among them people in showy dress hurried about their business, chattering and calling to each other like a flock of colorful birds. Somewhere nearby a woman's voice rose in raucous song, with a rattling drum and clapping hands keeping time. The noise was deafening; the riot of color blinding. Kristan blinked as Kennet continued to bawl in his ear: "The palace is in the southwest part of the city, my lord. Shall I ride ahead and announce you?"

"Which way is the harbor?"

"Downhill and straight ahead, my lord."

"The harbor first."

Kennet nodded and led off with Mitchell. Kristan brought Malvo in line after them, with Walter and Geoffrey flanking him, Astéria and the two children behind, and Matthew bringing up the rear. The crowd jostled and pushed against them as they descended toward the harbor, with its flotilla of ships rocking in the blue-gray chop of Seagirt's half-moon bay. Some ships lay at anchor well out; others jounced against their moorings at the dozens of docks that thrust out into the water like reaching fingers. Risking another bout of nausea, Kristan looked over his shoulder at Astéria. She was sitting bolt upright in the saddle, craning her neck and biting her lower lip.

"Do you see it?" Kristan asked. "The merchant ship?"

She shook her head. Her eyes were bright with sudden, hopeless tears. Serle reached over and patted her hand comfortingly. "Maybe it's too soon," he said. "Maybe tomorrow."

"Tomorrow," Astéria echoed, and tried to smile.

"Well, I'll be," Sir Geoffrey said. "Look over there."

At a nearby dock, troops were disembarking from a warship while a bow-legged man bawled abuse at them. "On the double, on the double, you disgraces to the crown and the Stone," he cried. "Quick march back to the castle and assemble in front of the barracks, where you'll drill until dinnertime. Maybe then you'll remember to follow orders when you hear them."

Mitchell grinned. "Why, it's Captain Ommald."

"And that's Dell Curry with him," Walter said. "What's he got in his arms?"

"Looks like a fish," Matthew said, and started to laugh.

The troops scrambled into ranks and started toward the castle, with Ommald baying at them like an angry hound and Dell meandering in their wake, clutching a large, scaly fish to his chest. As the troops came abreast of Kristan's company, several men caught sight of Astéria and slowed to ogle her, causing those behind to run up their heels. The entire column came to an uneven halt, and Ommald's leathery face went almost purple. "What are you about, there?" he bellowed. "Get into step, get into step and march on. And you gawkers there," he added, whirling to face the knights, "next time you see troops coming, get out of the w . . ." He caught sight of Geoffrey and his voice failed.

"Now, Ommald, is that any way to treat an old comrade?" Geoffrey said.

"Geoff!" Ommald cried. "Well, I'll be boiled. And young Mitchell, too. What in the world are you doing in—"

Geoffrey gave his head an almost imperceptible jerk in Kristan's direction. Before Kristan could object, the old soldier's mouth dropped open and he sagged to one knee. "StoneKing," he said, and although he did not speak loudly, passersby wheeled to stare. An instant later, Ommald was on his feet and roaring in the faces of his startled troops. "ATTENTION! Come to attention before the StoneKing!"

"Oh, no," Kristan said under his breath.

The soldiers jerked upright. Carts and litters careened to a stop, but the people of Seagirt pressed forward, squawking like a flock of excited chickens. "That crooked little man?" a woman cried. "That's not the StoneKing."

"It is!" said another. "I heard he has a terrible scar on his face."

"I see the scar, but where's his Stone?" a fat man said. "He's supposed to have some kind of Wiche Stone."

Dell stood in their midst with a bemused expression, clinging to his fish. Kristan was overwhelmed with sudden anger: at the curious, skeptical faces, at Dell's absurd appearance, at the way his Reach stood without speaking, ignored and even shouldered aside by the crowd. Ommald was bellowing at the people to *kneel, kneel before the StoneKing*, but no one paid him any heed. The knights had drawn their mounts close about him, and as a result Astéria was too near; her human legs were almost brushing Kristan's thigh. "Watch out, watch out!" Nolle cried.

In desperation, Kristan pulled fiercely on Malvo's reins, causing the great black horse to rear. The crowds recoiled. Walter's eyes went wide with the realization of what Kristan was doing and why, and he pulled Astéria's horse clear just as Malvo landed on all fours again. Kristan let go of the reins long enough to rise in the stirrups and throw back his cloak. "Look!" he shouted, yanking the Stone from beneath his tunic. "Look, you fools! Is that proof enough for you?"

The crowd went quiet. For perhaps three breaths there was no sound but Malvo's indignant snorting and the hammering of Kristan's own heartbeat in his ears. At last, someone chuckled softly.

Kristan glared in the direction of the sound. A small, dark-skinned old woman had pushed her head through the curtains of a passing litter and was smiling at him. "Well, this is an unexpected pleasure, StoneKing. Did you come to Seagirt to escape Fandrall's winter weather?"

Kristan's rage dwindled. He released the Stone and sagged back into the saddle. "Mali Uzuri. Hello."

"Is it really him, Guild Mistress?" asked a woman in the crowd.

"It is indeed," Mali Uzuri said. She put out one hand, and several people hurried to assist her from the litter. Once she was on her feet, she waved everyone off with absent disdain. "Silly people, greet the StoneKing properly," she said, and bent slowly and carefully into a deep curtsey. "My lord, welcome to Seagirt."

Everyone faced Kristan. The men swept into elaborate bows, flourishing their hands gracefully. The women curtsied so low that they were very nearly sitting. Then, they held those postures, bent over with heads humbly bowed although they flicked curious, calculating glances at Kristan from beneath their eyebrows. Even Dell was bowing, bent double over his ridiculous fish.

Kristan knew they were waiting for him to acknowledge them, release them from their obeisance, but the incident had made him feel spiteful, and he sat in the saddle without responding. The shrewd glances turned anxious. The soldiers' faces went red as they strained at attention. The women's curtsies began to wobble and the men's knees started to shake.

It was only when he noticed Mali Uzuri trembling that Kristan relented. "Get up," he said gruffly. "Go about your business."

"Get along, get along there," Ommald said, waving his hands at the crowd as if shooing birds. The people rose and moved away, but they lingered at the roadside, in shop doorways and windows, studying Kristan and his company and whispering to each other behind their hands.

Kristan nudged Malvo toward Mali Uzuri's litter. The rest of his company followed. Mali Uzuri wore her usual impish smile, but as he drew closer, her eyes narrowed and her expression grew grave. "I hope all is well with you, my lord," she said.

"Well enough," Kristan said.

"And that your journey here was an easy one."

"Easy enough."

Mali Uzuri eyed Astéria, a hint of her former smile playing about her lips. "And may I ask if you've come for business or pleasure, my lord?"

"Business."

She nodded. "Of course. May I assist in any way, my lord?"

"I'm looking for a sea trader. He may have arrived in the last day or so."

"We have ships in and out of our harbor all the time. Do you know the trader's name?"

Kristan glanced at Astéria. She was leaning forward in the saddle, one hand pressed to her heart. "I don't," he said.

"Then, perhaps, you know what his ship looks like?"

"*To paní,*" Astéria said, and with both hands, sketched a square shape in the air.

Dell started, nearly dropping his fish.

"*To paní eínai rigé,*" Astéria went on, and with one hand, made a series of parallel lines in the area she had defined.

"*Paní, nai?*" Dell said. Astéria wheeled toward him. He stuffed the fish under one arm, raised his free hand and blew into it, letting the hand drift toward her. "*Ti chrómata?*"

Astéria let out a cry of relief. "*Kókkino kai chrysó,*" she said. "*To échete dei?*"

"*Ochi,*" Dell said, shaking his head. Astéria's mouth quivered.

"What?" Kristan demanded. "What?"

Dell looked at him and shrugged. "No ship with a red and gold-striped sail has been here."

"But that's good," Serle told Astéria, patting her hand. "That means we got here ahead of it."

"A red and gold-striped sail?" Mali Uzuri said. "That would be Lorz. He travels far and wide, and only comes to Seagirt once or twice a year, usually with a cargo of exotic fruits and strange creatures. We're about due for a visit from him."

Dell was studying Astéria. He opened his mouth, as if to ask a question, but Captain Ommald interrupted. "Pardon, my lord, but have you been to the palace yet?"

"Not yet," Kristan said.

"Then shall I send someone ahead to announce you? Or my

troops and I can escort you there now."

"The latter, please," Kristan said. He crooked his finger at Dell, and the Reach came to his side as Ommald began to bawl out orders. "Keep your questions until later," he said quietly, and Dell nodded.

The soldiers formed into ranks facing the castle and stood silently with Ommald at their head, awaiting orders. Kristan turned to Mali Uzuri. "If you hear news of this trader Lorz, I would be grateful if you'd send a messenger to me."

"Of course, StoneKing," Mali Uzuri said. "And if you find time weighing heavy on your hands while you wait, come and visit me. The Uzuri family home is a simple one, but your presence would honor us."

"Thank you." Kristan nodded to Ommald, who roared at the troops, and the whole cavalcade set off toward the castle at a slow march.

Dell walked alongside Malvo, still carrying his fish and wearing a thoughtful expression. He had slung his chain of office behind him, so that it hung down his back, clear of the scales and slime that smeared the front of his tunic. Sir Walter drew up next to him, grinning. "That your dinner?"

"I was bringing it back to show Raul." Dell raised the fish close to Kristan. "Look here. See those sores? Many of the fish in the bay have them now. I keep telling Raul the new jetties are hurting the fish."

The fish smelled faintly of decomposition. Kristan winced and waved it away. "Jetties? The ones I approved in the fall?"

"The same. They're causing parts of the bay to silt up."

"I hadn't heard that."

Dell's mouth went tight. "No one seems to think it's important—no one in the merchant guilds, that is."

"You should have written me about it."

"Raul and Piri Neff write the reports."

"You should have asked them to include your concerns."

"I did my part. I told them what I'd observed."

Dell fell back so that he was alongside Astéria, and a moment later, Kristan heard them conversing quietly in *Kentávron*. Sir Mitchell drew up next to Malvo in the place Dell had vacated. "Sir Dell learned a lot more of that lingo than I ever could, my lord," he said in a low voice. "That'll make things easier."

"Dell always manages to surprise me," Kristan said. *And it was certainly a surprise to discover one of my Reaches wearing his chain backward and carrying a fish through the streets,* he thought crossly. He fixed his attention on Malvo's ears, trying to ignore the people gathering in great clusters to watch his company pass. Many of them were eating—meat skewered on sticks, buns glistening with honey, some yellowy fruit that dripped juice down their hands—and the munching jaws below the staring eyes seemed the height of insolence. Mumbled through mouthfuls of food, their half-audible comments buzzed around his ears like flies.

" . . . not much to look at . . ."

" . . . thought he'd be a lot bigger . . ."

" . . . more men . . ."

" . . . that beat-up horse . . ."

" . . . carrying a standard, at least . . ."

" . . . scruffy little fellow . . ."

I'd like to cut out all your tongues; cut them out and roast them on a spit, and then stuff them down your gullets. The sudden viciousness of the image, and his immediate shame on conjuring it up, made his guts roil. *Stop it. Controlcontrolcontrol . . .*

Ommald bawled an order and the troops wheeled right. They were turning onto a broad thoroughfare, paved in stone rather than cobbled, and lined with elegant buildings. At the end of it, nearly a mile in the distance, rose the palace of Seagirt.

Kristan blinked. Instead of the moats and imposing stone fortifications of his other castles, the palace was surrounded by a low, arched wall of whitewashed brick that curved before a generous lawn planted with willowy trees. Instead of a daunting buttressed gatehouse, a grand double archway topped with rows of banners on poles stood open and welcoming. In place of looming battlements were a number of slender rounded towers, each capped with a cambered roof of some shining metal that reflected sunlight as brightly as a mirror. And the keep, rather than the massive, angular structures in Needwood, Moordock and Kingsmere, was a series of expansive, airy buildings, all arches and windows and softly curving walls that seemed to bend and bow like ocean waves.

"Ooo," Nolle breathed.

"It's quite something, isn't it?" Sir Matthew said.

"Worst defenses I've ever seen," Sir Geoffrey muttered. "Like a great whore, lying there wide open to anyone."

"Geoff, please," Kristan said, but in his heart, he had to agree. There was something sluttish about the palace sprawling before him, something that smacked of laziness and excess. A throng of pikemen hurried through the gates and onto the thoroughfare. One of their number called an order, and the men swiftly formed two precise columns facing each other on either side of the road, their weapons upright, their white and gold uniforms blinding even under the meagre winter sun.

"My word," Walter said, chuckling.

Captain Ommald heard him and dropped back to join Kristan's company. "They do this sort of thing well. Neatest formations I've ever seen." His lined features twisted into a grimace. "But they've got no stamina. Can't quick march more than a few miles without getting winded, whatever I do."

Another order rang out. The pikemen rapped the butts of their weapons three times against the stone roadway. A third order, and the pikes snapped up so they pointed at the sky. A final order, and every pike tilted at a precise angle, forming an archway.

"Pretty work," Sir Kennet said, as their company passed beneath the pikes and through the gates.

Ommald's response was lost in the sudden blare of horns from within the palace courtyard. The courtiers of the palace were massed before the broad steps of the palace's main entrance, and as they bowed and curtsied they looked like a bed of bright flowers nodding in the breeze. Ommald and his soldiers came to a stamping halt, Kristan and his company reined up, and a dozen young men, mantled in white and gold, came to take charge of their horses.

A familiar face materialized out of the well-dressed, well-fed crowd: Raul Ferrador, wearing an expression that mingled delight and dismay. He hurried forward with hands outstretched. "Kristan!" he cried, and then corrected himself quickly. "My lord! What a surprise! What a wonderful surprise!"

Kristan dismounted stiffly, eyeing his Reach. Unlike Dell, Raul was clad in an elegant tunic the color of good wine. His face was carefully shaved, his hair neatly combed, and his chain of office lay bright across his shoulders. Behind him, the councilor Piri Neff smiled and nodded, although he, too, looked somewhat disconcerted.

"Hello, Raul. Hello, Piri," Kristan said. "I'm sorry to arrive unannounced." He glanced around at the assembled courtiers, still frozen in their positions of obeisance. "Although it seems I wasn't entirely unexpected. Get up, get up," he added, somewhat querulously, and the courtiers rose.

"Word travels quickly here in Seagirt, my lord," Piri said. "Mali Uzuri sent word that she'd met you near the docks." His gaze drifted past Kristan, and his polite smile wavered a bit at the sight of Dell's fish. "Please, my lord, come inside out of this winter weather."

Geoff let out the tiniest snort, and Kristan shot him a warning look. "Thank you," he said, and with Raul and Piri leading, his own company around him and the courtiers of Seagirt falling in behind, he entered the palace.

Once inside, he was dazzled by the flickering, dancing light of candles set within globes of faceted glass. The light bounced from furnishings glazed with bright colors, wall hangings shot with gold and silver thread, and fixtures of metal dimpled and dinted to create even more reflective surfaces. To escape the light, Kristan looked at the floor, but even it was laid with some kind of stone laced with glittering flecks. His head began to pound as he followed blindly in Raul's wake. His Reach was almost chattering, gesturing at this tapestry, that room, those courtiers. The rest of Kristan's party made appreciative noises, but Kristan stayed silent, registering none of it. At last, everyone stopped moving, and all the noise ceased, as if in expectation.

"And this is your throne," Raul said.

Kristan looked up. Before him rose a tall, steep dais of pale stone rimmed in gold, its steps laid with a carpet loomed with swirling colors and laced with still more gold and silver thread. At the top of the steps was an enormous chair of white marble, the stone worked so carefully that not a single hard angle remained. The back and arms were sculpted with an openwork pattern that resembled the twisting skeins of thread that were Dyer's symbol. Its seat was cushioned in soft golden velvet edged with jewels, and a luxuriant white fur was draped across it. The whole thing was overhung by a canopy of weighty, colorful fabric, tasseled and tucked into graceful, looping folds.

"Have mercy," Kristan whispered.

"My lord," Piri Neff said, bowing low and sweeping his hand toward the throne. "Won't you be seated?"

Reluctantly, Kristan mounted the dais. He was stiff from riding and his bad knee ached with each step. He realized how he must look: a small, crooked man, drab and travel-stained, with straggling, uncombed hair and five days' growth of beard, limping and laboring up to the showy luxury of Dyer's throne. As he gained the top of the dais, his face was hot with embarrassment and annoyance, and it was with a certain pettishness that he thrust the white fur aside and seated himself.

The courtiers applauded, smiling at him even as they whispered to each other. His knights nodded proudly. Astéria was wide-eyed, Nolle gawped and Serle stood with his hands clasped worshipfully to his chest. But the gems decorating the cushion bit into the backs of Kristan's knees, the canopy made him feel caged and suffocated, and the great height of the dais seemed both pompous and foolish. He was just about to make an ill-considered remark about trying to rule from a mountain-top when there was a sudden flurry of activity at the doorway, and a group of large, prosperous-looking men elbowed their way toward the throne. "Greetings, my lord Gemeta!" called the largest of the men, leading the rest in an elaborate bow, all twirling hands and extravagantly-extended legs and humbly lowered heads contrasting with their scheming eyes. "The guilds of Dyer welcome you!"

"Fedro Vincenze," Kristan said, with a cool nod. "Please rise."

"Welcome, my lord, welcome," Fedro said. "How good it is to see you again, my lord, after so many months, and what an honor to witness the StoneKing gracing Dyer's throne at last!"

Like a turd on a golden plate, Kristan thought.

"Mali Uzuri told us you were at the docks, my lord, looking for the trader Lorz," Fedro went on. "Captain Lorz usually deals with me when he has business to transact. I'd be happy to act as your agent when he arrives."

"Thank you, Fedro, but I prefer to handle this business myself."

"Of course, my lord, of course. But perhaps what you seek from Lorz is already in Seagirt. Our marketplace is full of goods from all over, and I'd be happy to show you—"

Kristan stood up. "Perhaps later," he said, and started back down the stairs. As soon as he stepped to the floor, everyone bowed again; all but his own company, who looked at the bent backs in bewilderment, and Dell, who was scrutinizing Astéria even as a servant tried to discreetly extricate the dead fish from his arms. "Get up, get up," Kristan said, losing patience. Looking perplexed, the Dyerians righted themselves, and he forced himself to smile and show some semblance of good manners. "I look forward to conversing with each of you later, but right now I'd like to speak privately with my Reaches."

"Of course, my lord," Raul said. "There's a chamber behind the throne for private audiences. Won't you come this way?"

"Meantime, I'll see to your retinue, my lord," Piri Neff said, as the crowd of courtiers dispersed. In a lower tone, he added, "Shall I arrange for adjoining rooms for you and the lady, my lord?"

"What?" Kristan said, and then realized what Piri was implying. He was about to voice a vehement *no* but reconsidered. "Yes," he said. "Yes, please. In fact, I'd be grateful if you'd put my entire company close at hand."

"King Claude's former chambers can be made ready in an instant," Raul said, but his smile was a bit fixed as he considered Astéria.

"Very good," Piri said, and ushered Kristan's company away. Dell stood looking after them, but at a pointed *ahem* from Raul, he fell in behind his fellow Reach and accompanied Kristan to the private chamber behind the throne.

"Is anything wrong, Kristan?" Raul asked, when they had closed the door on the rest of the palace.

"Not exactly, no," Kristan said. "But it would be best if the reason for my visit is kept quiet. Where is Marcus?"

Raul and Dell exchanged a look.

"I'm not entirely sure," Raul said. "I sent someone to find him as soon as we got word of your arrival."

"Well, how soon will he be here?"

"Oh, any moment, I'm sure."

"Or not," Dell said. "Kristan, which of the children is Wiche?"

"What?"

"You've got a woman with you who's fluent in *Kentávron*," Dell said, with a touch of impatience. "She rides—even walks—as if she's unused to both. My guess is that she's a centaur, with some kind of disguising spell on her. I know none of your

169

knights are Wiche, so that leaves the children."

Kristan snorted out a laugh. "Nothing gets past you, does it, Dell?"

"The boy seems an utter bumpkin, all big eyes and gaping mouth," Dell went on. "So that leaves the girl. She's got a sly look."

"Nolle is Wiche," Kristan said, "and she shifts. How did you know?"

Raul said nothing, but his eyes were round with astonishment.

"The woman stays close to you, but you avoid touching her," Dell said. "You even made Malvo rear up to avoid contact with her which would, of course, break any spell."

"A centaur? Where did you find this centaur?" Raul asked.

"The princess of Malchea brought Astéria to me as a gift," Kristan said. "Apparently, there are some who believe Torrin belonged to me—a kind of pet. King Lockward thought I might want breeding stock. Astéria was purchased from this sea trader Lorz. He has eleven more centaurs. I was told he might be making his way to Seagirt. With luck, he'll be docking here in the next few days. I'm hoping he won't have sold any more of his cargo, and I'll be able to take all of them to Torrin in *O Tópos*. That's the reason for all this secrecy."

"In that case," Raul said, "it might be better if Marcus doesn't know."

"Why?"

Once again, Dell and Raul glanced at each other. "Out with it," Kristan said. "Why shouldn't Marcus know?"

"Well, perhaps just as a precaution, more than anything," Raul said. "Marcus is . . . he sometimes—"

"Marcus is a drunk," Dell said.

An unpleasant tremor ran through Kristan's guts. "Explain, please."

Raul turned up his hands. "Kristan, for some men, even a little bit of money and power is too much—"

"Explain with less philosophizing."

"Marcus spends most of his time in the taverns and doxy-houses, where he's a great favorite," Dell said. "He's not here because Raul's messenger can't find him—or even more likely, he's been found, but can't be roused. He often drinks himself insensible."

"And how long has this been going on?"

"Not long—maybe since mid-winter," Raul said.

"It's been going on longer than that, Raul, and you know it," Dell said, with uncharacteristic sharpness. "But it's only been since mid-winter that we realized he couldn't be trusted."

Controlcontrolcontrol. Kristan's head began to pound again, and he reached for the Stone. "What do you mean?"

Raul sighed. "Some have discovered that when Marcus is in his cups, he'll share information that should have been kept in the council chamber."

"He'd already begun missing council meetings—" Dell said.

"He wasn't the only one," Raul said under his breath, and Dell glared at him.

"Go on, please," Kristan said.

"Piri discovered what was going on," Raul said. "After that, it just seemed best to . . . to have the meetings without him."

"Why am I only hearing about this now?" Kristan said. "Why wasn't I informed earlier?"

"I . . . we didn't want to trouble you," Raul said. "I'd hoped we could sort things out ourselves. Things have been running pretty smoothly—even without all the Reaches in council," he added, with a pointed look at Dell.

"Yes, things run smoothly because you ignore any dissention," Dell said.

Raul threw up his hands. "I wasn't going to trouble the StoneKing with your reports about fish!"

"Because *you* decided the fish weren't important."

"Piri agreed with me, and so did Marcus."

"Yes, you'll listen to *him*, when he bothers to show up."

"Stop it, both of you," Kristan said sharply, and the two Reaches fell silent. Kristan folded his arms across his chest and concentrated on the splendid floor, counting his breaths and waiting for his stomach to settle. He heard Dell and Raul shift from foot to foot; sensed that they were watching both him and each other warily. "All of this comes as a surprise," he said at last, and could not keep the edge out of his voice. "An unpleasant surprise, especially given the current circumstances. We'll discuss it further, but not until I've had a chance to talk to Marcus and Piri. Meanwhile, you're to keep what you know about Astéria and the reason for my visit to yourselves. You can tell Piri, but no one else. How many of my warships are in Seagirt's harbor now?"

"Eight," Dell said.

"Arrange for them to patrol the harbor. Once Lorz is spotted, his ship is to be intercepted and word sent to me immediately. I don't want him to come into port, but he's not to be boarded, either. His ship is to be kept isolated until I can get out to it and speak to him, is that clear?"

"Yes, my lord," both Reaches said.

"That's all, then." Kristan strode to the door, threw it open and was not surprised to see Piri Neff standing a discreet distance away. *Just like Quinn Logan*, he thought, and found himself wishing with all his heart that his chief councilor was there to advise him.

"My lord," Piri said, bowing. "If you're finished with your meeting, may I escort you to your chambers? You must be weary after your journey."

Kristan was weary, suddenly and utterly. "Yes, please."

Piri flicked a look at the two Reaches, but merely bowed again and with Kristan following, set off at a sedate pace. Servants and courtiers hastened out of their path, averting their eyes. Whispered warnings and the sound of scampering feet echoed ahead of them as they passed into an airy hallway. "What's going on?" Kristan asked.

Piri shortened his stride so that he and Kristan were side by side, but he kept his gaze fixed straight ahead. "Sir Geoffrey told me you don't like being stared at, my lord. The Dyerians have an unfortunate habit of doing just that, so I've taken the liberty of ordering them out of your sight unless they've been summoned. I hope that's acceptable."

Kristan only grunted. They were ascending a broad staircase, and his knee was complaining vociferously. "Your company is settled in the royal chambers," Piri said, slowing his pace even further. "You've brought so few servants with you, my lord; if you'd like I can assign some of the palace servants to you as well. There are several who are efficient as well as circumspect."

"That won't be necessary." Kristan shot him a sidelong look. "And you can set your mind at rest about the woman Astéria. It's not what you think. Dell or Raul will explain."

"Very well, my lord."

"I should send word to Quinn Logan that I've arrived safely. Will you arrange for a courier?"

"A runner was already scheduled to take reports to Fandrall in the morning, my lord. Your message can go with him. Would you like to see the reports first?"

"Is there anything pressing? Anything, perhaps, that might have given me some idea of the discord between my Reaches?"

Piri winced. "My lord, I apologize. I advised Reach Ferrador any number of times to make a clean breast of the situation, but he didn't want to trouble you. And although he's been working largely alone, he's kept things running smoothly."

"Dell doesn't seem to think so."

Piri's mouth tightened. "If I may be so bold, my lord, both Reach Curry and Reach Tasgall have personal agendas which keep them from seeing what's best for the kingdom as a whole."

They gained the top of the steps, and Kristan paused to catch his breath. Piri Neff kept his eyes carefully averted, but his brow was furrowed. "My lord, a feast in your honor is being arranged for this evening, but if you're too tired, it can be canceled."

Kristan blew out an impatient sigh. "Is it important, this feast?"

"With respect, my lord, it is. The Dyerians set great store by show. You entered the city very modestly. It would be best if your next appearance was a bit more . . . regal."

"You sound like Quinn."

"Ah, Quinn." Piri smiled, rather wistfully. "I confess that I miss him, my lord. I often wanted to write him for advice on the situation here."

"Why didn't you?"

Startled, Piri looked him full in the face. "That would have been wrong, my lord. Wrong in the first place for me to pass on privileged information in private correspondence, and wrong in the second because it would have put Quinn in the awkward position of choosing between betraying my confidence and withholding information from you. And make no mistake, my lord; no matter how strong our friendship, Quinn would have informed you immediately."

Kristan snorted. "I wish someone had."

A short, wide hallway led from the landing to a pair of elaborate doors. Before them, two guards in white and gold snapped to attention at Kristan and Piri's approach. They faced each other and with a stamp and a ceremonial flourish, opened the doors. A burst of laughter came from within, and Kristan found himself resenting his party's high spirits when he himself was so troubled. "When is this feast, Piri?" he asked.

"At sundown, my lord. Or sooner, if you're hungry now."

Kristan shook his head, remembering how difficult the arrangements for Princess Jelena's feast had been, and envying Piri's confidence in the skills of the palace staff.

"Very good, my lord. If you need anything further, or if the rooms don't suit, please send word via the guards." Piri bowed and hurried off, and Kristan passed between the guards and entered the room. In quiet unison, the doors closed behind him.

Before him was a spacious chamber decorated in white and gold and sumptuously furnished. A number of doors and a single broad hallway opened onto it. At the far end of the room was a large, polished stone hearth in which a cheerful fire crackled. His knights, Nolle and Astéria were gathered near it, the men chuckling over some joke. Astéria, still in human form, caught sight of Kristan first, and her smile disappeared. "Kreestan," she said. "I make trouble for you?"

The knights turned to him, suddenly somber. "No," Kristan said. "You're the least of my worries, Astéria."

"Can I release her from the shift?" Nolle asked. "I'm tired."

Kristan nodded. Nolle twirled her finger and Astéria's true form took shape. It was a relief to be able to look at her and not feel sick. A low, richly upholstered couch stood nearby; he sank onto it and massaged his aching knee. "Where's Serle?" he asked, as Astéria pranced a bit, clearly happy to be back on four legs.

"In your bedchamber, my lord," Sir Kennet said, pointing down the hallway. "I told him to unpack your things and air your clothes."

"It's a magnificent room, my lord," Sir Matthew added. "Beautiful hangings, a big comfortable bed, and two great windowed doors that open onto a balcony. The view is nothing short of spectacular."

"All the rooms are wonderful, my lord," Sir Mitchell said. "Piri Neff said the royal family and their retinue once lived in these chambers. All of us have bedrooms of our own, even Serle and Nolle, and there's more to spare."

"There's a big bathing room through that door," Sir Geoffrey said, indicating with a thumb. "But your room has its own bath."

Sir Walter crossed to a large table. "Cakes and wine here, my lord, if you'd like a bite. May I serve you?"

"Thank you, no."

Nolle let out a tiny whimper, and he remembered that none

of them had eaten since their morning porridge. "But please, help yourselves," he said. Nolle rushed to the table, grabbed a cake and stuffed it in her mouth. "Don't gorge," he added sharply. "There's a feast at sundown. All of you should bathe and make yourself fit to eat with these fancy folk." A sudden chill breeze made him shiver. "Where is that terrible draft coming from?"

They all looked around, puzzled, and then a look of awful realization flooded Kennet's face. He bolted down the broad hallway to Kristan's chamber. A moment later, he let out a roar. Kristan struggled to his feet and hurried after him, with everyone else hard on his heels.

A bewildered Serle stood in the middle of a vast bedchamber. The doors to the balcony were open and the elaborate wall hangings, heavy brocaded bed curtains and even the enormous bed's fur and silken coverings flapped in a stiff sea breeze. Kennet hustled in from the balcony, carrying an armload of Kristan's clothes. "What's the matter with you?" he shouted. "You don't hang the StoneKing's clothing outside like some peasant's washing! Matthew, Mitchell; get the rest." Kennet turned to Kristan. "He's draped all your things on the balustrade, my lord."

"But you said to air them," Serle said, in a small voice.

"I didn't mean outside, you little fool!"

Mitchell came back in with the rest of Kristan's clothes. "I'm sorry, my lord, but a pair of your leggings blew off and are snagged in a tree branch just below the balcony. Matthew's trying to get them now."

Kristan crossed to the balcony doors and looked out. Matthew was lying on his stomach, straining to reach the wayward leggings, but they were just out of his reach. In the courtyard below, a number of passersby had stopped to stare at the spectacle.

"Pardon, my lord," Walter said, nearly elbowing Kristan out of the way in his haste. He pushed Matthew aside and with his longer arms, was able to tug the leggings loose, although Kristan heard fabric tearing in the process. The two knights hustled back into the room, and Kennet banged the balcony doors shut.

Astéria, Mitchell and Nolle froze in the act of folding Kristan's clothes. Walter stood with the ripped leggings in one hand. Geoffrey, Matthew and Kennet loomed over Serle's cringing figure, their faces scarlet with rage. For three long breaths, no one moved or spoke.

And then Kristan began to laugh.

He could not help himself. His laughter was no more than a wheezing snicker, but it shook him from head to foot, so much that he could barely stand. He made his way to the absurd bed, like a ship in full sail in the middle of the room, and sat down. The feather mattress was so soft that it was like trying to sit on a cloud. His backside sank, his feet flew up and he went sprawling. He lay on his back amid the feather pillows and silken covers, giggling when what he really wanted to do was put his head in his hands and weep. But he could not weep; had not wept for as long as he could remember, and so he laughed helplessly while the others stood staring at him.

At last, he controlled himself and struggled upright. The sight of all the goggling, fearful faces almost set him off again, but he choked back his mirthless hilarity. "Go," he said, fanning his hands at the company. "Go get ready, all of you. Leave me be. Not you," he said, as Serle started to follow the others out. "Close the door and come here."

"Kreestan—" Astéria started to protest, but Geoffrey and Kennet hustled her out before she could say more.

Serle shut the door and came to Kristan. His face was so pale that his freckles were like flecks of dirt on snow. His teeth were buried in his lower lip, and his eyes shimmered with tears.

"Why are you crying?" Kristan asked. "Do you think I'm going to beat you?"

Serle shook his head.

"Then why?"

Serle took a shuddering breath. "Because I shamed you, sir—my lord," he whispered. "Because I made you look foolish."

"I'm capable of doing that on my own. You made a mistake, Serle. That's all."

A tear spilled down Serle's cheek. "I'm sorry, my lord."

"I know you are. But the next time you don't understand what someone means, promise me you'll ask for an explanation. That's the only way you'll learn." He looked around the room. "Now, Geoffrey said I have my own bath here."

Serle smiled tremulously and trotted to a door in the far wall. "In here, my lord." He pushed the door open, and a cloud of scented steam drifted into the bedchamber. "The bath in the other room is a lot bigger, but it doesn't have heated water like this one. There are towels and sponges and soap and pretty glass lanterns and one wall is even all over mirrors. And you have your own private shithole, too."

Another hysterical giggle rose in Kristan's throat, but he swallowed it. "Garderobe," he said. "That's what it's called in a castle, Serle."

"Garderobe," Serle repeated. "Anyway, it's behind a little wall in the corner." He hesitated. "Sir Kennet said I should assist you bathing, my lord."

Kristan's skin crawled at the idea. "That's not necessary. Lay out my best clothes for the feast and put the rest away neatly. Once I get my boots off, you can clean them, and when that's done, you can have your own bath and get ready. Do you have a change of clothes?"

"Oh, yes, my lord. Sir Randolf gave me a nice new tunic and leggings before we left."

"Very well, then. Get to work."

As Serle busied himself with the clothing, Kristan pulled off his boots, then padded across the room in stockinged feet and looked into the bath. It was a small room, with three walls of white marble and the fourth lined from floor to ceiling in small mirrored tiles. In the middle of the room was a round pool of bluish marble, large enough for several people and nearly deep enough to swim in. At either end of the bath was a tall metal stand with many gracefully arched arms. From every arm hung a small lantern of glass and gold. Beeswax candles glowed brightly within, emitting their own pleasant aroma. Curved benches of some sweet-smelling wood flanked the pool, and a little table of the same wood held a stack of neatly folded linen towels, a basket of sponges and brushes and a golden bowl filled with soft, creamy soap. Ewers of fresh rinse water stood nearby.

Kristan closed the door and sat down on one of the benches, feeling suffocated by all the luxury. He pulled off his travel-stained clothing and sat for some moments staring at his reflection in the mirrored wall opposite. *Ugly*, he thought. *Princess Jelena was right. Ugly and graceless and ill-tempered. And foolish and naïve into the bargain.*

He dug a handful of the soft soap from the bowl, picked up a sponge and stepped into the pool, turning his back on the mirrored wall. The water was pleasantly warm and soothing to his aching joints and muscles, but he could not enjoy it, or the buttery lather of the soap as he washed, nor the play of light on the rippling water. *Fool, fool, fool*, he thought, dousing his head and scrubbing his scalp so fiercely that it tingled. *What kind of king are you, not to know what goes on in your own kingdom?* He grabbed one of the ewers and upended it over his head, inhaled sharply at the shock of cool water and sucked water up one nostril. He sputtered and coughed, and when at last he could breathe again, he sagged against the side of the pool, berating himself for his stupidity, his lack of judgment, his arrogance.

At last, a faint sound broke through the wall of his misery: Serle, singing a simple tune as he worked in the bedchamber beyond.

> *Little woolly head*
> *Make your woolly bed*

In clover and in thistle and in dew
Your mam will keep you warm
While I guard the flock from harm
And you grow into a woolly ram or ewe
Never mind the hawk
Never mind the wolf
Never mind the rain or dark of night
Rest your woolly head
In your woolly bed
Your mam and I will keep you safe 'til light

Serle's reedy voice faded to a hum, but the gentle rhythm of the song seemed to flow along Kristan's taut neck and shoulders, down his back and into his legs. He closed his eyes and cupped one hand over them. Slowly, his headache began to ease. With Serle's humming a soft counterpoint to the lapping of warm water around his body, Kristan nodded off.

CHAPTER TWELVE

Fedro Vincenze stood too close, glittering with gilt and jewels and reeking of the perfume he had swiped over his jowls, leaving greasy streaks along the shaking blubber of his neck. *These Dyerians*, Kristan thought, clenching his teeth behind his smiling lips. *All show and no substance. If I looked at this man cross-eyed, he'd piss himself.*

He was tired and irritable. He had been on his feet for some time as Raul and Piri Neff introduced all the councilors and officials of his Seagirt court. Then, they had moved on to Seagirt's most prominent citizens, all in glittering and eager attendance. Fedro had been presented first, and he hung over Kristan's shoulder as his fellow guild heads and other moneyed Dyerians bowed and murmured their greetings. Kristan wished fervently that he had listened to Piri and received his visitors from the towering throne instead of in this silly line, but the idea of the throne had seemed too formal, too distant, although at least it would have spared him the stink of Fedro's perfume.

Dell stood silently nearby, staring into space, but there was still no word from Marcus, and Kristan was already framing the reprimand he planned on giving his third Reach. *That is,* he thought, *if Marcus ever shows up.*

He glanced down the line at his own party. Sir Kennet and Sir Geoffrey stood just beyond Piri, bowing stiffly as they were introduced. Next were Walter, Astéria, Matthew and Mitchell. Kristan had briefly considered keeping Astéria secluded, but decided that her omission from the reception would create even more curiosity. He had placed her in Matthew's care and cautioned her to speak as little as possible. Now, addressed simply as 'Lady Astéria,' she stood between the knights, smiling shyly. Nolle, no doubt inspired by the fantastic dress of the Dyerian court, had altered Astéria's appearance somewhat, substituting a gown of blue and silver for the copy of Jelena's cream-colored dress and an elaborate headpiece of opals for the pearl circlet. The result was so spectacular that no one seemed to notice Astéria's silence, even without Walter and Matthew's diverting stream of chatter.

Nolle herself stood just behind Astéria, wearing a sullen look and the dull gray dress that had been provided for her. Before the company descended to the feast, she had attempted to shift herself into a more attractive form and been reprimanded by Kristan. "I need you to focus all your attention on holding Astéria's shift," he had told her.

"You're just supposed to be a maid, not a courtier," Serle had added, a bit smugly.

The squire had been delighted with his new clothing: leggings and tunic of brown, with a modest trimming of green braid at the hem and sleeves. He, too, stood behind Astéria, ready to fend off any approach from behind, but his eyes were on Kristan, as if eager to be called to his lord's service.

"And here is Mali Uzuri, my lord!" Fedro boomed out, even as Raul murmured the name in Kristan's ear.

"I'm sure the StoneKing's sight and hearing are in full working order, Fedro," Mali said crisply. "And even if they weren't, he has help enough here without you." Fedro's face went red, and he stalked off to join the other guild heads. Mali grinned at Kristan. "Well, your looks are much improved since the last time we met, my lord."

"Just a wash and shave," Kristan said.

"More than that, my lord," Mali said, in a lower tone. "You show these peacocks what proper finery should be."

Kristan only nodded, although the compliment pleased him. He was wearing the clothing made for the great ceremony in Hogia the previous summer, when he had sworn in his Reaches and knights. The tunic was a little lightweight for even Dyer's mild winter, but it was of fine fabric in a dark, rich green, subtly embellished with gold and silver thread. He was secretly grateful Quinn Logan had not packed any of the beautiful but outdated wardrobe Princess Jelena had mocked. *Perhaps I should buy new clothing while I'm in Seagirt*, he thought.

Mali Uzuri had brought some of her family along and was introducing them: tall, handsome men and women with proud bearing, dark velvety skin and the same high cheekbones and shrewd eyes as their matriarch. All were dressed in jewel-bright clothing, but their trappings were kept to a tasteful minimum: a broad cuff of gold on a graceful wrist, a single large gemstone in a brooch, a subtle sprinkling of tiny silver beads on a comb set in wiry black curls. Something about their manner was both comforting and yet strangely unsettling, and Kristan tried to puzzle out why as he returned their bows.

"They're a handsome crowd, aren't they?" Mali said. "Our home is on the southwestern side of the city. You must visit us, StoneKing, and know us better."

"I would like that," Kristan said, and meant it.

A sudden commotion drew his attention to the main doors. Over the protests of others, a man was pushing his way through the crowd, leading a dainty woman in a cloak and hood of rich purple lined with downy white feathers. On Kristan's left, Piri let out a soft moan; on his right, Raul sucked in a breath through his teeth. "He's brought that woman with him," he muttered.

"Make way, make way!" Marcus Tasgall shouted, his flushed face split by a broad grin as he shoved his way toward them.

Kristan had to make a conscious effort to shut his gaping mouth. The third Reach of Dyer wore brightly striped leggings and a vivid yellow tunic edged with tippets of white and black fur. His chain of office lay crooked across his shoulders. He sported several rings set with showy gemstones, and his straggling hair, grown long, was tied back to reveal ears pierced with rakish gold hoops. Occasionally, he paused to slap someone's back or shoulder and guffaw a greeting. Those he touched drew back, faces creased with embarrassment. In contrast, the woman he led kept her head demurely bowed, her face hidden within her hood, but even so, her passage was marked with scornful eyes and curled lips. Their clever faces suddenly expressionless, the Uzuri family stepped aside.

As Marcus came closer, Kristan could smell him: a combination of wine and some sort of heavy, acrid perfume that made him want to sneeze. Marcus' eyes were bloodshot and his face tinged an unhealthy yellow, but his grin was raffish as ever. "Kristan Gemeta! What a surprise!" he said, as he stumbled to a halt. His bow was so low and extravagant that the homage seemed almost mocking.

"Reach Tasgall," Kristan answered coolly.

"We've been waiting for you, Marcus," Raul said. "Didn't you get my message?"

"Oh, I did, I did," Marcus said, staggering upright. "I came as fast as I could get my clothes on. By way of apology, I've brought a surprise of my own for the StoneKing." He pulled the woman forward. "Say hello, my dear."

The people surrounding them murmured in distinctly disapproving tones. "I don't think this is the proper time or place—" Raul started to say, but the woman was already dipping into a low curtsey, and as she did, she put back her hood and lifted her head. Her green-eyed gaze met Kristan's.

Green eyes staring up at him, wide with guilt; round bare breasts squeezed in Owen's hands, skirts rucked up to the waist, shapely legs parted and Owen's thick-muscled body between them, both of them pillowed in a warm, golden bed of hay—

Kristan caught his breath. "Tansy," he said. "Tansy."

A trembling smile curved Tansy's full lips. "Kristan," she said, her voice no more than a whisper.

"You know her?" Raul said.

"Know her?" Marcus crowed. "They were sweethearts once; isn't that right, Tansy? And not so very long ago."

"A lifetime ago," Tansy said, still looking up at Kristan. Without thinking, he put out his hand. She placed her fingertips in his palm and came to her feet, to a chorus of bewildered mutters from the crowd. Tansy's lips parted, as if to say more, but before she could speak, Raul signaled to someone across the room. A sudden blast of horns made everyone jump, and Tansy's fingers slipped from Kristan's.

"Dinner is ready, my lord," Piri Neff said. "Shall we go in?"

With Piri and Raul flanking him and loud processional music pressing in on him like pushing hands, Kristan let himself be guided into still another elaborate chamber. Here dozens of tables had been placed end to end, forming seven long rows that ran nearly the length of the room. Perpendicular to these was another row of tables on a low dais, which placed them slightly higher than the rest of the room. The tables furthest from the dais were simply laid with plain linens, cutlery and cups, with benches for their occupants, but those further up were progressively finer, with goblets and plates and embroidered linens and cushioned stools instead of benches. Closest to the head table, the linens were of glossy brocade, the trappings of gold and silver. At the head table, twelve gilded chairs faced the rest of the room, with manservants in white and gold poised to assist those of greatest rank to their seats. In the middle of this row stood a single ornate chair with a towering back and great curved arms, and it was to this chair that Raul and Piri steered him. The tallest, grandest-looking manservant bowed and started to pull the chair out, but was unceremoniously elbowed aside by a determined Serle. The chair was too heavy for the boy, and its legs squawked against the floor as Serle heaved at it, but at last there was enough room for Kristan to slip between it and the table. With an ungracious gesture to the tall manservant, Serle allowed him to push the chair back in, then took up a jealous stance behind it, just within Kristan's eyeshot. Kristan gave him a nod, and Serle beamed.

Up and down the room the guests were being seated, but the method of this seating varied. On either side of the room's entrance, a doorward mantled in gold and white held a list inscribed on parchment. As each guest passed through the doorway, the doorwards would consult their parchments carefully. Sometimes a page would be summoned to escort the guest to one of the higher tables, but more often the doorward, with an elegant gesture, would indicate one of the middle tables. Some guests' only acknowledgement was a haughty jerk of the chin toward the lowest seats. Occasionally, a guest would slip a few coins to one of the doorwards and receive better seating in return.

"It's a long-standing tradition here, the buying of status," Raul said, keeping his voice beneath the blaring music as he took the seat on Kristan's left. "I don't care for it, but it's hard to break old habits."

Dell was seated on Raul's left, and one of the splendid manservants had pulled out the next chair for Marcus, but Marcus was nose-to-nose with Piri Neff. The councilor shook his head and Marcus' already flushed face grew redder still. He waved one hand at Tansy, who kept her gaze modestly on the floor, then pointed to Kristan, while beyond him manservants and guests waited in consternation.

"Damn it," Raul muttered. "She can't sit at the head table."

"Why not?" Kristan asked.

Raul cupped one hand over his mouth and leaned in to him, a gesture so like the whispering Dyerians' that Kristan's skin prickled. "Kristan, I'm sorry to tell you this, particularly if she's an old friend, but Tansy is a notorious courtesan, from one of the largest doxy-houses in Seagirt. Marcus has been in her thrall for months." He hesitated, then added, "Were you really sweethearts?"

Kristan did not answer. The argument between Marcus and

Piri was growing more heated, and at last, Tansy looked up, but not at them. Her green-eyed gaze locked on Kristan in mute appeal.

"Let her be seated with Marcus," Kristan said.

Raul's eyes went wide. "Kristan, it wouldn't be proper."

"I said let her be seated."

"But it would look as if—"

"Must I buy status for her?" Kristan snapped.

Raul swallowed hard. "No, my lord."

"Then do as I say."

Raul half stood, gestured to Piri and nodded solemnly. Piri gawked at him for a moment, then heaved a sigh and waved Tansy toward the seat next to Marcus. A manservant took her purple cloak, his nose turned up as if the garment smelled bad. Beneath the cloak Tansy wore a neatly fitted, high-necked gown of an even deeper purple that, at first glance, seemed overly modest among the other Seagirt women's finery. But the high neck of her gown stood open, revealing her pale throat, and the purple fabric had been cleverly slashed at the shoulder, breast, waist and hips with filmy cloth the exact color of Tansy's creamy skin, fooling the eye into believing she was half-naked. The people who had sneered at her arrival were now sneaking glances at her, open-mouthed.

Tansy nodded her thanks as the manservant drew out her chair. Piri took the place next to her, shooting a pointed look at the two courtiers who stood waiting for the single remaining seat. The two exchanged a glance, and with ill grace the younger one found a chair at a lower table. Marcus dropped carelessly into his seat, draped his arm across Tansy's shoulders and kissed her on the cheek. She accepted the kiss with a regal tilt of her head, but she looked past Marcus at Kristan and smiled.

Kristan looked down the other side of the table. Sir Geoffrey was seated on his right, with Kennet, Walter, Astéria, Matthew and Mitchell beyond him. Nolle stood behind Astéria's chair, looking less thrilled with her assignment than Serle. Astéria herself seemed oblivious to the curious and even admiring looks the other guests were turning on her. Her apprehension was clear as she studied the array of dining implements before her. Walter patted her hand reassuringly as Matthew shook out her napkin and draped it across her lap.

"So, who's your pretty friend, Kristan?" Marcus called.

Raul quickly raised his hand and the servants surged into motion, bringing forth towels and basins of water. The lowest tables received pottery basins, beautifully enameled but earthenware nonetheless, while higher up the basins were of some bright, faceted metal that sent reflections of candlelight dancing into their users' faces. The tables closest to Kristan received basins of silver and the head table basins of gold, both metals extravagantly engraved with Dyer's symbolic skeins of thread.

Kristan's own basin was golden, with a rim inset with small, sparkling diamonds. The tall manservant presented it with a flourish, while Serle stood by jealously, holding the fine embroidered linen towel (*more skeins*, Kristan thought absently). The entire hall went silent and still. "They're waiting for you to wash first, my lord," Raul murmured, barely moving his lips.

Kristan bathed his fingertips, resisting the urge to wrinkle his nose at the heavily scented water. When he was finished, the manservant hesitated, a questioning look on his face, and Raul leaned a little closer. "It's a Dyerian custom for the master to show favor by sharing his basin," he whispered.

Kristan deliberated as he dried his hands on the towel. His first impulse was to send the basin down the right side of the table, to share with his knights and Astéria, but he sensed the gesture would be viewed as a slight to his Dyerian hosts, and he did not want to draw further attention to Astéria. *Sharing with the Reaches would be best*, he thought, but he was still annoyed with all three. With bitter amusement, he imagined the reaction if he sent the basin to Tansy. *By the Stone, can these people not even wash without worrying about status? I ought to share with*

Serle and Nolle, just to show how little I care for their custom.

He was on the verge of simply ignoring the ritual when his eye fell on Mali Uzuri. Seated at one of the closest tables, she watched him with good-humored interest, her small dark eyes sparking, her lined face creased in a mischievous grin. He smiled back. "Send the basin to Mali Uzuri," he told the man-servant.

The other guests murmured in approbation or envy as Mali bathed her gnarled old hands in the gem-encrusted basin and dried them with the embroidered towel. Kristan glanced to his left. Raul was watching with a polite smile, although there was a trace of hurt in his eyes. Dell was impassive and Marcus was paying no attention at all, busy nuzzling Tansy's neck while she stared down at Mali, her eyes narrowed. Beyond Tansy, Piri Neff scrutinized the scene with a raised eyebrow and pursed lips; he glanced at Kristan, as if feeling his gaze, and gave him the tiniest, approving nod.

With the ritual concluded, the rest of the basins were presented, or in the case of the lower tables, merely passed. The splash and slosh of washing filled the air for some moments. Then, the basins and towels were whisked away, replaced by a parade of brimming pitchers borne by more servants. They filled goblets with wine at the upper tables and tankards of ale at the lower ones. When everyone was served, Raul stood and cleared his throat. Everyone went quiet.

"My lord," he said, bowing to Kristan. "Your very good health. Welcome to Dyer."

"Health to the StoneKing!" Fedro Vincenze shouted, and every guest echoed the words and drank heartily. Other toasts followed until at last Raul nodded, and from some distant kitchen a fresh procession of servants entered, bearing bowls of honeyed fruits, tureens of exotic soups, mounds of bread and cakes, stuffed chickens, ducks and geese, large fish roasted whole, skewers of squab and enormous platters of suckling pig, shining with grease. All of these were carried with great pomp past all the other guests, straight to Kristan so that he could be served first. The sight of so much food sickened him, and after the first dozen dishes, he began to wave some away, only to discover that other guests then refused the dishes as well. *So much waste*, he thought, and signaled the puzzled servants to bring the spurned dishes back. Even taking only the smallest morsel from each filled his plate to brimming, but he forced himself to sample everything, even though the oily richness of Dyerian food made him even queasier.

Raul seemed aware of his discomfort. "It's a lot, isn't it?" he said quietly. "Dyerians set great store by having plenty to eat, and King Claude was no exception. I understand he was a man of large appetite." He glanced at Kristan's plate. "It's good of you to try every dish, my lord. It will mean a great deal to the kitchen staff."

"I'm sure they've worked very hard," Kristan said.

"They're capable of even more extravagance if given sufficient notice. The feast they produced for Dell and Marcus and me on our arrival last summer was extraordinary. I thought we'd never be done eating. They'll be waiting for the chance to show you their very best, my lord."

Kristan's stomach heaved. "Surely, there won't be more feasts?"

"Not of this magnitude, no. But more intimate dinners will be expected. For example, Fedro Vincenze and his fellow guild heads are already clamoring for invitations to dine with you. And it would be good for you to sit down with Captain Ommald and his officers. And then there's the Seagirt town council, and some of the elders—"

"Better hope this trader Lorz shows up soon, my lord, or we'll all be fat as pigs," Sir Geoffrey muttered in Kristan's other ear.

The feast went on and on, the meats giving way to a cavalcade of sweets, cheeses and sugared nuts. The chatter of the diners grew louder and more raucous. Revolted by the excess,

Kristan had already begun slipping portions of his food to Serle, who ate them with alacrity that bordered on outright greed. Following his example, Astéria fed Nolle the same way, but there was nothing to be done about the wine, which was strong and honey-sweet. Kristan finally asked for a goblet of water, but even that had been sweetened and scented, and after one taste he pushed it aside. He envied his knights their good appetite, their easy conversation.

At last, the flow of food and drink eased; the diners sat back from the ruins of their meals and the conversation grew louder still. Many guests rose to visit other tables, but Kristan felt trapped by the big chair and the servants who still circled like vultures, looking for the opportunity to serve him. Raul had moved to Kristan's right and was chatting with Sir Kennet. Dell remained in his seat, silently examining the half-eaten remains of a squab. As Kristan watched, his Reach lifted the bones from his plate, held them up and flexed the wing back and forth, his mouth twisted thoughtfully. Beyond him, Marcus leaned over the table to engage in loud, animated conversation with one of the guests at a lower place. With a final guffaw, he drained his wine goblet, slammed it down, dropped into his seat and began nibbling Tansy's ear while his fingers burrowed into her lap. Piri Neff took one look and quickly engaged the councilor on his left.

With an effort, Kristan pushed back his chair and stood up. After all the wine and food, the sudden movement made him unpleasantly dizzy. Throughout the hall, the guests went quiet, turning their faces to him like flowers to the sun.

"Good ladies and gentlemen," he said. His tongue felt fat and fuzzy in his mouth, and it was an effort to speak clearly. "You have given me a rich and royal welcome to Dyer—one I will never forget." *Try though I might*, he added silently, as the guests cheered. He raised his hand for quiet and continued: "I thank you for your company this evening, and bid you a pleasant journey to your homes and your beds."

An uncomfortable silence greeted his words. "So soon, StoneKing?" Marcus bawled out. "Why, it's the shank of the evening!"

Kristan gritted his teeth in what he hoped passed for a smile. "It's a pity, but I fear I don't have the stamina for a long evening; not tonight."

"Of course you wouldn't, my lord, not after five days of winter travel," Raul said, his solicitous tone at odds with the fierce look he shot at Marcus. He bowed gracefully to Kristan. "A refreshing night's sleep to you, my lord."

Following his example, the other guests rose and bowed, murmuring their goodnights as they departed. Startled from his contemplation of the squab's wing, Dell stumbled to his feet. Marcus shrugged and took Tansy by the elbow. "No matter," he said. "The festivities can go on elsewhere easily enough."

"I think not," Kristan said. "I'd like to meet with my Reaches and Dyer's council, tomorrow morning at daybreak."

"Very good, my lord," Raul said. Piri Neff nodded in grim agreement.

"Daybreak?" Marcus squawked. "No one in Dyer is afoot at daybreak. No one does anything of import before noon."

"Then tomorrow should make for an interesting change," Kristan said. "Good night."

* * *

For some time Kristan lay in the great soft bed with his eyes shut, hoping the comforts of the elaborate room would lull him to sleep, but it was no use. The pillow had been scented with a fragrance he found oppressive. The room was too warm for the furs that had been laid atop the covers, and when he shifted position, the silky linens stuck to his skin. No sound came from his companions, peacefully asleep in their own chambers, but parts of Seagirt were still awake. Strains of music and occasional bursts of song and loud conversation drifted up from the city below.

As Kristan lay staring up at the bed's heavy canopy, a faint tap came from the balcony doors. At first, he thought he had imagined it, but then a second tap sounded, followed by a quick rattle, as if something had bounced to the balcony floor. As he threw back the covers, a third tap sounded. A fine, fur-trimmed robe lay on a nearby bench and Kristan hurried into it, wondering if it had belonged to King Claude. *More dead kings' leavings,* he thought, with a touch of resentment. He limped to the balcony doors and pushed them open.

Three small pebbles lay on the balcony floor. The moon was a brilliant silver coin in the sky, its light glittering on the great Seagirt bay below and the hundreds of craft anchored there. Some were mere dark smears on the water; others twinkled with lantern light as they rocked on the swell. A sudden gust of cold, damp wind whipped Kristan's hair about his face; he pulled up the fur-trimmed collar of his robe as he stepped out to the balustrade.

"I wondered if you were awake," said a quiet voice.

Standing in the shadows beneath his balcony was a slender, hooded figure. It stepped into the moonlight, raised gloved hands to the hood and turned it back. Tansy's green eyes looked up at him.

The old memory jolted through Kristan's brain again, and his hand sought the comforting shape of the Stone beneath his robe. "What are you doing here?"

Tansy smiled. "We didn't get a chance to talk at the feast. I knew this balcony led to your room. I slipped the guards a few coins to let me pass."

"Did you?"

His tone was cold, but she only tilted her head, her smile deepening. "It's the way of the world, here in Seagirt. Money can get you everything you want."

"How much does Marcus pay, to get what he wants?"

"Don't be cruel, Kristan. We used to be friends, back in

Fandrall. More than friends."

"Much has changed since then."

"I know that—all too well."

They stood in silence for some moments. In the moonlight, Tansy's face was pale, her eyes and parted lips bathed in its faint bluish light. "It's cold out here, Kristan," she said at last.

"Then go back to Marcus and get warm."

"Are you angry that I'm with Marcus?"

Am I? Kristan wondered. Aloud he answered: "I'm angry because Marcus idles with you when he should be attending to the kingdom's business."

"He'll attend to your business tomorrow."

"Will he? Why?"

"Because I took away his wine. Because I paid several servants to get him awake and alert in plenty of time for council tomorrow. Because I told him I was going home to sleep in my own bed, and don't want to see him again until he's back in your good graces."

Kristan snorted. "He must care for you a great deal."

"He does."

"And do you care a great deal for him, or for his money and position?"

Tansy did not answer. Another blast of wind made both of them wince. Kristan's bare feet were growing numb against the cold stone floor.

"You think ill of me," Tansy said at last.

"You've never given me any reason to think otherwise. You haven't even asked about your mother and father."

"Mother and Father," Tansy echoed. "How are they?"

"Well enough, for two people whose hearts are broken. Feva and Lyko think you're dead. They've been grieving. Why didn't you write, at least to tell them you were alive?"

"If they knew what I was, they'd wish me dead," Tansy said, her voice so low that Kristan barely caught the words. He was suddenly ashamed of himself.

"They wouldn't," he said. "They would be so glad to hear from you . . . so glad to know you're alive."

"Are you glad, Kristan?" she asked. "Glad that I'm alive?"

"Of course I am."

"Then let's be friends again. I wish we could sit and talk quietly, as we did when we were children. Do you remember how we'd lay on the grass and look at the sky and talk about our dreams?"

No, Kristan wanted to say; *no, I can't remember any of it, and the only dreams I have now terrify me.*

"Let me come up to you," Tansy said, and moved as if to climb the tree alongside the balcony.

"No," Kristan said.

"Then come down to me."

"No."

"Why? Is that woman in your bed now?"

"What woman?"

"The woman in your company. Lady Astéria." Tansy's eyes narrowed. "Or perhaps it's the little servant girl who lies beside you."

"Neither," Kristan said. "My bed is empty."

"Marcus said you had a lover. A girl you left behind in Hogia. Don't you miss her?"

Heather's somber face rose in his mind's eye; a fragment of his nightmare. He shook it off before the memory could take full shape. "That's none of your concern."

Tansy stood looking up at him, her face framed by the soft feathered lining of her hood. "You look like your father," she whispered.

Father.

Kristan had not thought of Robert Gemeta in a long while, not since he realized any attempt at remembering him would only unsheathe razor-sharp images of his death. He knotted his hands around the balustrade and leaned toward her, suddenly starved for some softer recollection. "I look like my father . . ."

he repeated. "How?"

"Stern," Tansy said. "Sad. But your father could smile, too. Once, when we were very young, I blew you a kiss. Your father caught it before you could. He smiled then, but I think he was protecting you. You were such an innocent little boy—your face was like an open flower." She took a step closer to the balcony and tilted her head back, so the moonlight fell full on her face. "Your mouth is so different now—hard when it used to be soft. And your smiles never reach your eyes. So much has happened to us in two years, Kristan. I've heard only a little of your story, and you almost none of mine. Is there no way we can talk together, as old friends? You can't visit my house, not without setting a thousand gossiping tongues clacking. Could you invite me to dine?"

"No." The breeze freshened, and he shivered. "It's late and it's cold. We shouldn't be out here, talking. It isn't right."

"I want to see you again, Kristan. I'll think of some way."

"Go home, Tansy," he said, although he longed to say *stay; stay and tell me more of what you remember. Give me back some of my past.*

"As you wish," Tansy said. She drew up her hood. "Good night, StoneKing."

She slipped into the shadows. Her soft tread retreated, faded and was gone. In the town below, a sudden burst of laughter echoed through the crisp night air. A melancholy ache knotted Kristan's throat, and he bowed his head against the bright moonlight.

CHAPTER THIRTEEN

The dawn council meeting began well. Raul, Piri Neff and the other councilors were already present when Kristan entered the chamber. They were all neatly shaven and combed and well-dressed. Many wore jewelry, only simple rings or bracelets, but even these subtle adornments made Kristan conscious of his own drab appearance. Marcus arrived shortly after, a little bleary-eyed but sober, and Dell joined them just as sunrise brightened the windows with a wash of gold.

At first, all three Reaches were attentive and engaged, but as the morning wore on, Marcus began to yawn and fiddle with his clothes, while his contributions to the discussion grew increasingly flippant and trivial. Dell stared out the window as if longing to be somewhere else, his involvement limited to the occasional nod, the infrequent grunt. Only Raul stayed engrossed, his small dark eyes darting from face to face, from ledger to ledger as he led a discussion on taxes. Kristan kept silent, listening and watching. Gradually, the councilors edged their chairs around to face Raul, effectively excluding Dell and Marcus from the debate. Dell did not seem to notice or even care, and after a few more ineffectual remarks, Marcus laced his fingers atop his belly and stared at them. In time, his eyelids began to droop, his head to nod.

"That's enough," Kristan said. Marcus' head snapped up, and everyone jumped and started to their feet as Kristan rose. He waved them back to their seats. "Please continue without me, gentlemen. And thank you for an enlightening morning."

Deep in thought, he made his way back to his chambers. Once again, servants and courtiers cleared the halls before him, and he was grateful to be spared their scrutiny. At the main doors to the royal suite, a fresh pair of elegant guards came to attention, and he nodded at them absently. As they opened the doors for him, a sudden, telling clatter of hooves and the slam of a door within the chamber told him that Astéria had been startled while in her true form, and he made a mental note not to arrive so quietly in future.

"It's only me," he called, once the doors were shut behind him.

Astéria peered from her room, wide-eyed and breathless. "You scarce me, Kreestan."

"I'm sorry. Where is everyone else?"

"Most go out. Nolle ees . . . ees . . ." She waved her hands helplessly, then mimed washing under her arms. "*Pos to léte, kánei mpánio?*"

"Bathing," Kristan said. "And Serle?"

"This word I know," Astéria said, with a proud smile. "Serle ees *shitting.*"

Before Kristan could respond, Mitchell came down the hallway from Kristan's chambers. "There you are, my lord! I wondered how long you'd be in council."

"Long enough," Kristan said. "Where are the others?"

"Geoffrey, Kennet and Matthew went down to the docks to see if there was any word about Astéria's ship. Sir Walter is checking on our horses. And I was just out on your balcony. Someone was tossing pebbles at the doors, but when I came out, no one was there." He held up a bit of folded parchment, sealed with a blob of colored wax. "I found this. There's no name on it."

Kristan took it from him, broke the seal and opened it. Inside was a brief message, written in a fluid, feminine hand.

Fedro Vincenze has a house near the palace.
If you wish to meet me there, let him know.—T.

He closed the note and stood pondering. Seeing Tansy had awakened a deep yearning to talk to someone who knew his past and could provide him with some shreds of the memories Daazna had taken from him, but the idea of a clandestine meeting was troubling.

"Is anything wrong, my lord?" Sir Mitchell asked.

Before Kristan could answer, Serle came into the room, adjusting his clothing. "Good morning, my lord!" he said cheerfully.

"Actually, it's nearly noon," Mitchell said. "Should I ask the guards to have some food sent up?"

"Yes," Kristan said absently.

Astéria let out the tiniest sigh, and he realized how numbingly dull her confinement in the suite must be. At the same time, the idea of spending another moment in the suffocating splendor of the palace was suddenly more than he could bear. "No," he said. "No, I want to go out. Let's all go out and have a better look at this city."

"We'll have to pry Nolle out of the bath first," Mitchell said. "She's been in there all morning."

Tucking the note into his tunic, Kristan strode across the room to the bathing chamber door. He knocked sharply, but there was no answer. "Nolle!" he called. "Nolle, get dressed. We're going out."

There was still no reply. Kristan pressed his ear to the door but heard nothing.

"You don't suppose she's gone and drowned herself, do you?" Mitchell joked, but his face was uneasy. Kristan pushed the door open.

The bathing chamber was empty and silent. Nolle's clothing lay on a nearby bench, but she was nowhere to be seen. Astéria, Serle and Mitchell crowded up behind him.

"Where's she got to?" Mitchell said.

A faint ripple disturbed the surface of the big communal pool, and Kristan stepped forward to peer into it. A small, slender fish swam near the bottom, flicking its tail lazily, the larger, wavering form around it almost obscured by the water. "There she is," he said. "She's too deep to hear us." Leaning down, he thrust his hand into the water and splashed noisily.

With a surge and splatter, Nolle materialized, palming her wet hair out of her face. When she saw them staring at her, she quickly crossed her arms over the small buds of her breasts. "Can't a person bathe in peace here?"

Astéria laughed and fanned her hands in an imitation of fins. "Nolle ees *psári!*"

"Fish," Serle said.

"Feesh," Astéria repeated.

"What on earth were you doing, girl?" Mitchell said.

"Trying a new shift. It took some getting used to. I thought I'd choke before I got the hang of it." Nolle made a face and spat. "Ugh. This scented water tastes bad."

"You're not supposed to drink it, stupid," Serle said, with a smirk.

Nolle's eyes blazed and she thrust one hand at Serle. "*Marra marra marrapatta!*"

In an instant, Serle's fish form was flopping helplessly at the edge of the pool. Kristan lunged for it, but it tumbled into the bath and sank just beneath the surface, twisting and splashing.

"Nolle, stop it!" Kristan shouted.

Nolle only laughed as she watched Serle struggle. "How do *you* like the taste of it, know-it-all?"

"Nolle!" Kristan said again. With a roll of her eyes, Nolle raised her finger to undo the spell, but at that moment Serle's fish form righted itself in the water and with a flick of its tail, shot toward her. She squealed and scrabbled toward the opposite edge, but Serle was already darting in and out, nipping her heels, her legs, her backside. As she heaved herself from the bath, Serle's fish form leaped halfway out of the water after her, then dropped back and began swimming round and round the perimeter of the pool, as if in triumph.

"I guess he showed you," Sir Mitchell said, tossing Nolle a towel.

Serle flung himself out of the water again, all shining scales and wiggling fins, and Astéria clapped her hands and waded into the bath. "Nolle, Nolle, you do to me!" she cried. "You make me feesh!"

Nolle shot a look at Kristan. "Can I try? I've never done two shifts at once."

He shrugged. "If you like. At least she hasn't any clothes to get wet."

Nolle let out an excited giggle, then immediately became sober as she worked the spell again. With a great splash, Astéria shifted into a larger and quite lovely fish, with elegant stripes along its sides. She thrashed in the water while the Serle-fish swam encouragingly around her. At last, she rolled onto her belly and began to chase him. Sir Mitchell leaned over the bath, laughing as the two fish flashed past. "That's amazing," he said. "I always wished I could swim."

"I bet I can do you, too," Nolle said, her eyes still fixed on the fish.

Mitchell glanced sidelong at Kristan. "No . . . I shouldn't . . ."

"Go ahead," Kristan said.

With a grin, Mitchell stripped off his boots and tunic and stepped to the edge of the pool. A breath later there were three fish in the water: the small Serle-fish, the striped Astéria-fish, and the Mitchell-fish, which looked a bit like a brown trout.

Kristan sat down on one of the benches and studied Nolle. The Wiche girl's face was pale and her mouth was set tight. "How hard is it, maintaining all three?"

She grunted, still focused on the shifts. "Not as bad as I expected."

The three fish chased each other merrily around the big

bath, and then, all at once, they leaped out of the water, their bodies flashing in the lamplight. The wild blurring of their true forms made Kristan's stomach lurch, and he looked away.

"I want to see if I can hold their shifts and change myself at the same time," Nolle said. "Can I try?"

"Are you sure that's safe?"

"If anything happens, you can touch us and break the spell."

"Very well." There was a mutter, a splash, and when Kristan looked back at the bath, Nolle's towel was in a heap at the edge and a fourth fish had joined the three. Nolle's fish was a little different this time, larger and covered in shimmering silver scales. He watched the four graceful forms dart playfully around each other and felt a pang of forlorn envy.

The four fish swam together for only a few moments before the multiple spells gave way: Astéria reappeared first, sitting on her haunches in the middle of the bath, then Serle materialized, followed an instant later by Mitchell. All three sat in the water, sputtering and laughing, while the Nolle-fish made one final circuit of the bath, and then shifted back. She caught up her towel, fumbled it around herself and sat on the edge of the bath, trembling and panting. "Are you all right?" Kristan asked.

She swallowed hard and nodded. From the central chamber of the suite came the sound of the main doors opening and closing. "Anyone home?" Sir Walter's voice called.

"In here," Kristan answered.

Walter's large form filled the doorway. He gaped at the giggling threesome in the bath. "What in the world—"

"Nolle was experimenting with multiple shifts. They were all fish, for a bit."

"Sorry I missed the fun," Walter said, not looking sorry at all. "The horses are in good shape, my lord; recovering well after such a long winter journey. Malvo was stuffing himself with oats when I left."

"Good. I want to go into the city and have a look around, but we'll go on foot and let the horses keep resting."

Walter raised his eyebrows. "There are plenty of other horses available. Or I could arrange for a litter, like the one Mali Uzuri was using."

"On foot, Walter."

"As you wish, my lord. But you might get mobbed. We should probably have an escort."

"Very well. Arrange it, please, but quickly. The rest of you, get dried off and ready to go."

"Thank goodness," Nolle said, with an impudent toss of her head. "This place is boring." As Kristan heaved himself to his feet, her expression softened into something like pity. "I'm sorry you couldn't be a fish, too. It was fun."

He shrugged. "I already know how to swim."

While everyone made ready, Kristan went into his chamber. From his cache of money, he took a few coins, then hesitated. *I'm sick of frugality*, he thought. He took a generous handful of coins, placed them in a soft leather bag and thrust it into his tunic.

His fingers encountered Tansy's note. He pulled it out and placed it on a nearby table, then reconsidered. *Someone might see it,* he thought, and dropped the note into the dying embers of the fireplace. As the parchment burst into flame, he felt a sudden flare of bitterness. *The meeting would be perfectly innocent. Besides, I'm the StoneKing. I can do as I please, no matter what anyone thinks.*

Even as the arrogant words formed in his brain, the Stone grew cold against his chest. Its disapproval made him both ashamed and resentful, and when he rejoined the others, he was almost surly.

At the main doors of the palace they were met by a score of pikemen, with a grinning, bowing Captain Ommald at their head. Kristan resisted the urge to roll his eyes at what seemed excessive precaution, but as soon as they stepped into the streets of Seagirt, he realized Walter was right. People came at the run, crowding close for a better view of the royal party, elbowing and treading on each other's toes in their eagerness. At a barked order from Captain Ommald, the pikemen surrounded the company. "Now then, my lord, where would you like to go?" Ommald asked. "The marketplace near the docks, perhaps? Everything in the world for sale there."

Kristan nodded. With the pikemen pushing back the curious and shielding the company somewhat from all the staring eyes, they made their way to the clamor and bustle of Seagirt's marketplace. The breeze off the harbor was cold and fresh on Kristan's face, but as soon as they passed among the tents and stalls and little shops, the cool air gave way to the heat of braziers and cookfires and massed bodies, the mingled odors of food and people and animals. Men and women stood haggling over crates of fruit, trays of fish fresh from the sea, cages of exotic beasts and kegs of wine and beer. Many people were eating as they bartered, talking with their mouths full, spewing bits of half-chewed food with each shouted offer and counter-bid. *All these people do is stuff their faces*, Kristan thought. *It's a good thing we got here before Lorz. If someone here bought one of the centaurs, they'd probably try to eat it.*

Deeper into the marketplace the food stalls gave way to pavilions featuring vast displays of the cloth for which Dyer was famous. Kristan and his party paused to finger soft velvets, shimmering silks and nubby linens, dyed in every color imaginable, woven in every conceivable pattern. Obsequious merchants bowed and showed off their finest wares, promising Kristan *the best, only the very best for you, my lord, and at a price I couldn't dream of offering to anyone else.* He lingered over a bolt of crimson so dark it was almost black, like the color of dried blood, but when the merchant began recommending tailors who could fit tunics *like skin, my lord, like a second skin, and have the finished product to you before nightfall*, he turned away, the idea of anyone touching him raising the hair on the nape of his neck.

After the cloth came jewelry, trays and trays of it: first cheap necklaces and bracelets and earrings, brooches and clasps and combs glittering with gilt and colored glass, then finer, more costly adornments brought out from under counters for Kristan's inspection. A beautiful ring caught his eye: a single large sapphire; not faceted, but smoothed into a graceful curve and set deep into a thick band of silver. Its seller was a woman, heavy-jowled with deepset eyes, and she leaned over the counter with a confidential air as Kristan slipped the ring on his first finger. "Feel the weight of it," she whispered. "That's a ring of substance, my lord; and the stone is without parallel. I've had it in my stock for some time, but you're the first I've let try it on. How well it looks on you, my lord."

"It's a handsome ring," Sir Walter said, as Kristan raised his hand to the light.

"You should buy it, my lord," Serle said, breathless with awe. "Look, it's got a star in the middle of it."

"*Omorfo*," Astéria breathed, leaning over his shoulder to look. "Pretty."

"Everyone in Dyer has fancy things," Nolle said. "You're more important than they are. You should have fancy things, too."

"It's the truth," Sir Mitchell said, keeping his voice low. "I hate to see you so plain amongst all these peacocks, my lord."

Kristan shook his head. "I'm a plain man," he said, but the ring's gleam woke a strange yearning in his heart. *It's the color of Heather's eyes*, he thought. *Exactly the color of her eyes. I could look at it and think of her, and that would be some comfort.* "How much?" he asked the woman, and she whispered a price he found outrageous. *But why shouldn't I have it?* he thought defiantly. *Why must I always be so prudent? I'm the StoneKing and I can have what I want.*

He put the money on the counter, and the jeweler bowed deeply. "You do me great honor, my lord. Please, take the ring as my gift, as a token of my respect." But she was already scraping the money into her hand, and Kristan turned away, the ring an unfamiliar weight on his finger.

They had moved on to a stall featuring maps and books, and were bent over a fine map of Malchea when Matthew, Geoffrey and Kennet shouldered through the crowd, looking glum. "No word, my lord," Kennet said. "We quizzed every merchant and fisherman on the harbor, but no one's seen a ship like the one Astéria described, not for months."

Even before Serle turned to Astéria to translate, the look of happy interest was fading from her face. "*Lypámai*," Serle said, patting her hand. "I am sad. *Eímai* limp . . . *eimai* lump . . ."

"*Eímai lypíménos*," Astéria said, trying to smile and failing. She laid a hand on her chest. "I say to me: *Na eísai ypomonetikoí*."

"What does that mean?" Nolle asked.

"It mean . . ." Astéria put up one hand, palm out, as if trying to halt some unseen person approaching. "It mean be quiet. Wait."

Sir Geoffrey leaned close to Kristan. "Some say this Lorz might not show up until spring. They say he sometimes continues south, and then doubles back to Seagirt when his hold is full."

Kristan's heart sank, and although he tried to keep his expression neutral, Astéria turned to him, clutching her cloak against her chest. "What Geoffrey say? What?"

"Nothing important," Kristan said, even though his mind was already scrambling for solutions. "Lorz will be here soon, Astéria; don't worry."

She looked so miserable that Kristan's pleasure in his new purchase faded. *Selfish*, he thought. *Selfish and foolish. I can't keep clinging to something I can't have.* Impulsively, he pulled the ring off and held it out to her. "Here. A present."

The people peering past the pikemen murmured excitedly.

"No, Kreestan," Astéria said. "Ees yours."

"It will look better on you. Prettier. 'Omorfo. Please take it . . . as a gift."

Astéria's lower lip trembled. "You are kind, *Vasiliá* Kreestan."

She started to reach for the ring. "Wait," Walter said, interposing his bulk between them. "If we do it that way, all our hard work will be for naught. With your permission, my lord?"

He held out his own hand. Kristan gave him the ring and with a genteel bow, the knight presented it to Astéria.

"Which of them is courting her?" someone in the crowd whined.

"Thank you, Walter; I wasn't thinking," Kristan murmured.

Astéria slid the ring onto her hand; it was too small for her forefinger, but it fit her little finger perfectly. "Thank you, Kreestan," she said softly.

They lingered in the marketplace for some time. Kristan bought Serle a neat little dagger in a leather sheath; Nolle received a thin cuff of copper that just fit her skinny wrist. He purchased tankards of a robust brown ale for his knights, sweet pear cider for the children, a pale, fragrant wine for Astéria and himself. They sampled peculiar fruits and nuts coated in piquant spices. They tasted a tart with a thick yellow filling that was both sweet and sour, and a kind of hot pickle that made them gasp and fan their fiery mouths. The pikemen kept the curious far enough back that Kristan was able to ignore the stares and the murmurs, but while he took a distant satisfaction in his companions' pleasure, he was too worried to enjoy it himself. *What am I to do if this Lorz never appears? I can't wait here for him indefinitely. I'll have to take Astéria on to O Tópos. I could tell Torrin about this Lorz; could he mount a search for the ship himself? Would it put his people at greater risk? Can their ships even travel on the open ocean? Should I send ships of my own after Lorz? Can I spare the ships and the men? I could leave my Reaches here in charge of the search, but they're not working together as it is. What am I going to do about that situation?* Like a dog chasing its tail, his worries pursued each other around in his brain without clamping onto a solution. Astéria, too, had grown quiet; she twisted her new ring on her finger and gazed into space as the children and knights exclaimed over each gustatory discovery.

"Are you tired, my lord?" Matthew asked at last. "Shall we go back to the palace?"

Before Kristan could answer, a sudden clamor rose from the dockside end of the marketplace: a scream, a chorus of shouts, the crash of something being knocked over. "What in the world . . . ?" Matthew muttered.

"Some squabble over prices, no doubt," Geoffrey said.

"Folk here might yell when they barter, but they don't come to blows," Captain Ommald said. "I'll go have a look." He snapped his fingers at one of the pikemen. As the pair started toward the disturbance, their way was blocked by a crowd of people trying to flee from it. "Brigands!" someone shouted. "Thieves!"

The merchants shoved their wares beneath the counters, slammed lids on crates, pushed the most valuable items into their own pockets. The crashing and shouting was getting closer, and people surged past the royal party, elbowing them in their panic. The knights and pikemen surrounded Kristan, Astéria and the children, trying to protect them, but they were being squeezed back against one of the stalls, and Kristan found himself pressed closer and closer to Astéria. "Keep apart!" Nolle cried. "I can't hold it if you touch!"

Serle forced his skinny body between Astéria and Kristan, trying with all his might to keep them separated. At the same moment Nolle suddenly shifted into a bird and shot straight up, relieving some of the pressure on the group. "Wiche!" someone cried, pointing at the fluttering form. "She's Wiche!"

The crowd, startled by this new disturbance, shied back, creating even more room. "Pikes out!" Captain Ommald roared. "Stand clear of the StoneKing, you fools!"

The sharp tips of the weapons thrust out and the crowd fell back even further, just as a nearby stall went over with a crash and a familiar voice bellowed, "Out of the way, you *hrokafull* Dyerians! I have a right of free passage from the StoneKing!"

The crowd parted, and there stood Olaf Sigurdson.

One arm was loaded with cloth, a haunch of meat and loaves of fresh bread. In the other was his battle axe. On his chest was the glittering medallion Kristan had given him, engraved with the symbols of all four countries of the realm. Behind him were more Northmen, their arms piled high with looted goods. At the sight of Kristan and his guard, they froze. Everything went suddenly silent.

"Olaf," Kristan said. His voice sounded plaintive and far away.

Olaf's ruddy face went pale. His mouth opened and closed, until finally a single word came out, in a voice that was little more than a startled croak. "*Fiskur?*"

"Olaf, what are you doing?"

Olaf cleared his throat, grinned sheepishly and lowered his axe. "Just getting supplies," he said. "Just getting a few supplies for a voyage. What in the world are you doing here, *Fiskur?*" He cleared his throat again and dropped the loot he carried. "I mean StoneKing."

Another Northman let out a braying laugh, shoved his way to Olaf's side and regarded Kristan with a sardonic smile. "So, *bróðir*—this is your famous friend?"

There was no mistaking the resemblance between them. They were both big men, bearded and blond, with the same heavy brow, fleshy nose and high cheekbones. Sigurd Sigurdson was a little shorter than Olaf, a little less broad through the shoulders, but the greatest difference between the two was in their eyes. Olaf's gaze was sea-blue, good-humored and forthright; Sigurd's a shifting, menacing blue-gray. Within his beard, his mouth was a mere slash, lips so thin they were almost invisible. "This is the reason you forsook your ship and the sea?" he went on, looking Kristan up and down. "This little runt is the StoneKing?"

"Watch your tongue, Northman," Sir Geoffrey growled.

"Geoff," Walter said under his breath.

"I'm Kristan Gemeta, and I am the StoneKing," Kristan said. Sigurd raised one bushy eyebrow. "Well, I'm Sigurd

Sigurdson, and I bow to no man."

"I didn't expect you would." Kristan turned to Olaf. "Do you and your brother have everything you need?"

Olaf swallowed hard and darted a look at his brother. Sigurd only crossed his arms and stared at Kristan, the mocking smile still in place. "I think . . . I think so," Olaf said.

"Good." Kristan turned to the gaping onlookers. "Olaf Sigurdson is my great friend and has been given the right of free passage throughout my realm. He and his company are to be shown every courtesy. Pass the word that the bills for the items taken, and any damage done in the taking, should be sent to the palace." His gaze lit on the small brown bird perching on the awning just over his head. "Come down from there."

Sigurd guffawed. "You talk to birds, StoneKing? Do they talk back?"

"Now, please, Nolle." Kristan put out one hand and the bird fluttered to him. The instant its small clawed feet touched his fingers, the spell broke and suddenly Nolle was standing beside him, her hand in his. The Northern crew muttered in amazement and Sigurd's eyebrows shot up, although Olaf grinned, looking more like himself.

Kristan let go of Nolle's hand. "Olaf, my friend, I'd be pleased if you and your brother would dine with me at the palace tonight. Clearly, we have a great deal to talk about. Are your ships docked nearby?" Olaf nodded, and Kristan gestured Ommald forward. "Captain, would you and your men kindly help my Northern friends carry their supplies to their ships? And then would you mount a guard to keep the curious away from them? Thank you. Olaf, I'll look for you and Sigurd at sundown. Good day."

He strode through the marketplace, and the people gave way before him, like a school of fish parting before a ship's bow. Astéria, the knights and the children hurried in his wake, but he did not slow down until they were well away and climbing the hill back to the palace.

"That was well handled, my lord," Walter said, as Kristan paused to catch his breath.

"That man is your friend?" Nolle demanded, her eyes still ablaze.

"Was," Geoffrey said.

"He still is," Kristan said. To his dismay, his voice was trembling and his legs felt as if they might give way at any moment.

"What on earth was he doing, roaring through the marketplace like that?" Matthew said. "He knows full well Dyer is part of your realm. Why would he terrorize your people?"

"It's that brother of his, that Sigurd," Mitchell said.

Astéria stepped close and peered into his face. "Kreestan, you sick?"

"You're very pale, my lord," Kennet said. "Shall I get some kind of conveyance for you?"

Kristan waved one hand impatiently. "I'm fine. Let's move on before these damned Seagirt gawkers start gathering again."

But he was not fine; his head was spinning, his stomach churning. *Olaf*, he thought, as they hurried on to the palace. *My friend. My comrade. My ally. Why has he turned against me?*

Raul and Piri Neff met them at the palace's main entrance. "I was told you went out to see the city," Raul said, smiling. "I hope it didn't disappoint."

"No," Kristan said. "Piri, be prepared for an influx of outraged creditors in very short order."

Piri's brow furrowed. "My lord?"

"Olaf Sigurdson and his brother just cut a rather broad swath through the marketplace."

"Olaf?" Raul repeated. "What in the world—"

"Both Sigurdsons will be joining me for dinner tonight," Kristan went on. "Please see that appropriate arrangements are made. I'd like all three Reaches in attendance. You as well, Piri. I think this meeting may be a difficult one."

* * *

"Everything all at once," Bastian muttered, as he thumbed through the latest messages from Hogia. "First, the courier from Malchea, then the packet from Norwinn, and now this. My brain is awhirl, I tell you."

"I was hoping we might hear from the StoneKing today," Randolf said. "But I suppose it's too soon."

"Too soon by a few days," Quinn Logan said absently, his eyes darting back and forth over the message from Malchea.

"So what does Lockward have to say?"

Quinn grunted. "It's an apology—a rather abject one—for his daughter's behavior."

"I expect the additional troops at the border did the trick," Randolf said, grinning.

"There's a postscript from the lady herself at the end." Quinn cleared his throat and read aloud: "*Father is ashamed of me, and rightly so. I made a great fool of myself, and I hope with all my heart you will forgive my arrogance and bad temper.*"

"I'll wager he made her write it," Randolf said.

"I'll wager he dictated every word," Bastian said, with a chuckle. "Now what in the world is this? Has Alister run out of fresh parchment?"

Both knight and councilor craned to look at the document Bastian held. "It's struck through on the one side," Randolf said.

"Oh, dear," Bastian said, bending his head to study the missive more closely. "Oh, dear. I know the StoneKing said to approve anything Lady Heather asked, but this is . . . different."

Quinn Logan peered over the scribe's shoulder. "She's considering Ravelin Seachlan's offer of marriage?" he muttered. "Oh, dear, indeed."

"What on earth is she thinking?" Randolf said.

"She's an independent woman of means," Quinn said, sitting back with a shrug. "She can do as she likes."

"But she doesn't like Ravelin. Or at least, she didn't."

"Things change."

"She turned Sir Kennet down last summer," Bastian said. "It broke his heart; he was mad for her." He lowered his voice to a whisper. "Rumor has it that she and the Gemeta were lovers."

"Let's not gossip about the StoneKing's personal life, shall we?" Quinn said, a little too crisply. "A great deal has happened since last summer. A rebel girl has grown into a formidable soldier, an outcast boy into a powerful king. Youthful longings give way to more mature demands; it's the way of the world."

"But wouldn't marrying Lady Heather allow Ravelin to take control of Hogia's military?" Randolf asked.

"I think it's more likely Lady Heather will take control of Ravelin," Bastian said drily. "All the same, should I put this aside until the StoneKing can be consulted?"

"He said to approve any request she makes," Quinn said, rereading the message from Malchea. "Besides, Lockward's conciliatory tone makes me think that an alliance between his daughter and the StoneKing is still very much a possibility."

"I don't think he likes Princess Jelena one bit," Randolf said.

"Be that as it may, such a match would be of great advantage to the realm. And the realm comes first; he knows that." For a breath, Quinn's stern expression wavered. "If the StoneKing has any lingering feelings for Lady Heather, her request to marry Ravelin would put an end to them."

"He still won't like it," Randolf insisted.

Quinn put down the parchment, folded his arms and leaned toward the old knight. "All right, Randolf, let me put it to you this way. If Kristan Gemeta was sitting here right now, what do you think he would say? 'Tell her no?'"

"Well . . . I suppose you're right."

"So then." Quinn nodded to Bastian. With a little sigh, the scribe dipped his quill in the ink. At the bottom of Lady Heather's message, in his most careful hand, he wrote a single word:

APPROVED

CHAPTER FOURTEEN

Kristan sat across the table from Olaf, watching as his friend worked his way through a breast of goose, a steaming heap of root vegetables, a thick loaf of bread and a great flagon of ale. Conversation thus far had been desultory, centering mostly on the food and the weather. Sigurd ate heartily as well, but each time he stabbed his knife into a cut of meat or swallowed a goblet of wine in a single gulp, he eyed Kristan as if to say *I could devour you, too, little king—in one bite, and not even have to chew.* Raul, Dell, Piri and Kristan's knights kept largely quiet, but Marcus had kept up a steady stream of jokes and gibes that had initially been welcome, but grew more tiresome with each refill of his goblet.

Serle was in his place just behind Kristan's chair, but Astéria and Nolle had remained in the royal suite; Nolle sullen but Astéria visibly relieved by Kristan's reprieve. "I am tired for this thing," she told Kristan. "This smiling, not talking—ees *hard.*"

Kristan had to agree. He was still coldly angry about the Northmen's pillage of the marketplace, still wondering how to broach the topic, but as he studied Olaf, he saw how haggard and dispirited his friend seemed. Unlike his brother, he avoided meeting Kristan's gaze. There was something desperate in the vigor with which he ate.

Sigurd thrust his knife into a great joint of meat and dropped it on his plate as he eyed Kristan's barely-touched food. "You're not much of an eater, StoneKing."

"My appetite has always been small."

"That's not what my brother tells me. He says you're a greedy little fellow—at least, when it comes to crowns."

Olaf's knife clattered onto his plate. He stared at Sigurd, making inarticulate noises through a mouthful of meat and bread.

"Some may think so," Kristan replied evenly. "But I do what I must."

Sigurd pointed his knife at Kristan's head. "So where are your crowns? I thought you might wear all four at once, heaped up on your head like a pile of dogshit."

On Kristan's right, Geoffrey's fingers knotted around his own knife. Olaf groaned through his food.

"I don't wear a crown," Kristan said.

"That's right, that's right." Sigurd's knife drifted down to point at the Stone. "You have your magical Stone. You can change a bird into a girl."

"No. The Stone does no magic itself. It's a talisman. It negates magic. The girl Nolle is Wiche—a shape-shifter. She cast a spell to turn herself into a bird, but when I touched her, the Stone undid the spell."

Sigurd narrowed his eyes and smiled. It was not a pleasant expression. "So . . . if I took your Stone, I could undo magic, too?"

"No, no," Marcus guffawed. "It only works for him. Otherwise, why would they call it the Gemeta Stone? If it worked for everyone, they'd have to call it the Everyone Stone." He laughed again, but no one joined in.

Sigurd began to saw at his meat. "I and my brother and our men—we're plagued with magic."

"How so?" Kristan asked.

"This *sprunga* that keeps us from our home."

"Sprunga?" Matthew repeated. "What's that?"

"In Hogia you call them Cracks," Kristan said. "The Wiche call them Reavings." He turned back to Sigurd. "Olaf told me about this *sprunga*—how you sailed into it during a storm, and afterward found yourself in a place you didn't know. And how you've kept going back there, trying to find your way home."

"Aye, back and back and back again," Sigurd muttered. He pushed a gobbet of meat into his mouth. His expression grew distant as he chewed and swallowed. "Four times we've been back since Olaf rejoined us, and yet the accursed place still spits us out in the same ill-starred sea. Its magic gave us a safe harbor in the storm, but now it won't let us go back."

"Four times," Kristan repeated. "You must be weary of the journey."

Sigurd twisted a hunk of bread off the loaf in front of Olaf. "Many of my men—even my own brother—want to give up."

"Not give up, bróðir," Olaf protested.

Sigurd only stared at the bread as if he hadn't heard. "They say it's no use," he said, his voice rising. "They say we should accept our fate and make a life here. Wherever here is. Whatever a life here would be, without our families—our wives and children." He flung the bread aside and slammed both fists on the table. "Be damned to them! As long as I'm captain, we'll go back as many times as it takes. We'll ram our ships down that bölvaður sprunga's throat until it's forced to swallow us down!"

He snatched up his joint of meat and began to gnaw at it, his teeth scraping loudly against the bone.

Olaf looked across the table at Kristan, desperation etched in every feature of his face. "I'm afraid we're going to lose the men, Kristan. They mutter behind our backs. They look to the shore and talk about how one place would make a fine place to build a home, how another has good meadows for pasturing. We've lost two from Sigurd's ship already; they jumped overboard after our last voyage and tried to swim for shore, but they sank like stones. If we lose many more, we'll have no chance to get home. No chance at all."

"Cowards," Sigurd growled. "They deserved to die."

"That's why we came to Seagirt," Olaf went on. "We've run out of places to poach; the people know us now and they hide their goods and themselves whenever they spot us."

"Where?" Kristan said, suddenly uneasy. "Where have you been poaching?"

Olaf went red to the roots of his hair. "Our usual places," he said. "Stratheden . . . and Norwinn."

"You've been poaching on Norwinn?" Kristan's insides seemed to knot into a tight ball. He gripped the arms of his chair.

"Not poaching, exactly," Olaf said quickly. "I show the medallion you gave me, and the people give what they can. Or at least, they did."

"That's how you're using the medallion? As a permit to rob my people?"

Sigurd looked up, his teeth still fixed in the joint of meat. Olaf's expression turned mulish. "It's our way, Kristan. I told you that a hundred times."

"Olaf, I offered you money. Time and time again. If you were in need, all you had to do was ask."

Sigurd snorted. "You'd like that, wouldn't you? To have the *Norðurmenn* come to you with their hands out and their eyes downcast, begging for scraps? So the rest of the world can see how the little StoneKing has tamed the brigands?"

Geoffrey shot to his feet. "You mind your tongue—"

"Mind yours, you Norwinnian *stykki af skit*!" Sigurd said, rising so abruptly that his chair went over with a crash.

"Gentlemen, gentlemen," Raul said, raising both hands in a placating gesture. "We're all friends here—"

"Your stinking ships have dogged us along the coastline for the last month," Sigurd snarled. "Three days ago one fired on us. They used incendiaries!" He barked out a mirthless laugh. "Lucky for us Norwinn archery is as poor as its seamanship."

"Hold on, hold on there—" Mitchell started to say. All the knights were on their feet now, shouting, along with Raul and Piri Neff, whose attempts at calming the situation were lost in the uproar. Serle's mouth was agape; Dell sat watching, his head tilted to one side; Marcus smirked and poured himself another goblet of wine. Olaf bent his head and knotted both hands in his hair.

Kristan clutched the Stone, trying to quell his rising rage and nausea. *Controlcontrolcontrol*, he told himself, but other thoughts crowded close. *A month. My ships have been pursuing them for a month, perhaps longer, but never a word about it in Norwinn's reports. Why didn't Melissa tell me? Why didn't I know?*

"Sit down." He did not speak loudly, but his men quickly obeyed, leaving Sigurd alone on his feet. "Master Sigurdson, please sit down," Kristan continued, in a more moderate tone. "Serle, help him with his chair."

Serle scurried to obey, but Sigurd waved him off, righted his chair and dropped into it. He sat glaring at Kristan, breathing hard, the great veins of his neck throbbing. Kristan gazed back, waiting for his own pulse to slow.

Olaf raised his head. "I'm sorry, Kristan."

"I'm sorry, too," Kristan said, but he kept his eyes on Sigurd.

"You'll get no apology from me," Sigurd said. His voice was low and guttural, as if wrenched from the very bottom of his soul. "I curse the day my *hálfviti bróðir* met you and let you make a fool of him. I curse the day you pulled him out of the Mor and made him your lapdog." With a shaking hand, he poured himself more wine. "You should have let him drown."

"*O bróðir minn . . .*" Olaf whispered.

Sigurd drained his goblet and put it down with a bang. He did not answer. No one spoke.

"How long will it take to outfit your ships for your voyage?" Kristan asked, breaking the uncomfortable silence.

Olaf cleared his throat. "Another two days, maybe three. We need to make some repairs."

Kristan turned to Raul. "See that they're given every assistance. Pay all their expenses—" Piri Neff let out an inadvertent squeak, but Kristan fixed him with a hard stare. "Out of my personal treasury."

Sigurd guffawed. "That eager to see us go, are you?"

Kristan turned the same cold gaze on him. "What else can I do to help you?"

Sigurd opened his mouth as if to retort, but then he hesitated. A strange, desperate light filled his eyes. "You could come with us."

"Come with you?"

"Yes." Sigurd banged his hands on the table. "Yes! Your Stone can undo magic. Maybe it can undo the *sprunga's* magic."

"It's a talisman. It protects me from magic. That's all it does. It can't undo a Reaving."

"Have you ever tried?"

Dell had been so quiet that his question made Kristan jump. "What?"

"Have you ever tried?" Dell said again. His face was blandly curious, his tone reasonable.

"Tried?" Kristan echoed, his voice scaling up. "Of course not. It wouldn't work."

"You can't know for sure. Not until you've tried."

Kristan gaped at him. "Dell, I've stood over Reavings again and again. In Hogia and in Fandrall as well. Nothing happens."

"Come with us to Stratheden and try, *Fiskur.*" Olaf's face was suddenly alive with hope. "If you really want to help us. It's north of Stratheden's castle town—only about seven days' voyage from here."

"I'm sorry, Olaf. I can't."

"Can't?" Sigurd said. "Or won't?"

"Both. I can't leave my realm. I won't. Even if there was a chance the Stone could somehow send you home again, I have too many responsibilities to chance such a dangerous journey. It would be madness to try."

The instant the words were out of his mouth, he wished them unsaid. Sigurd stood up slowly, his manner so menacing that all five of Kristan's knights rose with him. But it was to his

brother that he turned. "I'm done. Sit here and exchange pleasantries with your friend the StoneKing if you like, but I'm going
back to my ship."

He strode from the room. Olaf got up as slowly as an old
man. "*Fiskur*," he said, spreading his big hands. "*Fiskur*, please.
Even if it doesn't work . . . even if the Stone can't send us
back . . . maybe then Sigurd will realize it's over. Maybe he'll
finally accept that we have to start a new life here."

"Olaf, I've been king for less than a year; far less. A journey like that would keep me away from my realm for a month
or more." Kristan glanced down the table at his three Reaches:
Raul alert and attentive, Dell staring into space again, Marcus
grinning lazily, as if enjoying the show. The sight made his guts
writhe. "Everything is still too unsettled. I can't risk it."

Olaf heaved a great sigh and started to go.

"Olaf, wait," Kristan said, hating himself for what he was
about to do. "I'll create an account for you here in Seagirt. And
I'll set up a similar one in Moordock. You can draw funds from
them to outfit your ships and crews, at any time, in any amount.
But the poaching on my lands and the intimidation of my people—it stops now. Do you understand?"

Olaf slowly straightened up. He seemed to grow larger: his
big shoulders spread, his chest swelled, his jaw clenched and
his sea-blue eyes went cold. "I understand," he said, his voice
so soft that it was barely audible. He turned and walked out of
the room.

Kristan pushed his plate aside, folded his hands on the glossy
tabletop and stared at them, overwhelmed with guilt and anger
and sorrow. The knights sank into their chairs. No one moved
or spoke. At last, Serle stepped quietly forward, picked up a
pitcher of wine and refilled Kristan's goblet. Kristan nodded his
thanks. He lifted the goblet to his lips, but his hand shook so
badly that the golden cup's rim rattled against his teeth.

"I'm sorry, Kristan," Raul said. "That can't have been easy
for you."

Again, Kristan nodded. He took a sip of the wine, but it was bitter on his tongue, and he set it aside. "Piri, kindly assign someone to track and record whatever expenses the Northmen incur. I don't want every opportunistic merchant and trader in Seagirt claiming the Sigurdsons owe them money."

"At once, my lord."

"And I need to write to my sister. Now."

"Yes, my lord."

Piri hurried from the room, and Marcus laughed as he poured himself more wine. "You're quite the juggler, my friend." His mocking grin faded as Kristan glared at him. "It was a joke, Kristan."

"You seem to regard much of what I do as a joke."

"Not at all, not at all; it's just all this balancing and steadying and trying to keep everything from toppling over. There's a juggler who turns up in the Seagirt marketplace on occasion—he puts metal plates on poles, and then spins them. Gets a dozen plates going at once, and then runs back and forth between them to keep them all going. But he's an amateur compared to you." He raised his goblet to Kristan. "I salute you, Master Juggler."

It's a joke, it's a joke, he doesn't mean to insult you rattled through Kristan's brain, but the turmoil in his stomach drowned out rational thought. "Perhaps if my Reaches did their jobs, my running back and forth could be kept to a minimum."

"So, will you be off to visit your sister next?" Marcus asked, oblivious to his rising anger.

"What for?" Kristan's head was beginning to pound—*naturally*, he thought. *Cramps and nausea, then the headache.*

"I thought that's why you wanted to write her. I thought you might want to introduce her to your new companion."

"What are you talking about?"

Before Marcus could answer, Piri came back in, bearing ink, quills, parchment and sealing wax. "Shall I write for you, my lord?"

"I'll do it myself," Kristan said. He had dipped his quill and was deliberating on just how to frame Melissa's reprimand when Marcus spoke again.

"I'm talking about Lady Astéria, of course. She's an extraordinary beauty, Kristan; I congratulate you."

"On what?"

"On your conquest. I'm a bit surprised, though. I never thought your tastes ran to the big, buxom, docile type. I always thought you preferred your women small and scrappy."

"Marcus . . ." Raul said, in a voice laden with warning.

"Oh, Raul, all Seagirt is abuzz with the news that the StoneKing gave a ring to his lady friend today—even if he did have Walter pass it to her."

"It isn't what you think," Kristan said.

"She's not your mistress? Not even your sweetheart?"

As the denial rose to his lips, Kristan hesitated. Even the most meager explanation might arouse further curiosity, and he was in no mood to sidestep the questions that would inevitably follow. "I don't have to explain my relationship with Lady Astéria to you," he said crossly. "Leave off talking about it."

Marcus smirked but said no more, and Kristan bent over the parchment. *Sister*, he wrote:

> *I have met with the Sigurdsons and was distressed to hear of their raids on coastal villages of Norwinn. To render further incursions unnecessary, I have set up an account for them in Seagirt so they can draw funds as needed. Please see that a similar fund is created for them in Moordock, to be drawn against my personal treasury. Why was this news kept from me? I remind you that as my Reach, your responsibility is not only to deal with such matters, but to keep me informed of them.*

He signed his name and thrust the parchment at Piri Neff. "See that this goes to Norwinn promptly."

"We can send a speedy little sailboat out first thing in the morning," Raul said. "One can generally make its way up the Mor faster than larger ships."

"Always so much hurry," Dell muttered.

Kristan threw down the quill. "If you have something to say, Dell, then say it out loud."

"Everything we do is in a hurry," Dell said, unperturbed. "Realm riders, realm runners, fast little realm messenger boats. Sometimes I think it would behoove our messengers to go a little more slowly."

Marcus hooted. "What, you want realm walkers now?"

"What purpose would that serve?" Raul asked, his mouth in an irritable twist.

"So they could see. So they could observe. There's so much that we miss because we're in such a hurry. A slower messenger would be able to see so much more."

Only if you walk slow as we do, with your eyes and your ears open, with your skin feeling and your nose smelling and your tongue tasting the air like a snake . . .

The words swept through Kristan's memory like a spring breeze, soft with promised warmth but accompanied by a chilly undercurrent that made him shiver. He shook it off and stood up.

"Yes, that would make a change. I have an even better idea: messengers who bring me *all* the news from my kingdoms, instead of just what my Reaches think I should hear."

He stalked from the chamber, with Serle and the knights on his heels. Just as Kennet drew the door closed, Marcus' voice drifted after them: "Well, what a temper he's in. I guess the boy isn't getting any after all."

Kennet shut the door quickly. The knights looked at the floor, the wall, anywhere but at Kristan.

"Was he talking about me, my lord?" Serle asked. "What does he mean, I'm not getting any?"

Kristan's face was hot with embarrassment and anger. "I'm going out," he said. "Get Malvo ready."

"I'll arrange an escort—" Walter started to say.

"No escort."

Geoffrey frowned. "My lord, someone should accompany you. Maybe just a few of us—"

"Are you deaf?" Kristan nearly shouted. "I said no escort! I'm sick of making a spectacle of myself every time I set foot out of this palace!"

"Of course, my lord," Kennet said quickly. "It's dark out, and with your hood up you can probably pass unnoticed. But may I suggest you take Serle with you?"

"Why?"

"He needs the practice," Matthew said.

"And he could hold Malvo while . . . if you decide to go inside . . . someplace," Mitchell added.

They think I'm going to a doxy house, Kristan realized, and he choked back a derisive laugh. "All right, I'll take Serle. And you can set your minds at rest. I won't be gone long. I'm going to pay a call on Mali Uzuri."

* * *

Kennet was right: in the dark, with his hooded cloak covering his own figure as well as Malvo's scars, Kristan was able to pass through the streets of Seagirt without attracting notice. To quiet his knights' concerns, Kristan was wearing his sword, and Serle, trotting ahead on his pony to ask directions, had thrown back his own cloak to display his new dagger. *Yes, we're a formidable pair*, Kristan thought sourly; *me with a sword I haven't touched in six months, and Serle with a dagger he has no idea how to use.*

Serle was still a nervous horseman, yanking at his pony's bit and kicking it too sharply when he wanted to go faster. Kristan reminded himself that the boy would need additional instruction. *Not that he shows any promise as a squire. The knights are right about that. I was a sentimental fool to choose him. I can't keep letting sentiment overrule sense.*

In answer to Serle's piped questions, passersby pointed the way to Mali Uzuri's home, a surprisingly modest dwelling on a slight rise overlooking the harbor. It was fronted by a low stone wall that enclosed a simple graveled courtyard. In the yellow lamplight near the front doors, a single small figure grunted and feinted with a sword.

Now that's a likely boy, Kristan thought. The child was young, perhaps only nine or so, but there was nothing of youth's awkwardness in the way he handled his weapon. He was so intent on his practice that he did not notice their approach until their shadows overwhelmed his own.

"Good evening," Kristan said, putting back his hood. "Is Mali Uzuri at home?"

The boy gaped at him. Just then the front door opened, revealing a tall, willowy young woman. Kristan recognized her as one of Mali's granddaughters, but before he could speak, she dipped into a graceful curtsey. "My lord," she said, "please, come inside. Desta, stop staring," she added to the boy. "Put that foolish sword away and tell Grandmother the StoneKing is here."

The boy sheathed his sword and pushed past her into the house.

"Serle, stay here with the horses," Kristan said. "I won't be long."

Just inside the doors was a warm, pleasant anteroom. "You do us great honor," the young woman said, as she took his cloak and gauntlets. "Grandmother will be so pleased."

"Pleased indeed!" Mali Uzuri entered the anteroom with both hands extended in welcome. "A good evening to you, StoneKing. I feared you might be too busy to visit."

Absurdly comforted by the sight of Mali's lined face and twinkling eyes, Kristan smiled. "And I feared I might go mad if I didn't find a few moments to spend with the only sensible person in Seagirt."

Mali let out a snort. "I heard about the Northmen's arrival in the marketplace. I imagine matters have grown even more complicated, but I won't quiz you about them. Come and sit with me, and we'll talk of other things. Ebele, see that the StoneKing's servant is given a hot drink, and send Desta to my work chamber with refreshments.

"You interrupted me when I was working, StoneKing," Mali went on, as she led him down a long, low-ceilinged hallway. "Normally, I'd ask you into the main part of my house, make a great fuss of you and show off my home and family. But my guess is that you wouldn't enjoy that, not tonight."

"You were working this late?"

Mali smiled at him, but it was a kind smile. "I keep forgetting you come from a farming country, my lord, where the workday begins at sunrise and ends at sunset. But I also expect you're no stranger to working into the night yourself." She showed him into a large chamber, brightened by a good fire in the hearth and candles set in mirrored sconces. A large table stood in the center of the room. Its perimeter was covered with small samples of cloth, each stained with a different-colored dye. A jumble of pots, jars and stoppered bottles stood on a tray in the middle of the table, giving off a pungent odor. "My family's wealth comes from its long history as dyers—the profession which gave this country its name," Mali said. "Most of our work is done in a warehouse closer to the docks—that's where I was going the day I met you in the street—but here at home I often experiment, trying to find new blends, new hues. That's what I was doing when you arrived." She spread a small piece of linen on her palm and pointed to a splotch of milky blue color in the middle of it. "Isn't that pretty? But it fades so quickly. I've been trying different fixatives on it, but they alter the color." She clucked regretfully and put the cloth aside. "But enough of that. Come and sit down."

They seated themselves on either side of the fire, on a pair of long, low couches covered in bright cushions and pillows. "May

I offer you some water, my lord?" Mali said, lifting a pitcher from a table at her elbow.

"If it's more of that flavored, scented stuff, no, thank you," Kristan said.

"You don't care for our water?"

"The Dyerian penchant for embellishment is something I can't understand. Even a simple cup of water is made complicated."

Mali laughed. "Actually, there's a good reason for it. Seagirt lies on the edge of the ocean. Water from our wells is often brackish—unpleasant to taste and smell. Hence the flavoring and scenting." She replaced the pitcher and folded her hands in her lap. "Don't judge us too harshly, StoneKing. The customs you find excessive often have very good reasons for being so."

"Is there a reason for the scrabbling for status? The jostling for position? The staring and the whispering and the gossip?"

"You find the Dyerians a difficult people to love, don't you?" Mali tilted her head to one side and studied him. "I remember how you dealt with us last summer in Hogia. So blunt—even brusque. You had no patience with formalities. Farmers and pasturers need no formalities; neither do miners and herders, nor fishermen. But Dyer is populated with merchants, and our lives are a constant stream of bartering and dealing. The more information we have, the stronger our bargaining position. Information is the coin of our realm. Information, along with status and position, give us the advantage when we sit down to negotiate." She grinned at him. "You did well enough at the great feast—made the appropriate faces, said the appropriate words—but it was clear you disapprove of us, of our excess. I disapprove of excess myself, although I appreciate luxury and quality as much as anyone."

"I noticed that your granddaughter answered the door. Do you keep no servants?"

"That's correct, but not because I'm frugal. I hire what and who I need when I need them—bearers for my litter, for example—but they don't live under my roof."

"Why is that?"

"Servants are prone to talking amongst themselves, and of carrying information to ears that will pay for that information. You see, there's that pesky need for information again, my lord. My wealth comes not just from good business sense, but from keeping my dying methods and discoveries within the family—all of whom have a vested interest in maintaining that secrecy." Mali smiled. "Then again, I have a large family, and I raised them to take pride in being self-sufficient. Ah, Desta, there you are."

Kristan looked over his shoulder. The boy Desta stood in the doorway, holding a tray containing a pitcher, two goblets and a bowl of dried fruit and sugared nuts. "Don't just stand there staring," Mali went on. "Bring the refreshments here."

Desta crossed the room to them, and in the bright light Kristan was able to get a better look at him. Unlike the rest of the velvety-black Uzuri family, Desta was tawny-skinned and hazel-eyed. His kinky reddish hair was cropped close to his head, and he was dressed in mud-splattered leggings, low boots and a green tunic trimmed with golden braid. Mali frowned. "Little fool, why are you wearing those clothes to wait on the StoneKing?"

Desta's chin rose defiantly. "What's wrong with them?"

"They're not appropriate, and you know it. Do you want to bring shame on the Uzuri household? Go and change this instant."

"It's just a little dirt," Kristan said. "The boy looks fine to me."

Both Desta and Mali looked at him sharply. The old woman's wrinkled face was startled, but Desta's eyes were suddenly bright with hope. He offered the tray with a graceful bow. "Thank you, my lord. It's an honor to serve you."

Up close, there was something familiar about the boy. His cheekbones were high, his nose broad, his lips full, and the proud assurance in his posture stirred a vague memory in Kristan's brain.

Mali took the tray from the boy and handed him the water pitcher. "If the StoneKing doesn't object to your clothing, then I suppose there's no harm done. Take this back to the kitchen."

"I like your horse," Desta said, ignoring her. "But your squire doesn't know how to handle him."

"Serle is young and still learning, I'm afraid," Kristan said.

"He's a lot older than me, and I could do it, easy," Desta said, with an ill-concealed air of disgust. "I've been riding since I could walk."

"And boasting since you first took breath," Mali snapped. "Do as I told you, Desta."

His lower lip outthrust, Desta bowed and carried the pitcher out. Again, something about the boy's long, confident stride seemed familiar. Mali sighed and sat back in her big chair. "Willful and proud, that one."

"How old is he?" Kristan asked.

Mali studied him for a long moment before she spoke. "Not quite nine."

"He's tall for his age. Is he your grandson?"

Mali shook her head. "A cousin. I'm sure you've noticed the child is different from the rest of the Uzuris. The lineage is . . . well, a bit checkered."

"How so?"

Mali seemed to be weighing her words carefully as she answered. "Some years ago, one of our guild heads took himself a new wife. She was quite beautiful: fair and blue-eyed, with hair so pale it seemed touched by starlight. But she was also very young, and far too flighty to be saddled with such an old man. I had a cousin who was a bit of a rascal . . . well, more than a bit. He carried himself as if he thought everyone was watching, and much of the time they were; the women, at least. Oh, he was a handsome fellow, who could charm the birds right out of the trees."

Come down, Kinglet.

The voice echoed faintly through Kristan's brain and was gone.

"My cousin took a fancy to the new wife, and she to him," Mali went on. "It was a recipe for trouble. Many whispered behind their hands about the two of them. Some even whispered to the husband, but he was captivated and wouldn't hear a word against her.

"In time her belly began to swell, and her husband strutted around as if he was the first man ever to get a woman with child. But when Desta was born—well, it was clear that some other man had primed the wife's pump. The husband thrashed her, and she took the baby and fled. She came looking for poor foolish Bamidel, but so did the husband and his friends, and they caught my cousin here in this house and beat him bloody while she stood with the baby in her arms, screaming."

"Bamidel," Kristan muttered. The name rolled off his tongue with ease, and he felt the same flutter of familiarity. "What happened then?"

"Bamidel managed to escape, with a mob of the husband's friends on his heels. They never caught him, even though the husband offered a generous bounty. Rumor had it he fled to the Exilwald. We haven't seen him since."

I'm a born rascal and deserve to be outcast . . .

"Gabriel," Kristan whispered.

"Is something wrong, my lord?"

Gabriel's smile. The flash of an axe. See you soon . . .

With an effort, Kristan thrust the memory aside. "I think . . . I think I knew Desta's father. We met in the Exilwald."

Mali's face went slack. She sat back slowly. "I had forgotten. I had forgotten you lived there. Are you sure, StoneKing?"

"The man I knew called himself Gabriel. I knew he'd fled Dyer for some reason, but little else. Desta resembles him strongly. Mali, where is Desta's mother? May I speak to her?"

"I don't know where she is. For a while she lived with

us—she had no place else to go, not with Desta—but one day she walked out the door and never came back. She was seen boarding a ship to who knows where. We never heard from her again." Mali leaned toward him, in her eagerness placing her hand on his wrist. "StoneKing, is it possible my cousin could be found and brought back to Dyer? The old merchant is dead now, and his friends would leave Bamidel alone if he was under your protection. Then Desta would have a father, at least."

Kristan withdrew his arm and averted his eyes from her hopeful face. "Gabriel is dead."

For some moments Mali did not speak. "Ah," she said at last, and when Kristan dared to look at her, he found her composed, her features as blank as a closed door.

"I'm sorry to be the bearer of such sad news," he said.

"To be honest, I expected it. For all his charm, Bamidel was a scoundrel at heart. I always knew he'd come to no good end."

"You're wrong, Mali. He died in my service, in the Wichelord's stronghold in Hogia. He died a hero's death."

. . . see you soon seeyousoon . . .

The room seemed to shift and sway, and Kristan caught hold of the Stone to ground himself. "Mali. Did you never approach King Claude about employing Desta as a page at the castle?"

"Claude and his lot would never have allowed Desta to be a page."

"Why not?"

Mali squinted at him. "Not suitable."

"Illegitimacy seems a poor reason to turn away such a likely boy. I could speak to my Reaches and have it arranged."

Once again, Mali Uzuri seemed to choose her words with care. "The people of Seagirt know Desta's history too well, my lord. The child has always been mocked, and in the public eye would be mocked even more."

"Then perhaps a change of scenery is in order."

"What do you mean?"

"Perhaps Desta would do better in a place where his history

isn't known. A boy of his skill would be welcome in my service." From the corner of his eye, Kristan caught a glimpse of Desta in the shadows just outside the doorway, water pitcher tilting in his hand, listening with all his might.

Mali followed his gaze and snapped her fingers irritably. Desta started and hurried off. Mali waited until his footsteps receded, then turned to Kristan. "My lord, Desta is very young, and dreams a child's dreams. A child's dreams shouldn't always be indulged. They may change with age and experience of the world."

"I would hate to see his dreams denied because of his lineage. Promise me you'll think about what I've said, Mali."

Mali shook her head slowly. "You're young yourself, my lord, and perhaps still idealistic in spite of your worries and woes. Not everything can be fixed as easily as we wish. And not everything is as we perceive it to be." Her wrinkled lips pursed as she considered him. "But I'll think on what you've proposed."

"Don't you trust that I'll take care of the boy?"

"I think you will. In fact, I'm sure you will." Mali's eyes began to twinkle. "Perhaps there's a place for Desta in your realm after all. You're a forward-thinking fellow, StoneKing; with your Reaches and your lady commander we've heard so much about. The idea of elevating three tradesmen into such positions of responsibility . . ."

Her voice trailed off, and Kristan was sure it was deliberate. He said nothing, and Mali grinned. "Ah, you think I'm trying to trick you into revealing your feelings, StoneKing, so you don't speak. But your silence alone speaks volumes. It was clear the night of the feast that you were unhappy with your Reaches here." Kristan started to protest, but she held up one dye-stained finger. "Hear me out. If you were from Seagirt, you wouldn't risk silence when someone asks you a leading question. You might say, *you honor me with your presence, my friend*, or *how is your beautiful family*, or even *my, this dish is tasty*. You would smile and deflect, smile and deflect. All of us in Seagirt—councilors and merchants, assuredly, but everyone else as well—all of us keep eyes and ears open, but when we observe something, we pretend that we haven't, and tuck the information away to use later." Her smile broadened. "And I can see from your face that you don't like this idea at all."

"You make me feel like a bumpkin."

"Only by way of warning, my lord. For example, I'm aware that the woman Tansy bribed her way past the guards last night, in an attempt to see you. No, don't ask me how I know; I told you, gossip is the coin of the realm here. But the fact that I know means that others know, just as I know you admired a particular bolt of deepest crimson in the marketplace today. I should thank you for the compliment, by the way; that color is one of my particular blends, and someone bought the bolt the moment you moved on. I also know you tried on a silver ring with a blue stone and seemed to like it very much, and paid full price, without bargaining. You should always bargain, my lord. I also heard that after you bought it and wore it on your own hand, you presented it to your lady companion. You can imagine the conjecture that caused. People are quite curious about your Lady Astéria."

Kristan turned his attention to the bowl of sweets. "My, this is a tasty dish."

Mali laughed and clapped her hands. "Well done, my lord, although I can tell dissembling isn't your nature. But it's our way here. And while not all Dyerians gamble, every one of us is a gamer at heart. We love the ruses, the maneuvers, the schemes and strategies. We love them for their own sake, but if there's something to be gained along the way, so much the better." She was silent for a few moments, and her manner became more somber. "But I see you have a great deal on your mind, my lord, and didn't come here to talk about my family, nor about Dyer's peculiar ways. And now that I've warned you about our trade in gossip and secrets, perhaps you no longer wish to unburden yourself to me."

"It's not an unburdening that I need so much as your opinion."

"I'm at your service, my lord."

"You've sat in meetings with my Reaches. Do you think they're in over their heads?"

Mali blew out a long breath. "They're three different men with three very different approaches to their jobs. It's difficult to judge, my lord."

"I would appreciate it if you'd try."

"Well, then: no, not in over their heads, exactly. Reach Ferrador is hardworking, listens well and takes his duties seriously. He's a bit unimaginative and somewhat naïve, but he keeps an open mind and has managed to avoid being swayed by any particular guild head." She picked up one of the dried fruits, considered it, and then popped it into her mouth. Kristan waited while she chewed and swallowed. "Reach Curry has been equally difficult to sway," she went on, "but his interests lie outside the council chamber and indeed, outside most of the subjects we normally discuss. On the other hand, he has strong powers of observation and isn't afraid to speak his mind." She poured herself a goblet of wine and sat peering into it for a few moments before continuing: "And Reach Tasgall is popular with the guild heads; of all three Reaches he's the one who's fit in most easily, although that may be because he's the most malleable of the three Reaches. But he's very much in Fedro Vincenze's pocket."

Perhaps others are as well, Kristan thought, remembering Tansy's note.

"But still, he's affable and approachable, even if you may not approve of his drinking and carousing." Mali's mouth twisted impishly. "Although you don't seem to disapprove of the company he keeps."

Kristan started. It was as if Mali had been reading his mind. "Are you speaking of Tansy Yeomans?"

"I am. You don't seem to be an impulsive young man, and

yet allowing her to sit at your table was an impulsive act, one that has caused a great deal of talk."

It was on the tip of Kristan's tongue to confess to Mali about Tansy's message, but he kept silent.

"Perhaps I've touched on a sore subject," Mali said.

"Not at all," Kristan said. "Tansy and I were playmates as children. Her parents still live in Kingsmere, where her father is master mason. She disappeared over a year ago, and they feared she was dead. It was a shock to see her, that's all." Kristan rose, and Mali stood with him. "Thank you for your opinion on my Reaches."

"You're welcome. Bear in mind that it's only one opinion, my lord, and there are plenty of others: a veritable garden of them, yours for the plucking."

"Yours, I feel, is honest."

A look of distress flickered across Mali's face and was gone. "I'm just as capable of trickery as the next Dyerian, StoneKing."

Kristan shrugged. "We all do what we must, I suppose. Good evening, Mali." He nodded at her work table. "I hope you find a way to make that blue color stick. It's very pretty."

"If I do, I'll have a bolt dyed for you and send it to Fandrall."

Outside, Desta stood holding Malvo's bridle with one hand and stroking the horse's broad black nose with the other. "Where's my squire?" Kristan asked, and Desta jerked his head contemptuously to the far side of the courtyard, where Serle was trying to catch his pony. The squire's face was flushed and miserable as his mount flirted away from him every time he tried to grab its dragging reins.

"May I help you mount, my lord?" Desta asked.

Kristan raised one eyebrow. "You can help my squire catch his pony, if you please."

Desta nodded and strode across the courtyard. He gave Serle a not-too-gentle push out of the way and in short order, cornered the pony and caught up its reins. Speaking to it sooth-ingly, he brought it back to Kristan, with Serle following, wide-eyed.

"Well done," Kristan said. "You handle horses well, Desta."

"I know swordplay and archery, too," Desta said. "I'm better at it than some of the older boys."

Kristan nodded and swung himself into Malvo's saddle. With an air of disdain, Desta held out the pony's reins to Serle. "Thank you," Serle said, mounting awkwardly. "I wish I knew as much about horses as you."

Desta's only response was a grunt, but he watched with jealous eyes as Kristan and Serle turned their horses toward the palace.

As they clopped slowly through the darkened streets, Kristan tipped his hood back enough to see Serle's dejected expression. "Don't sulk," he said rather sharply. "Desta comes of a wealthy family and likely had plenty of idle time to learn those skills. You've had to work for your living."

"But I still wish I was as good as him," Serle almost whimpered. "Malvo was giving me such a hard time, my lord, jerking his head and nipping, and my own horse got away while I was trying to calm him, but I couldn't catch her and hold Malvo at the same time. Then Desta came along and he got Malvo to behave right away."

"Well, Desta probably couldn't herd sheep to save his life," Kristan said. "You've been my squire for less than a fortnight. You won't master everything right away. Give yourself time." Serle's downcast face brightened, and Kristan repressed the urge to roll his eyes. *So hopeful, so ready to believe the impossible.* A sudden image of Heather fluttered through his mind, no more than a wisp: her bruised and dirty face bathed in the mellow golden light of a summer sunset as she stood looking toward Hogia's castle, blue eyes soft with hope. *Stop it,* he told himself, twitching his mind away before the vision could transform into the silent, despairing Heather of his nightmare. He fixed his gaze on the road ahead and turned his thoughts toward Tansy's note. He had barely begun weighing the advantages and disadvantages of seeing her when a large form on horseback loomed up next to him, so suddenly that he jumped. Serle let out a squawk and scrabbled for his much-prized dagger.

"Put your knife away, boy," Sir Walter said. "Sorry to startle you, my lord."

"Have you been following me?" Kristan demanded, putting back his hood.

The knight's broad, good-natured face turned sheepish. "A bit, my lord. Just to make certain you came to no harm."

"Are the others prowling around Seagirt as well?"

"Mitchell and Matthew stayed with Astéria, but Kennet and Geoffrey rode out with me."

"Where are they now?"

"There's some sort of row at the docks, down where the Northmen are berthed. They went to have a look at what's going on, but I thought I'd better wait for you."

"By the Stone, if Sigurd and his men have started a fight . . ." Kristan muttered, and nudged Malvo into a trot. Walter fell in easily with him, but Serle let out tiny yips of dismay as he struggled to keep pace and stay in his saddle.

As they crested the hill overlooking the docks, the bright moonlight made it easy to spot the two Northern vessels, their sinuous lines at odds with the portlier merchant ships riding at anchor some distance away. Kristan had only a moment to wonder if all their captains had decided to give the Northmen as wide a berth as possible when he realized that another silhouette rode just to the Northern ships' starboard. This one had a vaguely familiar look.

Walter let out a surprised grunt. "That's a Norwinn warship, my lord. Wonder what it's doing here?"

Two clusters of shadowy figures faced each other on the dock, voices raised in argument. Geoffrey and Kennet waited nearby with their horses, leaning attentively toward the knot of people as if ready to intervene. The Sigurdson brothers, flanked by their crews, were squared off against the other group, but all the broad shoulders blocked Kristan's view of the opposition. He reined up and rose in Malvo's stirrups for a better look, and as he did, Olaf took a step back, raising his hands defensively as a small, cloaked figure advanced on him, fist raised. "Tell me where he is, Olaf!" the figure shrilled. "He went out to find you! I know you've seen him!"

Serle let out a giggle. "That's a fierce little lady."

Walter turned to Kristan, his eyes wide. "My lord, that's . . . that's . . ."

Rigid with anger, Kristan lowered himself slowly into the saddle. Below, Olaf was shaking his head and saying something in a placating tone, but his answer only seemed to infuriate the Reach of Norwinn further. "Lying Northern dog!" Melissa cried, and sprang toward him. Her companions restrained her. The Northmen and the warship's crew began to roar at each other.

Controlcontrolcontrol . . .

He nudged Malvo into a slow walk and descended toward the fracas, clenching his teeth before the bile rising in his throat. Serle, still giggling, started to say something more but was shushed by Walter. Kennet and Geoffrey looked up at their approach, but Kristan passed them without a word and continued straight toward the crowd.

In mid-shout, Melissa caught sight of him. Her voice died and she shrank back. The Northmen fell silent and the crew of the Norwinn warship came to sudden, straining attention.

"Kristan," Melissa finally squeaked, "what are you doing here?"

"I might ask you the same question, sister," Kristan replied. His own voice was little more than a growl.

She did not respond, and in the silence Sigurd snorted and turned to Olaf. "You seem to be plagued with Gemetas, *bróðir*."

"Why are you here, Melissa?" Kristan said. "Why aren't you in Norwinn?"

"Nigel," Melissa choked out. "I'm looking for Nigel."

"And where is Nigel?"

"I don't know!" she cried. "A month ago, he left . . . I mean he went . . . I sent him to investigate reports of Northern raids on our coastal villages. And he hasn't come back!" She spun to face Olaf. "He hasn't come back! Why won't you tell me if you've seen him?"

"I told you, Missy, we skirmished with Norwinn warships," Olaf said. "But I've no way of knowing if Nigel was aboard any of them."

"He went to find you! To talk to you!"

"Quiet," Kristan said. "Olaf, when did you last see a Norwinn warship?"

"Three nights back, near the mouth of the Mor," Olaf said. "The one that fired incendiaries at us."

"That was us," Melissa blurted, then clapped a hand over her mouth. Kristan turned a cold stare on her.

"My lord, we didn't fire on them," said one of the Norwinn crew, stepping forward. "They didn't answer our hail and we shot . . . well, we shot *near* them, but not at them."

Sigurd let out a loud, derisive laugh.

"We were trying to get them to stop, my lord, so we could ask them if they'd seen Sir Nigel's ship. And when they didn't stop, we followed them. But we fouled our rudder, and then we ran aground, and then—"

"Who are you?" Kristan demanded.

"I beg your pardon, my lord; I'm Captain Saratt, second-in-command of your fleet in Norwinn."

"And where, may I ask, is the first-in-command of Norwinn's fleet?"

"He's with the First Advisor, my lord. With Sir Nigel."

Sigurd laughed again, and it took all Kristan's willpower not to shriek his outrage: at Captain Saratt, at Olaf, at Sigurd, at Melissa, at anyone within range of his voice. He thrust his hand beneath his cloak and took hold of the Stone with such force that the chain bit into the back of his neck.

"Very well, Captain Saratt. Kindly take your men, board your ship and dock elsewhere."

"My lord?"

"Somewhere not directly beside the Northmen," Kristan said through his teeth.

"Yes, my lord. At once, my lord." Captain Saratt shot an anxious look at Melissa. "And the princess, my lord?"

"My Reach will be accompanying me to the palace at Seagirt."

"Kristan . . ." Melissa started to say, but Kristan held up his hand.

"Wait with your ship until you get further word from me, and only from me. Is that clear, Captain Saratt?" Kristan turned to Melissa. "Are you traveling with an escort?"

His sister looked startled. "Wh . . . what?"

"An escort. A few of Norwinn's ladies, perhaps?"

Melissa's eyes darted away from his. She shook her head.

"A maidservant, at least?"

"No," Melissa whispered.

"By the Stone . . ." Kristan muttered. He shot a hard look at Captain Saratt, who was twisting his fingers together. "Captain, you're still here."

"Sorry . . . sorry, my lord," Saratt said. He flapped his hands at his crew and they nearly fell over each other in their haste to gain the safety of their ship.

Kristan turned to Olaf and Sigurd. "I apologize for the disturbance. Good evening."

Sigurd smirked; Olaf only nodded. They returned to their ships, their crews in tow. Melissa alone stood on the dock. "Kristan—" she started to say.

"Not one word," he replied. "Kennet, ride ahead and let the palace know that the Reach of Norwinn will be joining me in the royal suite. Walter, kindly give your horse to my sister and let's get back to the palace before we attract the usual Seagirt gawkers."

Kennet kicked his mount into a gallop and disappeared into the night. Walter dismounted and helped Melissa onto his horse. The other knights dismounted, and after a glare and a snap of the fingers from Geoffrey, Serle got down as well. Leading their horses, they walked ahead, allowing Kristan and Melissa some semblance of privacy.

Kristan's throat was too tight with anger for conversation, however, and Melissa was equally silent. She kept her head lowered, and at one point, Kristan was sure he saw a tear shining on her cheek, but he resolved not to speak until they were alone.

At the palace they were greeted by all three Reaches as well as Piri Neff, every one of them smiling although it was plain that they were equal parts confused and wary.

"So good to see you again, Princess," Raul murmured, bending over Melissa's outstretched hand with surprising grace.

"You look tired, Missy," Dell said, forgetting to bow.

And Marcus, naturally, laughed. "Seagirt is overjoyed with Gemetas, it seems," he said, as he gave her one of Seagirt's elaborate, hand-twirling bows. "Lovely as ever, my dear."

Piri Neff's bow was formal, and his eyes sought Kristan's as he rose. "The princess' room has been prepared in your suite, my lord."

I hope Nolle and Astéria had fair warning, Kristan thought. He struck off for the royal chambers, leaving the others hurrying in his wake. To his dismay, Marcus offered his arm to Melissa and came along, too.

In their rooms, Astéria waited in human form, with Nolle sleepy-eyed and irritable at her side. Melissa's eyebrows shot up at the sight of them, but with Marcus in the room Kristan could not explain, and dismissed the pair with a curt nod. With another near-mocking bow, Marcus bid them good night and departed. Matthew and Mitchell said the proper things, in a properly discreet way, then everyone hustled off to their respective rooms, leaving Melissa and Kristan gazing at each other.

Melissa sank onto one of the low couches and put one hand

to her head. "Don't shout at me, Kristan."

"I wasn't going to. But I would like an explanation, please, and I would like it without embellishments or excuses. What are you doing here?"

"I told you, I'm looking for Nigel."

"Putting aside for the moment the issue of why, may I ask who's governing Norwinn while you're out chasing Northmen?"

"I left Vadden Yale in charge," Melissa said, with a defiant tilt of her chin.

"You left V . . ." Kristan slapped his forehead. "What were you thinking? I left Norwinn in your care, and you run away and leave an underling in charge?"

Melissa snorted. "Well, if you're here, who's in charge in Fandrall?"

"That's neither here nor there."

"You find fault with me for the very thing you're doing. Whatever it is you're doing. And who is that Astéria woman anyway?"

"It's complicated. For now, all you need to know is that I had no choice but to bring her to Dyer."

"And no one else could do that for you?"

"No."

"Well, I was in the same situation with Nigel," Melissa said, her voice rising. "It's my fault he's gone; I sent him away when I was . . . when I was in a temper. What was I to do? Send some underling off to find him and order him back home? I had to find him and bring him back."

"Your job is to rule Norwinn in my stead."

"Why won't you stop judging and listen to me?" Melissa shouted, leaping to her feet.

The outburst so startled him that he recoiled. His sister pressed forward, almost on tiptoe, so that they were nearly nose-to-nose. "You stand there like you're carved out of stone and condemn me for what I've done when you don't know anything about it. I'm not going home until I find Nigel."

"Yes, you are," Kristan retorted. "As quickly as you can get your ship repaired, provisioned and turned back around. Whatever went on between the two of you, your presence in Norwinn takes precedence. Send out ships to search for Nigel if you must, but you must stay in Moordock."

Melissa's soft mouth tightened. "I won't go back without Nigel. And if you try to force me, then I won't do anything, do you hear? Vadden can run your kingdom for you; I'm done!"

She stood before him with her small fists clenched and her chest heaving. Kristan's own anger faded into frustration, mingled with bitter self-pity. *And now my own sister turns on me,* he thought. "Enough," he said. "You're tired, I'm tired, and we're not going to accomplish anything by threatening each other. Are you hungry?"

Melissa shook her head and sagged back down onto the couch. It was only then that he saw how thin and pale she was. "I should never have sent him away," she whispered. "I spoke in anger and grief. I was such a fool." Sudden tears welled in her eyes. "Brother, what am I to do?"

He knew he should comfort her; take her in his arms and hold her and let her weep, but his skin crawled at the idea of such close contact. He compromised by giving her shoulder the briefest of squeezes. Melissa reached up, as if to take his hand, but he flinched away and was instantly ashamed of his cowardice. "Missy, I'm up to my eyes in problems right now, with no simple solutions to be had," he said. "Whatever happened between you and Nigel, you're still my Reach. You must go back to Norwinn and assume your duties again. Now please—go to bed. We'll sort out a plan tomorrow."

Melissa stood up, dropped him a peremptory curtsey and stalked off to her room. Kristan half expected her to slam the door, but she did not. He went to his own chamber, dismissed a drowsy-eyed Serle, and sank down on the edge of the ridiculous bed. He sat for a long time, his head in his hands, but at last he rose, as he knew he would, and began to pace. Back and forth he walked, back and forth the length of the sumptuous room, his uneven tread on the soft carpet a mocking echo of his burdensome, halting thoughts.

CHAPTER FIFTEEN

The messenger from Fandrall nodded to Heather as he hurried through the courtyard and up the keep steps, but she forced her attention back to the drill. "That's the way," Sir Eaden was saying in a bright, encouraging voice. "Lunge . . . and recover. Lunge . . . and recover. Nicely done."

The women of the castle and the women of Needwood moved in something approaching unison, but there was still a clear division among them. Isobel, Lily and Annys stayed in their own cluster, the Needwood women in theirs, with Bayla and the castle servants forming a sort of neutral territory between them. Heather clasped her gloved hands behind her back and paced through their ranks, trying to shut her brain to the racket of her own thoughts: *Did he answer? Did he answer? If he did, what did he say?* She stopped to adjust the angle of one woman's wrist, took up a practice sword to demonstrate to another how to keep her weight balanced during the thrust, nodded and smiled and tried to be attentive, all the while trying to swallow the knot of anxiety in her throat.

The Home Guard was coming along; she had to admit it. Although some of the women were timorous and others undeniably clumsy, most of them had, at least, mastered the basic defensive moves. *But I want more*, Heather thought, clenching her mind against her own fearful thoughts. *I want them to be willing to attack.* Her gaze drifted toward a group of her own idling soldiers, a dozen or so, who jigged against the cold and smirked as they watched the women drill. "You men come here," she called, suddenly impatient with the careful, studied moves of the exercise.

Eaden turned away from the drill as the men trotted toward them. Taking advantage of his inattention, some of the women slackened their efforts. Isobel even paused to lean on her sword, panting.

"Oh, you're ready to stop, are you?" Heather said. "Very well, give up your weapons to these men. That's right, go on and take them," she added, as the men hesitated. "On the double."

The men moved among the women, relieving them of the practice swords. "Good," Heather said. "Now go over to the gatehouse and wait. Eaden, go with them." She turned back to the women. "Home Guard, we're going to try something different. Line up in front of the keep steps."

"You said we wouldn't have to drill with the men," one of the Needwood women complained.

"You won't be drilling with them. They're a band of rogue soldiers from Stratheden, and they're attacking Needwood. They're after your homes, your shops, your farms. They're going to take anything and everything they want. Everything, understand? There are no men around to defend you, no soldiers. It's up to you to stop them."

"But they have all the swords!" Lily cried.

"They would, wouldn't they? You're going to have to find weapons of your own. Look around; use whatever's available. In a real attack, that may be all you have. Don't just stand there, move!" As the women scurried off, a few of the men grinned and hefted the wooden practice swords in mock menace, while others looked dubious. "The women are going to guard the keep doors," she called to them. "On my order, your task is to gain those doors. You have the weapons; use them how you see fit."

"Oh, now, my lady," said one of the soldiers, pointing to a buxom, rosy-cheeked young Needwood woman who was hustling back to the steps clutching a barrel stave. "That's my sweetheart. I don't want to hurt her."

The young woman grinned. "I'd like to see you try."

Lily returned from her search with a pike, gotten who knew where. The goatherd brandished her staff, and the scullery maid a length of chain that Heather was fairly certain had come from the kitchen well. With ill grace, Isobel was gathering a heap of loose cobbles. Annys came running with a shoeing hammer and the castle's blacksmith close behind, protesting vociferously. Heather waved him to one side as the rest of the women assembled before the keep steps with their makeshift weapons at the ready.

"Now then," she said. "Do whatever you must to keep these men away from the door. They have the advantage of you in experience, but you outnumber them."

"Only by five or six," said Lily.

"That may be so, but bear in mind that they're only fighting for gain. You women are fighting for your lives." Heather's gaze fell on Bayla. Her maidservant's face was pale and her hands were knotted tight on the long handle of the spade she carried. *This exercise may cut too close to the bone for her*, Heather thought, suddenly remembering the circumstances of their first meeting. She was about to excuse her maidservant from the exercise, but the grim determination on Bayla's face stopped her. *She'll endure it*, she thought; *Bayla will endure it and come out the stronger.*

"Right, then," she said. "Is everyone ready?"

The soldiers whooped and brandished the practice swords; the women nodded. Heather stepped out of the way. "Then have at it," she called, and winced as, without preamble, her soldiers charged.

Bayla was the first to move. With her height and reach, she had the advantage over the other women, and she practically leaped forward, her spade raised. It smashed into the lead soldier's practice sword, shattering it, and the man retreated with

Bayla right after him. With a yowl of glee, the scullery maid whirled her chain overhead and let it fly, fetching the next soldier a hard wallop in the shoulder. His weapon dropped from his benumbed fingers. When he dived to recover it, Lily jabbed her pike into the ground just short of his hand, and he scrambled out of reach on hands and knees. As Lily struggled to recover her weapon, another soldier darted forward, sword raised, but with surprising accuracy Isobel hurled a cobblestone and caught him just below the right eye. He dropped like a felled ox.

"That's the way, that's the way!" Eaden shouted.

"Look out!" Heather called, as the buxom young woman with the barrel stave was tackled by her own sweetheart. He wrestled her to the ground, but she locked her legs around his waist and whacked him soundly about the shoulders with her stave, laughing all the while. The goatherd let out a screech and hurried to help, but was waylaid by another soldier, who knocked her staff aside and grabbed her. Annys stepped in, flourishing her shoeing hammer, and the soldier took one look and fled. The other soldiers were also backing up, all but the one felled by Isobel's cobblestone and the one still locked within his sweetheart's ferocious embrace.

"Well done, ladies!" Heather cried, clapping her hands. "Eaden, make sure Isobel hasn't killed that fellow. You there with the barrel stave, let your prisoner go."

With Eaden's assistance, the victim of Isobel's stone got to his feet, hand clapped to his swelling cheekbone. The soldier kissed his sweetheart noisily and rolled off her. She smacked him on the backside with her stave, still giggling.

"Let us try again, my lady!" shouted one of the soldiers.

"Sure you can take it?" the scullery maid called back. The other women cheered, and even Isobel smiled as she hefted another cobblestone.

At that moment, Heather caught sight of Alister standing in the keep doorway. He waved a sealed message at her, and even from a distance she could see the long diagonal ink stroke that cut through the writing on the exterior. She had to swallow and wet her lips before she addressed Eaden. "Gather up all the practice swords and see that the borrowed weapons are returned, would you? Well done, everyone."

As the women and soldiers congratulated each other, Heather climbed the steps to meet her cousin, hating the trembling of her knees, the rapid tattoo of her heart. "Here you are," Alister said, presenting the message with a flourish. "The StoneKing is as thrifty with paper as you. I hope you got the answer you wanted." As he handed her the message, he leaned closer. "And your father wants to see you when you have a chance. Fair warning: he's getting twitchy about your upcoming trip."

"Thanks," Heather said. Alister lingered for a moment, as if waiting for her to open the message, but when she did not, he shrugged and hurried back into the keep.

Heather stood with the message in one hand. Her instinct was to hurry to someplace private—a deserted anteroom, a secluded corner of the castle wall, even a garderobe—but she could not move. She tried to take a deep breath but it was as if her lungs had collapsed, and all she could do was suck in tiny, rapid sips of air. The noise of courtyard and castle faded to a muted roar. She made herself focus on the red wax that sealed the message. It was an irregular blob that resembled a fat red fish, and as she stared at it, it wavered before her eyes, as if it would swim away. *I'm going to faint*, she thought; *I'm going to faint if I stand here one moment more.*

She ran one finger carefully beneath the seal, popping it loose without breaking it. The parchment crinkled as she opened it and stared down at the words. Her own handwriting stared back at her but at the bottom was a different hand: Bastian's elegant lettering, spelling out the word APPROVED.

A wail of anguish bubbled up in her throat. She choked it down. With numb fingers she closed the parchment, and then folded it on itself, over and over, until it was a hard, thick packet with the little fish of red wax hidden in its middle. She bent and pushed it well down into her right boot. *That's it,* she told herself. *That's all there is. You were a fool to think there would be more.*

She forced herself upright, unlocked her clenched teeth and drew in a great gulp of air. *And now you know,* she thought. *Now you know, and you have to carry on. Do your job. Teach the women. Drill the men. Plan the war games. There's nothing to do but carry on.*

Squaring her shoulders, she went back down the steps. The women and soldiers were still talking and joking in the court-yard, all except the bosomy Needwood girl, her soldier sweet-heart, and Isobel.

"Why is everyone idling?" Heather said, more harshly than she had intended, and every head swiveled toward her.

"Sorry, my lady," Bayla said. "We thought we were finished."

"The sun's going down," said the scullery maid. "I have to get back to the kitchen to help with dinner, my lady, or Cook will have my hide."

"And I've got to get my animals home," said the goatherd.

"Go on with you women, then," Heather said. "You soldiers are dismissed as well. Sir Eaden, a word with you, please."

They crossed the courtyard together, through the long shadow of the keep's western wall. "They're improving by leaps and bounds, my lady," Eaden said. "The Home Guard, I mean."

"Yes," Heather said. She forced herself to speak with a brisk-ness she did not feel. "I'm pleased with them, and with your work. I'm giving you command of the castle while we're away on exercises, Eaden, but I also expect you to keep up with the Home Guard's drills until I return."

Eaden beamed. "Of course, my lady."

"Very well. We'll have more to discuss over the next two days, but for now you can go about your business."

"Yes, my lady. And thank you, my lady. Thank you for your trust."

Heather nodded again. Her face felt as if it had turned to stone, her mouth and eyes mere slits in its cold blank surface. "You've earned it. Go along, now. I'll see you at dinner."

Eaden hurried off. *No doubt to tell Jerrold and Bran*, Heather thought. She walked slowly through the gatehouse, returning the guards' salutes with a half-hearted one of her own. She crossed the drawbridge and stood looking toward Needwood. In the distance the goatherd guided her bleating charges along one of the side streets. *Headed toward her home and a good fire and maybe someone to share it with*, Heather thought. *How I wish I had someone to talk to*. As she turned back toward the castle, she caught sight of a couple deep in a shadowy niche of the castle's curtain wall. In spite of the cold, the two were locked in an amorous embrace.

It was the Needwood girl and her soldier sweetheart. Their mouths were pressed together and she clutched the back of his neck with both hands. Her skirts were rucked up, exposing one plump thigh, and the soldier's hand was buried deep in the cleft of her legs. Cheeks burning, Heather averted her gaze and started back, but an answering heat was rising in her belly, setting her legs trembling. Just before she entered the gatehouse, she stole a last look at the couple. The soldier's other hand was at the woman's breast now, kneading the abundant flesh as he pressed himself between her legs. The woman threw back her head, and although Heather could not hear her gasp of passion, she felt it in her own throat, and was overwhelmed with longing.

She hurried past the guards, head down, aching with the need to be touched, to be held and caressed. She could not remember the last time a man had touched her. Her father and cousin were not given to displays of physical affection. Her knights often clapped each other on the back or gripped each other's shoulders in friendship, but they would never extend so familiar a gesture to their commander.

Only Ravelin had ever dared lay a hand on her, and that only the lightest touch of passionless lips on the back of her hand. *Could I be content with that?* she wondered. *Content with a companion instead of a lover for the rest of my life? Or will I be alone until the end of my days, with nothing to fill this emptiness where Kristan used to be?*

In his work chamber, Colin was busy putting away his papers and ledgers for the day. "There you are," he said, as she came in. "Have your women and soldiers finished brawling in the courtyard?"

"It was an exercise, not a brawl," Heather said, but she was too despondent to argue the point. "Alister said you wanted to see me."

"Are you still planning to leave for your war games the day after tomorrow?"

"Barring bad weather, yes. I'm leaving Sir Eaden in charge of the castle's defenses."

Colin grunted. "How many did you finally decide to take with you?"

"Two hundred soldiers, along with Sir Jerrold and Sir Bran. And Ravelin, of course."

"And that's all?"

"Pardon?"

"Two hundred men, Jerrold, Bran, Reach Seachlan and you. No one else?"

"And Bayla. I'm taking Bayla."

"So . . . two women and two hundred men. Daughter, do you never think about appearances? About propriety?"

"Oh, not this again," Heather said. "Father, I'm the commander of the army."

"You're also a young woman—an unmarried young woman," Colin said, his brow lowering ominously. "It isn't right for you to travel without a female escort."

"Bayla is escort enough."

"Bayla is a servant and your employee. And while I know you don't like to hear these things, her reputation is less than spotless."

"What happened to Bayla was not her fault."

"You know that, and I know that. But other people don't know that."

"Or they choose to overlook it," Heather muttered.

"Don't be thickheaded about this, daughter. Would it hurt to take one or two of the court women with you? Take Isobel, perhaps, or Annys. Both of them are widows, and respectable. It's not as if I'm asking you to take an old maiden auntie. They've been training with you, after all."

Heather had no energy for further argument. "All right, all right. If it'll set your mind at rest and put an end to this discussion, I'll ask one of the women to go with us."

Colin nodded, an exasperating look of triumph on his face. Heavy-footed with melancholy, Heather went to her room to clean up for dinner. She tried to reply cheerfully to Bayla's few questions, but it was an effort. For her part, Bayla seemed unusually subdued. "So, what's the latest from Sir Walter?" Heather asked, making an effort to rouse herself from her own gloomy thoughts.

"I don't know." Bayla wound Heather's braids into a fresh coronet and pinned them in place before continuing. "There wasn't anything from him in today's messages, and none in the packet before that."

"He's just busy, no doubt."

"No doubt," Bayla echoed, but when she tried to smile, her lips trembled. She turned away quickly, but not before Heather saw the shimmer of a tear on her cheek.

"Here now," she said, catching her maidservant by the hand. "What's the matter?"

Bayla kept her face averted. "Oh, I'm just being foolish."

"Bayla, I've never seen you cry before. Tell me what's wrong."

"It's just . . ." Bayla sat down on the bench before the hearth and clasped her hands in her lap. "A fortnight ago . . . I may have opened my heart too much, my lady. Wrote things that were impulsive. I shouldn't have assumed that Walter's feelings for me . . . are as strong as mine for him."

Compassion broke through Heather's own misery. "Well, that makes no sense at all. Last summer it was plain to see he cared for you, and he's never missed a chance to write to you since then."

"I know that," Bayla said. "But Walter is not just a knight; he's part of the StoneKing's personal retinue. A man of position. And I'm not only just a maidservant, I'm . . ." Bayla swallowed hard. "I'm damaged goods, my lady."

Heather sat next to her. "You're worth three times any woman in this court, including me. A man would be a fool to let you slip through his fingers, and Walter is no fool. I'm sure there's a perfectly good explanation for his silence, and you'll find out what that is with the next packet from Fandrall. Meantime, you and I will be off on the war games, and we'll have so much to occupy us that we won't have time to think about Walter." *Or anyone else*, she added to herself.

Bayla gave her a shaky smile. "Thank you, my lady. I'm sure you're right. And now, what would you like to wear for dinner? I finished that new gown this morning—would you like to try it on?"

"Of course," Heather said, but as she stood before the mirror while Bayla laced up the back of the dress, her spirits sagged again. The gown was made of a soft pine-green fabric that Heather had picked for its warmth and durability, but it had no sheen. The brown beads and thin gold piping at the high neck and sleeve hems were so subtle as to be almost invisible. A neatly fitted bodice and a series of clever tucks over the hips gave her lean figure a more womanly shape, but even that could not disguise the breadth of her shoulders, nor her calloused hands, nor the drawn, sunburnt features of her face. *I'm only nineteen*, Heather thought, as she stared at her reflection, *but I look like a hard-used woman of thirty. There's no girlishness left in me.*

"Don't you like it, my lady?" Bayla asked.

Heather made herself smile. "It's lovely, Bayla. I can't wait to show it off at dinner. Such neat, even needlework on the trim, and the skirt hangs so beautifully." She swayed back and forth to demonstrate. "Before I go downstairs, though, I want your opinion on something."

"Of course, my lady."

"For appearance's sake, my father wants me to take one of the court ladies with us on maneuvers, to act as my companion." Bayla groaned. "I know, I know. But I flout custom enough as it is. He suggested Annys or Isobel, since they're older and widowed—which, in his eyes, gives them a certain respectability. Of the two, which would you pick?"

"If I was going to pick the one who'd be the least nuisance, I'd say Annys, my lady. But she'd be miserable. She's a poor rider and suffers in the cold. And she has the most responsibilities here in the castle. She'd be badly missed." Bayla made a face. "I hate to say it, but I think you'll have to take Isobel."

Heather heaved a sigh. "I think you're right. All right, Isobel it is. I'll talk to her as soon as I have a chance."

When she joined the rest of the court for dinner, everyone gaped at her. The female courtiers, in their usual dinner finery, recovered first. They gathered around to examine her dress more closely and gush over the fabric and workmanship, while all the time their eyes roamed over Heather with something like pity, making her feel like a crow mobbed by a flock of bright songbirds. Her knights eyed her surreptitiously, as if uncertain whether to praise her new attire or pretend they hadn't noticed it. Most opted for the latter, although Sir Jerrold got up to draw out her chair for her, something he had never done before. Colin beamed at her; Alister nodded his approval.

To her relief, dinner was served quickly and she was able to apply herself to her plate. Even though she was not hungry, she wolfed down her food from sheer nerves, raising her eyes only to reach for her goblet. As she did, she spotted Ravelin watching her. She froze, a fresh flush of embarrassment creeping up her neck. He lifted his goblet to her in a courtly gesture, making her ashamed of the way she had been gobbling, *like a pig at a trough*, she told herself. *When did being commander mean you stopped having manners?* With some trepidation, she raised her goblet back to him, and he smiled.

As they drank, Heather studied him over the rim of her cup. The hair at his temples was going silver, but the rest was still black, straight and shining. When he turned to speak to Sir Bran next to him, only the faintest sagging of the flesh at his jawline indicated his age. His tunic, elegant but not showy, was fitted carefully to his broad shoulders and chest. *He's still a fine-looking man*, Heather could not help thinking. *He's well-built, well-spoken, intelligent and mannerly when he chooses. Would it be so bad, being married to him?*

As if sensing her inspection, Ravelin suddenly looked at her. She dropped her gaze to her plate, overwhelmed by thoughts of being married to him: eating meals together, sitting side by side before the fire, lying beside him in bed. *Would it be so bad?* she wondered again, even as another blush warmed her face. *If marrying Ravelin allowed me to command without scrutiny, travel as I wanted, act without judging eyes on me, could I bear it?*

Of course you could, she told herself sharply. *You've borne far worse, and survived. You'll endure it, and be stronger for it. You can endure anything if you set your mind to it.*

She looked down the table toward Isobel, who was poking at her food, sour-faced. Heather groaned inwardly at the thought of traveling in her company. *But you can survive that, too. There's nothing you can't survive, if you can survive losing Kristan.*

* * *

"Well, I have some news," Isobel said, when they were finished.

Ravelin only grunted as he adjusted his clothes. Truth be

told, he was more than a little weary of Isobel. Her simpers, affectations and pouts had dulled her allure as a sexual partner. Gone too was the excitement of their illicit couplings, replaced by the thrill of the hunt as he pursued his new quarry.

The sight of Heather in her simple, severe dress had filled him with perverse delight. Yes, it had been an unattractive dress, and she looked gawkier than usual in it, but seeing her blushes and discomfort had been like watching a deer turn skittish at the scent of a predator on its trail. *I'll have you, my girl,* he thought. *In spite of all your wariness, I'll have you sooner or later.*

"I said I have some news," Isobel said again, with a teasing lilt to her voice.

She had propped herself up on her elbows and the moonlight from the anteroom window washed her sharp features in thin, cold blue. Her skirts were still bunched around her waist. "Well, what?" he said, averting his gaze from her parted thighs.

"Your little friend has asked me to accompany her on maneuvers." She smirked at his surprise. "Yes, I thought that might get your attention."

"Accompany her?" He knew he sounded like an idiot, but the idea that Isobel would be underfoot just when he was closing in on his prey was not at all what he wanted.

"Apparently, her father is concerned about the impropriety of his precious girl marching off with all her virile soldiers and only her tart of a maidservant for an escort," Isobel said. "For appearance's sake, she's asked me to go along—respectable widow that I am." She swung her legs coyly. "Isn't that convenient?"

"Convenient?"

"For you and me, of course."

He turned away, making a show of tugging his tunic straight so she could not read his expression. "You do realize it won't be a pleasant trip, don't you? We'll be out on maneuvers from dawn until dark."

"I know. I won't try to come to you on the journey; that would be too difficult. Once we've arrived, though . . ." A slither of fabric and the slight thump of her feet on the floor warned him that she had gotten down from her perch on the table. A moment later, her arms encircled him from behind and she pressed the length of her body along his. "The waiting will make it that much more enjoyable . . . my lord," she whispered, and nibbled his earlobe.

He fought the urge to shrug her off. Isobel still had the potential to be useful to him, and he could not afford to sour her allegiance now. He pulled one of her hands to his lips and kissed it with all the passion he could muster. "Be patient, my dear. This little game with Lady Heather is at a delicate juncture, and a false move could upset all our plans. Wait and watch. I'll let you know when it's safe for us to meet."

CHAPTER SIXTEEN

Even with the fur covers kicked off, Kristan's luxurious bed was still too warm, and he slept fitfully. He woke for the last time, sticky and miserable, just as dawn turned his vast chamber from a shadow-filled cave into a dull gray prison. His skin prickled as he pulled on his woolen undergarments, and with a soft oath, he stripped them off again. *This foolish Dyerian winter*, he thought. *Who needs all these layers?*

Once dressed, he went into the main room, where he found Geoffrey poking up the fire. "Morning, my lord," he murmured. "Can I get you a bite of breakfast?"

"Thank you, no," Kristan said, keeping his voice equally low. "I've got council with the guild heads this morning, but I'm going to go have a walk to clear my head first. Until I get back, my sister and the others are to stay within the chambers, understand? Do what you have to do to make that happen."

He slipped through the main doors, nodding to the guards as they snapped to attention. With his hands clasped behind his back, he paced the palace halls until time for council, scattering early-rising servants before him like startled birds.

In council, his low spirits sank still further. Although there was a certain interest in observing the guild heads' strategies as Piri Neff guided the conversation from topic to topic, he was too weary and disheartened to care. Once again Raul was the only Reach who stayed attentive throughout the meeting, listening to each complaint and suggestion, asking questions and making copious notes. Dell only came alive when the issue of the harbor's silting was on the table, and he subsided as soon as it was dismissed after a cursory discussion. But for the occasional joke, Marcus contributed nothing to the conversation. He cleaned his nails with a small knife, fiddled with the papers before him, scratched at his scraggly beard and yawned repeatedly. Only when Fedro Vincenze introduced a topic for debate did the Reach pay attention, and even then, he spoke only to agree with the guild head.

Mali Uzuri was in attendance, but she held her tongue throughout the meeting. On occasion Kristan found himself pinned in her bright-eyed gaze, as if she was expecting him to speak. *And I should speak*, he scolded himself; *I should make my presence felt.* But he could not bring himself to care about any of it: not the harbor silting, nor the collection of taxes, nor the fish nor the roads nor the docking fees nor anyone seated at the table with him.

At least the tedium of the meeting was preferable to returning to the royal suite. He dreaded dealing with Melissa's anger and Astéria's melancholy and his knights' apologetic servility, as if the entire situation was somehow their fault. He glanced out the window toward the shining bay in the distance. *Just let Lorz arrive today*, he wished silently. *And let him arrive with his cargo intact, so I can take Astéria and her people to Torrin and be done with all of this.*

Well past noon, the discussion began to stutter and wane, as bellies accustomed to being filled regularly growled for their missed lunch. Kristan had no appetite himself, but at last he cleared his throat and rose. "I'm sure all of you are anxious to return to your businesses. Thank you for your contributions to this morning's discussion. Council is dismissed. Good day."

Most of the merchants hurried away, but Fedro Vincenze sidled up to Kristan with an unctuous air. "What a pleasure it is to have you among us, my lord. We accomplished so much more than usual."

"I thought there was a great deal of talking simply to hear oneself speak," Mali Uzuri said from the doorway. "My lord, I hope you have more pleasant things planned for the balance of your day."

Kristan only nodded, and Mali left. Dell followed her from the chamber. Marcus was already gone, although his raucous laughter rang in the hallway. Raul lingered at the table with Piri Neff, going over the meeting's notes, but Fedro still hung close by Kristan. "Speaking of pleasant things, my lord," he said softly, "our mutual friend is eager to meet with you. She wondered if tonight, at my home, would suit."

It took a moment for his words to sink in, and in the silence Fedro leaned even closer, showing his teeth in a conspiratorial smile. "My household is a discreet one and you won't be disturbed. If you'll pardon my saying so, my lord, you look weary. You deserve a peaceful evening in the company of an old friend."

Someone to talk to, Kristan thought. *Someone who knows my past. Someone who can give me back a little of what I've lost.*

Still he hesitated. Fedro waved one hand nonchalantly. "I know you've a great deal on your plate, my lord. But let me tell her yes, shall I? That way if you have the time, she'll be waiting for you, and if you don't—well, Tansy is a bright young woman and knows the way things are. She'll understand."

Musing over the situation, Kristan made his way back to the royal chambers. As he entered the hallway leading to the suite, he noticed the carefully bland expressions of the guards and heard his sister's voice raised in indignation. "How dare you keep me in this room?" she was almost screeching. "How dare you treat me as if I'm a child—or a prisoner?"

"Princess, I'm only following your brother's orders," Geoffrey's voice rumbled.

Kristan's guts clenched. *By the Stone, am I never to have a moment's peace?* He nodded to the guards, and they swung the doors open, revealing Geoffrey's broad back and Melissa's small, angry figure just beyond it. As the doors clicked shut behind Kristan, Geoffrey turned, and his face flooded with relief. "There you are, my lord. I was just trying to explain to the princess—"

Melissa pushed past Geoffrey. "How dare you tell your lackeys to keep me trapped here?"

Kristan's own temper flared. "Moderate your tone and your language when you speak to me," he almost snarled, and Melissa shrank back. "Where are the other knights, Geoff?"

"They all rode down to the harbor to see if there was any news." Geoffrey's glower suggested there would be payment extracted from his fellow knights for abandoning him with Melissa.

"And Astéria?"

"She's hiding in her room with the children," Melissa said. "For such a big woman, your doxy hasn't much spine."

"Kindly hold your tongue," Kristan snapped. "Astéria, come out here."

The door to Astéria's chamber opened. Serle and Nolle came out first, glaring at Melissa, followed by Astéria in human form. It was clear Nolle had been studying Seagirt fashion and had adjusted the centaur's shift accordingly. Astéria was more magnificent than ever in a ruby gown slashed with white and trimmed in gold, and this time her hair was crowned with an elaborate circlet of gold wire strung with hundreds of tiny, flashing diamonds.

"Don't you think that's a bit gaudy for daytime wear, my dear?" Melissa said sweetly.

Astéria turned to Kristan with a helpless shrug. "I am sorry, Kreestan. Nolle make me look like this."

"Soft fool," Melissa muttered.

"Change her back, Nolle," Kristan said.

"Do it," Serle hissed, giving Nolle a hard nudge with one bony elbow. Nolle only smirked.

Melissa let out a snort of disgust. "She can't even change her clothing by herself?"

Controlcontrolcontrol . . .

In three strides Kristan crossed the room, thrust Nolle out of the way and laid one hand on Astéria's shoulder. With a rustle of fabric, a jingle of jewelry and the customary hiss, the shift collapsed and Astéria gave herself a shake that made all four hooves clatter on the marble floor.

Melissa's mouth dropped open and both hands went slowly to her head. "What . . . what . . .?"

"I told you I'd explain," Kristan said.

"Why didn't you tell me last night?"

"Because Marcus was here—"

"Marcus? What does he have to do with it?"

"If you'll let me get a word in edgewise, I'll tell you everything. Sit down. Astéria, please join us. Geoff, ride down to the harbor and tell Captain Saratt to attend on me in the throne room. Serle, go to my room and . . . and find something to do. You too, Nolle."

Serle hustled off, but Nolle stamped one foot. "I'm sick of being stuck in these rooms. I'll go with Sir Geoffrey."

"Not a chance," Geoff muttered, and slipped out quickly. Nolle stormed into the bathing room and slammed the door. Kristan's head rang from the impact. A slow steady ache swelled behind his eyebrows as he attempted to explain the situation to Melissa. Her cold stare unnerved him; every action he'd taken suddenly seemed foolish, and he began to stammer. To his relief, Astéria took over the narrative. Her passionate words, broken and mangled as they were, were far more effective than his own blundering attempts, and he was content to sit back and watch his sister's reaction to the tale. Melissa listened, nodding but largely expressionless, although at one point her gaze wandered off and her nose wrinkled with distaste.

"What is it?" Kristan asked.

"This place isn't as clean as it looks," Melissa replied, jerking her chin toward the bathing room door. A small gray mouse was creeping along the wall, surrounded by the familiar blur of Nolle's true form. With an oath, Kristan grabbed the nearest cushion and flung it with all his might. The cushion slapped against the wall and the mouse let out a squeak. It scuttled back to the door and slid beneath it, dragging Nolle's true form behind. The sight of the quivering shape constricting and twisting as it squeezed through the narrow opening made Kristan's already unsettled stomach heave, and he averted his head, grimacing.

"It Nolle," Astéria said, in answer to Melissa's startled look.

"Good heavens," Melissa muttered. "I wonder you keep her around, brother."

"I need her," Kristan said. "At least until I can recover the rest of Astéria's people."

"Well, you should keep her under control."

Control.

"So until this Lorz fellow appears, you're stuck here in Seagirt?"

"Yes."

Melissa's brows knotted. "And you had to do this all yourself? Mitchell knows where to find *O Tópos*. Why didn't you just send him?"

"I made him swear an oath, Missy. The same oath you took. The same one I took. If anyone is going to break it, it has to be me."

"My, you're important," Melissa said, with a slight toss of her head.

Kristan's fingers twitched with the sudden urge to strike her. He took hold of the Stone instead. With its cold weight filling his palm, he forced himself to count three slow breaths before he answered. "Melissa. You may not think much of me right now, but I'm still the StoneKing. I won't ask you again to moderate your tone."

Melissa did not answer, but she knotted her fingers in her lap and kept her gaze fixed on them as he picked up the thread of the tale. He outlined the situation with the Northmen, touched but did not elaborate on the strife between the three Reaches of Dyer, and explained why Marcus had to be kept ignorant of Astéria's true nature. Only when Tansy's name was mentioned did Melissa look up, a derisive curl to her lips. "Oh, her. You always liked her, but even as a child I thought she was common as dirt. It's no surprise she ended up a doxy."

"You call me this thing, *doxy*," Astéria said. "What is doxy?"

Melissa had the good grace to look embarrassed. "I apologize; I shouldn't have said that. But I was upset and didn't understand the circumstances."

"But what is doxy?" Astéria insisted, turning to Kristan.

The Kentravron probably don't even have a name for it, he thought. "It . . . it's a woman who takes money from a man. In return, she lets the man . . . well, lie with her."

Astéria shook her head, clearly confused. A hot flush crept up Kristan's face. He made a fist with one hand and thrust the index finger of the other into it. "She lets him mate with her."

"But this woman, she . . . she . . ." Astéria shook her head again, patted her chest, then clasped both hands over her heart. "*Ton agapá?* How you say?"

"Love," Melissa said.

"She . . . love . . . this man?"

"No," Kristan said. "She'll lie with any man, in exchange for money or gifts."

Astéria's mouth trembled. She raised her hand and pulled off the ring he had given her.

"Wait, that's different," Kristan said. "I gave you the ring because you were so sad. I wanted to make you feel better."

She held the ring out to him. "It make you sister and all people here say I am doxy."

"Astéria—"

"Take back, Kreestan. I not want."

Kristan plucked it from her hand and stood up. "Fine," he said, unreasonably hurt, and thrust it into his pocket. "Fine."

Astéria extended her hand, as if to touch him. "Kreestan—"

"Never mind; it doesn't matter." He stepped out of her reach and raised his voice. "Nolle! Serle!"

Serle hurried in from Kristan's bedchamber; Nolle stuck her pouting face out of the bathing room. "Serle, I want you to come with me and my sister. Nolle, stay here with Astéria."

"I'm tired of being stuck here!" Nolle shouted.

Before he knew what he was doing, Kristan crossed the room and grabbed Nolle by both shoulders. "You address me as 'my lord,' and you do as I tell you!" he snarled in her face. "Do you understand?"

Nolle nodded, eyes huge. In the sudden silence, Astéria whispered a single word.

"*Ragis.*"

The hissed syllables seemed to rattle through the room. Kristan pushed Nolle away and strode toward the chamber doors, his vision swirling, his insides churning like a turbulent sea. Astéria ducked into her room just as he threw the doors open. He limped through the hall and down the stairs, scattering courtiers and servants before him. Behind, Melissa and Serle struggled to keep pace.

In the throne room, Captain Saratt was just arriving in the company of Geoffrey and the other four knights. They bowed as he approached, but he ignored them and lurched up the steep dais steps to Dyer's throne. He threw himself into its fur-and-velvet depths, gripped the elaborate carved arms with both hands and willed his roiling guts into submission. Knights, captain, squire and sister assembled in a row below him, waiting anxiously.

He took a deep breath. "Sir Kennet, any word on Captain Lorz and his ship?

"Nothing yet, my lord. I'm sorry."

Kristan resisted the urge to pound the arms of the throne with both fists. Instead, he glared at Captain Saratt. "How soon will you be ready to leave?"

Saratt came to rigid attention. "By tomorrow, my lord. Our stores are replenished and our repairs should be completed by sundown."

"As soon as the princess is on board, you're to set sail for Moordock." He held up one hand as Melissa began to protest. "No stops along the way, no deviations from the route. Straight back to Moordock, understood?"

Saratt shot a sorrowful glance at Melissa. "Yes, my lord."

"Good. Return to your ship and carry on with your preparations."

"Am I to have no say in the matter?" Melissa demanded, as Captain Saratt left.

"That is correct. And once you're back in Moordock, you're to stay there. I authorize you to send out additional ships to search for your First Advisor, but you're to remain at the castle and resume your duties. Do you understand?"

"What's to stop me from disobeying you and doing as I please?"

A sudden vision swelled in Kristan's brain; a vision of shaking his sister until her teeth rattled. In response, his stomach cramped so hard that he gasped, but at the last moment he was able to turn the reflex into a long, deep breath. "Don't try me, Melissa," he said, fighting to keep his voice level. "I'm warning you. I asked if you understood."

"Yes, my lord," Melissa said, but her eyes were blazing.

"Good. The Sigurdson brothers will be setting sail soon. Chances are they'll encounter Nigel as they make their way back toward Stratheden. If you write a message to Nigel, I'll ask them to give it to him." From the corner of his eye, Kristan saw Raul enter the throne room, then hesitate. "What is it, Reach Ferrador?"

Raul was already backing out. "It can wait, my lord."

"Speak."

"It's truly not important—"

Kristan clutched the arms of the throne so hard that his

knuckles went white. "I said speak."

Raul swallowed hard. "I thought . . . with your permission, of course, my lord . . . I thought a welcoming dinner for your sister might be in order. Your courtiers are quite eager to meet her."

"What an excellent idea." Kristan stood so abruptly that his head spun, and he had to steady himself before he could descend from the dais. "It will have to be both a welcome and farewell, since my sister leaves tomorrow."

"She does?"

"And you'll have to host in my place this evening. I have another engagement."

"Another engagement?" Melissa sputtered. "I'm to sit and exchange pleasantries with your courtiers while you're off at another engagement?"

"Indeed, you are. You'll smile and make yourself pleasant. And if I hear a word of you being haughty or sullen, I swear I'll have you sent back to Norwinn in irons. Right now, though, I suggest you start writing that letter. I'll wait here until you're finished. You can use the anteroom just behind the throne. Raul, set her up with parchment, quill and ink."

"Of course, my lord."

Melissa's face crumpled. "I can't . . . I can't say what I need to say in a letter."

"You'd better try, and do it quickly. I'm going to the harbor to speak with the Sigurdsons as soon as Serle can get Malvo saddled and brought from the stables. Fortunately for you, he's utterly inept at the task, so you'll have a little extra time."

Melissa let out the tiniest sob. *Loathsome creature*, Kristan thought, but he was not certain if he was addressing himself or her. His stomach heaved again, and he clenched the Stone in one fist. "Sister, I'm running out of patience. If I don't have your letter in my hand before Serle comes back with Malvo, the Northmen can sail off without it."

Raul hurried Melissa away, and Kristan turned to Serle, who

stood with open mouth and wide, hurt eyes. "Go to the stables. Get Malvo and your own horse ready. And this time I want you to do the job yourself. No one is to help you, understand?"

"Yes, my lord." Serle ran from the throne room, and in the ensuing, uncomfortable silence, Kristan forced himself to breathe more evenly.

"Shall we go with you, my lord?" Sir Kennet asked.

"No. Stay here and escort my sister to her dinner. Astéria too, if she wants to go, although I doubt she will." He let out a mirthless laugh. "I seem to be making everyone unhappy today."

"Since Serle is busy, shall I get your cloak and gloves for you?" Sir Mitchell offered.

"Yes, thank you."

"I could speak to Captain Ommald and arrange an escort for you," Sir Walter said.

A rude response rose in Kristan's throat, but he choked it back. "I'm going to be asking a favor from someone who'll have no reason and no desire to do it. The less show of military might, the better."

Walter cleared his throat. "My lord, with respect, you know how these people like to mob you."

"By the Stone—" With an effort, Kristan controlled himself. "Fine. Fine. Tell Ommald a small escort, and they're to keep at a distance while I talk to the Sigurdsons."

Relief flooded Walter's broad face, and he hastened out just as Sir Mitchell returned with Kristan's things. "The weather's turning, my lord," he said, as he helped Kristan into the cloak. "The wind's picked up quite a bit and the sky is lowering. It wouldn't surprise me if we had snow tonight."

Kristan snorted. "This day just gets better and better."

His bitter mood seemed to make the knights even more miserable. They stood shuffling their feet and gazing at the floor as they waited. At last, Sir Walter returned at a run. "Your escort is waiting outside, my lord, and Serle just arrived with the horses," he said. All five knights turned toward the ante-room door, as if willing Melissa to come through it. Several moments passed in tense silence.

"Melissa, I'm leaving," Kristan called at last.

Melissa burst from the anteroom with Raul on her heels. She hurried up to Kristan and held out a single sheet of parch-ment, folded over. Tucking his gloves into his belt, he looked at her ravaged face, then at the letter. It was sealed with a blob of red wax. A cruel impulse overwhelmed him, and he broke the seal and opened the letter.

The writing within was uneven and blurred with tearstains, but still legible. *I'm sorry*, it read:

> *I'm so sorry.*
> *Please come home.*
> *Please.*
> *Please.*
> *Please.*

The abject misery of her words struck him to the core, but he was still too angry to have pity on her. "Well done," he said. "Short and to the point."

Melissa's lips curled back from her teeth. "I hate you," she whispered.

He shrugged, thrust the letter into his tunic and left the room, feeling every eye drilling into his back.

Outside, a blast of damp, chilly air hit him, and he pulled his hood up. Serle waited at the foot of the stairs, holding Malvo and his own horse by the reins. Next to him, Captain Ommald stood with an escort of a dozen pikemen. "Half of them, Ommald," Kristan said, as he descended.

With a jerk of his head, Ommald dismissed six men. Kristan circled both the horses, examining their tack. Serle's horse stood placidly enough, but Malvo's ears were laid back and he was stamping and rolling his eyes. "His girth is loose," Kristan said. "Tighten it, please."

Gnawing on his lower lip, Serle glanced from one set of reins to the other, as if unsure what to do. "Drop the reins; the horses will stand," Kristan said.

Serle did as he was told, but as soon as he laid hold of the girth, Malvo flung his head up and reared slightly. Startled, Serle's mount skittered sideways. "Whoa now," Kristan called, grabbing Malvo's bridle. "Serle, get your horse under control."

Serle scrambled after his horse's reins, and Kristan let go of Malvo's bridle to do up the girth himself. As he did, Malvo swung his head sideways and bit Kristan's shoulder.

It was not a hard bite, but Kristan was so shocked that for a moment, all he could do was clutch his shoulder and gape. All at once his rage erupted. He snatched the gloves from his belt and hit Malvo in the face with them. Malvo squealed and tried to break away but Kristan grabbed the reins and struck him again. The great horse dropped his head and stood shivering, and Kristan yanked the girth snug.

"Oh, sir, I'm so sorry—" Serle started to say.

"Mount up," Kristan snapped. "We've wasted enough time." He pulled on his gloves, swung himself into the saddle, turned Malvo sharply toward the gates, and kicked him into a gallop. Captain Ommald bellowed to the escort, and they came jogging after him, with Serle bringing up the rear on his pony.

Kristan knew he was riding too quickly for the crowded Seagirt streets, but he did not slow; instead, he took perverse pleasure in seeing the staring people scatter out of his way. It was not until his thighs and arms began to cramp that he realized a seizure was taking hold. Quickly, he slowed Malvo to a trot, forcing himself to breathe deeply and bring his emotions under control.

The sun was already setting and a raw wind had blown the harbor into chop. The Northern ships jounced up and down at their moorings. Olaf stood on the dock with Sigurd, watching as their crews stretched canvas across their freshly loaded stores and battened them down. Kristan reined up and dismounted as the escort, Captain Ommald and Serle caught up to him. He tossed Malvo's reins to Serle and limped out onto the dock.

Sigurd caught sight of him first. Sneering, he nudged Olaf. "Look, *bróðir*, your good friend the StoneKing has come for a visit."

Olaf turned an expressionless stare on Kristan.

"To what do we owe this honor?" Sigurd said.

"I've come to ask a favor," Kristan said.

Sigurd's eyebrows shot up. "Have you now? You refused to help us, but we're supposed to help you?"

"I've helped you as much as I'm able," Kristan said.

"As much as you care to, you mean."

"Leave off, Sigurd," Olaf said. "What do you want, Kristan?"

"I assume Nigel is still patrolling Norwinn's seacoast," Kristan said, producing Melissa's letter. "Chances are quite good that he'll be looking for you. This message is from my sister, asking him to return home. Would you be good enough to deliver it?"

Sigurd let out a bitter laugh. "And run the risk of being fired on again?"

"They didn't fire on us, brother," Olaf said. He plucked the letter from Kristan's fingers and tucked it inside his tunic. "We'll be leaving in the morning. Tell Melissa if I see Nigel, I'll deliver her message."

"Thank you," Kristan said. His anger had dwindled, leaving him tired and melancholy. "Thank you from both of us."

Olaf only nodded and moved down the dock to check his ship's moorings. Sigurd stepped closer to Kristan and grinned down at him. "You're a cocky little shit, StoneKing, coming down here with your soldiers to demand favors of us. If you'd had the courage to come alone, I would have dragged your scrawny ass aboard my ship and taken you to that *sprunga* by force. I'd have made you prove to me that your Stone's magic couldn't send us home."

"All the force in the world can't make the Stone what you want it to be," Kristan said. "Good evening, Sigurd."

"*Éttu skit*, StoneKing," Sigurd answered, still grinning.

"Everything all right, my lord?" Ommald asked, as Kristan returned to his escort.

"Fine," Kristan said. He took Malvo's reins from Serle and mounted wearily. In spite of his certainty that the Stone could not possibly send the Northmen home, he was troubled by a niggling worm of doubt, and ashamed of his unwillingness to help his friend.

He nudged Malvo into a plodding walk toward the palace. Twilight was turning the sky an unsettled blue-gray, and the windows he passed were already bathed in golden light from the lamps and candles within. The citizens of Seagirt hurried to their evening's appointments, and among them Kristan caught a glimpse of the boy Desta, slipping through the shadows with foxlike grace. Somewhere nearby a door opened, and the pleasant sound of mingled music, laughter and conversation came to Kristan's ears, filling him with envy.

As they approached the palace, a sudden blur flashed over Kristan's head, and he realized that Nolle had left the royal suite and was exploring the city in bird form. He took a breath to shout after her, but she had already flown out of sight down a side street. *What difference does it make?* he thought. *Why shouldn't she go out? And why should I make a fool of myself, shouting at a bird?*

Ahead, the graceful curves of the palace flickered as fast-moving clouds hid, and then revealed the pale face of the moon. *I can't do it*, Kristan thought. *I can't stand to go back to the palace; not now.*

"Captain Ommald," he said, "do you know the house of Fedro Vincenze?"

"Yes, my lord," Ommald said. "It's just ahead—the big house on the left."

"Thank you. I'll be stopping there. You can take the escort

on to the palace."

"We can wait for you, my lord."

"That won't be necessary. I won't be long." He glanced over his shoulder at Serle. "I'm going to pay a visit up ahead, Serle. I want you to wait with the horses while I do."

Serle made a pathetic attempt to smile. *No doubt he's dreading being left alone with Malvo*, Kristan thought, although Malvo had been strangely subdued since Kristan had struck him. *The big brute deserved it*, Kristan told himself, but his heart ached at the thought that his camaraderie with Malvo had turned sour along with everything else.

"This is it," Captain Ommald said, jerking his head toward a fine house set back from the broad promenade. "Fedro Vincenze's place."

"Thank you, Captain. Good night."

The escort marched on as Kristan turned his horse into the courtyard of Fedro Vincenze's sprawling home. As he dismounted, Fedro himself flung open the door and descended the steps, arms spread wide. "My lord! How good of you to grace my humble home with your presence!"

"Good evening, Fedro," Kristan said, handing Malvo's reins to Serle.

Fedro bowed, grinning broadly, and gestured Kristan into the house. Inside the front hall all was splendid marble and gilt, washed in warm yellow lamplight, but the home seemed oddly quiet. "I've restricted my family and servants to the southern side of the house," Fedro explained. "You'll have free use of our northern wing. Respect for your privacy is of great importance to us, my lord." The guild head's grin spread even further as he glanced over Kristan's shoulder. "And here is our friend Tansy. Please, don't let me intrude on your visit." Still bowing, he backed from the room.

In the warm lamplight, Tansy's green eyes were more vivid than ever. Her hair hung loose but for a single lock caught back from each temple. Her gown was of brown velvet, so soft and rich that it practically begged to be touched. Its broad open neckline exposed her collarbones and throat. She wore no jewelry to distract the eye from the perfection of her skin.

"I was afraid you wouldn't come," she said, smiling. "I saw you ride by earlier. You looked so grim. You look grim still, and tired." She stepped backward into the room behind her. "Won't you come in? Come in and be comfortable?"

He followed her into the chamber. It was an airy room, draped with light fabrics that floated in the slight puff of air as she closed the door. To one side, half in shadow, stood a large, low couch, covered in soft cushions. Dominating the rest of the room was a table covered in snowy white linen. A single large chair stood at one end, with a smaller chair to its left. Dozens of candles in branched silver stands shed their light on an array of covered serving dishes, but only a single goblet and plate were in evidence, and that only before the large chair.

"I thought you might be hungry," Tansy said. "I instructed Fedro's kitchen staff to entice and entrance you with their finest dishes. Here, give me your cloak and gloves and sit down." Tansy pulled out the single chair for him.

"Am I to eat alone?" he asked, watching as she draped his cloak on a chair near the low couch. The scent of her perfume—a sweet mingling of roses and berries—swelled as she came back to the table.

"You are, with no one to bother you but me," Tansy said. She laughed, showing her teeth, and caught up a small, slender crystal pitcher. "I'll wait on you myself. We'll begin with this wine—it comes from a vineyard far to the southwest, and its maker is very close about how it's crafted, but I think you'll like it. It tastes like sunshine and sea air." She poured the wine into his silver and gold goblet, raising the pitcher high so the wine tumbled down, catching the light. It was not the hearty red wine Kristan was accustomed to, but a sparkling pale liquid, like molten gold, and Tansy watched the level carefully, her moist lips parted, the soft tip of her tongue just visible between her teeth.

"There," she said, handing it to him. "Taste it and see if I'm not right."

He took a sip of the wine. It was sweet and light and tingled on his tongue. "It's very good."

Tansy seated herself in the smaller chair, propped her elbows on the table and cupped her chin between her palms. "Do you remember a harvest festival long ago? We were only little children, you and I, but you had a tankard of sweet cider. Do you remember?"

Standing in the shadows near the cider-seller's tent, out of sight of Father and the knights, Tansy's breath on his face, Tansy's lips pressed against his. Then a voice behind them, mocking and hate-filled—

Kristan wrenched his mind away before the memory could show its venomous edge. "I'm afraid not."

"A shame. The day was nearly over, but the cider was still cool and delicious, and we shared it, by turns, until it was all gone. Like this." She took the goblet from his hand and raised it to her mouth, and when she lowered it, a faint dew of wine shimmered on her lips. Her tongue crept out and licked it away. "And now you," she said, and handed him the goblet. He drank again, trying to recall the flavor of cider on a late summer's evening, but there was only the taste of wine, and Tansy watching him. "I stood in the crowd to watch the bouts, but you sat in the pavilion with your father."

Father. The dreadful memory of Robert Gemeta's death rose up so suddenly that Kristan could barely breathe. "Tell me what you saw," he choked out, desperate for some gentler vision. "Tell me how he looked."

Tansy giggled, oblivious of his pain. "Oh, I barely looked at him. I was looking at you. You were such a beautiful boy, so gentle and graceful, so different from all the other boys. I couldn't take my eyes off you, even when I was supposed to be watching Owen."

Owen . . . it was Owen who had spoken, Owen who mocked him, tormented him, pushed him while Tansy watched . . .

Kristan's stomach knotted. He made himself concentrate on Tansy's face. "Why did you leave Kingsmere? How did you end up here?"

She took the goblet from him again and sipped from it before answering. "It was hard to live there. The Daaznans had all the power and the people of Kingsmere hated them so. If you chose one side, the other was against you. I couldn't live like that. Owen . . ." She lowered her gaze to the goblet. "I know you didn't like him, and you'll think less of me for what I did, but I knew he'd gone to Dyer with the Daaznans. So, I followed him. I thought he might look after me, and he did, for a bit. But he was only a common soldier, and poor. He couldn't get promoted because his officers didn't like him. They all liked me, though. I wanted to be more than a soldier's woman, so . . ." She shrugged. "Eventually, Owen was assigned elsewhere, and I haven't seen him since. I sometimes wonder what happened to him."

A nightmare vision of Owen's face, battered and hacked out of all recognition, swelled in Kristan's brain. He took the goblet from Tansy and drained it, too quickly. It made his head spin. "So, you became an officer's woman."

His voice was harsh, but Tansy only smiled. "For a while. But then I met Fedro, and everything changed."

"You became his woman, then?"

"Oh, no, no. My relationship with Fedro is strictly business."

"And what business is that?"

Tansy plied the crystal pitcher again. "As a guild master and one of Seagirt's most prominent merchants, Fedro must frequently entertain guests—fellow guild heads, business associates, potential trading partners and so forth. His wife, a good woman who's given him a number of children, lacks the . . . oh, how shall I put this . . . the polish to handle such events. So, I help him provide a congenial mood. I choose the food, the drink, and how it's presented. I welcome the guests, see to their comfort, provide diverting conversation and something pleasant to look at. I arrange the entertainment—musicians, dancers, singers—"

"Whores," Kristan said, before he could stop himself.

Tansy's smile never faltered. "Sometimes. When a guest is content, he's much more willing to see things Fedro's way."

"And Marcus? Does he see things Fedro's way?"

"He does."

"And is this dinner supposed to make me see things Fedro's way as well?"

"I'd be lying if I said Fedro wasn't hoping you'd look on him more kindly. But this dinner was my idea." Tansy sighed and folded her hands in her lap, like a scolded child. "We can talk of Marcus and Fedro if you like, but it's making you look grim again, and I was so hoping to make you smile instead."

"I have little to smile about these days," Kristan said, and hated the petulant sound of his voice.

"Won't you let me try?" She leaned toward him, and her sweet perfume filled his nostrils. "That's why you came here, isn't it? To find something to smile about?"

Her eyes were so soft, so pleading, that he was ashamed of his ill temper. "I'm sorry. I fear I've been an ungracious guest."

"Let's begin again, then." She nodded toward his goblet. "Don't you like the wine? If it's not to your liking, I can bring another."

"It tastes expensive."

Tansy laughed. "It is. But you should have only the best, my lord. That's one of the beauties of Seagirt. Anything you want can be yours."

"If you have the money to pay for it."

She looked at him slantwise. "If you have the means to pleasure yourself, why shouldn't you? I heard you bought yourself a ring in the marketplace, but then gave it away to your Lady Astéria."

He pulled the ring from his pocket. "This one, you mean? She gave it back to me."

"Why?"

"It was just a simple gift, from one friend to another. But because others misconstrued its meaning, the gift became tainted."

"So, she's not your woman."

Kristan put the ring back in his pocket. "No. I told you that the first night I was in Seagirt."

"So you did." She crossed her arms on the table. It was impossible not to look at the rounded tops of her breasts. "I watched you all through that dreary dinner. You were surrounded by the best of everything, all the wealth and pomp and splendor of Seagirt's palace, and yet you took no pleasure in any of it."

"It was too much. Too much of everything."

Tansy laughed, caught up his napkin and draped it in his lap, so quickly that he had no time to recoil at her nearness. "It's the Dyerian way, to take pride and pleasure in excess. I'd rather have just enough of something splendid. This, for example." She uncovered a single dish and placed it before him.

Upon its shining silver surface, a single little bird lay on its back. Its feet were missing, but its tail and wings were intact and fanned out decoratively, as if the small creature was in flight. In the middle lay the bird's tiny breast. It had been skinned and boned, poached pale white and sliced thin, and sprinkled with spices and tiny slivers of herbs.

"There," Tansy said. "What do you think?"

With a forefinger, Kristan touched the bird's head. It shifted, revealing a minute crest of red feathers rising from its skull.

Kinglet.

Martin's voice hissed through his memory. Gorge rose in his throat.

"Isn't it a lovely little dish?" Tansy said.

For some moments Kristan could not speak. "Why?" he said at last. "Why would you eat this?"

Tansy laughed again. "Because it's delicious. Because it's pretty. Because it's rare and expensive."

"It's barely a mouthful. It took more time to prepare than it would to eat."

"That's the pleasure of it. Taste it and see."

Kinglet.

Gabriel's winking face rose in his memory; Gabriel the moment before the axe hewed off his head.

Seeyousoonseeyousoon . . .

Kristan forced himself to concentrate on the delicate dish before him. He studied the pattern of feathers on the outspread wings, the delicate down at the bird's throat. He picked up a sliver of meat. It was tender between his fingers. A riot of scent assailed his nostrils as he raised it to his lips.

"Go ahead," Tansy said. Her voice was soothing and warm as honey fresh from the comb. "Life is full of so many delicious things, Kristan; so much to taste and eat and enjoy. You've earned it. You deserve it. It's yours for the taking." She leaned close and laid her fingers atop his raised hand. The hair rose on the back of Kristan's neck.

Kinglet.

She pressed the morsel to his lips. He took it on his tongue and tasted all its flavors: the grassy tang of fresh herbs, the prickle of peppery spices, the mellow smoothness of expensive oils. Drowning beneath all this was the faint taste of flesh, barely cooked. Kristan's mouth filled with saliva; he could not tell if it was from nausea or appetite. He chewed; swallowed. "Good," Tansy whispered. She raised his hand to her mouth, put out her tongue and delicately licked the crumbs of seasoning from his fingers. His skin prickled with revulsion even as he grew hard beneath the napkin in his lap.

With her free hand, Tansy lifted the goblet of shimmering wine. "Now a little more of this," she said, and took a sip. Her green eyes watched him over the rim. She put the cup aside, but did not swallow. Instead, she leaned toward him again.

Her face was too close, and Kristan shrank away until his skull was pressed against the high back of the chair, and yet she still came on, and he could smell her again, her sweet perfume and beneath that, a faint seashore scent. Her lips met his, pillowy-soft and yet insistent, and under their pressure his own lips parted. A trickle of wine, still cool, passed from her mouth into his. He swallowed, and felt her lips curl into a smile. "So many delicious things," she whispered. "Let me comfort you, Kristan. Let me make you smile."

She pressed his hand to the warm heavy roundness of her breast. She inhaled, caught the tip of his tongue between her lips and sucked it gently. Gooseflesh rose on his arms and he averted his face. "Stop it," he growled. "What about Marcus?"

"Don't talk about him." She pulled up her skirt, exposing bare legs, and straddled his lap. "Marcus means nothing to me."

His guts began to roil even as the pressure of her body aroused him further. *Controlcontrolcontol* reverberated warningly through his brain, but running underneath it, like a discordant countermelody, was the echo of Tansy's voice saying *yours for the taking, yours for the taking . . .*

She was trying to open his tunic now; he lifted his hands to bat hers away but she began to rock her body, back and forth and side to side. The sensation was so overwhelming that he groaned. His hands clamped onto her hips instead, pressing her heat tight against him. Tansy brushed the Stone aside and scrabbled at the remaining fastenings of his tunic. "Yes, my love," she whispered, "my love, my Kristan, how I've dreamed of this—"

She yanked his tunic open and froze. Her eyes went wide and her lips pulled back from her teeth in a snarl of revulsion as she stared at his mutilated chest. Then she recovered; she closed her eyes quickly, threw back her head in an imitation of ecstasy and thrust herself against him with a vigor that was almost frantic. "Take me, Kristan," she cried. "I love you. I've always loved you."

She was lying; he knew she was lying, just as she had lied to him before, when she had told him she loved him, and then gave herself to Owen in the haystack. The grief and humiliation of that memory mingled with the knowledge that she found him repulsive, and his desire turned bitter in his mouth.

And still he was hard with wanting her, but the wanting was marred by the need to hurt her, punish her, to make her suffer as he had. He grabbed her buttocks. "Oh, yes, yes, my love, my Kristan," she cried, as he staggered to his feet.

He flung her onto the tabletop, among the shining silver platters and the sickening, expensive foods. He saw the triumph in her smile and hated it, hated her. He plunged his hand into a bowl of thick sticky sauce and smeared a handful of it down her face. Her eyes popped open and her practiced smile faltered, but only for a moment; she moaned and tried to grapple him closer. Guts churning, he slammed himself against her so hard that everything on the table rattled. He wanted to do it again, again and again, but instead he grabbed one of the silver platters and upended its oily, dripping contents onto her face and chest. She sputtered a bit but lifted her face as if to kiss him. "Do what you want with me," she whispered. "I'm yours, I'm yours."

He seized her wrists, pinned them above her head with one hand and put his face close to hers. "You're not mine, you lying bitch."

She froze in mid-writhe. Her lips opened and closed, as if trying to form another lie. He knotted his free hand in her hair and yanked her head back. "You've never been mine. You're a whore. And you mean nothing to me."

His insides heaved and he thought he might choke on his rage. He released her and stumbled back from the table. She sat up slowly, wiping her soiled face on her sleeve. Her smile was gone, replaced by a look of cool calculation as she studied him. "You want me," she said. "I can see it."

The floor seemed to sway beneath his feet. "Get out."

She slid off the table and stood facing him. "I can be anything you want, Kristan. I can be a virgin, never touched, with downcast eyes and timid hands. I can be a sophisticated lady of court, all wit and wile and games." She flicked at the slime clinging to her bodice. "Or I can be your sow. Choose how you want me . . . StoneKing."

The room shifted, tilted, but her hard, green eyes never moved. "I want no part of you."

"Liar."

Take her.

"You want me."

Hurt her.

The Stone was freezing cold against his bare chest. She stepped toward him, her eyes on the pulsing bulge between his legs. Her satisfied smile shone through the slick of oil and crumbs of food. "You want me," she said again, so close that he could smell the wine on her breath.

She reached for him.

His hands shot out and slammed into her shoulders. She staggered back and crashed against the wall. He was on her before she could fall; she laughed in his face, but the laugh turned into a squawk as he flung the door open and threw her into the hall beyond. She went sprawling, and when she looked up, her eyes were like ice on the Mor. "You want me," she said again.

"Get out of my sight."

"You want me. I see it. Any fool can see it, especially on a skinny little man like you." She laughed. "Take me. I'm yours."

"You're a whore. You've always been a whore."

She laughed again as she rolled to her feet, but her smile was like an animal baring its teeth. "You'd better take me, Kristan Gemeta. You were a pretty boy, once, but now you're hideous. Repulsive. No woman will want you. Oh, you'll find women who'll bed you, but they won't want you. They'll only endure you."

"Get out!"

"One day you'll come to me on your knees, StoneKing. On your knees, do you hear?"

He slammed the door on her and threw the bar across it. He had barely stepped away when the first cramps hit. He fell to his hands and knees, gagging, as the thudding ache of his loins spread through his hips and buttocks and down his thighs, convulsing in counterpoint to the spasming of his insides. The Stone swung in and out of his vision like a red pendulum. His body bucked and heaved as if it would wrench itself to pieces, as if his belly would split open and spill his bowels onto the shining floor.

Someone was hammering on the door, calling out to him. *Any moment*, he thought, in the midst of his agony. *Any moment now I'll black out*, but while his vision smeared and shifted, the merciful release of unconsciousness did not come. The paroxysms jerked him across the room; threw him onto his back and arched his spine like a bow, and then yanked his knees up into his belly. He rolled onto his side, facing the door, and tried to rise, but the cramps rippled down his limbs, knotting his fingers and toes.

Beyond the door voices rose: Fedro and Tansy shouted at each other and Serle cried, "My lord! My lord!" At the same time something small was squeezing beneath the door, a little gray mouse surrounded by a wavering blur that suddenly hissed and stretched and materialized into Nolle.

She stared at Kristan for a moment, then whirled to the door. "No," Kristan said, but his voice was no more than a croak. Nolle hesitated with her hands on the bar. Another spasm took him; his body bucked and twisted, but he managed to make his knotted tongue form words. "Only . . . Serle . . ."

Nolle nodded, unbarred the door and opened it only long enough for Serle to push into the room. Someone else tried to crowd in behind him, but Nolle and Serle threw themselves against the door and managed to work the bar back into place.

Both ran to his side and knelt next to him. Nolle tried to touch his forehead, but Kristan's hand rose of its own volition and slapped the girl's fingers away.

"Don't touch him," Serle snapped. "He can't stand being touched."

"What are we supposed to do, then?" Nolle said. She was almost whimpering.

"Just be quiet, be quiet!" Another spasm shook Kristan from head to toe, and Serle leaned close to him. "My lord, do you want us to fetch a healer?"

Kristan tried to answer, but his jaw muscles were cramping, sealing his teeth tightly together. A froth of saliva bubbled onto his lips. He made a gurgling sound of dissent and managed to shake his head.

"All right now, sir, just breathe," Serle said. "Just breathe. Nolle, get his cloak. That's it, sir, nice and easy. I'm going to put your cloak over you so you stay warm on this cold floor."

Someone pounded on the door. "What's going on in there?" Fedro called, his voice high and hysterical. Another paroxysm shook Kristan so hard that his elbows, heels and skull drummed against the floor. Nolle let out a tiny squeak of dismay.

"Don't listen; don't you listen to all that noise," Serle went on, in the same soothing voice. "You just think about breathing in and out, in and out. Easy does it, sir." He began to hum, then to sing softly, and through his torment Kristan recognized the tune from their first night in Seagirt.

Never mind the hawk
Never mind the wolf
Never mind the rain or dark of night
Rest your woolly head
In your woolly bed
Your mam and I will keep you safe 'til light

Serle's thin voice cracked on the high notes, but the tune

gave Kristan something to concentrate on. Gradually, his spasms eased and slowed. It helped that Fedro had stopped pounding at the door, but muffled conversation in the hall beyond signaled that he had not left. Kristan shut his eyes and finally drew a full breath.

"That's the way, sir," Serle said. "You just rest now." He sang the tune again, more slowly, in a voice that was little more than a murmur. Kristan found the simple rhythm of the song and breathed with it. His knotted muscles began to relax.

"Is he asleep?" Nolle whispered.

"Hush," Serle said. "Maybe."

"Did you see his chest? It's awful—scars all over."

Kristan shuddered.

"Hush, I said. Can you slip out to Desta? Ask him to wait?"

Nolle's skirts rustled as she stood. Her footsteps receded quickly, and her faint murmur of *marra marra marrapatta* was followed by a shout of surprise on the opposite side of the door.

Kristan opened his eyes. "Desta?" he croaked.

Serle smiled down at him. "Yes, sir. He was passing by and stopped to talk. He told me horses will sometimes hold their breath and make themselves fat so you can't tighten their girth. He showed me how to give Malvo a poke in the belly to make him behave." His smile faded. "Then we heard that lady screaming at you, and Fedro Vincenze shouting. Desta held the horses so I could run to see what was happening, but it was Nolle who got us into the room." He leaned a little closer. "Don't be mad, sir, because she snuck out of the palace."

Kristan pushed himself upright. His head throbbed. A final spasm shook him, but it was not as severe and over quickly. His tunic still hung open, exposing his lacerated chest, but his fingers trembled so that he could not fasten it up. Serle raised his hands, then hesitated. "Please, sir," he said. "Please let me do it for you."

Defeated, Kristan nodded. He pulled the Stone out of the way. Serle leaned close, his fingers fumbling over the elaborate fastenings. Kristan averted his face. *Breathe,* he told himself, *count your breaths,* but he could not help shivering at the boy's touch.

"I'm sorry, sir," Serle whispered. "So sorry."

"Why?" His voice came out as a snarl. "Because I'm such a weakling that I shiver like a baby bird when I'm touched?"

"No, sir." Serle let out the tiniest sob. "Because someone did that to you. Because someone hurt you so terribly."

Kristan shut his eyes. He wanted so badly to weep himself, but no tears would come. *What have I done?* he thought. *What kind of monster have I become?*

He rolled to his hands and knees and with an effort, heaved himself to his feet. The room pitched and heeled, but he made himself focus on his breathing and in a few moments, everything settled into place. Outside the door Fedro was whining and apologizing, and a breath later Nolle's mouse form slipped into the room and she rematerialized. "Desta says he'll wait as long as it takes. Fedro is still out there but he sent that woman away." She shook her head, mouth prim. "She said swear words I've never heard before."

"Can you ride, sir?" Serle asked.

Kristan nodded. Serle helped him into his cloak, and then hovered at his elbow as he made his way toward the door. Nolle ran ahead to remove the bar, and as she opened the door, Fedro tried to push his way in. "My lord, I'm so sorry—"

Nolle raised both hands threateningly. "Shut up and get out of the way."

For a large man, Fedro could move with startling speed. When Kristan and Serle came into the front hall, he was pressed against the far wall, eyes huge in his fat face, hands raised defensively. "I do apologize most abjectly, my lord—"

"I said shut up," Nolle said. She opened the main door. Outside, alert and seemingly impervious to the blustery weather, Desta waited with Malvo and Serle's pony.

"Shall I help you mount, sir?" Serle asked.

"No," Kristan said. "Get on your own pony and take Nolle up behind you."

"I'll fly back," Nolle said. Desta turned toward her, as if eager to watch the transformation.

Through his misery, Kristan felt a distant amusement. "I'd rather you didn't," he said. He pulled on his gloves and held out a hand for Malvo's reins. "Thank you for your help, Desta."

Desta beamed. "I'm happy to be of service. May I escort you to the palace, my lord?"

"That won't be necessary. Go home. It's cold, and I'm sure everyone is wondering where you are."

"They won't miss me, my lord, and I'm not cold."

"Do as I say, Desta," Kristan said wearily. "I won't forget what you did tonight, never fear."

Desta's shoulders sagged, but he made a pretty bow all the same. "As you say, my lord. Good night."

Desta disappeared into the darkness. Kristan guided Malvo out of the Vincenze courtyard, with the children following behind on their shared mount. The pony was skittish, but Malvo trudged along like an old horse, his once-proud head carried low. *I'm sorry, old friend*, Kristan thought, and patted the sleek black neck, but Malvo flinched at his touch.

The bitter wind had driven most of Seagirt indoors. The promenade leading toward the palace was largely deserted, and Kristan was grateful. He was ashamed of himself: ashamed of his lust, ashamed of his viciousness, ashamed of his frailty. He felt the children's pitying gazes on his back, and drew up his hood to hide his face. *I'm going to go mad*, he thought. *If I don't get home soon, I'm going to go stark mad, in front of all these staring eyes.*

The approaching clatter of hooves yanked him from his misery. He raised his head just as Sir Walter reined up before him. "There you are!" the knight said. "I know you said not to bother you, my lord, but I thought you'd want to know right away."

"What is it?" Kristan said dully.

Walter's grin was so broad that his teeth sparkled in the moonlight. "He's here at last, my lord. The merchant Lorz just arrived in the harbor."

CHAPTER SEVENTEEN

Lorz' ship was well out in the harbor, but even at a distance and through the cacophony of wind and waves, his outrage was evident.

"What do you mean by this? In all the years I've been coming into Seagirt, this is the only time I've ever been refused entry! Not even the Daaznans kept me from conducting my business!"

The shouting, complaining voice continued as Saratt's ship nosed toward the other realm warships, which hemmed in the merchant vessel like a pack of wolves surrounding a large, fat cow. "Make way, there!" Saratt called.

A rattle of pikes from the nearest ship answered. "Bear off," came the warning cry. "No one is to approach, by order of the StoneKing!"

"The StoneKing is aboard my vessel," Saratt shouted back. The bellowing aboard the merchant ship abruptly went silent.

"Prove it," said the voice from the nearest warship.

Saratt turned to Kristan. "My lord?"

"Show a light here," Kristan said, and stepped into the bow. As members of the crew illuminated his head and shoulders with lanterns, he pulled the Stone from beneath his cloak and held it up. "I am the StoneKing," he said. "Now give way."

"At once, my lord!"

Kristan made his way back to the aftcastle. His five knights stood outside, squinting against the mingled rain, snow and salt spray. Just within the low doorway, Astéria waited in human form, hands clasped together and eyes bright with hope. Serle and Nolle flanked her, jiggling from foot to foot with excitement. Melissa was seated inside, wearing an expression of cool disinterest.

"You could have stayed ashore," Kristan said to her.

"Oh, I wouldn't have missed this for the world," Melissa answered, with just the faintest sardonic bite to her words.

"Kreestan, you think my people there?" Astéria asked in a low voice.

"I hope so," Kristan said.

"The ship is riding low in the water," Mitchell said. "That means they're carrying a full load of cargo in their hold."

"They'll be there," Serle said, patting Astéria's arm. "I'm sure of it."

"Easy there," Captain Saratt called, as the Norwinn warship eased alongside Lorz' ship. Even riding low, the merchant vessel's sides rose well above their heads, and Saratt turned an anxious face to Kristan. "Are you sure you want to do this, my lord? The darkness and this weather are going to make boarding tricky. You might fall in, or be crushed between the boats. And it's even more dangerous for the lady," he added, glancing at Astéria.

"I do it," Astéria said, with a fierce stare.

"I'll help you," Sir Mitchell said. "I've done this before."

"Serle, too," Astéria said, taking the squire by the hand.

The crew of the merchant ship lowered a rope ladder, and Sir Mitchell, with the help of some of Saratt's crew, caught hold of it as the warship rocked in the waves. "It would be best if you went first, my lord," Mitchell said. "Serle can follow you, then Astéria. I'll bring up the rear."

Kristan nodded. "As you say."

With the end of his journey finally in sight, he felt almost reckless with elation. He grappled onto the rope ladder and with the wind whistling in his ears, began his ascent. It had been so long since he had exerted himself that he arrived at the top of the ladder out of breath and trembling. He endured the touch of the merchant crew as they helped him over the ship's rail, then found himself facing a broad barrel of a man with a weathered face, a bristling black beard and an expression of mingled annoyance and curiosity.

"Are you the merchant Lorz?" Kristan asked.

Lorz gave him a graceless bow. "I am, StoneKing. Welcome aboard."

Kristan glanced over the side. A white-faced Serle was coming slowly up the ladder, with the shadowy forms of Astéria and Mitchell behind him. A sudden blur and flutter of brown feathers burst up from the deck of the warship below. It winged past the three on the ladder and a moment later Nolle was standing next to Kristan. Lorz uttered an oath and his crew drew back.

Kristan opened his mouth to reprimand Nolle, but she leaned close. "Astéria is nervous," she murmured. "I thought I'd better stay close. And I altered her shift, just in case one of these fools might recognize her."

"Very well," Kristan said.

"A Wichie?" Lorz was sputtering. "You brought a Wichie aboard my vessel?"

Before Kristan could answer, Serle clambered over the rail and reached back to help Astéria, but the very crew members who had recoiled at Nolle's appearance surged forward, elbowing Serle and each other in their haste to help her. To Kristan's astonishment, instead of Astéria's tall form, the figure that stepped on deck was that of the princess Jelena, from her luxuriant shape and creamy dress right down to her red gloves. Serle gasped, and Sir Mitchell, topping the ladder behind her, stopped short, mouth agape.

"Princess!" Lorz exclaimed, and bowed low—*far lower than he bowed to me*, Kristan observed sourly. "Well, this is a pleasant surprise!"

Astéria was too busy staring from her red gloves to her jutting bosom to answer. Nolle stepped quickly forward. "Don't you worry, Princess, you're just a little wet," she said. She shot a hard glance at Mitchell and the knight suddenly seemed to come to his senses. He leaned over the rail to wave the Norwinn warship off, but Serle stayed where he was, still gawping. With an insincere smile, Nolle took hold of his arm. "Come along, boy," she said, and gave him a hard pinch.

He let out a squawk. "What'd you do that for?"

"Serle," Kristan said warningly, and the squire subsided. "Sir Mitchell," Kristan went on, "kindly escort the princess."

"Yes, indeed; come out of this weather," Lorz said, gesturing toward the ship's deckhouse. "I can guess now why you're here. Princess, your gift must have been a great success." He smirked at Astéria, but she only gave him a blank stare. "Your gift to the StoneKing," Lorz said helpfully. "Such a fine, strong beast."

Astéria's eyes blazed with sudden comprehension, but before she could respond Kristan cut in. "Indeed. Princess Jelena tells me you have more. I'd like to see them."

Lorz did not answer. He twisted his mouth to one side and rubbed his beard thoughtfully. Astéria's hand rose to her throat, and Kristan's heart sank.

"Well," the merchant said at last, "I have them, my lord, but they're not in a fit state to be inspected. We've had nothing but bad weather since we left Malchea, and the creatures are sick from the rough seas. For all their strength and size, they aren't very hardy. May I suggest instead that you come into my cabin? I'm carrying a store of a particularly robust honeyed wine from a far western port. You and the princess can sample it, and we can do a little preliminary bartering."

"I'd rather see the stock now."

"But this wine, my lord—I can guarantee you've never tasted such a fine drink—"

"I didn't come out here to taste wine."

Lorz spread his hands in appeal. "My lord, I beg you; give my stock a chance to recover from the voyage. If you wait until morning to inspect them, they'll be rested and in far better spirits, I assure you—"

"Now," Kristan said, unable to keep the edge from his voice.

Lorz' face fell, and he gestured to one of his crew for a lantern. "As you wish, of course. But please, my lord—bear in mind that you won't be seeing them at their best."

They followed the merchant into the depths of the pitching, heaving ship; down ladders, between barrels and crates roped tight against the ship's hull, past seamen snoring in their hammocks. As they descended, the stench of mold and wet wood began to mingle with another odor; a fetid stink that crawled up Kristan's nostrils and lodged just behind his watering eyes. Lorz paused at the top of a final ladder. "Because of the weather, we haven't been able to clean this hold lately. It's a bit rank."

"A bit?" Sir Mitchell muttered.

"Continue, please," Kristan said. With a sigh, Lorz started down the ladder, and Kristan turned to his company. Astéria was clinging to both Serle and Mitchell. She was trembling, and all three were white to the lips from the stench and the pitching of the ship. "Look here," Kristan whispered. "Whatever we find down below, everyone is to keep calm. Astéria, it would be best if you didn't speak, understand?" He put a finger to his lips to emphasize his words, and she nodded.

As Kristan descended after Lorz, the odor seemed to creep up his body like a rising tide. He tried to breathe through his mouth, but the stench was so strong he could taste it. It was all he could do not to gag.

"Well," Lorz said, his voice bright with false heartiness, "here they are."

The merchant had hung his lantern on a hook and was lighting a twist of straw from its flame. In the sudden flare Kristan glimpsed a series of tall, narrow cages. Astéria let out a tiny whimper, and Serle murmured to her soothingly. Lorz moved through the hold, lighting other lanterns with his twist, and the yellowy light revealed filthy straw, piles of vomit and excrement, and the centaurs huddled miserably in their prisons.

Some stirred, moaning and squinting against the light.

Lorz caught up a long pole and prodded the nearest centaur, a thin adolescent female with a sorrel hide and tangled red-blonde hair. She rolled onto her chest, heaved herself onto all four legs and stood, arms crossed tightly over her small breasts, head down. Her tail was matted with liquid feces, her hocks were raw and oozing and her bony frame trembled as if in the throes of ague.

"She's a fine creature," Lorz said. "A bit under the weather at the moment, but once she's feeling better and we get a chance to clean her up, you'll see. She may be a bit young for breeding, but she's meeker than the others. She has beautiful lines, doesn't she?" He poked the centaur girl again. "Look up, pretty thing, so the StoneKing can see your face."

The centaur girl lifted her head. Her large, slightly tilted eyes drifted toward Kristan, regarded him dully, then suddenly flicked beyond him. She snarled and threw herself at the bars of her cage. *"Poú eínai?"* she cried. *"Poú eínai i Astéria?"*

She was not shouting at him, but at Astéria in her Jelena-form. At her outburst, some of the other centaurs looked up, then staggered to their feet and joined in the uproar.

"Ah, the creatures must recognize you, Princess," Lorz called, grinning like a corpse as he used his prod to strike at the angry centaurs. "Get back, there!"

"Astéria! Ti tis échete kánei?" shouted a male centaur.

Astéria let out an inarticulate moan, and at the same moment her Jelena-form began to waver. "She's fighting it," Nolle hissed. "She's trying to break free."

"Get her out of here," Kristan ordered in an undertone. "Get her back on board the warship."

Mitchell and Serle hustled Astéria to the ladder. With Nolle close behind them, they ascended, and the centaurs seemed to go mad with rage. They roared and shook the bars of their cages until they rattled. Some turned and began kicking the bars with their hind legs. In the tumult, Kristan took the opportunity to count them. *Eleven*, he thought, overwhelmed with relief. *Six females and five males. In terrible shape, but by the Stone, they're all here.*

"Back, back!" Lorz shouted, as he jabbed at them. One of the males grabbed the prod, and as he and Lorz struggled for it, Kristan leaned as close as he dared to the young female. "*Chairete*," he whispered.

She froze in mid-kick, then whirled to face him, eyes wide and lips parted. Kristan pressed a finger to his lips. "*Eíste ypomonetikoí*," he said, hoping he had not mangled the pronunciation. The young female swallowed hard and nodded.

Kristan swung to Lorz. "Stop upsetting them. I can see the condition they're in."

Lorz yanked the pole free of the male centaur's hands and staggered back, but he was still trying to grin. "Yes, indeed; they're a lively bunch, aren't they?"

"They're sick," Kristan said.

"I tell you, it's from the weather."

"And starving," Kristan went on, waving his hand at the centaurs. "Look at them. Their ribs are showing."

Lorz' grin wavered. "My lord, I haven't been mistreating them, I swear to you. We've tried everything—hay, oats, all manner of greenstuff—but they won't eat."

The merchant began to enumerate all the ways he had tried to care for his difficult cargo, but Kristan was barely listening. The young female had sidled up to the centaur in the nearest cage and was speaking to him, keeping her voice low. He cast a startled look at Kristan, then shifted to the other side of his cage and spoke to the next centaur, who nodded and passed the message on.

" . . . shut away down here for their own protection, my lord. Some of my men were pestering the females and I suppose you can't blame them; being at sea and away from women so long, it's hard for them to resist tweaking a nipple when they see one—"

"Shut up," Kristan said absently. All eleven centaurs were watching him now. *How to get them off this ship and to O Tópos?* he wondered. *How to do it without attracting attention or being followed?*

He turned back to Lorz. "I'll take all of them." Even as he spoke, he imagined Quinn Logan groaning at the expense, and Piri Neff telling him that he was stretching his personal finances to the breaking point, and finally, Mali Uzuri saying *you should always bargain, my lord.* "But at a tenth of the price Princess Jelena paid," he added quickly.

He had no idea how much Jelena had actually paid for Astéria, but to his satisfaction Lorz' jaw dropped. "Oh, now, my lord . . ."

"A tenth, Lorz. You charged the princess a ridiculous price and got away with it, but you won't find another buyer for the *Kentav*—the creatures, I can guarantee it. Oh, you might sell one or two, but not all eleven, not as unruly as they are, and not in their condition."

"My lord, have mercy. You've no idea what it's cost me to keep these things: the delicacies I've had to buy to tempt their appetites, the repairs to my ship when they go wild, as they so often do, the iron cages—I had to delay my departure from Malchea to have the things built—the increases I've had to pay to my crew just to coerce them into sailing with these monsters—they think they're bad luck and some wouldn't sail with them for any amount—not to mention the space they take up, which I could have used for more profitable cargo—"

"All the more reason you should accept my price, and be rid of them."

Lorz' features settled into a stubborn scowl. "I'd be selling them at a complete loss, my lord."

"A tenth of what the princess paid, Lorz." The surge of energy Kristan had felt on learning of Lorz' arrival was fading, replaced by leaden resentment, a growing headache, weakness in the knees and the familiar swirl of nausea. *I am the StoneKing.*

How dare you presume to barter with me?

"Surely you won't begrudge me a little profit, my lord. The best I can do is sell them at half what the princess paid. Even that will barely cover my expenses."

"A tenth of the price, I said." Kristan's fingers twitched with the desire to strike the merchant. *Control. Controlcontrolcontrol.*

"A third of what I charged in Malchea, and I'll throw in a crate of that honeyed wine."

Kristan sucked in a deep breath. "Lorz, you don't seem to understand your position. You're in my harbor, in my waters, surrounded by my ships. You can accept my offer, or . . ." A sudden, spiteful idea struck him. "Or I can simply take what I want."

Lorz goggled at him. "My lord, you can't . . . you couldn't possibly—"

"Can't I? I could take your entire cargo—your entire ship, for that matter—and have you and your crew pitched overboard." His stomach knotted, overwhelming his satisfaction at besting the merchant. He moved toward the ladder to hide his discomfort. "One tenth, or nothing at all, Lorz. You choose."

He ascended through the ship, with Lorz whining and complaining behind him the whole way. On deck, Sir Mitchell waited by the rope ladder, his fingers tucked into his armpits for warmth, the raw wind tumbling his hair and cloak. "How goes it?" Kristan asked, raising his voice to be heard over the churning of the sea against the ship's hull.

Mitchell put his mouth to Kristan's ear, and Kristan had to clench his teeth against the impulse to shy back. "All in the warship, my lord. Nolle changed Astéria from the princess form to her own human shape while they were going down the ladder. What with the dark and the wind and waves, neither crew was the wiser. Slick as snot, that girl."

Below, Captain Saratt's warship still rode alongside the merchant vessel, and the captain himself was gazing up at them, his anxiety over the worsening weather evident in spite of the darkness. Mitchell cleared his throat pointedly, and Kristan turned to find Lorz before him, wringing his hands. "All right, my lord, all right," he said. "Twenty pieces of gold each, but it isn't fair, my lord."

"Very well," Kristan said. "Let's go, Mitchell. Lorz, I'll be back with the money shortly."

"But . . . my lord, shouldn't we follow you to the docks, to offload the creatures?"

"No. You're to wait here for further instructions."

"But my lord—"

The merchant's protests faded as Kristan descended the rope ladder, with Mitchell following. "Captain Saratt," he said, as soon as his feet were on the warship's deck, "head back to the dock. And pass the word to the other warships that they're to keep Lorz here, under the same conditions as before. Tell them we'll return as quickly as we can." He beckoned to his knights, and they followed him to the aftcastle, where the rest of his party waited. "We're going to have to move fast," he said, gesturing everyone close as the ship turned toward the shore. "Sir Mitchell, can you captain this warship?"

The young knight gaped at him. "Well . . . I . . ."

"Can you or not?" Kristan demanded.

Mitchell swallowed hard. "Yes, my lord."

"Can any of the rest of you sail?" Kristan went on, turning to the other knights.

"A bit, my lord," Sir Geoffrey said. "I'd be a disgrace to Norwinn if I couldn't."

"Kennet? Walter? Matthew?"

"No, my lord," the other three knights murmured, looking absurdly ashamed.

Kristan swore softly. "I need more sailors."

"Why?" Melissa said. "You've got Saratt and his men."

"I don't want them. I only want people I know and trust near *O Tópos*. Astéria, can your people sail this ship?"

She stared at him, clearly still shaken. "*Aftó to skáfos?*" she finally said. "*Naí.* Yes."

"Then we can offload Saratt and his men as well," Kristan said to Mitchell.

"But they're my crew!" Melissa protested.

"Keep your voice down," Kristan said. "Once you're in Norwinn, you can send a ship back for them. Until then, they'll have extended shore leave in Seagirt. I can't imagine they'll object." He flicked his gaze around the ship. "This thing is too big to navigate into *O Tópos*, isn't it, Mitchell?"

"Yes, my lord, but it's got a little launch of its own. We could anchor a little way off on the Mor and send someone into *O Tópos* in the launch, to let them know where the warship is so they can come get their people."

"Very good. As soon as we're back at the dock, you're to take command of this warship. Offload everything but provisions, understand? You're going to have to make room for our mounts as well as the centaurs. Geoff and Kennet, you're to prepare the horses. Walter and Matthew, see to our own belongings. The rest of you, help them get everything packed."

"And what am I to do?" Melissa demanded.

"Get ready with everyone else. As soon as the centaurs are safe in *O Tópos*, you'll be going back to Moordock, I'll be going back to Fandrall, and everyone can get back to work."

"But Nigel—"

"I've already told you what to do about him, Melissa, and I've neither the time nor the patience to argue it further."

She crossed her arms and turned her back on him.

"My lord," Geoffrey said, "how can we move the centaurs from Lorz' ship to this one? I know you don't want to do it at the docks, where people will see and talk, but transferring them at sea will be well-nigh impossible."

"Leave that to Nolle, Astéria and me."

They left Sir Mitchell at the dock, to deal with Captain Saratt and his crew, and hurried to the palace. Geoffrey and Kennet hustled off to the stables while Kristan led the others inside.

The doors had barely closed behind them when they were beset by Marcus, red-faced and the worse for drink, with Raul and Piri trying to restrain him while Dell watched impassively and servants and courtiers peered from nearby doorways.

"There he is!" Marcus shouted, flinging himself toward Kristan. "There he is at last, the despicable little shit!"

"Marcus, for pity's sake—" Raul started to say.

"Pity? He had no pity, not for her!"

To Kristan's astonishment, great tears were welling in Marcus' eyes. "What on earth is going on?" he demanded.

"As if you didn't know!" Marcus shook both fists at him.

"Please, Reach Tasgall, not here—" Piri Neff said, clinging fiercely to Marcus' arm.

"It should be here! It should be in front of everyone, so everyone knows what the great StoneKing did to a helpless woman!"

Kristan's stomach clenched. A slow, insistent tingle of rage crawled up his spine.

Control control control.

"Come into the throne room," he said, trying to keep his voice level, but the words sounded cold and arrogant.

In the throne room, he mounted the dais and seated himself in silence. Marcus stood at the foot of the steps, fists clenched and chest heaving. Piri and Raul stood nearby, as if ready to leap on him if needed. Dell waited with the rest of Kristan's party.

"Now," Kristan said, taking hold of the Stone. "Explain yourself."

"I don't have to explain!" Marcus shouted. "You know what you did to my Tansy!"

Kristan made himself look Marcus squarely in the eye. "What did she tell you?"

"She wouldn't talk to me. She shut herself in her room. But I saw the condition she was in. I talked to Fedro. I know what you did!"

"I ruined her dress and hurt her pride."

"Liar! You raped her!"

The words jarred the air like the reverberation of a great, cracked bell. Someone gasped—it might have been Melissa.

I wish I had my sword, Kristan thought; *I would step down from this throne and lop your squawking head from your body.* His muscles were beginning to twitch; the Stone was like a lump of ice in his hand. *Stop it. Control. Controlcontrolcontrol.*

He forced himself to lean back in the throne's ornate embrace. He counted his breaths as he ran his free hand along the slick, cool curves of its arm. "Tansy dared to put her hands on me," he said at last. "You may be fooled by a whore's blandishments and caresses, Marcus, but I am not. And even if your claim was true, remember this: I am the StoneKing. I do as I please. I don't have to explain or excuse my actions. Not to you, nor anyone in this room."

"How could you—"

"Shut your mouth." Kristan propped his elbow on the arm of the throne, rested his chin on his upturned palm and considered all the faces watching him: Marcus crimson with fury, Raul stricken, Dell still detached in spite of the furor, Piri Neff carefully expressionless. His own company could not seem to decide whether to look at him or avert their eyes. *I'm sick of you all*, he thought, *sick of your judgment, sick of your watching eyes.* "I'm setting sail this evening," he went on. "My business in Dyer is nearly completed. Piri, I'll need a considerable sum from my personal treasury—two hundred and twenty gold pieces. Please see that it's brought to me immediately. Before you go," he added, raising his hand as Piri started to leave, "one more piece of business. I've been here long enough to see that three Reaches in this realm are two too many. The partner proxy is a failure. I admit it, and as of this moment I dissolve it. Raul, you'll remain as sole Reach. Dell and Marcus, I release you from my service."

He was prepared for Marcus' sputter of fresh outrage and

Raul's pale-faced yet somber nod, but not for the sudden grin that lit Dell's face. *By the Stone, he hated this*, he thought. *He hates it as much as I do*. The realization softened his anger and eased the churning of his guts, and he continued in a calmer tone: "The two of you will maintain your status as knights of the realm and your wages for that service. In addition, I'll stand by my promise of last summer and give you the funds to set yourself up in whatever business you like, wherever you like. But this partner proxy is finished." He rose and descended the stairs. "Piri, hurry with that money, if you please. Those in my company, go and pack. Marcus, not another word. Raul, a moment of your time."

Marcus stormed out as Kristan met Dyer's remaining Reach at the bottom of the dais and beckoned him into a secluded corner. "I know this seems a sudden and capricious decision. Let me assure you it's neither. Are you ready to take on your duties alone?"

Raul swallowed hard. "I am, my lord. I hope I prove worthy of your trust."

"I trust that you will. You've proved yourself more than capable of managing the kingdom on your own. But on peril of your life, never keep information from me again, understood?"

"Understood, my lord. And I'm sorry to have disappointed you in that regard." Raul leaned closer. "Kristan, are you truly leaving this instant?"

"As soon as the funds are in my hands. I'll be taking the Norwinn warship to *O Tópos*, then on to Moordock, and finally to Fandrall's shore. Meantime, the Norwinn crew will be at liberty on your shores until they're sent for. See that they're treated well, especially Captain Saratt. And once Lorz has docked, you're to show him every consideration. Make certain he gets a more than fair price for whatever the palace buys from him. I'm sure he feels I've robbed him of his most valuable cargo, so to make up for it, grant him some official title—'personal purveyor of fine goods to the StoneKing' or some such nonsense.

That should go a long way toward salving his wounded pride. Oh, and send a messenger to Quinn Logan letting him know that I've left Seagirt and will be back in Kingsmere in the next seven days or so, depending on the weather."

Raul nodded somberly. "I'll take care of it, Kristan. I hope your journey is swift and uneventful, and the worst of this weather holds off until you're well away."

As Kristan started for the royal suite, he was waylaid by Dell, looking unusually determined. "Kristan, I need to talk to you," he said, catching Kristan by the sleeve.

Kristan pulled free. "Dell, I'm sorry. I had to do it."

Dell waved one hand impatiently. "You were right to dismiss me; I was no good as a Reach. I wanted to ask if I could sail with you."

"Are you going back to Hogia, then? I can put you off at Moordock and you can make your way to Needwood overland."

"I don't want to go back to Needwood. I want to travel."

"Travel? To where?"

"Everywhere. I want to study this land, the beasts and the trees and the weather. I want to find out why the wind blows the way it does, where the birds go when it's cold, what makes the tides go in and out. I want to know why long grass grows on the Plain but not in the mountains, what made the cliffs around Moordock, what causes the Cracks. I want to learn."

Too startled by the sudden burst of information to interject, Kristan could only gape at his former Reach. "I thought I might start with old Steffen in Moordock," Dell went on, a faraway gleam in his eyes. "He knows a good bit and I think he'd be willing to share that knowledge with me. And from there I could travel on, to different places, and see what I can see." Dell's gaze lit on Kristan, and he suddenly seemed to remember where he was and to whom he was speaking. "I don't expect you to pay me. You can revoke my knighthood if you want, and take back the money you've given me so far. I never felt I earned it, so I spent very little. Just let me go, Kristan. I don't expect anything more from you."

Kristan sighed. "Keep the money and the knighthood. I'll take you to Moordock with me, but you have to be ready quickly. We're leaving immediately."

"I don't need much," Dell said. "Just a cloak and a good pair of boots. Thank you, Kristan."

"Be at the docks as soon as you can," Kristan said, but Dell was already hurrying away.

Just as easily as that, Kristan thought. *Just as quickly and easily as that, he can drop all his responsibilities and walk away.* Overwhelmed by a burst of bitter envy, he hunched his shoulders and strode off to the royal suite.

* * *

Tansy was busy packing when Marcus burst into her room. "He dismissed me! The little shit dismissed me!" he cried, throwing himself into a chair.

She paused in the act of folding a shift. "What?"

"I said he dismissed me! When he came back to the palace, I challenged him—called him out in front of everyone for what he did to you."

"What did he say to that?"

"He looked me in the eye, cool as could be, and said he was the StoneKing and could do as he pleased!"

"Ah," Tansy said. "Well."

"And in the next breath he told us he was leaving, and that he was dissolving the partner proxy. He turned me and Dell loose and put Raul in charge. He left my knighthood intact, along with my pay for that, but without my Reach's wages I'll be ruined. The little shit! I was only just keeping my head above water as it was." He slapped his thighs, stood and began to pace, hampered somewhat by Tansy's belongings strewn about the room.

"That's unfortunate," Tansy said. She finished folding the

shift, put it into a sturdy leather satchel and turned her attention to her jewelry.

"Unfortunate?" Marcus echoed, pulling himself up short with a sardonic snort. "That doesn't even begin to describe it." He suddenly registered the disarray of the room. "What on earth are you doing?"

"What does it look like? I'm packing."

"Packing? Why?"

"I'm leaving Seagirt."

"Tansy, why?" Marcus tried to take her in his arms, but she shrugged him off. "What happened wasn't your fault, my darling; there's no need to be ashamed."

"I'm not ashamed. It's simply time for me to leave."

"But . . . what about me? What about us?"

She turned a cool eye on him. "Marcus, you're such an innocent. What we had was pleasant, but it's over now."

"Over? Tansy, I love you!"

"Don't be a fool. We were useful to each other, but that's done. I have to make a change now, and that change doesn't include you."

She stood, unmoving and unmoved, as Marcus sputtered and swore and even wept, but at last he stormed from her chamber and she was able to continue packing undisturbed. She picked through her belongings with a critical eye, choosing only what was essential. First was money, and she had a great deal of it. She distributed that amongst her bags and put the most valuable coins in a long narrow sack that she strapped to one leg, so that it would not ruin the fit of her dress. Next were her jewels, likewise secreted here and there. Next came her clothing; only her best and most luxurious, then her box of rouges, kohl and perfumes.

Finally, she took up the dress that she had worn earlier that evening. With a small but very sharp knife she cut a hand-sized piece from the greasy, soiled bodice. She rolled it up tight and tucked it in the perfume box, so she would see it every day, and every day be reminded of the reason she had left the spar-kling sophisticates of Seagirt for the backwater bumpkins of Kingsmere.

CHAPTER EIGHTEEN

By the time Lorz' money arrived from the treasury; by the time it was counted thrice, first by Piri, then by Raul, and at last by Kristan; by the time it was stowed in a large leather bag and sealed and a receipt signed for it (a time-consuming and annoying process that Kristan nonetheless resolved to put into place realm-wide upon his return to Fandrall), the rest of the departing company had already left for the docks. When Kristan arrived, they were swarming around the warship in the flickering yellow light of torches and lanterns, securing horses, stowing gear and generally making ready. The displaced Norwinn crew was lending a hand, and as anticipated, the men seemed not in the least troubled by their enforced shore leave, although Captain Saratt looked on with a long face.

Even though it was quite late, and the wind was increasingly bitter, the activity aboard the warship had attracted a crowd. Among them was the small, furtive form of the boy Desta, and to Kristan's surprise, Olaf also stood nearby. Melissa was beside him, speaking with some urgency, but when she caught sight of Kristan, she wheeled and stalked off to the warship. Kristan nodded to Olaf, but the Northman turned his back and disappeared into the shadows.

Sir Kennet came hurrying to relieve Kristan of the burden of the money sack. "Everything is loaded and all our people accounted for," he said, then leaned closer to add, "even your ex-Reaches."

"Both of them?"

"Sir Dell said you'd approved him joining us and got right to work helping us make ready. Sir Marcus is over there." Kennet indicated Marcus' figure, slouching against the starboard rail. "He came aboard with a bottle and the clothes on his back, nothing more. Sir Geoffrey is keeping an eye on him. My lord, I think you should put him off the ship. He's drunk and not to be trusted."

"I'll speak to him," Kristan said. He boarded, eyeing the preparations as he headed toward Marcus. Sir Walter was busy soothing the horses in the hold as the deck planks were relaid over them, while the other knights rushed here and there, under Sir Mitchell's direction. The youngest knight bantered with the warship's crew as they worked, and seemed to take pleasure in ordering the senior knights about. Astéria stood with the children right out in the bow, almost on her toes, as if by her very yearning she could move the warship toward the shadowy blob of the merchant vessel and the flotilla guarding it. Melissa alone waited in the doorway of the aftcastle, her heart-shaped face taut and unsmiling, and Kristan felt a pang of unease at the sight. *It can't be helped*, he told himself; *she's my heir and she has to learn that the realm comes first.*

"And there he is," said a sardonic voice. "The mighty StoneKing." Marcus threw back his head and drank deeply from his wine bottle.

Kristan stifled the impulse to strike his former Reach. "Why are you here, Marcus?"

Marcus belched and wiped his mouth with one sleeve. "Nowhere else to go. You said you'd set me up wherever I wanted. Well, I want to go back to Hogia. Back to Needwood."

"Very well. I'll put you off in Moordock with Melissa and Dell and you can make your way there overland."

Marcus peered toward Astéria. "Are you ever going to tell me what all this is about? You told Raul. You told Dell. You even told Piri Neff, but you wouldn't tell me. Why is that, mighty StoneKing?"

"If you're going to travel with me, Marcus, you'll address me properly. And in any case, you'll see for yourself soon enough." He turned away.

"Kristan," Marcus said, and something in his voice made Kristan look back. Tears shone in his former Reach's eyes. "Why her?" Marcus went on, his voice guttural with grief. "You could have had any woman in the realm. Why did you take her? Why did you take my Tansy?"

Kristan opened his mouth; started to protest, to deny, but then he reconsidered. *Let him believe what he wants. I'm the StoneKing and I do as I please.*

He plucked the bottle from Marcus' hand. "You're drunk. Once you're ashore, you can do as you like, but as long as you're on my ship, you'll stay sober and you'll hold your tongue. Or I swear I'll heave you overboard and you can sink or swim—it's all one to me."

He hurled the bottle into the water and strode across the deck to Sir Mitchell. "What's taking so long? Get these Norwinn seamen off the ship so we can get started."

It took some time to push off from the dock. In spite of Mitchell's bawled orders, the inexperienced knights blundered at their tasks, although Dell was less fumbling than the others. *He must remember what Olaf taught us last summer*, Kristan thought, and the memory of his final, cool parting from his friend overwhelmed him with mingled regret and anger. To shake it off, he joined the knights heaving at the lines, but his weary arms trembled with the effort. A pair of capable hands took hold above his, and he looked up into Astéria's rain-lashed face. "I do this," she said simply, and shouldered him out of the way.

He stepped back and watched her tall, powerful figure at work. *She knows what she's doing; that's a blessing. If the other centaurs are this capable, we'll be on the Mor in no time.* Serle and even Nolle hurried to help, and Astéria bent her head low to instruct them.

Only Melissa and Marcus did not offer to assist. His sister was huddled deep in her cloak within the aftcastle, head down, and Marcus stood above her on the poop deck, gazing back toward the receding lights of Seagirt. *Let him look*, Kristan thought crossly. *Let him yearn. I'm glad to wipe the dust of that place off my feet.*

Once the ship was under way, Kristan held a huddled conference with Astéria and Nolle, then a second one with his five knights and Serle. By the time they were nosing amongst the Dyer warships once again, Nolle had shifted Astéria to her Jelena form, transformed herself into a mouse and was riding on Astéria's shoulder, hidden in the rich folds of her cloak. As soon as they were alongside the portly form of the merchant ship, Sir Geoffrey secured the rope ladder and steadied it as Kennet, with the money bag strapped to his back, began to climb. Kristan followed him, with Astéria and Serle behind. Geoffrey brought up the rear and stood guard over the ladder, glowering at the merchant crew. Kennet unlashed the money bag and handed it to Lorz. The merchant hefted it, his face glum.

"No doubt you'll wish to count it," Kristan said. "Sir Kennet will accompany you to your cabin and witness the counting. You'll provide him with a receipt when you're finished. Meantime, the princess and I will inspect my purchase. No, we don't need an escort," Kristan added, as Lorz started to offer. "In fact, please gather your crew on deck, as far away from us as possible. Princess Jelena finds their ogling offensive."

"Of course, my lord."

With the crew gathered morosely at the far side of the ship, Geoffrey in position at the ladder and Kennet keeping Lorz busy in the cabin, Kristan and the others descended into the hold. As soon the centaurs caught sight of Kristan, they got to their feet, muttering; the moment Astéria appeared, the young female began to shake the bars of her cage again. "*Poú eínai í*

Astéria, kátharma?" she cried.

"*Kátse ísycha, Gaia,*" Astéria said sharply. The young female gasped. Nolle's mouse-form poked its head out of the cloak at the nape of Astéria's neck, an all-too familiar hiss filled the air, and a moment later Astéria stood in her true form, with Nolle at her side. The young female cried out and thrust both hands through the bars as if to embrace Astéria, and the other centaurs pressed as close as they could, their voices rising in joy and disbelief. "*Kathíste ísycha,*" Astéria said again, pressing a finger to her lips.

She began to speak in a low, urgent voice, gesturing frequently to Nolle. "Wait by the ladder," Kristan muttered to Serle. "I hope this rotten hulk doesn't have a ship's cat."

The centaurs goggled as Nolle changed from girl to mouse and back again, her growing exasperation evident with each shift. "*Poios tha páei prótos?*" Astéria asked. The other centaurs exchanged dubious looks. Astéria turned to the young female, her hands outspread beseechingly. "*Gaia?*"

The young female centaur swallowed hard and nodded. Nolle raised her hands and muttered the shift spell, and a moment later a small, reddish-brown mouse was blinking up at her from the filthy straw. "*Évge, Gaia,*" Astéria said, clapping her hands softly. "*Pígaine me tin Nolle tóra.*"

The Gaia-mouse did not move. With an impatient sigh, Nolle shifted into her own mouse form and scuttled into the cage. Her blurred figure ran around and around the wavering shape of the transformed centaur, making Kristan's head spin. He shut his eyes for a moment, and when he opened them, the two mice, surrounded by the flickering haze of their true forms, were passing him on their way to Serle. The squire stood very still as the mice leaped onto his boot and scurried up his leggings, but a nervous giggle escaped him as they burrowed beneath his cloak. "They tickle," he said.

"Go on, then," Kristan said. "Quickly and carefully. If anyone asks, you're fetching something for Princess Jelena."

Serle mounted the ladder, and Kristan stood with his head raised, listening to the boy's footsteps retreat through the ship. *"Poios eínai o epómenos?"* Astéria asked, turning back to the remaining centaurs. One of the younger males lifted a hand and said something in a questioning voice. Astéria was kept busy answering him, gesturing often at Kristan, until at last Serle's footsteps approached once more. As he hurried down the ladder, the Nolle-mouse jumped from his clothes, landed on the deck before him and rematerialized. "So slow," she said. "Who's next?"

Astéria pointed at the young male, and the same process was repeated: spell, transformation, mousy reassurance, dash across the floor, scramble up Serle's twitching body, ascend to the deck. This time the return was quicker ("they can run down the ladder to the ship faster than I can climb it," Serle explained) and the moment of encouragement unnecessary as the centaurs' faith in Nolle's spell grew. The next trip, Nolle transformed two centaurs, and three the trip after that. At last, she shifted Astéria back to her Jelena-form, then transformed the remaining centaurs into mice all at once. The creatures secreted themselves not only amongst Serle's clothing, but in Astéria and Nolle's as well. Kristan could hardly bear to look at his three companions, so sickeningly commingled were their forms with the shift-shapes. He led the way back to the deck and met Lorz coming out of his cabin with Kennet. "I trust your inspection was satisfactory, my lord?" Lorz asked.

"It was," Kristan said. "Kennet, do you have the receipt?"

"Yes, my lord," Kennet said, patting his tunic breast.

"Then kindly escort the princess and her servants to our ship and tell Mitchell to make ready. Lorz," he went on, turning to the merchant, "no doubt you feel ill-used now, but once you arrive in Seagirt, present yourself to my representative at the palace. I think you'll find that your losses this evening will be more than offset. One last thing: your ship is to stay here until daybreak."

"Until daybreak, my lord? I thought you were in a hurry to offload your purchase."

Kristan smiled a bit, in spite of himself. "Things change, Lorz. In ways and at times that can catch us by surprise. Good evening."

Lorz bowed, looking deeply puzzled, and Kristan hurried to the ladder. "Let's get out of here," he muttered to Geoffrey. They had barely set foot on the warship's deck before Sir Mitchell began to bellow orders. Their vessel slewed away from the merchant ship, paused among the Dyer warships long enough to pass on Kristan's order about keeping Lorz in place until morning, and then veered toward the harbor's broad entrance.

Sir Geoffrey blew out a long breath. "Glad that's over."

"Any difficulties?"

"None at all. Her cheekiness aside, that Nolle is a clever girl, and even Serle seemed to have his wits about him for once. He'd trot over to the ladder and stand there talking to me while the mice ran down to our ship. Once Nolle came back, he'd let her climb up his sleeve, and then go below decks again. The crew never suspected a thing." He chuckled. "I wish I could be there when Lorz goes into his hold and finds all those locked, empty cages."

"Where are the centaurs now?"

"Gathered below," Sir Matthew said, as he and Kennet joined them. "It was a sight to see, all those little mice scuttling across the deck. Once they got below decks with the horses, Nolle shifted them back. I think seeing the horses worried them, as if they thought they were going to be tied up with them. None of us knew how to tell them they only had to stay there until we got clear of the harbor, but finally Sir Dell settled them down—he knows enough of the centaur tongue to make himself understood."

"Walter got the galley fire going and stirred up some hot gruel for them," Kennet said. "They're in sad shape, my lord. Skin and bones, most of them."

"Seemed like Lorz was trying his best to feed them," Geoffrey said. "I wonder why they wouldn't eat."

"Imprisonment sickens them," Kristan said, remembering how shaken Torrin had been when tied up, even briefly.

A strong, salt-laced gust filled their sails as they headed out to sea. Geoffrey, Matthew and Kennet hurried to assist Sir Mitchell, just as Astéria popped her head out from below decks. "Kreestan!" she called. "It safe? We come up?"

Kristan nodded. With difficulty, the centaurs clambered from the hold, one at a time, arms and legs and hooves struggling for purchase as their comrades boosted them from below. Once on deck, some threw back their heads and closed their eyes, breathing deeply of the raw wind. Others held their faces and arms into the salt spray and gusty rain, then rubbed each other down, washing away the filth of their imprisonment. Still others laughed and pranced about the deck. Astéria clapped her hands sharply. "*Systitheíte kai na peíte efcharistó*," she said, pointing at Kristan.

Suddenly somber, the centaurs approached Kristan. The young female Gaia put one hand to her chest and bowed, right forefoot extended. "*To ónomá mou eínai Gaia. Sas efcharistó, Vasiliá* Kreestan."

Kristan bowed back, just as gravely. Gaia giggled, looked over her shoulder at Astéria and murmured something in *Kentávron*. Astéria shook her head in rebuke and turned to Kristan. "I am sorry. Gaia is *neari* . . . young. But *aderfí*. My . . . oh, how you say?" Melissa had come out onto the deck to watch, and Astéria waved toward her. "Sister, yes?"

"Gaia is your sister?" Kristan asked.

Astéria put her hand on Gaia's shoulder, and now Kristan could see the resemblance, in spite of the difference in coloration. "*Mikrí adelfí mou*," Astéria said. "This is why I feel sick when I first see her; when she call me bad things because she think I am Jelena."

"*Lypámai*, Astéria," Gaia murmured, looking sorry indeed.

The other centaurs presented themselves, murmuring their thanks. One of the males glanced at the knights struggling to bring the sails under control, and muttered something to Astéria.

"Zosimos says we sail this *várka* for you," Astéria said to Kristan. Kristan nodded.

Eyeing the sails, the sea and the sky, the centaurs trotted to the laboring knights and with smiles and bows and polite gestures, took over the lines. They brought the ship quickly under control and soon, its sails swollen with wind, it was slicing through the water like a knife. Although the centaurs were painfully thin, and their tails and the long mane-like stripes of hair down their spines were tangled and dirty, they were still magnificent creatures. "I think some of them are even taller than Torrin," Matthew said, as the knights returned to Kristan's side.

"More slender, though," Kennet said. "They don't have our friend's sheer mass."

"We'll have to feed 'em up, so they're not so shaky on their legs."

"They don't look shaky to me," Geoffrey said.

"They can stay on deck as long as there are no other ships around," Kristan said. "But the moment there's a chance they could be seen, they'll have to go below. Where's Serle?"

Matthew laughed. "In the stern. He's looking a bit green."

"And Nolle?"

"All that shifting wore her out," Geoffrey said.

"I sent her to the galley, where it's warm," Kennet said. "She was white to the lips and shaking all over."

There was a sudden crash below decks, followed by cursing and the sounds of a scuffle. A few moments later Walter came on deck, dragging a small, struggling figure by one arm. Kristan's heart sank at the sight.

"Look what I found stowed away below," Walter said. "I was checking the horses and found this boy hiding behind the grain stores. He says he knows you, the lying little sprat."

"Desta, leave off," Kristan snapped, as Desta aimed a kick at the knight's shin.

"Ah, so you do know him?"

"He's a relative of Mali Uzuri's," Kristan said. "Let him go."

Walter released Desta's arm, and the boy recovered quickly and bent himself into a typical Seagirt bow, all flourish and show. "Oh, stop it," Kristan said crossly. "What in the world were you thinking, Desta?"

"What do you want to do with him, my lord?" Walter asked.

Geoffrey snorted. "We should pitch him overboard and make him swim back to shore."

"We can't turn around and go back, not now," Matthew said.

"Perhaps an inbound ship could take him back," Kennet said.

"It'll have to wait until we get to Moordock," Geoffrey said. "We need to steer clear of other craft as long as we have the centaurs aboard."

Desta said nothing. He had straightened up and fixed Kristan with a look that mingled entreaty and defiance.

"There's nothing to be done about it now," Kristan said, with an irritable sigh. "I'll decide what to do with him later."

"And until then, my lord?"

"Bunk him with Serle, I suppose."

"I'll sleep in the hold with the horses, my lord," Desta said. "I can look after Malvo for you."

"That's Serle's job," Kennet said.

Matthew glanced astern. "Serle is being sick over the side as we speak. I doubt he'll be much use, my lord, at least until he gets his sea legs."

Kristan resisted the urge to roll his eyes. "Very well, Desta. And don't smile," he added, as the boy beamed. "You may be a resourceful, capable boy, but you're a nuisance right now. And Mali Uzuri must be worried sick about you."

"She said I could go," Desta said.

"What?"

Desta shuffled his feet. "She caught me when I was sneaking out. She said I was just like my father and if I was bound to do something, there was no talking sense to me. She said she supposed you'd forgive her and that you'd look after me, if only out of respect for my father."

See you soon, see you soon . . .

Kristan concentrated on the horizon, where the sky was growing lighter with the coming dawn.

"Please don't send me back, my lord," Desta said. "Please let me stay. I could be your squire. Serle doesn't know how to be a good squire, but I do."

Kristan glared at him. "Not another word about it, Desta. You show great insolence by criticizing my choice of squires, and ill manners by belittling his abilities."

Desta ducked his head. "I'm sorry, my lord. I won't do it again."

"You had better not, or by the Stone, I'll let Geoffrey pitch you overboard." Kristan took a deep breath and brought his temper under control. "We're on a mission of great secrecy, Desta."

"I understand, my lord. I saw the creatures and how that girl Nolle brought them aboard."

"They aren't creatures; they're *Kentávron*. Their kind helped me during last summer's struggle, and you're to treat them with respect."

"Yes, my lord."

Desta bowed again, and Kristan winced at the elaborate gesture. "Once a day is sufficient, Desta."

"And there's no room on this ship for all those Seagirt flourishes," Sir Walter said. "You might knock someone overboard."

"Enough, Walter. Desta, we're comrades on this ship and we must all work together to get the *Kentávron* to safety. If you conduct yourself well, I'll see if I can find a position for you in my realm. None of my knights have chosen squires yet; perhaps one of them will find you suitable for their service."

"But I—" Desta started to say, but wilted under Kristan's stern gaze. "Yes, my lord."

"Find some work for him, Geoffrey, and keep an eye on him. Walter, check on Serle. The rest of you, try to learn from Astéria's people about the sailing of this ship. Once they've left us for *O Tópos*, we'll have to make our way to Norwinn on our own."

Desta started to bow again, but Geoffrey took him by the shoulder, spun him about and pushed him toward the hold. As the knights hurried off, Kristan turned toward the aftcastle and found Marcus standing in his way, a broad grin on his face.

"Well, what?" Kristan demanded.

Marcus' smile only widened further. "You told me to hold my tongue, my lord," he said, and then bent into the most elaborate of Seagirt bows. Kristan swallowed his irritation and brushed past.

To his surprise, Melissa was still standing outside the aftcastle, gazing out to sea. Her dark hair was so misted with rain it looked almost gray, and her face was so haggard, so desolate, that Kristan's resentment at her gave way to pity. "Missy, get some rest. You can have the captain's cabin here; I'll sleep elsewhere."

She neither answered nor looked at him.

"Sister, I know you're angry," Kristan said. "But I do what I must."

"So do we all," she said, but her voice was thin and distant. Kristan threw up his hands in exasperation and went below.

He found Nolle curled up beside the galley stove, wrapped so deep in her cloak that only her nose showed. At first, he was not certain if she was awake or asleep, but as he hesitated in the doorway, she pulled away the cloak to peer at him out of one bloodshot eye. "What is it?"

"Walter said you weren't feeling well."

"You try turning a bunch of silly, frightened creatures into mice and back again and see how you feel."

"Nolle—"

"I know, I know. I'm supposed to say *my lord*."

Kristan was too weary to chide her for her insolence. *When did I last sleep?* he wondered. He sank down beside Nolle, braced his back against the bulkhead and propped his hands on his knees. "I came to thank you. You were invaluable tonight, Nolle. I don't know how we would have gotten the centaurs off that ship without you."

"It was the most shifting I've ever done at once." A sudden cunning glitter rose in her eyes. "I got all those centaurs aboard with no one the wiser. You should give me my reward now."

The thought of giving up the scrying ball was like a blow to the heart. "That wasn't our agreement."

"What difference does it make? I did what you asked, and did it well. Why not give me the scrying ball now?"

Because it's all I have left of my childhood. All I have left of Simeon. Why should I have to give it to this ill-mannered chit? "Nolle, I've a lot on my plate right now," he said aloud. "Don't try me."

"I heard the ruckus when Sir Walter found Desta. I knew you'd be mad."

"You knew Desta was in the hold?"

She snickered and sat up. "I saw him when I brought Gaia down there. He was petting Malvo. When we shifted out of the mouse form, you should have seen him jump! He hid behind Malvo, but I still saw him."

"Why didn't you tell anyone? We could have put him off the ship before we left Seagirt."

She shrugged. "I was busy. And afterward I was too tired. Besides, I like him. He helped us when you were sick. You owe him."

"I owe him? Nolle, you make my head ache." Kristan heaved himself to his feet and started for the ladder.

"My lord?"

The honorific, coupled with Nolle's suddenly meek tone, made him turn back. "What is it?"

"What will happen to me? When we get back to Fandrall, I mean? Serle will go on being your squire, and I expect you'll make Desta a page or something, but what about me? Will I have to go back to the kitchen? Back to being a scullery?"

"Was the work too hard? Was Dru unkind to you?"

"No . . . but after all this . . ." She waved vaguely at the galley, at him. "It'll be hard to go back to that kind of slog."

He thought of his own drudgery waiting in Fandrall: the endless daily grind of councils and taxes and decrees and reports. "Oh, very well. Let me give it some thought. Only promise me you won't plague me about it."

She clapped her hands. "I promise, I promise! And you know what?" she added, as he started up the ladder.

He breathed a silent sigh. "What, Nolle?"

"What that Sir Marcus said about you? I don't believe it." She was up on her knees, her hands clasped. "I don't believe it for a moment. You may lose your temper sometimes, like when you shook me, but you could never do something like that. Something that bad."

Couldn't I? A wave of shame and uncertainty washed over him. *What would have happened, if the fit hadn't taken me?*

"Get some sleep, Nolle," he said aloud, and went up the ladder.

CHAPTER NINETEEN

"Second unit, forward!" Heather called. Skapi danced a bit as the archers dashed ahead, and Heather reined her in, watching closely as the soldiers passed the first unit, which crouched at the eastern side of the trail with bows at the ready.

"You see?" Ravelin said. "The first unit watches over the second, keeping an eye on the enemy and providing covering fire if necessary. Now the leader of the second group will determine if it's safe for the first group to move forward. Some call the maneuver 'leapfrogging'; I prefer the term 'bounding,' myself."

Heather stood up in the stirrups to watch the unit's progress, as did Sir Bran on her left and Bayla just behind her. Isobel did not rise to watch; she sat sidesaddle and looked exquisitely, politely bored. Still standing, Heather turned to Ravelin. "And this is how you advanced toward the Stratheden troops, during the war?"

Ravelin nodded. "My father and King Aldo both preferred the traditional wedge formation, but in this terrain, it simply wasn't practical. The maneuver took Aldo by surprise; when we were hammering out the terms of our treaty, he told my father that it wasn't an honorable way to conduct a battle, and that I wasn't a gentleman for employing it." He grinned, but there was a forbidding light in his eyes. "We almost started a new war right there at the table."

The leader of the second unit signaled the first unit to move ahead. There was still no sign of the troops under Sir Jerrold's command, which had been sent ahead to play the part of the enemy forces in this war game. The troops carried only practice weapons: blunted swords and untipped arrows. The troops under Bran's command wore armbands of red cloth around their right arms, while those under Jerrold's command wore blue, with the object of the day's exercise to collect the greatest number of enemy 'colors' as evidence of their 'kills.'

The first unit hurried into the lead position, and Heather sank back into Skapi's saddle. "Was that the source of the ill will between you and the Hudnalls of Stratheden?"

"The ill will between our families and our kingdoms predates even my father's reign, but Aldo has never missed a chance to heap fuel on the fire." Ravelin snorted. "He even mocked me before a gathering of other kings."

"When was that?"

"Some fifteen years ago, when the StoneKing's mother died."

At the mention of Kristan, Heather was suddenly, acutely aware of the thick wad of parchment tucked deep inside her boot leg. Rather than burn the message approving her marriage to Ravelin, she had kept it and carried it with her every day, even though its bulk worried her, even though its sharp edges scraped her, even though its touch was like sand in an open wound. *You're going to learn to bear it*, she told herself. *You're going to let it chafe you until you grow calloused and indifferent to its touch.* She swallowed hard and forced herself to concentrate on the exercise. They were coming abreast of the second unit. Its leader looked toward her for a command, and she recognized him as the soldier with the Needwood sweetheart. She swung herself out of the saddle and tossed Skapi's reins to Sir Bran.

"Where are you going, my lady?" the knight asked.

"I can't see." She shouldered her way through the startled second unit to its leader. "What's your name, soldier?"

"Wortness, my lady," the soldier said. "I'm sorry, my lady, did I do something wrong?"

She shook her head impatiently. "Move your unit forward, Wortness. Take the lead position."

Wortness nodded, looking puzzled, and Heather fell in with the men as they hustled up the mountain trail. They passed the first unit, and Heather was annoyed to see every soldier staring at her. "Eyes ahead, you men," she growled. "The blues could be advancing on us this moment."

Even as she spoke, the tree line just ahead erupted with howling blue troops, swirling down the mountainside toward them. "No, no, no!" Heather roared, as the red units froze. "Don't just stand there, form ranks! Nock your arrows and shoot!"

Stumbling and fumbling, the two units tried to follow her commands, but it was too late. The blue troops were already on them, led by a wild-eyed Sir Jerrold, who urged them on with ferocious bellows. The blues laid about them with their practice swords, swatting the red troops with gleeful abandon, snatching off red armbands and brandishing them with bloodthirsty yells. One enthusiastic combatant caught Heather a hard blow across the shoulders and knocked her face-first into a drift. She sat up, cloak askew, clothes caked with snow, one braid hanging loose, and found herself eye-to-eye with a dismayed Jerrold. "Stop, stop, stop!" he shouted to his men, waving his arms. "Don't hit the Lady!"

The men halted in the midst of their battle and watched sheepishly as Heather struggled out of the drift. "Why did you stop, Jerrold?" she demanded.

"I'm sorry, my lady, I didn't realize you were with the advance unit."

"What difference did that make? You should have continued the attack. You would have routed us."

"But I didn't want to hurt you—"

"My sweet mother's life, you're not going to hurt me with a practice sword!" She pulled off her gloves and tried to tuck the errant braid back into the careful coronet Bayla had plaited that morning, but her cold, fumbling fingers only loosened the entire construction. With a muttered oath, she yanked both braids down, scattering hairpins in the snow. "All right, all right; it's done now," she continued, over Jerrold's apologies. "How many armbands did you get?"

Jerrold consulted quickly with one of the junior officers. "Eight, my lady."

"That makes twenty-nine, then. Bran has thirty. Well done, Jerrold; you've almost caught up."

"Actually, Sir Jerrold has surpassed Bran."

Heather looked over her shoulder. Ravelin had ridden up and was watching from horseback, with Sir Bran at his elbow, Bayla and Isobel just behind and the balance of the red troops hurrying to catch up. "How so, Reach Seachlan?"

"You're the commander, Lady Heather, and in this exercise, I think it's fair to say that you've either been captured or killed."

"But she's not wearing an armband—" Sir Bran started to say.

"It doesn't matter. She joined the advancing unit and was overwhelmed with them."

Bran's face fell, and Heather was both vexed with herself and irritated with Ravelin. "Very well; then the reds and blues are tied now."

Ravelin smiled ruefully. "With respect, my lady, since you're the commander, your capture or death would be worth a great deal more than a single armband."

Jerrold smirked and Bran began to sputter in protest. Heather's annoyance swelled, but she tried to keep her tone light. "Capturing an inept commander is worth nothing. However, I joined the unit as a footsoldier; therefore, I'm worth a single point. The score is even and we're wasting daylight. Jerrold, marshal your troops here and take over the advance. Bran, move your men ahead to the defensive position. We'll try the exercise again, and this time I'll stay out of the way."

She heaved herself into Skapi's saddle, and as the army hurried to follow her orders, Ravelin leaned close to her. "Your pardon, Commander. Perhaps I should have held my remarks until we could speak privately."

"I wondered why you felt it necessary to correct me before my men," Heather answered, more crossly than she had intended. Ravelin nodded and looked away, making her regret her brusqueness. "I'm sorry. Tell me why you spoke up."

"With respect, my lady, a commander should never go with the troops into battle. Not unless things are desperate. Not unless the men are so badly demoralized that their leader has to show them where their duty lies, at the risk of his—I beg your pardon; *her*—own life."

"I see your point," Heather said. "But in my own defense, this is a war *game*. I'm a young commander and have as much to learn as my soldiers do. I wanted to see for myself what this 'bounding' advance was all about. If I don't understand how it works—the advantages, the drawbacks, the risks to my troops—then how can I judge when best to use it?"

"Fair enough. You're not afraid to get your hands dirty, I'll give you that. But bear in mind that a commander among the common soldiery is always going to be a distraction—game or no." He flicked a sidelong look at her. "Young woman or no."

Heather's irritation flared. "Reach Seachlan, I would think by now you would've realized neither my sex nor my youth have been a detriment to my command."

Ravelin inclined his head gravely. "Of course, my lady. And I shouldn't presume to second-guess the StoneKing's decisions. I'm sure he knew exactly what he was doing when he appointed you."

Heather felt the wedge of parchment dig into her calf. "Of course he did," she said coldly. Turning Skapi northward, she nudged her into a brisk trot, with Bayla on her heels. She made her way uphill, to a vantage point overlooking the trail below, where she could see both Bran's units scurrying ahead and Jerrold's assembling alongside Ravelin.

"My lady," Bayla said, drawing up next to her, "would you

like me to put your hair back up?"

Heather started to say no, then realized they were alone. "Where's Isobel got to?"

Bayla grimaced. "She stopped to relieve herself, my lady. She said she'd be right along."

Downhill, Isobel's horse stood riderless beside Ravelin, and Isobel herself was just trudging out of the underbrush toward it. Ravelin dismounted and with a polite nod, helped Isobel onto her horse. "Well, let's hope she has enough sense to follow our tracks up to this ridge," Heather said, and turned her attention to the soldiers.

* * *

"I thought I told you to stay with her," Ravelin said under his breath, as he handed Isobel the reins.

"She's got her maidservant keeping watch on her," Isobel answered, barely moving her lips as she arranged her skirts in careful folds about her legs. "Besides, we've barely spoken these past two days. I've missed you."

"And I you," Ravelin said, although it was untrue. It had been a pleasure to lie alone in his own snug tent, while Isobel, playing the part of chaperone, was quartered in Lady Heather's much larger pavilion along with Bayla. "Anything new?"

Isobel feigned a great interest in her gloves, while Ravelin tugged at her horse's girth, which was already tight. "She's close-lipped even with her maid. But last night I noticed something strange."

"What's that?"

"She's got a piece of parchment hidden inside her boot. It's all folded up. I thought maybe she had something wrapped in it; coins or who knows what. I saw her slip it under her pillow when her maid was helping her undress."

Ravelin straightened up. "What do you suppose is in it?"

"Nothing," Isobel said, not looking at him but with a smug

smile curling her lips. "There's nothing in it."

"What do you mean?"

"I mean it's just parchment, folded up. It's a message of some kind." Ravelin grunted and turned to his own mount, fidgeting with a stirrup as he listened. "I woke up before sunrise this morning," Isobel went on in a murmur. "There she was, already dressed and crouching over the lamp with it. She had it unfolded, and she was peering at it with the most ridiculous, dismal expression. As soon as she realized I was awake, she folded it up and poked it back into her boot."

"A message, eh?" Ravelin mused. "Get it for me."

"How? It's either in her boot or under her pillow."

He mounted up. "Find a way," he said over his shoulder, and nudged his horse after the troops.

* * *

At noon, with the cold winter sun glaring brightly off the snow, Heather called a halt and gathered the troops for a quick meal. The mess wagons dished out heaping portions of thick pottage, cooked that morning and kept warm in lidded iron pots nested in hay-lined wooden boxes. The horses got a ration of oats, and Heather watched in amusement as Skapi munched her portion with ladylike deportment—that is, until Ravelin's mount, tethered next to her, tried to steal some and barely escaped being bitten.

"Impudent fellow," Ravelin said.

"Skapi likes to keep what's hers," Heather said, digging her spoon into her own meal.

"Perhaps one day she'll learn to share."

Sure she was being baited, Heather shot a hard look at Ravelin, but he was stirring his pottage with a pensive air. "I'd like to know more about relations between Stratheden and Hogia," she said briskly. "You mentioned earlier that Aldo insulted you in Fandrall. What happened?"

Ravelin's lips hardened into a thin line. "We had all gathered for Rose Gemeta's burial—Landon of Norwinn, Claude of Dyer, Lockward of Malchea and even Aldo Hudnall, though it was a far journey for him. Even on such a solemn occasion, Aldo couldn't resist twitting me."

"What about?"

Ravelin did not answer. He raised his filled spoon to his mouth, considered it, then lowered it as if repulsed. "What about?" she said again.

"My lack of an heir," Ravelin said in an undertone. "It was only out of friendship and respect for Robert Gemeta that I didn't make Aldo pay for it then and there."

"So Robert Gemeta was your friend?"

Ravelin glanced at her. "You wear such a grave expression, Commander. Yes, he was my friend. We were close in age, and we served together during the Stratheden war." He stared at his spoon. "And now you're wondering how I could have killed him. No one understands how badly I wanted an heir. No one understands what it was like, after all those years—to have the chance for one dangled before my eyes. No one understands how Daazna could trick you . . . how he could make you believe . . ."

"Perhaps I do," Heather said quietly. She looked down into her own bowl, unwilling to meet Ravelin's gaze. "Daazna was *Impulii*. He could sense another person's desires and corrupt them for his own use."

"How do you know that?"

"Phelan told me." The falseness of the words made Heather suddenly furious with herself. "No, that's a lie. I know because Daazna used me the same way. To get to Kristan."

She shoveled a spoonful of pottage into her mouth and forced herself to swallow it, along with the bitter memory of her betrayal. As she dug her spoon into her bowl again, Ravelin put his hand gently over hers, arresting the motion. "What a relief," he murmured. "What a relief to know that someone as strong and good-hearted as you could be fooled just as I was. To know you share the same grief and guilt, the same knowledge that what you did was so terrible that you can never be forgiven for it."

"Kristan forgave me," Heather said gruffly, even as her brain whispered *did he?*

"But have you forgiven yourself? I can't."

Heather's eyes tingled with rising tears. She bit down hard on her tongue and pulled her fingers free, but Ravelin was already moving away, his bowl clutched in both hands, his head lowered.

They barely spoke the rest of the afternoon. Ravelin rode stony-faced at her side as they continued both the war games and their journey into the mountains, adding only a few words of advice or commentary as she ordered her troops into first one exercise, then another. It was not until the sun was low on the horizon that he looked ahead and finally smiled. "There's the lodge," he said, pointing into the distance. "You can just see its battlements above the tree line. We should be there by nightfall."

Heather peered ahead. "It's far larger than I realized."

"It's quite beautiful, if I say so myself. I had it built after the Stratheden war was over."

Heather turned to Sir Jerrold, who was riding to her left. "Send a messenger ahead to Sir Bran. Tell him the day's exercises are finished and to have his men start gathering kindling for our fires tonight."

"No need," Ravelin said. "We always left the lodge well-stocked with firewood before we closed it up at the end of the season."

Behind Heather, Isobel cleared her throat lightly. Something in the sound made Heather turn to look at her. Isobel wore a strangely guarded expression, and she cleared her throat again as Ravelin turned as well. "Some of us lived in the lodge for the two years Daazna was in power, Reach Seachlan. All the firewood was used up."

"Ah, I'd forgotten," Ravelin said. "Of course you would have used it."

Isobel nodded and averted her eyes.

"Shall I send the messenger, Commander?" Sir Jerrold asked.

"Yes, please," Heather said, "and put your own men to work gathering kindling as well."

Ravelin was gazing toward the lodge again. "I'm looking forward to showing the place to you, my lady. I'm unreasonably proud of it. Every king wants to build, but as Hogia's castle was already complete, my energies went into the lodge. I chose the site and spared no expense in the construction and furnishings. Paneling on the walls, beautiful arrases, fine furnishings and a great round table in front of a stone hearth. We used to bring sizable parties up here to hunt in the fall. We'd stay for a month, and our efforts kept the castle in meat all winter long. After a day's hunt, my knights and captains and I would sit in the main hall, the hounds at our feet, flagons of ale in our fists and a great roaring fire at our backs."

"It sounds very pleasant."

"It was indeed." Wistfulness softened Ravelin's sharp features, and Heather could not help feeling sorry for him. *He's lost so much: his crown, his throne, his wealth, his birthright, his self-respect. I only lost my heart.*

Their nooning over, the army wound its way northeast through the mountains, with the lodge growing ever closer. As the setting sun filtered through the trees, casting long blue shadows on the snow, the small army clattered past a low stone wall and into the lodge's forecourt.

Up close, Heather was surprised at how forbidding the lodge looked—*more like a fortress than a pleasant retreat*, she thought.

She turned to Ravelin to ask why, and was startled by his sudden pallor. "The outbuildings . . ." he whispered. "The stables and kennels and barracks . . . what happened to them?" Following his gaze, Heather realized that every outbuilding was gutted, leaving only the stone walls standing like empty shells.

Behind them, Isobel cleared her throat again, and Ravelin reined his horse around to glare at her. "Where are the roofs? The doors? The floors and windows?"

Isobel shrank back in her saddle. Her lips moved, but no sound came from her throat.

"Where are they?" Ravelin almost shouted.

"Burned, my lor—Reach Seachlan." Isobel's voice was no more than a squeak. "We had to burn what we could to stay warm and cook our food."

The harsh bark of Ravelin's laughter made Heather wince. "The lodge is surrounded by trees. Trees as far as the eye can see."

"None of us knew how to cut them down. And the servants who came with us were all house servants, and none of them would learn."

"I see," Ravelin said. He kept Isobel pinned in his gaze for several long moments. "But there's more, isn't there?"

Isobel swallowed, nodded. Ravelin swung from the saddle, threw the reins at Sir Bran and strode toward the lodge's great double doors. Heather dismounted and passed Skapi's reins to Bayla. "Hold her, please. Jerrold, bring a light and follow me." She hurried after Ravelin, who had already disappeared into the lodge.

She entered the building and paused, squinting in the dim light filtering through cracked, filthy glass. Before her was a large, echoing hall, empty but for a large table and a few chairs that stood before a great stone hearth. The walls had been stripped of their paneling, leaving only studs and bare nails. The stone floor was strewn with debris and thick with ground-in dirt. Before the hearth lay great mounds of material, wadded into rude beds, and over one of these Ravelin stood, prodding it with one foot. "This used to hang on the eastern wall," he said, barely audible. "It was a tapestry illustrating the final battle between my forces and Aldo's. I spent so many pleasant evenings sitting before it, admiring its colors and fine needlework. And they ruined it. My own courtiers tore it down and slept in it, like pigs wallowing in the mud—"

His voice caught. He sank into one of the chairs and put his head in his hands. Jerrold came in with a lantern, and Heather took it from him with one hand while with the other she pressed a finger to her lips. "Get the supply wagons unloaded and see if you can rig some sort of roof for the stables," she whispered.

"Yes, my lady. Shall I set up camp on the lodge grounds? Another night sleeping under the stars won't hurt us."

"I'll have a look around first. Get everything unloaded and wait for my orders."

"Yes, my lady," Jerrold muttered, and with a worried glance at Ravelin, hurried out.

Heather prowled around the great room, examining the damage. In their two years of residence, the courtiers had burned everything they could reach, but high on the walls some of the costly paneling remained, and the surviving furniture, although used hard, was handsome and well-made. A door led to a filthy kitchen, its lone table strewn with crusted dishes, goblets and utensils. Another large stone hearth dominated the room, dirty straw mattresses and blankets heaped before it. Off the kitchen was a pantry, with hooks for hanging game and shelves for other foodstuffs, but nothing remained but a few rusted cooking pots, an array of empty bottles and a scattering of mouse droppings. A narrow door led to a snug room that might have been a bedchamber for kitchen servants, although the furnishings had probably been burned for fuel. A final door led to a rear courtyard with the remnants of a woodshed and a well, with a few battered pitchers and basins perched on its stone rim. Beyond it rose a tall stone tower.

When she returned to the main room, Ravelin was sitting as she had left him. "How bad is it?" he asked, without lifting his head.

"Not so bad it can't be fixed." She lifted the lantern to peer up a dark stairwell.

"The bedchambers are up there," Ravelin said. "I shudder to think what's been done to them."

She started up the steps, then paused. "You should come with me. Sitting there feeling sorry for yourself isn't going to make it any better."

Ravelin looked up then, his mouth twisted into a bitter smile. "I'm overwhelmed by your sympathy."

"I'm sorry for what happened," Heather said, "but the quicker we determine what needs to be done, the quicker we can get to work. Come on."

She continued up the staircase. At the top was a large, low-ceilinged room. Ravelin's heavy tread sounded on the steps, and she sensed him looming up behind her. "This was where my men slept," he said. "My knights and captains. Not a bedstead nor a table nor a chest left."

"I expect they burned everything they could lay their hands on," Heather said. "Where do those two doors lead?"

"The one on the eastern wall opens onto the garderobe. The one in the northern wall leads to my room."

Together they walked across the echoing chamber. Ravelin pushed the northern door open and Heather held up the lantern. Its light flickered on bare walls. Ravelin let out a strangled laugh. "No surprise here. My bed was massive; it must have taken all day to break it up for firewood. If they'd expended half the effort cutting down trees, they could have heated the whole lodge for a fortnight."

"None of them knew how to use an ax or a saw," Heather said.

"And none of them would dirty their hands to learn how. I wonder if they were able to burn my favorite view."

"Sorry?" Heather said, but Ravelin had already pushed past her and was descending the stairs. She hurried after him as he crossed the great room below and entered the kitchen. A blast of chill air struck her as Ravelin opened the rear door and stepped outside. "At least my view appears to be intact," Ravelin said. "Give me your lantern."

She followed him to a narrow doorway in the tower's side. Within was a flight of stone steps that spiraled around a central post. Ravelin started up the stairs, taking them two at a time; Heather struggled in his wake, puffing a bit. At the top was another doorway, and Ravelin waited only long enough for her to join him, then stepped into the cold blue twilight.

The tower's summit was ringed by chest-high battlements. Far below was the kitchen courtyard. Straight ahead was nothing but sky. "My view," Ravelin said. "I built it high, so I could look down on Aldo Hudnall." He pointed toward the northeast. "On a clear day, you can see all the way to Hull's Contrivance, Stratheden's castle town. Hull Hudnall was Aldo's great-grand-father. The town sits on cliffs overlooking the sea, with a rocky beach and a bit of a harbor below. Terrible anchorage, but legend has it that Hull was determined to settle there. He built a series of great winches and pulleys and used them to lift stones from the beach to build his castle. They're still in use today, to bring up goods from any merchant captain skilled enough to bring his ship into the harbor."

Heather was only half listening. A stone pillar jutted from the center of the tower; atop it was a broad, shallow basin of metal. When Heather stood on her toes to peer into it, she discovered a messy array of twigs and dried grasses, all woven together. "What in the world is this thing?" she asked.

Ravelin's thin lips curled as he looked into the basin. "A hawk must have nested in it last spring. Probably my former courtiers never came up here; they would have burned it along with everything else."

"I can see the nest. But what's this basin for?"

Ravelin opened the hasp of the lantern door. "Break off some of that nest, and I'll show you."

Heather pulled a handful of dry twigs and pine needles from the nest. Ravelin took it from her, lit it from the lantern's flame and thrust it quickly into the middle of the basin. With a crackle and snap, the old nest caught fire, and they both stepped back as the flames leaped up, gobbling the small mound of fuel. "My little joke," Ravelin said. "Whenever I came here, the first thing I'd do was set this signal ablaze, just to let Aldo know I was on his border."

"On his border?" Heather repeated. "Just how far away is Stratheden?"

"Just beyond the kitchen courtyard." Heather gaped at him, and Ravelin's smile broadened. "If you push through the shrubbery, you'll find a steep drop-off into a ravine. The River Strath runs through that ravine. Cross it, and you're in Stratheden."

"I knew we were close. I didn't realize just how close."

"Close enough for the shit from my garderobe to fall into it."

Heather gaped at him, and he shrugged. "I put the lodge here for a reason. I wanted Aldo to feel my presence. I wanted my shadow to fall over him at sunset." As he spoke the words, the last embers of the signal light winked out, and darkness fell about them like a curtain. Heather raised the lantern and found Ravelin staring toward Stratheden, his face set in harsh lines and his hands gripped tight on the stone battlements. "And now I cast no shadow at all," he muttered.

For a few moments they stood without speaking. At last, Ravelin looked at her over his shoulder. "You're chewing on your lip, Commander."

"I was thinking," Heather said. "Bran's units are behind by five points, so they'll have clean-up duty. Jerrold's men can hunt for the pot, take care of repairs and knock together some rough furniture—tables, benches and so forth. It'll take a day or two from our exercises—"

Ravelin grabbed her by the shoulders, so suddenly that she nearly dropped the lantern. He thrust his face close to hers and gave her a shake. "Don't you pity me; don't you dare," he whispered fiercely. "I have little enough pride left as it is."

Heather wrenched free. "Reach Seachlan, control yourself."

He drew himself upright. "I beg your pardon," he said, but while his voice was steady, his hands were clenched and his whole body shook with ill-contained emotion.

Heather was trembling herself; but it was not anger that had unsettled her so much as the unexpected pressure of Ravelin's hands, his hot breath on her face, the nearness of his eyes. The lantern was clattering in her hand; she set it on the battlements and took a deep breath. "If we're to use this lodge as a staging area for our exercises, then it's got to be habitable. Once we get it cleaned up, the cooks can serve meals from the kitchen and we can sleep warm and dry. If the men are well-rested, with hot food in their bellies, they'll be better able to learn from the exercise."

"Of course," Ravelin said.

He was still standing too close, but she held her ground. "The soldiers can sleep in the main hall. Bran and Jerrold and their captains can share the large bedchamber. You'll have to sleep with them. Bayla and Isobel and I will need the privacy of your room."

"Of course," Ravelin said again. "Forgive me, my lady. I mistook your pragmatism for patronage. I know your head will always rule your heart."

Stung, Heather caught up the lantern.

"And I forgot this is the StoneKing's property now," Ravelin went on. "As his servant, you're bound to see to its upkeep."

The wad of parchment in her boot was suddenly huge and heavy against her leg. "That's my father's job," she retorted. "My job is to train my soldiers."

"Of course," Ravelin said once more, with a slight bow.

The formal gesture, coupled with the hurt in Ravelin's eyes, struck her to the heart. She started to turn away, then wheeled back. "Do you think I have a heart of iron? Do you think I'm so much the StoneKing's man that I can't see how, day in and day out, you struggle to keep your anger and grief under control? Yes, you were right—I pitied you. And if kindness turns your stomach, I pity you even more."

For some moments they stood facing each other without speaking. Ravelin's eyes bore into hers; his nostrils flared and the veins in his temple and neck throbbed. Heather's own pulse rattled in her veins and she found it hard to breathe. Ravelin raised his hands, and she thought wildly *he's going to kiss me, he's going to kiss me* and she could not tell if she found the idea repellent or exciting.

Instead, he took her free hand in both of his and went to one knee. He pressed his lips to her fingers; not coolly, as he had in the past, but with a passion that spread like fire through the back of her hand, up her arm, through her neck and into her face. "I'm sorry, Heather," he said. "I'm so sorry. You're a good friend to me. I think you may be my only friend. I'll try to be worthy of your compassion."

He rose, and in silence they descended from the tower. Heather led the way with the lantern, but she felt Ravelin's hot gaze on the back of her neck, and her knees wobbled beneath her the whole way down.

CHAPTER TWENTY

Kristan stood by the helm as Sir Mitchell eased the warship into the wind. "We're about half a mile downstream of *O Tópos*, my lord," the knight murmured, wiping his mist-dampened hair from his brow. "You'll have to row against the current, but it isn't very strong tonight, and since their harbor entrance faces downstream, you'll be able to access it more easily. Will you be able to find it in the dark?"

"Of course," Kristan said, but in his heart, he was not so certain. He had been in and out of *O Tópos* in darkness several times; in a distant, detached way he knew what landmarks to look for and how to navigate through the centaur realm's river gates, but his memories of the place were dry and crumbled as dead leaves.

And he was tired, tired to his bones' marrow. His worries and constant faint nausea, coupled with the uneasy motion of the ship, had made sleep nearly impossible. He had catnapped when he could, but nightmares loomed every time he closed his eyes. Even in the calmer waters of the Mor his knees shook, and his hands sometimes trembled when he tried to eat. He knew his knights were troubled by his growing frailty; whenever he moved about the ship, one of them, or Serle, or more often the boy Desta would be at his side, ready with an outstretched hand when he stumbled, deaf to his querulous demands to let him be.

Even now Mitchell was eyeing him with concern. "Are you

sure you don't want me to go instead, my lord?"

"I've told you time and again—no." Kristan glanced around the ship. The centaurs were out of sight, waiting below with the horses until it was safe for them to come on deck. At the port side Desta, Dell and the other knights were busy lowering the small launch into the water, while Astéria, in human form, waited at the rail with Serle and Nolle. Marcus lounged nearby, watching the proceedings without offering to help, but Melissa remained in the aftcastle. *Still sulking*, Kristan thought, but his irritation was overwhelmed by guilt over his harsh treatment of his sister. *By the Stone, this trip can't be over too soon.*

Astéria smiled as Kristan joined her at the rail. "This boat *polý mikró*, Kreestan," she said, and held up one hand, thumb and forefinger close together.

"It's large enough for you and me. But we'll have to be careful not to touch each other. The shift has to stay in place until we're off the Mor, in case we're approached by another vessel. Nolle, you'll have to hold the spell even with Astéria out of your sight."

"I told you, I can do it," Nolle said, with a shrug. "But we haven't seen another boat since sunset."

"Just humor me. Serle, would you fetch my pack?"

Serle's eyebrows shot up. "But I thought . . . I thought you weren't . . ."

With a roll of his eyes, Desta ran off.

"No, I'm not staying in *O Tópos*," Kristan said. "But I need to take care of some business before I go."

"My lord, are you sure you don't want one of us to go with you?" Kennet asked. "I don't like you making this journey unaccompanied."

"Mitchell could go," Walter said. "He's already been to this *O Tópos* place—"

Kristan blew out an impatient sigh. "For the hundredth time—no. It's bad enough I'm breaking my own oath; I don't need to involve anyone else. Thank you, Desta," he added, as

Desta hurried up with the pack. "At least someone does what I ask promptly, without question."

"It's my pleasure, my lord," Desta said, shooting a triumphant look at a crestfallen Serle.

"How long do you want us to keep the centaurs below decks, my lord?" Matthew asked.

"Until I get back," Kristan said, as he rummaged in his pack. "No point in running the risk of someone seeing them when we're so close to our goal." He pulled out a small, round object swathed in a piece of cloth. Nolle gasped and put both hands to her chest.

"I can have it?" she said. "I can have it now?"

"You fulfilled your part of the bargain," Kristan said, but as he pulled the cloth away, revealing the scrying ball, he was flooded with bitter melancholy. *It's the only part of Simeon I have left. Why did I bargain it away to this child? I'm the StoneKing—she should have done what I told her, without a reward.*

Nolle snatched the ball from him. She cupped it in both hands, gazing at it greedily.

"Pretty," Astéria said, but she watched Kristan with an uncertain expression, as if she sensed his mood.

"My lord, this mist is getting thicker by the moment," Mitchell called softly.

Kristan thrust the pack at Serle. "Put this back, please. Astéria, you board first. The sooner we get there, the sooner we'll be back." He gestured toward Geoffrey, who was waiting in the launch to help them board.

"Goodbye, Astéria," Serle said, in a small voice.

"No make sad face," Astéria said, ruffling Serle's hair. "I come back with Kreestan friends. We say goodbye then."

With the knights' assistance, she climbed over the rail into the launch and Kristan followed. Geoffrey squeezed past them and heaved himself back aboard the warship. Kristan moved to take the oars, but Astéria grabbed them first. "I row, Kreestan. You show way."

"But—"

"She's right, my lord," Sir Geoffrey said from the warship's rail. "You'll need to navigate and keep watch. Besides, she's heavier than you. She needs to be in the middle so the launch will trim properly."

The knight's voice was matter-of-fact, and if Kristan could have seen his face in the darkness, he knew it would be equally dispassionate, but he was stung all the same. *None of you think I'm strong enough to row.* His irritation gave way to helpless resignation. *And you may be right.* "Very well," he said aloud, and situated himself in the bow.

"Safe journey, my lord," Sir Walter said.

"Be careful, my lord," Sir Kennet echoed.

With sure, smooth strength, Astéria pulled on the oars. A half-dozen strokes and the warship was only a shadow on the water, relieved by glimmers of light from the lanterns on deck and in the forecastle; another dozen strokes and even that gleam was absorbed into the foggy night. Head erect and cloak thrown back from her shoulders, Astéria rowed the launch with ease, but the chill air pierced Kristan's flesh and settled deep in his bones. He huddled deep in his cloak and directed his gaze to port.

The Exilwald's looming mass did nothing to ease his discomfort. Images of Martin and Gabriel, of fear and flight, of grief and hardship swirled in his mind's eye. He clenched his hands on the gunwales and willed the thoughts away. "More to port," he whispered, pointing left. "I can't see."

Astéria adjusted their course, and for some time the only sounds were the creak of the oars and the swirl of water.

"Kreestan," Astéria said quietly.

"What?"

"I am sorry."

"Sorry for what?"

"Sorry I make this trouble for you."

"Nonsense."

"For me, you leave home and make this bad trip. For me, you pay Lorz so, so much money. For me, you work and worry until you are sick."

He snorted. "I should thank you. If it hadn't been for you, I wouldn't have known what was happening in my realm. I would have stayed in Fandrall, trusting the reports and blithely unaware that my Reaches were keeping the truth from me. You showed me what a simpleton I've been."

"Kreestan, do not say this bad thing. You are good *vasiliás*, good king."

"I've been a gullible fool. But no more. This trip has opened my eyes. I'll never trust what I'm told again."

"Kreestan—"

He turned his back on her.

"*Ragis*," she whispered.

He glanced at her over his shoulder, but she avoided his eyes and bent to the oars once more.

Ahead, the blurry mass of the Exilwald was separating into distinct landmarks: a jut of land here, a forked treetop there, a cluster of bushes, a distinctive boulder, a subtle break in the tree line. A strange thrill ran up Kristan's spine. "There," he said, pointing. "There it is."

They eased out of the current and into what appeared to be a deep, narrow cove lined so thickly with evergreens that it was like sailing into a tunnel. "Ees nothing," Astéria said.

"It's meant to look that way. Head toward the far end."

Astéria rowed the launch deeper into the cove. The creak of the oarlocks and the faint clop of the oars in the water seemed loud and intrusive. The forbidding mass of the Exilwald closed around them. By the time they reached the far end of the cove, Kristan was shivering with mingled anxiety and relief. *I'll see Torrin soon*, he told himself. *Calm, reasonable, steadfast Torrin. He'll take these centaurs off my hands and I can go home.* He rose to his knees and sucked in a deep, steadying breath. A faint scent of mingled musk and spice filled his nostrils.

Astéria gasped, and Kristan twisted halfway around to look at her. "*Boró na tous myríso*," she whispered. "I smell them. I smell my people."

At that instant something zipped past his head and plunged into the water just beyond the boat. Astéria flung the oars aside and struggled to rise. The boat lurched, and Kristan, already off balance, tumbled over the side and into the water. He surfaced, sputtering, just as another arrow thudded into the side of the launch. "*Stamatíste!*" Astéria cried, waving her arms so wildly that the launch rocked.

"Stop, stop, you'll capsize!" The water was so cold that Kristan could not breathe; the weight of his sopping cloak was dragging him under. He clawed at its clasp but his fingers were already numb.

As he began to sink, Astéria loomed above him. She gripped his shoulder, a shudder ran through her, and the shift collapsed. With a powerful heave, she pulled him aboard, then straddled him protectively, her four legs spread wide for balance. "*Stamatíste!*" she shouted again.

There was no answer. The Exilwald was silent but for Kristan's wheezing and the lap of water against the boat's sides. Just as Kristan raised his head to look, there was a rustle and a creak, and the wall of young evergreens before them began to swing away.

"*Eisélthete*," a voice called softly.

With one forehoof, Astéria nudged Kristan into the bow, then crouched over the oars. As she rowed them forward, Kristan heard the faint clank of the river gate's winch, voices in a quick, muttered conversation, then the rustle of brush and the thud of retreating hooves.

"Kreestan, what these thing?" Astéria whispered, as the river gate, with its plantings of shrubs and evergreens, swung closed behind them.

"It's a gate," Kristan said through chattering teeth. "There are two more."

He was still trying to unfasten his water-soaked cloak, but his fingers were numb and useless. Astéria stopped rowing long enough to open the clasp and drag the sodden mass out from under him, then unfastened her own cloak and threw it over his shivering form.

As they moved through the narrow channel, whispering resounded along the banks. Ahead, the second river gate swung open, and this time the darkness was broken by the occasional yellow flicker of lamplight. The third gate yawned wide, and the scent of the *Kentávron* grew so thick Kristan could taste it. Beyond lay the harbor of *O Tópos*, its calm waters reflecting the bobbing, dancing lights as the centaurs carried lanterns toward the harbor. Five ships lay at anchor; a sixth dock stood empty. *I owe you a ship*, Kristan thought with a guilty start, and remembered the centaur vessel he had borrowed the previous summer, no doubt still sitting in Moordock's harbor. As Astéria pulled toward the vacant anchorage, centaurs spilled out onto the dock, and at their head, holding a lantern aloft, was Torrin.

He was more massive than Kristan remembered. His hide, so sleek when they had last parted, was shaggy, and every muscle of his body was tensed and straining as he stared at Astéria, his lips parted, his nostrils flaring.

The launch bumped gently against the mooring. Not one centaur moved or spoke. Like Torrin, they only watched.

"*Chairete,*" Astéria's voice was soft and tremulous. "*To ónomá mou eínai Astéria.*"

For a moment, her words hung in the silence. Then, all at once, the centaurs erupted into joyous roars, startling Kristan so badly that he jumped. His own greeting died on his lips as Torrin reached past him, his eyes still fixed on Astéria. "*Kalós írthes, Astéria,*" he said, his deep, rumbling voice cutting through the din. "*Kalós írthes ston O Tópos.*"

Astéria took his hand. The boat rocked as she leaped to the dock, and Kristan had to grab for the gunwales to keep from falling out again. With Astéria's hand still clasped in his, Torrin pushed his way through the cheering, laughing crowd, from the harbor up to the great promenade. The rest of the centaurs streamed after him in an exuberant parade. Their voices, their strong scent and the yellow lantern light faded into the distance, leaving Kristan alone.

"Well," he said.

He grasped the edge of the dock and with the boat dipping and sliding beneath him, managed to lever himself out. With Astéria's cloak clutched around his shivering body, he started after the centaurs, then stopped, feeling both foolish and absurdly hurt. "Well," he said again, "I'd better find someplace to get warm."

He probed his memory cautiously and at last recalled the annex where he and his party had been housed during the summer. Boots squelching, he shuffled toward it through the thin crust of snow.

The white marble building was dark and silent, but Kristan let himself in and felt his way toward the great room's central fireplace. Wood and kindling for a fire were already laid in the hearth, and after a few moments of fumbling, Kristan located a fire steel. His hands shook so badly that it took several tries before he was able to strike a spark. As the flames flared and crackled, he pulled off Astéria's cloak, then sank to the floor and tried to work off his sodden boots. His chilled muscles made him twitch like a horse shaking off flies, while his teeth clattered together until his head ached from the din. *This is the thanks I get*, he thought. *I spent days and a small fortune to free Astéria's people, I nearly drown bringing them here, and then I'm brushed aside and left to fend for myself while they celebrate.*

His hurt gave way to dull anger, which lent him enough energy to peel off his sopping clothes. He used the hem of Astéria's cloak to dry himself as much as he could, then wrapped his naked, goose-pimpled body up in it and sat as close to the fire as he dared. *By the Stone*, he thought, shutting his eyes, *I'm done with all this. Just let me get these centaurs off my ship and my sister off my hands and I can go home . . . go back to Fandrall . . . back to work . . .*

"My poor friend," said a soft voice.

Kristan jerked awake. Aquila, the king of the centaurs, stood over him, his pearly hide gleaming in the firelight, a kindly yet pitying expression on his lined face. "What a sorry welcome we've given you."

"Lord Aquila, I didn't hear you come in—"

"And no wonder. Astéria has told us the trials you endured to bring her to us. You must be exhausted. No, don't get up," he added, as Kristan started to his feet. "Stay there at the fire while I deal with your wet coverings." As he bent to pick up Kristan's sopping leggings and tunic, the annex door crashed open and Torrin burst into the room, followed by Astéria and a few other centaurs. More centaurs pressed around the doorway.

"There you are!" Torrin cried. "We couldn't find you anywhere—"

"All you had to do was look for a human footprint," Aquila said, rather coolly.

"I'm ashamed of myself," Torrin went on, advancing on Kristan with both arms outstretched. "I was so overcome at the sight of Astéria that I didn't even notice you. My friend, forgive me."

Beset by Torrin's powerful scent, his booming voice, his sheer enormity, Kristan shied back before he could control himself. Torrin stopped in his tracks, his welcoming smile fading.

"There's nothing to forgive," Kristan managed to choke out, but the words sounded petulant, and his voice had a high-pitched, carping ring. He cleared his throat and tried again. "I should ask your forgiveness for breaking my oath not to approach *O Tópos.* But I felt this was a special situation, and would go some way to paying the great debt I owe to the *Kentávron.*"

"There is no debt between friends," Aquila said.

"None indeed," Torrin said. "Kristan, Astéria says there are more of her people waiting in a ship on the river."

"Eleven," Kristan said.

"Pollux, ready a ship and a crew," Torrin said over his shoulder.

A male near the door nodded, and Kristan finally recognized the stern features of the *Kentávron* captain. Other centaurs clamored to go with him, but Aquila held up a hand and they fell silent. "Our friend Kristan is still soaked to the skin and chilled to the bone," he said.

"He doesn't have to come with us," Torrin said.

"I must," Kristan said. "I have to get back to my ship."

"What's your rush?" one of the centaur females said, tossing her chestnut hair. Kristan squinted at her, trying to remember her name. "You can stay here while we go after them."

"Chári," Torrin said reprovingly, and the woman fell silent. "But she's right," he went on, turning to Kristan. "Why not stay here, my friend? Get warm and dry while we fetch Astéria's people."

"Why not, indeed?" Aquila said. "Be our guest again. Stay with us as long as you like."

"My ship and my men are waiting for me."

"All your people are welcome in *O Tópos*."

Aquila's words were greeted with a sudden, stony silence from the other centaurs. *I am not welcome*, Kristan thought. *Whatever Aquila says, no human is welcome here.* "I can't linger," he said aloud. "I have pressing business and I've been kept from it long enough as it is."

Torrin drew himself up, as if affronted, but Aquila only inclined his head. "As you wish, of course. Let us get your things dry as quickly as we can." He indicated Kristan's wet clothes, and with ill grace, Chári and the other centaurs snatched them up and hurried out. "And bring towels and a hot drink for our friend," he called after them, but they had already banged the door shut behind them.

"I'll go," Torrin said. He turned to Astéria, who was waiting, her face half in shadow. "Come with me. I can show you more of *O Tópos.*"

He put out his hand, as if to take hers, but Astéria shrank away and averted her head. Torrin frowned and took a step toward her, but Aquila came between them. "Astéria and I will go," he said. "You stay here with Kristan." With a grateful look, Astéria hurried to the door, and Aquila took his son by the arm and spoke to him quietly in *Kentávron.* "*Nai, Patéra,*" Torrin muttered in response, but even when Astéria and Aquila were gone, he stared at the door as if he still saw them, nostrils flaring, muscles tensed, the mane-like stripe of hair down his spine bristling.

"You want her," Kristan said.

Torrin started, as if he had forgotten Kristan was there. His forehead and high cheekbones were flushed. "I do," he said in a low voice. "She is my life mate—my *sýntrofos tis zoís.* I know it. I feel it."

"You just met her."

Torrin's blush deepened. "This is the way it sometimes happens."

"And does she return your feelings?"

"She is not . . . receptive." Torrin swallowed hard. "She's worried. Perhaps even frightened. Father is right. I have to be patient. *O astéria mou,*" he added with a sigh. "I've been saying the words for years, never knowing that would be her name."

"I said it to her when we first met. I didn't know what it meant, but it was all the *Kentávron* I could remember."

Torrin wheeled toward him with a suddenness that was almost fierce. "You said that? What did she do?"

"Knocked me down and tried to trample me."

Torrin guffawed. The reaction was so coarse, so unlike Torrin's usual civility that Kristan's own temper rose. "What's so funny?"

Torrin laughed again. "I'm just relieved."

"Relieved? She tried to kill me!"

"You misunderstand. Her name—Astéria—it means 'stars.' *O astéria mou* means 'my stars.' She thought you meant she was yours . . . that she belonged to you. No wonder she was angry."

She did belong to me, Kristan thought sullenly. *She was given to me as a gift. And I bought the rest of them. They all belong to me.* He wanted to say the words aloud, but his stomach began to roil and his knees were suddenly weak. "Well, you have nothing to worry about on that account," he said, turning toward the fire. "And it's clear I'm not wanted here. I won't trouble you with my presence any longer than I have to."

"Kristan," Torrin said, but this time his voice was gentle. "Don't you realize how grateful the *Kentávron* are to you?"

"The *Kentravron* have an odd way of showing it."

Torrin sighed. "There are two things you should understand. I told you once that *Kentávron* blood runs hot in winter. It's because it's our *gónimes méres*—our fertile time. We can be . . . excitable. Sometimes even combative. We've had no true pairings in *O Tópos* for years. Now you've brought us new blood—twelve chances for life mates, twelve chances to produce young and increase our numbers. If we seem distracted, it's because our minds, our hearts—our whole beings—are focused on these new opportunities."

"Very well. What else?"

"The rest is . . . difficult." Torrin sat on his haunches and stared at the fire. "This autumn, when we went out on the Mor to trade, those who approached us weren't after our wine—they were after us."

"What?"

"Men in boats tried to hem in one of ours and board it. Pollux was at the helm and managed to elude them, but the humans gave chase. Our ship only managed to stay ahead of them by jettisoning the cargo, and even so, it took all Pollux's skill to avoid them until it was dark enough to escape undetected."

"Were they my people?" Kristan demanded. "Norwinnians? Hogians? If you can give me details, I can punish the offenders and put a stop to the practice."

"I don't know. It doesn't matter. The boats stayed on the Mor all through the autumn, watching for us—hunting us. We were trapped here. When winter set in, the hunters left, but we'd missed the trade season. In consequence, we've had to do without things we needed. The situation created more strain at a time that's already difficult enough. Some have blamed me for drawing attention to our kind last summer. They say the humans thought I belonged to you—a possession rather than a comrade—and now other humans want to catch one of us for themselves." Torrin cleared his throat and looked at Kristan sidelong. "Still others fear that because you took control of all the kingdoms surrounding the Exilwald, you likewise consider the Exilwald—and *O Tópos*—to be part of your realm."

"Nonsense," Kristan said, but at the same time he was startled by the idea. *Why shouldn't it be? It sits within my realm. It would be a simple matter to claim it, clear out the squatters and criminals and recluses, harvest the trees, use its resources to expand my—*

His stomach heaved suddenly. *Stop it. Stop it. You don't want the Exilwald. You don't need it. Think of the Kentávron. Think how much you're in their debt.*

"You and Astéria were lucky some of the more rational guards were on duty tonight," Torrin was saying. "They followed my orders and shot to frighten you away rather than kill you. They said that in the darkness Astéria looked like a human."

"She did look like a human. She was under a disguising spell."

"Ah. She said something about a magic girl in your company, but I wasn't sure I'd understood her."

"You don't understand *Kentávron*?"

Torrin's brow knotted, and too late, Kristan realized how

rude the question sounded. "Of course I do," Torrin said. "But in *O Tópos* we speak a combination of our language mingled with the common tongue, and reserve pure *Kentávron* for more formal occasions. Astéria speaks pure *Kentávron*, and her accent is quite thick."

"Ah." An uncomfortable silence fell between them. Torrin glanced toward the door, his face tightening with eagerness again. *He can't wait for her to come back*, Kristan thought. *He's already half forgotten I'm here. By the Stone, let me be rid of these centaurs and on my way again.*

As if in answer, the door banged open and centaurs poured into the room, led by the female Chári. She thrust a stack of linen towels at him. "Here, dry yourself," she said. Other centaurs surrounded him, holding out his tunic and leggings, his boots and even his cloak. "We squeezed the water out of your things and pressed them with hot stones," Chári went on. "They're dry now. Well, mostly dry."

"Put them on," said one of the males.

"Hurry up," muttered another.

The stench of burnt fur and leather filled Kristan's nostrils. The luxuriant lining of his cloak was singed and his boots were scorched. His clothing was stretched out of shape and still damp. "Come on, get dressed," Chári said. She took hold of Astéria's cloak and tried to yank it from his naked body. Kristan clutched the cloak tighter and looked to Torrin for aid, but his friend was staring at Astéria, who had come in with Aquila and stood slightly apart from the others, holding a steaming tankard. More hands were tugging at his cloak now, pulling him this way and that. Some of the centaurs were laughing. He was overwhelmed by the thought of being stripped bare, his hideous, mutilated body exposed before all the staring eyes. He tore free, stumbled backward and nearly fell into the fire. Chári stamped one hoof. "What's the matter with you? We saw you uncovered last summer!"

"Chári!"

The centaurs cringed back as Aquila advanced on them. No longer the gentle, enfeebled old centaur Kristan knew, he was at once bristling and enormous and terrifying. "You shame me!" he roared, and even Kristan flinched at the sound. "You shame *O Tópos* and you shame the *Kentávron*! Get out of here, all of you! Get out and go wait at the harbor!"

The chastened centaurs dropped Kristan's things by the hearth and clattered out. Only Torrin and Astéria remained, slack-jawed and silent.

"And once again I must apologize for my people," Aquila said, in a calmer voice, but his body was still rigid with anger. "Astéria, *to krasí, parakaló*."

Astéria hurried forward, offering the tankard, but Kristan threw up one hand to ward her off. "Leave me alone, please," he said, and was infuriated by how his voice shook. "Just let me dress in peace. I'll meet you at the harbor as quickly as I can."

"Of course," Aquila said. "Astéria, leave the drink by the hearth and come along."

He trotted out, with Astéria behind him, but Torrin hesitated. "I'm sorry, Kristan," he said quietly. "I should have remembered how you hate being touched."

Kristan let out a bitter laugh. "You clearly have other things on your mind." Torrin's mouth went tight, and Kristan instantly regretted his sarcasm. "Apologies, Torrin. I'm so tired I scarcely know what I'm saying."

Torrin sighed. "We both have a great deal on our minds. I'll wait for you outside."

Alone, Kristan dried himself as well as he could, put on his misshapen clothes, his damp boots and his ruined cloak and took a few hasty gulps from the tankard. It contained a full-bodied red wine that had been mulled with honey and spices. While he was grateful for its warmth, its strength made his head spin, and he dared not drink more. He picked up Astéria's cloak and joined Torrin outside, and in silence they hurried down to the harbor.

Astéria and Aquila were waiting with Pollux by the docks. "Every centaur in *O Tópos* wants to go with us," Pollux was complaining. "They all want to be the first to greet the newcomers."

"A single ship and a small crew will be sufficient," Aquila said. He no longer seemed angry, but his expression was grave. "We don't want to draw any more attention than necessary."

The crowd let out a collective groan. "My lord, we want to *see* them!" Chári cried. "Everyone wants to see them!"

"We'll need room for the eleven newcomers to board, my lord," Pollux said.

"Two boats, then, but that's all."

"I'll take command of one ship," Torrin said.

"Very well. Pollux, take the other."

"I go," Astéria said. "My people . . . they are *nevrikoí*."

"No need for them to be afraid," Torrin said. "They have no idea how welcome they'll be. I'll take Astéria on my ship," he added to Pollux.

"Of course you will," Pollux said, with a sly grin, and he moved toward the clamoring crowd. Torrin whisked Astéria's cloak from Kristan's hands. He settled it about her shoulders, helped her aboard his ship, and then hurried to join Pollux. Kristan was left standing on the dock, feeling foolish and a bit forlorn. A light touch on his shoulder made him jump.

"You look so tired, my friend," Aquila said. "Are you certain you won't spend a few days with us?"

Kristan eyed the centaurs fighting for Pollux and Torrin's attention as the two selected their crews. "I think I would be out of place, Lord Aquila."

Aquila's eyes twinkled. "Perhaps you're right. *O Tópos* is always a bit unsettled in cold weather, but this winter may be particularly . . . boisterous. It's all to the good, though, and we have you to thank for it." He shook his head as voices rose, crying out for the remaining positions on the ships. "You'd better get aboard, my friend, before things get out of hand."

To Kristan's surprise, some centaurs were shoving and even

striking each other in their eagerness to be among the first to greet the newcomers. Others had dashed off and returned bearing casks of wine and baskets of food. "Give them a proper welcome!" someone cried, as the foodstuffs were heaved aboard.

"All right, Chári; you're the last one," Pollux shouted, and the bold-eyed young female pushed her way onto the dock, thumbing her nose at those on shore.

"Not fair!" cried another female. "You chose her because she's your sister!"

Pollux blushed, but Chári only laughed. "Don't worry, Tacheía, I won't take *all* the new males. Watch out, little king; you're going to get trampled." She grabbed Kristan's arm and nearly threw him aboard Torrin's ship. He stumbled and went sprawling. With a clatter, the crew pulled long poles from brackets inboard as the centaurs ashore roared in excitement.

"Safe journey, Lord Gemeta," Aquila called.

The centaurs were already pushing away from the docks. One of Torrin's crew paused long enough to heave Kristan to his feet. "Stay out of the way," he said, and pushed him, none too gently, toward Torrin and Astéria at the stern.

With the centaurs thrusting their poles with abandon and each gate yawning wide well before they reached it, the ships bumped and rolled recklessly toward the Mor. As they approached the final river gate, Pollux's crew miscalculated a turn and their prow thudded into the lead ship's stern. With a yip of dismay, Astéria lost her footing, but Torrin quickly caught her around the waist. "Watch what you're doing back there," he ordered in a harsh whisper.

"Sorry," Pollux hissed.

Astéria pulled herself free. "I fine," she said, somewhat primly, and moved to Kristan's left, out of Torrin's reach.

At last, they burst onto the fog-shrouded Mor, and the centaurs put away their poles and hurried to raise the sails. "Which way, Kristan?" Torrin asked.

"South. In the middle of the river."

Torrin turned toward Pollux and pointed downstream. The sails bellied out, catching the light wind, and the ships turned south. "How far?" Torrin asked.

"Half a mile," Kristan said. "If it weren't for the fog, you'd be able to see it."

"You'd better go into the bow and guide us."

"I go too," Astéria said. She caught Kristan by the wrist and hustled him forward.

"What's the matter?" Kristan asked. "Don't you like Torrin?"

"He is *mia xará*," Astéria said in a low voice. "Fine. Handsome. But . . . how you say . . . he is hungry. For me. Too, too hungry. It is too much now." She shook her head. "When my people safe, maybe I like your friend better."

She fell silent, and it was only then that Kristan realized how quiet the ships had become. The only sound was the soft susurration of water parting before both bows. The centaurs peered ahead, their heads erect, their bodies tense. As if in response, the fog shifted and grew thinner.

Kristan caught his breath. The Mor was only empty gray chop. The ship was nowhere in sight.

The second boat swung up to port. "So where is this ship of yours?" Pollux called softly.

Astéria clenched both hands on the rail and leaned into the wind, eyes wide and still. "*Pou eínai?*" she breathed.

"Kristan?" Torrin said, raising his voice slightly.

"Where boat?" Astéria said, a frantic note in her voice. "Kreestan, where boat?"

Kristan could only stare, speechless. "Take the tiller," he heard Torrin say to one of the crew, but he could not tear his gaze from the empty river, not even when Torrin joined him at the rail. "Kristan, where is it?"

"Where's the ship?" Pollux called again, his voice rising.

At that moment a distant movement caught Kristan's eye. Something was flying toward them from the western shore, something small and brown and shimmering. Kristan leaned over the rail and waved his arms.

"What are you doing?" Pollux shouted. "It's just a bird."

The bird was almost upon them. Nolle's faint outline surrounded it, and within the wavering shadow her eyes rolled wildly. The bird flew past Kristan's reaching arms and struck his chest with such force that he staggered back. The next instant Nolle was clinging to him, shivering. "I locked," she cried. "I was so scared that I locked and I didn't know where to find you and I didn't know when you were coming back. I've been waiting in that tree . . . there were owls and it was so dark . . ."

The centaurs stared and muttered as Kristan detached himself from Nolle and held her at arms' length. "Where are the others?" he demanded. "Where's the ship?"

Astéria threw her cloak over Nolle's shoulders. The girl clutched it close. "The Northmen came up on our ship in the dark. It was that Olaf first. Your sister knew he was coming. She was waiting for him. She told the knights that she was going with Olaf to look for her husband, and not to stop her."

Kristan's insides lurched. His hand sought the Stone. He felt Torrin's eyes on him, as if waiting for an explanation, but his mouth was dry as sand and no words would come.

"Then while everyone was arguing with your sister, Sigurd and his men came up on the other side of our ship," Nolle went on. "They started to come on board. Sir Kennet ordered them off, but they wouldn't go. Sigurd wanted to know where you were, but no one would say. Desta kicked Sigurd in the knee, and Sigurd knocked him across the deck, and then there was a fight." Nolle's voice caught on a sob. "There were too many of them. The Northmen took everyone prisoner, but I shifted and flew up to the rigging. Then, the Northmen found the centaurs hiding below with the horses, and your friend Olaf looked surprised and said you might be in *O Tópos*. Sigurd started laughing and said that just made things better, and he put everyone below and bolted the hatch."

The centaurs, who had been listening intently, let out a collective growl that made Kristan's scalp prickle. "I can't believe it," Torrin said. "I can't believe Olaf would be part of this. We're friends."

"He didn't want to," Nolle said, "but Sigurd told him not to be a fool. He said the StoneKing had weighed the Northmen against the centaurs, and the Northmen weighed lighter. He said the StoneKing put the centaurs before even his own sister. And then he laughed and said if the centaurs meant so much to the StoneKing, he'd probably do anything to get them back. He shouted up to me that they were taking the ship to the Crack on the Stratheden coast, and I should fly to you and tell you so. He said if you follow them there, you can get your sister and your men and your horses and the centaurs back. I was too scared to fly—I didn't know where you were or how far I could go in the dark. Then Sigurd grabbed a bow and arrow and shot at me and I had to fly. And then they pulled up the anchor and all three ships sailed away."

With a wail of despair, Chári slammed both fists on the ship's rail, and the other centaurs began shouting. "Quiet," Torrin told them, and turned to Kristan. "Olaf is our friend. Why would he do such a thing?"

"He's under Sigurd's control," Kristan said. His voice was gravelly and seemed to come from far away. "And Sigurd is out of his mind. He thinks the Stone can send the Northmen back home."

"Can it?"

"Of course not. You know that. I told Sigurd the Stone doesn't have that power, but he didn't believe me. Olaf asked me to come with them to this Crack, just to try, but I said no." A fleeting look of surprise and disapproval flickered across Torrin's face, and Kristan clenched his fists. "Oh, not you, too. Torrin, I couldn't. I don't have time to make that kind of absurd journey, not even for a friend. I have a realm to rule."

Torrin said nothing. He studied Astéria, who was staring hopelessly southward, her hands clasped over her heart.

"Torrin, what are we to do?" Pollux called.

"Go after them, of course." Torrin turned his back on Kristan. "There's no time to lose. Pass over all the provisions you have. If you've got any weapons aboard, I'll take those, too."

"What?"

"One ship is sufficient, and one crew." He ignored the rebellious shouts from Pollux's crew. "My ship will go after the Northmen. Yours will return to O Tópos. Tell my father what's happened and where we're going."

Pollux's chin jutted out. "There'll be chaos when the people get the news."

"I know, and that's why I need you there—to keep order. Please, Pollux, don't argue. Let me have the food and weapons."

Pollux's crew began to hand over their stores, muttering angrily. Some glared at Kristan, and he wanted to shout at them *do you think this is my doing? Do you blame me for what happened?*

"Pay them no mind," Torrin said quietly. "This is a terrible blow for my people, and it will take some time for them to think sensibly. Would you like Pollux to take you back to O Tópos?"

"Why would I want to go back to O Tópos?"

"Father can have one of our ships take you to Fandrall. I know you're anxious to return home. As you've said, you don't have time for absurd journeys."

His words, repeated in Torrin's deep tones, sounded like a rebuke. Kristan masked his shame with a harsh laugh. "Do you really think I'd return to Fandrall, with my knights and my sister and Astéria's people taken prisoner? Do you really think so little of me?"

"You mistake my meaning," Torrin said, and to Kristan's further humiliation, the centaur's expression was pitying. "I can only imagine the demands on you, with four kingdoms to rule. I know how much you've already sacrificed to help the *Kentávron*. And I can see how exhausted you are," he added more softly. "If you'll entrust me with the task, I'll go after your men and your sister."

"And do what? Battle with Olaf and his brother?"

"I would do as you would," Torrin said. "I would try to reason with the Sigurdsons first."

The mild words, spoken without reproach, took the edge off Kristan's simmering anger. "Thank you for your offer," he said stiffly, "but if Sigurd is willing to steal my ship and kidnap my people and yours to get me to come to his damned Crack, then I doubt reasoning with him will work. I'll have to go with you."

Torrin nodded. "Then the sooner we're off, the better."

"That's the last of it," Pollux said, as a final cask was heaved aboard Torrin's ship. "You know our ships aren't suited for the sea. You're going to have a rough voyage."

"I know."

"All the *anypantroi* want to come with you," Pollux went on in a lower voice. "And I think you should take them. They'll put up with any hardship, if there's a chance they can get a life mate out of it in the end."

"All right. Give me Chári and your other unmated ones, and take the others back with you."

Chári let out a yell of triumph, and with one powerful thrust of her hindquarters, leaped from her brother's ship into Torrin's. Others followed, and the mated members of Torrin's crew took their places aboard Pollux's vessel, making both ships pitch and rock so wildly that Kristan and Nolle had to cling to the rail.

"Be careful, Torrin." Pollux said, as the ships moved apart. "*Kalí týchi.*" With a final wave, he turned his ship north and was quickly lost to sight in the mist. On their own ship, Chári had taken the tiller and was already navigating into the main current. Kristan stared ahead, the full import of what had happened finally sinking in. *Melissa and Olaf betrayed me. My sister and my friend betrayed me.*

"I don't think your sister knew what the Northmen were going to do," Nolle said, as if in answer to his thoughts. "She called after me when I flew away. She was crying. She said to tell you she was sorry."

Kristan only nodded. In the bow, Torrin put a comforting hand on Astéria's shoulder. She looked up at him, a single tear sliding down her face. *Failed*, Kristan thought. *Failed again. I saw Melissa's desperation and scorned it. I knew the danger in thwarting the Sigurdsons and ignored it. How could I have been so arrogant? What right do I have to call myself king?*

CHAPTER TWENTY-ONE

Isobel groaned on Heather's right and Bayla yawned on her left as they trudged up the steep trail toward the lodge, leading their horses. After a strenuous day's exercise, everyone was tired, and even Skapi was docile and clearly looking forward to her stall and oats.

Heather could barely set one foot before the other, but she was content. It had been a good day. The soldiers had thrown themselves into the exercises with a will, led with growing confidence by Bran and Jerrold. *I'll make real leaders of them yet,* Heather thought. *And a real flesh-and-blood commander of myself, too—not just a symbol of the StoneKing's authority.*

The thought of Kristan made her suddenly aware of the folded parchment wedged in her boot leg. She glanced over her shoulder. Ravelin was a few paces behind her, talking with determined geniality to Bran and Jerrold. The knights replied only in grunts and nods, but nearby soldiers listened with interest as Ravelin related the details of some past battle. *The troops seem to respect him, even if my knights don't. Is that a good thing, or bad?*

She was growing more and more uncertain of her own feelings about Ravelin. During the day, with her attention concentrated on the war games, she could be all business, but in the evening, during the boisterous dinners with the soldiers, she frequently found Ravelin watching her. At night she often lay awake, Bayla and Isobel's gentle breathing providing an accompaniment to the recollection of Ravelin's lips against her hand. *Is that a good thing, or bad?* she thought again.

In the courtyard, she relinquished Skapi's reins to Bran and waited as the men assembled in ranks for her formal dismissal, signaling the end of their day. Jerrold remained at the trail's head, urging the stragglers to hurry along. "Do I have to wait, too?" Isobel whined. "It's cold and I'm tired."

We're all cold and tired, Heather wanted to snap, but the sudden presence of Ravelin just off her left shoulder turned her throat dry. "Go inside, then," she said. "Tell Cook we'll want dinner immediately."

With a bob that approximated a curtsey, Isobel hurried into the lodge.

"Not everyone has your stamina, my lady," Ravelin said quietly.

"Bayla, you can go, too," Heather said, ignoring him.

"I'll wait with you, my lady," Bayla said, even though she was blue-lipped from the cold.

The last few men were at the entrance to the courtyard, but instead of coming inside, they were talking to Jerrold and pointing back down the trail. "Jerrold, what's the delay?" Heather called.

Jerrold gestured the men to wait and hurried up to her. "The men say there's a small unit of Stratheden soldiers coming up from the east. Maybe a dozen."

"Stratheden soldiers?"

"Yes, my lady. And the men say the soldiers are traveling under King Aldo's banner."

"Are you sure?" Ravelin demanded.

"They claim they could make it out even with the daylight fading. Big yellow sun with a jagged crown over it, they said, on a field of blue. They'll be here any moment."

"Attention!" Heather bawled. "About face!" The men, who had been at ease as they waited to be dismissed, snapped upright and with gratifying precision, turned to face the courtyard entrance. Heather strode to the head of the troops, Bayla, Bran, Jerrold and Ravelin hurrying behind her. "What do you suppose this is about?" she asked, flicking a glance at Ravelin.

Ravelin shrugged. "We've been on maneuvers here for two days. Someone on the Stratheden frontier was bound to notice, eventually. To be honest, I'm surprised it's taken Aldo this long to send someone to investigate."

Heather flung her cloak back from her shoulders and tugged her tunic straight, all too aware how muddy and disheveled she was. Bayla moved toward her with raised hands, as if to straighten her hair, but Heather waved her off as a clatter of hooves announced the visitors.

The footsoldiers entered the forecourt first, bearing Aldo of Stratheden's banner on a long pole. In their wake were three men on horseback. The man on the left was pock-marked and rangy and rode a piebald; the one on the right, shorter and stockier, was mounted on a nondescript brown horse. Between them was a huge, liver-colored mare which snorted and tossed its head, but her rider, massive as a boulder and nearly as motionless, paid no heed. Only his pebble-gray eyes moved in his stony face. As the column drew to a halt, Ravelin grunted deep in his throat, and as if in response, the gray eyes fixed on him. "Well," said the man, "if it isn't Seachlan."

"Captain Callum," Ravelin said, baring his teeth in the semblance of a smile.

Callum's answering smile was equally mirthless. "Oh, I was promoted to commander years ago. I'm sure you knew that. Then again, perhaps you lost your memory—along with your crown."

Ravelin's hands knotted into fists.

"But I heard you have a new title; a rather droll one," Callum continued. "What is it they call you now?"

Heather stepped forward before Ravelin could answer. "He is the StoneKing's Reach, and as such he is the StoneKing's representative. I must insist that you address him with the same deference you would show his lord."

The hard, gray eyes bore into her. "Ah," Callum said. "And you must be the StoneKing's wench—his girl commander we've heard so much about."

An angry rumble rose from the Hogians. "She's the Lady of the Sword, you great pig's buttock," someone growled.

"Silence in ranks," Heather said, barely raising her voice, but her men immediately obeyed. "I'm Heather Demitt," she went on, keeping both voice and expression carefully neutral, "and I am indeed the StoneKing's commander in Hogia. Welcome, Commander Callum. To what do we owe the honor of your visit?"

Callum's gaze drifted from the top of her messy hair to the toes of her muddy boots and back again. "Two nights ago, there were sightings of a signal fire in these mountains," he said at last. "And then reports of Hogian activity on our northwestern frontier. King Aldo sent me to find out the reason."

"We're conducting winter battle exercises."

"And how long will these exercises go on?"

"As long as I think necessary."

"Why must they take place on our border?"

"My men need experience with maneuvers in mountainous territory," Heather said evenly, in spite of her growing annoyance. "Please assure King Aldo there's no cause for alarm."

"So you say. But you serve a lord whose grasping nature is legendary."

"I beg your pardon?"

Callum turned up both palms in an elaborate shrug. "Maybe four crowns and four thrones are enough for the Gemeta. Or maybe not. You can't blame my lord for being wary."

Heather blew out a sigh. "Commander, all I can do is repeat that these are war games, nothing more. We can stand out here in the cold and argue about it—" A sudden idea struck her. "Or instead, perhaps you and your men could come inside and share our evening meal. It's nothing fancy, but it's hot and there's plenty of it. We can continue this conversation in comfort."

"What unexpected cordiality, Commander Demitt." The look Callum shot at Ravelin was so calculating that Heather was immediately on her guard. "We won't intrude on your dinner, but my captains and I would welcome a drink before we ride back to our camp."

"And your troops?"

"Oh, they'll wait here in the courtyard."

"Very well," Heather said.

As the Stratheden officers dismounted and handed their mounts off to their footsoldiers, Jerrold leaned close. "Do you want me to dismiss the men, my lady?" he murmured.

Heather resisted the urge to grind her teeth in frustration. "Not with these Stratheden soldiers in the courtyard and their leaders in the lodge. I hate to make the men stand in ranks in this cold, but that's what I want them to do, with their captains in charge. No one is to speak. No goading, no insults, no muttering amongst themselves. No matter what Callum's men may say or do, mine will remain silent and at attention. They'll conduct themselves like Hogians. And if any one of them disobeys, the entire army can stand out here until morning."

"Understood. Shall I stay with them, my lady?"

"No. Join me in the lodge once you've spoken to the captains." She forced a smile and gestured toward the door as Callum and his officers approached. "Gentlemen, if you'll follow me?"

As she led Callum and his captains inside, she was doubly grateful for the efforts her men had made to restore the cleanliness of the lodge, if not its former grandeur. The floor was swept and scrubbed, the walls washed down, the encrusted filth of the hearth scraped away. The windows and every other surface capable of reflecting light were polished until they gleamed. As was their custom, the soldiers had piled their bedrolls in neat pyramids on either side of the hearth before breakfast, and the sturdy trestles and benches they had built had been stacked precisely along the walls before they left for the day's maneuvers. A generous fire spread its warm glow on the large table that still dominated the room and the chairs ranged along either side. It was to these seats that Heather directed the party from Stratheden. "Please make yourselves comfortable," she said. Callum and his men settled themselves on one side of the table while Bran, Jerrold and Ravelin sat across from them. To Heather's relief, the Reach's high color had faded somewhat, although he looked far from friendly.

Callum leaned back in his chair, studying the bare walls. "This place has seen some rough times."

"Daazna's occupation of Hogia was difficult for everyone," Heather said. "However, we're on the road to recovery. Bayla, would you ask Cook to bring some ale?"

"There have been some pleasant changes, though," Callum said, eyeing Bayla's backside as she passed him on her way to the kitchen.

At the door Bayla nearly collided with Isobel, coming out with a goblet in one hand. "Watch where you're going," Isobel snapped.

Callum smirked. "And some things haven't changed at all. Hello, Izzy."

Isobel's goblet clattered to the floor, splattering her gown and Bayla's. With an exclamation of dismay, Bayla flinched back, but Isobel did not move. Eyes enormous in her pale face, she stared at Callum.

"You know each other?" Heather asked.

"Indeed, we do," Callum said. "How've you been, Izzy?"

Isobel's lips parted, but no sound came. Her eyes flicked from Callum to Ravelin and back again.

"Bayla, please get something to wipe up that mess," Heather said. Bayla picked up the goblet and squeezed past Isobel, who still did not move. *What's gotten into her?* Heather thought. "Isobel, would you care to join us?"

Isobel fixed her with a look of desperate entreaty. "No," she almost gasped. "No, thank you, my lady. I don't . . . I don't feel well. Excuse me." She hurried across the room and nearly ran up the stairs.

"Goodbye, Izzy," Callum called after her. Heather glanced at Ravelin for an explanation, but he looked as puzzled as she felt. She took the seat next to him as Bayla returned, with the cook and his assistant on her heels. They served out tankards of ale as she mopped up the spilled wine, then all three retreated to the kitchen.

"Gentlemen, your health," Heather said, raising her tankard.

With a perfunctory nod, Callum took a deep swig of his ale and banged his tankard down. "Good stuff, that."

"Hogian ale can't be beat," Sir Jerrold said.

"If ale's all you're after," one of his captains said, winking at Heather.

Jerrold and Bran leaned forward in unison, fixing the man with a cold stare. The captain grinned sheepishly and ducked his head. Callum only laughed. "It's nice, for once, not to have to bring our own provisions."

Heather lowered her own tankard. "I'm sorry?"

"Our own ale. Our own meat and bread. But when you're on the frontier, you take what you can get—no matter the price."

"What are you talking about?" Ravelin said.

"This lodge, Reach Seachlan. You don't know?"

"If I knew, I wouldn't ask."

"Oh, my." Callum let out a wheezing guffaw. "You didn't know that for two years it was the finest doxy-house for miles?"

Ravelin's shoulders went rigid.

"The *only* doxy-house," one of the captains snickered.

"The women here traded their favors for food," the other one said. "Sometimes just for firewood."

"At first, it was just the serving wenches," Callum said. "And they didn't show up until after the winter was over. My guess is they'd already broken up and burned every nonessential to keep warm and eaten everything there was to eat, even their horses. They started crossing into Stratheden territory. They said they were looking for firewood, but they'd fuck for a bowl of stew or a tankard of ale. Soon, they started bringing my men to the lodge instead. Nicer to fuck in a bed than under a tree or in a soldier's tent or barracks, with his comrades looking on. Word spread through the ranks that there was cheap tail just over the border." He paused, as if waiting for a reaction. All four Hogians were silent, although Heather felt as if her face was on fire. She was all too aware that Callum was using the coarsest language possible in an attempt to rattle her. "Once your courtiers realized what was going on, they demanded a share of the proceeds, so to speak," Callum went on, after taking another long pull at his tankard, "but the servants refused. Some entertaining squabbles, there. Eventually, they realized if they wanted to partake, they'd have to put out. But it was Izzy who finally took control of the whole thing—decided who'd do what to whom, when and for how much."

"Handful of grain for a quick squeeze and a pizzle-pull," said the pocky captain.

"Bundle of kindling to get sucked off," said the other, sniggering.

"Brace of hare or a jug of beer for a screw."

"And if you wanted one of the ladies—"

"—or one of the men, if your taste lay in that direction—"

"A load of firewood. A side of boar or venison. A cask of wine, at the very least."

"And not worth it in the long run," Callum said. "Most of 'em would cry the whole time. Except Isobel. She'd just lie there. Like fucking a plank." He leaned toward Heather, with a leer that made her want to cringe. "Pardon our blunt talk, Commander Demitt. But you're no doubt used to it—you're practically a man yourself."

Jerrold and Bran lunged to their feet, but Heather put up one hand to stop them before they could do more. She rose, with as much calm as she could muster, although her very insides were trembling. "I'm man enough not to be embarrassed by dirty talk," she said. "And woman enough to know when I'm being baited. Thank you for calling on us, Commander Callum. My next report to the StoneKing will include the details of our meeting. I'm sure he'll be most intrigued."

An uneasy light flickered in Callum's eyes, but then he guffawed again and stood up. "Goodbye, Reach Seachlan," he said, with a mocking bow, but received only a distant nod in return. As Heather and the knights escorted Callum and his men out, Ravelin remained at the table, staring straight ahead.

When Heather opened the outer door, she was assaulted by the sight and sound of the Stratheden soldiers mocking her troops. Some were nose to nose with the Hogians, insulting and jeering at them; others cavorted through the ranks, pulling faces and making rude noises; in spite of the cold, one wag had dropped his leggings and was wiggling his bare backside at the entire company. Heather clenched her fists, but at the same time a fierce pride in her own men, silent and expressionless in the face of such ridicule, warmed her from scalp to toes. "How interesting, Commander Callum," she said, her voice ringing through the cold air. "Is this typical of Stratheden discipline?"

Even in the thin light of dusk, she could see Callum's face go purple. "Get in ranks!" he bellowed. His captains ran into the courtyard, shoving and kicking their men, who stumbled over their own feet and nearly knocked each other down in their haste to obey. Callum stormed down the steps, flung himself onto his horse and kicked it so sharply in the ribs that it squealed and reared before bolting onto the trail. The captains threw themselves onto their own mounts and followed, shouting abuse at the soldiers, who formed straggling ranks and hurried after their leader at a near run. The Hogians waited, motionless, as the sounds of the retreating unit faded and the air grew still once more.

Heather walked down the steps and across the courtyard. With Jerrold and Bran behind her, she strode to the head of the ranks, pivoted sharply and faced the troops. The men remained at attention, but every eye was upon her. She clasped her hands behind her back and studied her army for several moments.

"Well done, men," she said at last. "You make me proud."

Broad grins spread across the men's faces, but they stayed as they were, heads erect, shoulders thrown back.

"Dinner is ready," Heather said. "I hope it's a good one; you deserve it. Jerrold, Bran: dismiss your men."

"DISMISSED!" Jerrold and Bran bellowed together.

The answering roar startled her so much that she jumped. She stepped back as the men hammered on each other's backs and pumped their fists in the air. As they swarmed toward the lodge doors, Jerrold and Bran fell in with them, shaking hands with some, clapping others on the shoulder.

Long after their shouts of triumph had faded, replaced by the clash and clatter of knives on plates, Heather stood alone in the courtyard. A rising ache of loneliness pierced through her satisfaction. "Practically a man yourself," she murmured. "But not enough, I suppose." She walked through the court-yard entrance and stood for some time gazing east, toward the Stratheden border.

"My lady? Your dinner's waiting."

Bayla's tread had been so quiet that Heather had not heard her approach.

"Set it aside for me. Where's Isobel?"

"Still upstairs, I think."

"Take a plate up to her, please. She said she felt ill. I doubt she'll come down." When Bayla did not respond, Heather turned to her. Her maidservant stood with her arms folded against the cold, her lips pursed, her eyes pensive. "What's wrong, Bayla?"

"I have a confession to make, my lady. That Commander Callum spoke so loud the three of us—Cook and his assistant and I—couldn't help but hear. What he said. About Isobel."

Heather blew out a sigh. "I know how she's treated you in the past, Bayla, and it must be a great temptation to strike back now that the shoe is on the other foot. But you have to keep this a secret. If it gets out amongst the men, it'll cause nothing but trouble."

"Isobel has nothing to fear from me, my lady, and I'm sure the cooks will keep silent as well, if you give the order." Bayla shrugged. "There were always rumors about what went on up here when Daazna was in power. Strange to think that every time Isobel called me a whore, she knew in her heart she was one, too. Lily and Annys as well."

"It was a desperate time. I'm glad it's over."

"That Callum—I didn't like the way he talked to you, my lady. Not one bit."

It was Heather's turn to shrug. "He was trying to provoke me and humiliate Ravelin. Speaking of Ravelin, where is he?"

"I think he's up in the signal tower, my lady."

"All right. Let's go inside; you're shivering."

Together they passed through the main room of the lodge, where the men joked and sang as they enjoyed their dinner. Heather paused long enough to whisper in her knights' ears that the information about Isobel was to be kept to themselves, and received a murmured, "yes, my lady" in response. In the kitchen, she made the same request of Cook and his assistant, and was gratified by how willingly the men acquiesced.

While Bayla dished up a plate for Isobel, Heather took a fire steel from the hearth and went out into the rear courtyard. High up on the tower, Ravelin's figure was silhouetted against the darkening sky. She thrust the fire steel into her pocket, gathered up an armful of logs and kindling, and made her way up the stairs. As she gained the top, Ravelin shot her a glance, then turned away.

"Don't do it," she said.

"Do what?"

"Dwell on it. It does no good." She put down the logs and filled the bottom of the metal basin with kindling.

"How can I not dwell on it? This was *my* lodge—my haven and my pride—and they turned it into a whore's den."

"They did what they had to do. They were cold and hungry."

"They were too lazy and stupid to learn how to look after themselves."

"It's past. It can't be undone. And it's a waste of time to wish it hadn't happened, or to hate Isobel and the others for it." Heather heaved the logs atop the kindling, then pulled out the fire steel. A few strikes sent a shower of sparks into the dry tinder. As the wood began to smolder, she blew gently on it. It flared up, and at last Ravelin turned.

"What are you doing?"

"Building a fire; what does it look like?"

"Why?"

"Why?" Heather stood back and admired the leaping flames. "Because I want them to see it. I want Commander Callum to see it. I want all the men at his outpost to see it. I want them to see it all the way to Hull's Contrivance. I want King Aldo to see it and know the Hogians are on his doorstep. I want him to realize we'll always be on his doorstep. Not big enough," she added, and started back down the winding staircase.

"Where are you going?" Ravelin called.

"To get more firewood."

She heard Ravelin coming down behind her, but she paid him no heed. She hurried to the woodpile and filled her arms. Brushing past Ravelin, she mounted the stairs again. She pushed the firewood into the basin and hustled back down for more. On the way, she passed Ravelin coming up, his arms loaded with wood, a fierce grin on his face. Back and forth they went, feeding the signal fire until it roared and leaped like a giant beast, until their hands were begrimed with dirt and soot. Back and forth they went, jostling each other on the steps, racing each other across the courtyard, giggling like children. At last, only a single stick of firewood was left of what had been the woodpile. Heather snatched it from beneath Ravelin's grasping hand, bolted back to the tower and bounded up the staircase just ahead of him. Hurling the stick into the flames, she turned to him in triumph. He grasped her arms and yanked her close. His mouth was on hers before she knew it. He crowded her against the battlements, pushing the length of his body against hers.

In her heart and head, she recoiled from him. In her heart and head, she did not want him, but her hungry, eager body betrayed her. Of their own accord her fingers locked onto his clutching arms; her lips parted before his probing tongue; her back arched so she was pressed against his hardness from navel to crotch. An animal growl rose from his throat. He pulled her tunic open and shoved his hands beneath her linen undershirt.

His cold fingers on her warm flesh were as startling as a slap. She turned her head, pulling free of his greedy lips. "Wait," she said, her voice low and guttural. "Don't. Someone will see." He let go of her and knelt at her feet. "What are you doing?"

Without answering, he yanked her leggings down and shoved her against the battlements. The shock of the cold stone beneath her buttocks made her gasp. A moment later, his mouth was on her flesh. "Ah, don't," she whispered, and tried to squirm away, but he only took hold of her thighs and pressed them apart. Pushing his face deep between her legs, he began to nibble and lick her. She knotted her hands in his hair, intending to force him back, but already her hips were rocking, matching the rhythm of his caresses, and instead of resisting him, she held him closer. Her gasps fogged the air before her and she was terrified that someone would come out into courtyard, look up and see her, but she could not stop. She could not stop, even when Ravelin's hands shifted, one moving behind to palm her buttocks as the other slid between her legs. Her teeth chattered as his cold forefinger tickled her and stroked her. Finally, he pushed just inside her and touched a sudden, secret pain.

She whimpered and went rigid. Ravelin looked up at her. At first, his expression was puzzled, but as he held her transfixed on his finger like a bird on a skewer, slow realization dawned in his eyes.

"You're a virgin," he whispered.

She averted her face, mortified. He rose, slipping his finger out of her but keeping his hand clamped between her legs. Its pressure forced her onto her toes. "Why, you little minx," he growled in her ear. "The rumors about you and the Gemeta were lies. You're nobody's mistress. You're still a maiden."

His fingers moved between her legs, no longer seeking to penetrate her but kneading and pinching her flesh. She could not control the pulsing jerks of her hips, nor the spasms that set her thighs and belly quivering. "A maiden," he whispered, "but a maiden with powerful desires."

With his free hand, he yanked up her undershirt, exposing her breasts. She tried to pull free, but he pinned her tight against the stone, squeezing her left breast as his hot mouth fastened on the right. She gasped as he sucked hard on her nipple, drawing it deep into his mouth. Below, his other hand still worked between her legs, and against her will she thrust against its pressure, harder and harder, until her climax shook her to the core and left her limp and gasping and half-senseless in Ravelin's arms.

He held her for some moments, looking down at her with a strange expression that mingled surprise, tenderness and calculation. At last, he raised his hand and licked the forefinger contemplatively. "You taste like salt and honey," he murmured.

She groaned and tried to pull away from him, but he caught her hand and pressed it to the hard ridge between his own legs. "See what you've done to me? I could take your maidenhead right now; you want it, you're ready for it. But I won't. Not here. Not now." He tugged her leggings into place, then turned and walked unsteadily toward the stairs. Just before he descended, he looked back.

"We should marry," he said.

As his footsteps receded, she sagged against the battlements. With trembling hands, she straightened her clothing and fastened her tunic. The heat from the signal fire was so intense that she felt as if she was being roasted. She turned from it and leaned into the night, sucking in long, deep breaths, letting the cold air bathe her cheeks. Far below, Ravelin came out of the tower, crossed the rear courtyard and disappeared into the trees beyond; the rustle of leaves marked his passage even when she could no longer see him, and after a few moments even that sound faded.

She turned back to the signal fire. Unthinkingly, she pushed a few errant sticks deeper into the blaze; with equal abstraction she circled the basin, picking up stray twigs and bits of bark and feeding them into the fire as well. Her hands were filthy, the fingernails rimmed with grime. Voices sounded in the courtyard below and then Bayla, Jerrold and Bran were silhouetted in the kitchen doorway. Bran raised his hand in greeting, and she gave him a perfunctory wave in return. After a final look around, she descended, noting with the same vagueness how weak her legs and arms were; how heavy her belly felt; how her flesh still throbbed where Ravelin had touched her. She wondered if her face would reveal what had just happened.

"There you are, my lady," Bayla said. "We weren't sure where you'd gone."

"That's quite a fire you've got there," Jerrold said. "Bright enough to keep Commander Callum awake tonight."

Bran snorted. "I expect that was the point."

"I . . . I used up all the firewood," Heather said.

Jerrold shrugged. "Easy enough to gather more when we're out on maneuvers tomorrow."

"Would you like your dinner now, my lady?" Bayla asked.

Heather nodded. In the kitchen, she handed the cook his fire steel in exchange for a bowl of meaty stew. As she started to sit down before the hearth, she was struck by the realization that Ravelin might come back into the lodge at any moment. The thought of having to face him was more than she could bear. "I'm more tired than hungry," she said, putting the bowl aside. "Bayla, is there water in our room? I'd like to wash."

"There's a bit in the pitcher by the hearth, but it's bound to be cold. I'll heat some for you and bring it up. And Isobel may be asleep, my lady. She was already in bed when I brought up her dinner."

"I'll be quiet. Bring the water up as soon as it's ready."

She slipped past the soldiers at dinner, acknowledging with a brusque nod the few who noticed her. Upstairs, the main room was silent and dark but for a thin reddish glow beneath her bedchamber's closed door. When Heather entered, she was grateful to find a fire crackling in the hearth. Isobel was a motionless lump in her bed, with only her hair showing above the blanket, but Heather sensed she was still awake.

She closed the door. "Commander Callum told us what went on here," she said quietly. "There's no need for shame, Isobel. I understand why you did what you did. I've instructed those who heard never to speak of it. And this is the last you'll hear of it from me. I swear it."

Isobel did not answer or even move.

Heather turned to the hearth. She unfastened her tunic, dropped it, and then pulled off her undershirt. She looked down and saw her bare breasts covered with sooty fingermarks.

Quickly, she stripped off her boots and the rest of her clothing and examined herself by firelight. Her body was covered with smudges and smears of grime. Her belly, thighs and buttocks proclaimed exactly where and how Ravelin had touched her.

She snatched up her discarded tunic and scrubbed herself with it, as if to scour away not only the dirt but the memory of how she had welcomed the touch of Ravelin's hands, his lips, his tongue. *Isobel isn't the only whore in this room*, she castigated herself. *You were like a bitch in heat, so starved for a man's touch that you risked everything. What if someone had spotted the two of you?*

By the time Bayla came in with a jug of hot water, soap, a towel and a wide, shallow basin, Heather's skin was stinging, but she was calmer. Standing in the basin, she soaped and sluiced herself. *At least Ravelin showed the restraint you lack. Maybe he's right. Maybe we should marry. At least then, when I feel this way, someone would be there for me. At least then I wouldn't be alone.*

She crawled naked into her bed and huddled under the covers. Bayla discarded the wash water in the garderobe, banked the fire and slipped into her own bed. The men downstairs quieted and the captains and knights came upstairs, talking softly over the day's events. Eventually, even these sounds were replaced by yawns and grunts and finally, snoring. The rhythmic sound lulled Heather into a leaden slumber, in which she was troubled by dreams of writhing in Ravelin's grasp before a gawking audience of knights and soldiers.

During one of these dreams she was disturbed by the pad of bare feet, followed by a soft rustling. Barely awake, she squinted at Bayla's bed, thinking the maidservant had risen to tend the fire, but Bayla lay with her covers pulled up to her nose, fast asleep. Heather twisted toward Isobel's bed and found it empty. A shadow crouched close to the banked fire, its back to Heather. As Heather tried to rouse herself enough to ask if everything was all right, Isobel stood up. With her head bowed and her fists knotted over her chest, she crept back to her bed, burrowed beneath the covers and lay facing the wall.

Heather let her head fall back and closed her eyes. The sigh of the wind outside, the faint crackle of the fire and the distant snores from the rooms beyond and below blended into an irregular hum that dragged her toward unconsciousness once more. She sank back into sleep just as another sound joined the dissonant murmur: sobs, muffled and yet anguished, from Isobel's bed.

THE END

StoneKing
BOOK THREE OF THE GEMETA STONE

DONNA MIGLIACCIO is a professional stage actress with credits that include Broadway, National Tours and prominent regional theatres. She is based in the Washington, DC Metro area, where she co-founded Tony Award-winning Signature Theatre and is in demand as an entertainer, teacher and public speaker.

ALSO BY
DONNA MIGLIACCIO

Kinglet: Book One of The Gemeta Stone
Fiskur: Book Two of The Gemeta Stone
Ragis: Book Four of The Gemeta Stone